"I thought you might⸻ ⸻⸻it of talent." Dian show⸻ ⸻⸻ teeth in a grin, as if it mattered not at all. "Guess I was wrong. Tomas, heel," she called and, pressing her boots into the horse's ribs, turned confidently out into the snow.

If the woman called, it would be within twenty yards, before Dian reached the stalls. The call did not come. Ten more seconds went by, seconds filled with the beginnings of bitter self-recrimination and her mind's angry demand for an alternative plan, when the voice followed her down the road. A single word: "Stop." It was spoken in a low voice, but a carrying one, and Dian did not think it a good risk to pretend she had not heard it. The owner of that voice would not repeat herself. She reined Simon in and circled him around to wait. In less than a minute, the "Strangers" door opened wide, and a woman stood within, darkly indistinct, but surprisingly small in the gloom.

Dian took a final look at the looming, ugly walls, and wondered if she would be able to maintain the matching façade of cold brutality that the next few weeks were going to require of her. Then she thought of Robin somewhere within those walls, and decided the attitude on her part would not be entirely a façade. She urged Simon forward, back to the city, to enter the city's gates.

CALIFIA'S
DAUGHTERS

LEIGH RICHARDS

BANTAM BOOKS
NEW YORK TORONTO LONDON SYDNEY AUCKLAND

CALIFIA'S DAUGHTERS
A Bantam Spectra Book / August 2004

Published by
Bantam Dell
A Division of Random House, Inc.
New York, New York

Chapter headings are taken from the translation of the *Sergas de Esplandián*, volume five of the *Amadís de Gaula*, by Garci Rodríguez de Montalvo, translated by William Thomas Little (Medieval and Renaissance Texts and Studies, Binghamton, NY 1992) as *The Labors of the Very Brave Knight Esplandián*.

Bantam Books, the rooster colophon, Spectra, and the portrayal of a boxed "s" are trademarks of Random House, Inc.

ISBN 0-553-58667-X

Manufactured in the United States of America
Published simultaneously in Canada

OPM   10   9   8   7   6   5   4   3   2   1

TO THE WOMEN WARRIORS

PROLOGUE

In the year 1532, Hernán Cortés sent an expedition west through Mexico to find a mysterious island which, rumor said, had brought huge wealth to the emperor Montezuma. When his man Mendoza came to the sea at last and gazed across the waters at what appeared to be an enormous offshore island, there was no doubt in his mind that this was the famed source of wealth. Nor did he doubt that this was also the land described by a Spanish novelist named Garcí Rodriguéz de Montalvo in an epic cycle of knights and nobility published some twenty years earlier. California (both the "island" Baja and, later, Alta California to the north) took the name from the epic's Amazon queen Califía, beauteous of face, powerful of arm, noble of heart.

The following story takes place five and a half centuries after Califía's story was written, and the irony is as cutting as the Amazon queen's blade: "They kept only those few men whom they realized they needed for their race not to die out," Rodriguéz de Montalvo writes. Little had he anticipated the rapid-fire series of plagues, wars, and environmental disasters that was to tip humankind into a downward spiral during the first century of the third millennium, slashing the world's population to a fraction of what it had been at the year 2000, overturning social orders, turning dearly held beliefs and mores to dust overnight. Particularly he could not have predicted the propensity of one virus to attach itself to the male of the species, one generation after the next.

By the time of this story, the world holds one male human being for every ten or twelve females.

BOOK ONE

THE VALLEY

ON THE RIGHT-HAND SIDE OF THE INDIES

THERE WAS AN ISLAND CALLED CALIFORNIA,

WHICH WAS VERY CLOSE TO THE REGION

OF THE EARTHLY PARADISE.

ONE

DIAN

FROM A DISTANCE, THERE WAS NOTHING ON THE HILL-side, nothing but the dry grasses of late summer and a smattering of scrub bushes beneath the skeleton of a long-dead tree. From a distance, no unaided human eye could have picked out the dun and dusty figures from the grass around them; nonetheless, they were there, one long, slim human and two massive dogs. They had been on the hillside since morning, and they moved little.

Their presence had not gone completely unde-tected. An hour earlier a small herd of white-tailed deer quartering the hillside had abruptly cut short its graze to veer nervously away. Twice, sentinel quail settling into the arms of the twisted stump had alerted their flock to direct their attentions else-where. And now a turkey vulture appeared above the far side of the valley, gliding in languid circles on the updraft that rose off twenty acres of crumbling as-phalt and debris, the remains of an office complex from Before. The bird spotted the three prone figures and sifted the wind through the distinctive fingers of her pinions, sidling across the currents to take a position a hundred feet above the invisible figures.

Hopeful thoughts flickered through her tiny brain and she dropped lower, then lower still, until one of the bodies jerked about to gnaw its flank, and another, the long one, turned its face to the sky and waved an arm. Faint avian disappointment came and went at these unmistakable signs of life, and the bird slid sideways toward the next valley. The three figures resumed their motionless watch.

Now, however, their stillness was one of alertness, even tension, rather than mere waiting. The human, no longer completely covered by the diminishing shadow of the grease bush, stared intently through a pair of large and ancient Artifact binoculars at the hillside ten miles away, where a faint haze of dust teased up from the ridge. In a few minutes the haze solidified into a cloud, its source coming clear: travelers. Eyes—blue human, yellow canine—focused on the spot, watching the drift of dust move down the face of the hill, saw the half-obscured wagons pause to weigh the temptation of the direct route through the Remnant against the unknown threats it could hide, saw the travelers turn to circle well clear of the tumbled remains. When the wagons had safely negotiated the dry streambed and regained the road, when it became clear that the travelers were firmly committed to the left-hand fork, the binoculars went into their case, the weapons were gathered up, and woman and dogs slithered over the top of the hill and disappeared.

JUDITH

Two hours later, near the place where the road's left fork dwindled to its end, another woman watched for another small cloud of dust to rise against a backdrop of trees, chewing her lip with impatience. Her name was Judith, and she sat perched on the top step of a sprawling old farmhouse that had once been painted white, shelling dried beans. Her bare toes were drawn back from the hot edge of the sun on the next step down; the worn boards and pathway below were thick with beans that had missed the bowl under the sharp, irritable jerks of her work-hardened fingers.

Judith didn't even see the waste she was making. Her eyes were on the Valley entrance, her inner gaze fixed on that vision of the morning's frantic activity— no, call it what it was: panic, mindless and dangerous, that had gone on far, far too long. Bringing the Valley into line had been like pushing a laden cart uphill, and Judith ached with the strain. But at last the long-unused emergency drills were recalled, and order jerkily took hold, and finally the gears meshed and things ran smoothly: guards out, weapons ready, all metaphorical hatches securely battened.

Now there was nothing left to do but wait. Forty minutes earlier she had found herself standing alone on the veranda, wishing she had gone with Dian, wondering if she shouldn't take a position at the Gates with a rifle, half-yearning for a return of the morning's upheaval just so she'd have something to keep her occupied—until she heard what she was thinking and berated herself: *For God's sake, you're a lousy shot, Dian's better off without you, and you should be grateful things finally calmed down. Go find something to do!*

So she'd found a mindless task and settled to it— badly, with shameful waste—and waited for Dian.

The worst part was the silence. She felt smothered under it, this strange, thick stillness where there was usually the workaday noise of an active community—children shouting and adult voices raised in work and song, the rumble and thump of the mill machinery, the echo of hammer and the rasp of saw and the jingle of harnessed horses pulling plow or cart. The myriad sounds that made up the daily voice of the Valley were gone, the core of its life locked up and guarded in the hillside caves high above the farmhouse. The oddly muted sounds of cow and goat drifted down from the upper pastures; the cock crowed in protest from the enclosed run behind the barn. Even the imperturbable blue jay that haunted the walnut tree seemed flustered at the impact his raucous voice made on the still air and flew off into the redwoods. Judith listened to the few voices of low speech, the crackle and patter of the beans dropping into the basket, the breath soughing in and out through her nose: no competition for the pervasive quiet. The hot air shivered with silence, and Judith watched the Gates.

Not actual gates, of course, not like Meijing had—there was no way to wall the area against determined invaders, although God knew they'd talked about it, especially, Judith gathered, during the early years. But the Valley was peculiarly well suited for defense, the hills at its back steep and heavily wooded, the low ground in front marshy where the creek spread out between a pair of rocky prongs. And then, when the worst of the riots had been raging Outside, the community had responded to an unspoken urge to strengthen those prongs and built them higher and thicker until the Gates came into being. Nothing high explosives or a concerted effort wouldn't push aside, but a few armed women atop the structure would slow an enemy down.

As now it seemed to be slowing Dian, damn it. The minutes crawled, beans continued to fall into the bowl and across the steps, and then finally, a faint suggestion of dust rising into the air down toward the Valley entrance. A minute later, sounds reached through the utter silence: a woman's faraway voice—Dian's, she was sure, calling a salute to her unseen sentries. In a minute Judith could hear the clear thud of cantering hooves on the planks of the lower bridge; her eyes shifted to the dam, the pond behind it as unnaturally motionless as the air without its usual midday complement of splashing bodies, the mill frozen against the weight of the collected waters. After four long minutes Dian appeared around the side of the mill, her horse at a trot. The smaller dog, a two-year-old brindle that stood thirty-four inches at the shoulder, shot away from her side to galumph like a mad ox through the shallow edges of the mill pond, heaving up great sheets of water at each stride until it stopped, belly-deep, to lap furiously. The other dog, fawn-colored and bigger by three inches and forty pounds, remained at Dian's left stirrup until she turned her horse's head to the water. Then he, too, waded forward to drink. Judith watched him closely for an indication of Dian's feelings, and was relieved when he appeared relaxed enough to snap playfully at the water.

Dian only allowed her animals a small refreshment before pulling the horse back onto the road and whistling the dogs to her side. Judith heard hoofbeats again as Dian crossed the mill bridge; as if the sound had been a signal, the rider shifted in the saddle to peer up at the house, then threw up an arm in greeting.

Judith started to rise, only to exclaim in exasperation both at the basket, which nearly upended down the steps, and at the awkwardness caused by her expanding belly. She thrust the beans to one side and stepped into the full sun to respond with a wide wave. In another moment Dian disappeared behind the apple orchard. Judith continued down the steps, pausing to bend laboriously and gather a few stray beans, then abandoned the project to set off across the stunted lawn to the entrance of the farmyard proper.

Dian would reach her in two minutes, and Judith compromised with her impatience by standing at the gatepost in the shade of the old walnut, the farmyard's guardian since the first rough shack had been raised there by her great-great-grandparents. The five-bar gate itself was so choked with weeds and walnut sprouts that it would have taken a crew to force it shut, but as other gates now kept livestock from the crops, there was no need. She leaned her arms on the top of the fence, which like everything in the Valley needed paint, and breathed in the acrid odor of the thick, oily leaves. Over and around her hung thousands of smooth green nuts the size of a baby's fist, still tightly wrapped in their husks, a good month yet from harvest. Her own time would follow theirs, by two or three weeks. She smoothed her belly and pictured the soft, pale infant walnuts straining against their spongy husks, then her mouth twisted in irritation and she moved out into the hot road. Think about something else. Think about the travelers.

It was Dian, inevitably, who had seen the approaching wagons, at dawn. She had been out on one of her increasingly frequent and far-ranging overnight forays and had spotted them many miles away, and waited only long enough to be reasonably sure of their destination before riding hard for home. At nine o'clock that morning Judith had been down at the mill contemplating an obstinate piece of machinery when there was a stir of alarmed voices along the road. She stepped out of the mill house to see Dian clattering up the road on a horse white with lather and shockingly near foundering, Culum gamely at her heels and no sign of the two other dogs she'd set out with. The sweaty rider reined in the instant she saw Judith.

"What happened?" Judith was demanding before Dian's boots hit the ground.

Dian glanced at the curious faces turned their way, and called to one of the youngsters.

"Patty, would you do me a big favor, and take Simon here up to the barn? You know what to do with a hot horse?"

"Of course," the child said, with the perfect disdain of a ten-year-old, and took the reins. She had to pull with all her weight to get the exhausted animal moving again.

"Thank you, Pats. Okay, Culum, you can go home now." The huge dog seemed to nod his shaggy head at her as he passed, ambling off at a bone-weary plod. Dian turned to the other adults.

"I need to talk to Judith for a minute," she said apologetically, and they faded away with curious glances and concerned remarks. Dian waited until they were out of earshot, then turned urgently to Judith.

"Jude, there are people on the road. Two wagons and a bunch of riders, at least ten or twelve."

"Coming here?"

"Where else is there?"

"Couldn't they just be tinkers or traders or something?"

"Didn't look right, and tinkers would know not to ride through the hill road. Besides, they looked, I don't know, purposeful. Tightly bunched, but moving as fast as they could manage."

"Two wagons, though—what's the worry? We stop them outside the Gates and see what they want."

"Last year it only took one wagon, with some kind of gun inside, to wipe out the Smithy village," she reminded Judith grimly. Judith winced at the memory of dry blood and buzzing flies, and studied her sister's face.

"You're nervous about this. In fact, I could swear you look frightened. You're having one of your Feelings

about those wagons, aren't you?" Judith's emphasis put
a capital letter on the word, recognition that, every so
often, Dian seemed to know things she couldn't.

"Yes, and no. They seem wrong, somehow. Not
necessarily dangerous, just very wrong. I don't like
the idea of them coming here with us all open like
this." Her hand gesture took in the scene: the nearby
field with its paused workers, the cluster of gaping
children, the slim young man walking down the road.

Judith's eyes thoughtfully followed this last figure,
her cousin Philip, before returning to Dian.

"You want me to call an alert," she said flatly.

"Yes."

"When we're all working from dawn to dark to get
the crops in, you want me to declare a day off, so
everyone can go play in the caves."

Dian heard the thread of capitulation hidden beneath the protest, and looked sideways at Judith,
summoning a faint air of mischief.

"We'll have some nice babies in May," she suggested.

"It's no joking matter, damn it!" Judith exploded.
"I can't go around calling alerts because someone
feels nervous, even if it is you. This is serious."

Dian's attempt at humor faded.

"You can't honestly think I don't realize that?" she
asked quietly.

"Oh, no, Di, I know you do. Sorry to be so touchy.
The heat." Dian nodded. "It's a strong feeling, then?"

"It is."

"Strong enough to nearly kill a horse and abandon
two dogs," Judith noted.

"They'll find their way home—Maggie bruised her
foot—but, yes, that strong."

"There's going to be screaming about this."

"But you'll do it."

"Yes, damn it, I'll do it. We need a break anyway,

and I suppose it'll do us good. When do you think they'll be here?"

"The road's bad and they've got two creeks to ford—if the wagons and riders stay together, they won't arrive until dark. If they abandon the wagons and ride hard, they could be here in four, five hours. I'll talk to Laine and Jeri, and if Carmen will trust me with another horse I'll go back and watch the road. I don't think we should wait too long to clear the place. At least get the menfolk out of the way."

Judith glanced nervously down toward the entrance to the Valley.

"You're sure about this?"

"No," Dian answered unhelpfully.

"Your hunches are usually right."

"Maybe this time I'll be wrong," she said, but her voice said she did not think it likely.

"All right, then, we'd better get on with it. What do you want me to do?"

Four minutes later the assembly bell rang (five strokes, just short of a drop-everything-and-run emergency) and twenty minutes after that Judith glimpsed Dian, on a fresh horse and followed by two dogs (one of them Culum, who would not allow a little thing like exhaustion to keep him from Dian's side). Her sister rode against a rising tide of alarmed adults and frightened children, turning her back on the shouts and confusion of the Valley's alert.

It had taken nearly two hours for the quiet to settle, for sentries to set out and the livestock to be rounded up, for the menfolk, the pregnant and nursing mothers, and the girls under fourteen years of age to climb to the caves. When they were finally away, Judith and the others looked at one another, and went off to their tasks. Judith's job in theory was to be available when someone needed instructions, but in practice what it had meant was waiting and chewing her lip, sitting on the front steps of her house while her fingers worked their way through a heaping basket of dried beans.

Now she could hear Dian's voice from behind the head-high corn, speaking words of praise and encouragement to dogs and horse. As Judith walked past the remnants of the farmhouse's picket fence, they rounded the final corner, the horse at an easy trot, barely sweating. The dripping dogs, tongues lolling, spotted Judith; the brindle broke into a run to greet her, while big Culum satisfied himself with a wag of the tail from his place at the horse's side. Dian quickly whistled the young one off and gave them both the signal for "home." The dogs obediently circled around Judith, looking somewhat apologetic at their muddiness, to lope on up the hill toward the cool and shady pond behind the old barn.

Dian dropped off next to Judith, and the two women started up the road to the barn, leading the horse.

"They're coming, then?" Judith asked, although it was not really a question. "How many?"

"They're coming. Should be here around nightfall, unless they can speed up, which didn't look likely. And they're playing it cautious—they went around that Remnant where Kat was killed."

"That could be a good sign."

"Or it could mean that they're smart enough to know that guns won't do much against booby traps. And it's a well-scavenged site, which means a lot of traps. Anyway, there's just the two wagons, both with canvas sides—no seeing what's inside, but only two horses on each, so the loads can't be too heavy. Ten riders, two drivers, three more horses tied to the wagons. All the animals looked tired. Unlikely there's more than twenty women altogether."

"Unless it's a Trojan horse."

Dian nodded. "In which case the wagons are full to the brim with women and guns. The Smithy's gang looked innocent too, from all accounts."

"Just the argument I used this morning whenever anyone objected to the alert." Judith accepted the reins from Dian, who walked ahead to pull open the heavy barn door; Judith spoke to her sister's back. "You were right last week when you said we were getting slack. Between the arguments and collecting last-minute things and trying to decide who was going where, it took nearly two hours."

"Shit. If it'd been a right-now emergency . . ."

"I know. We haven't had so much as a drill in months, so even if this is a false alarm, it's good practice."

"How many of the boys had to be bodily carried off when they found you weren't going to let them stay and fight?"

Judith gave a tired grin. "Three."

"You can't breed hormonal impulses out of males in a couple of generations."

"It would make life a hell of a lot easier for us if you could."

A person could argue, Judith reflected as she handed the reins back to Dian, that male hormonal impulses were precisely what had gotten the world into its present condition, that in a horrendous sort of cosmic joke, menfolk were bearing the brunt of actions chiefly their own. However, to say that, one would have to assert that women lacked the aggressive tendency, and no one with a sister like Dian was about to make that particular assertion. No, violence and belligerence were at home on either set of chromosomes.

The ancient wooden barn the two women entered was a dim and fragrant place redolent of twelve decades of horse and hay and childhood games, its air placid with the rustle of mice and the patience of cats; once inside, Judith's taut apprehension lessened a notch. She lowered herself onto the bench that stood against the wall, letting her head fall back against the rough boards, her hands laced together under the round of her belly. From beneath half-closed eyelids she watched her sister flip the reins around the stanchion, into the groove worn by countless reins, then remove her weapons from the horse: rifle for distance, bow for silence. As Dian leaned both in the corner and reached for the cinch buckle, Judith allowed her gaze to rise into the vast reaches of the building, to the web-draped rafters that had been cut from trees on the surrounding hills and raised, thick and bright and hopelessly anachronistic in an age of aluminum siding and prefabricated girders, by her grandmother's grandfather. She had never met the old man in person, but she met and used his handiwork every day of her life, from the bed she'd awakened in that morning to the time-black bench underneath her now. She followed a shaft of light from one of the ventilation holes he had cut in a corner of the hayloft.

"Hey, Di—you remember the owl?"

Dian let the saddle thump down onto the top of the stall partition, then turned to look at her sister.

"The nest, you mean?"

Yes, there had been a nest. It was an oddly disjointed memory, as if it had been from early childhood, although she must have been, what, fifteen? sixteen, even? when she had slipped into the barn on Dian's heels late one night, a night when a huge full moon flooded the Valley with depthless blue light, seconds after the barn owl had dropped from the high opening of the hayloft and disappeared on silent wings down the fields. They scurried, noiseless as the owl—or at any rate, Dian did, with clumsy Judith, nearly twice her sister's age and half again her size, stumbling behind. Two girls, Dian's inseparable four-legged shadow for once left behind, running across the barn floor and up the ladder, to bury themselves into the hay and wait.

Even then, Judith had been bad at waiting: moonlight crept an infinitesimal path across the boards while she stifled sneezes and itches and boredom, and then without warning the owl was there, a brief outline against the bright night in the loft window before it swooped noiselessly through the barn. Tiny hatchling cries rose up over their heads, then came a faint rustle from where eight-year-old Dian lay. Suddenly a mouse was twitching across a bare patch of boards—it must have been late spring, the hay nearly gone—scrabbling and squeaking and behaving in a suicidal fashion. The owl dropped from its nest in the darkness above, only to meet bare boards, a pile of hay, and—a hand. Holding her breath, Judith saw the bird flap its wings to land on the loft floor, then eye the closed fist that protruded from the hay. Its face was a flat blue-white surface set with two unamused black holes; it seemed very large. Slowly Dian's hand rotated, and opened, until the dead mouse was proffered between two fingers. The barn waited. After a long minute the owl took a step forward, its claws brushing the old wood with a faint scritch that Judith felt up her spine. It paused, then took another step, and a third. Inches from Dian's hand it stopped, settled its wings in a sort of decisive shiver, and reached forward delicately to seize the offering. When it had the mouse, it retreated a step to study the empty hand. For a moment the owl was both a rather stupid bird and a visitant from the divine. Judith must have made a noise, for the owl spread its wings and was gone.

And the child Dian had laughed, had scrabbled out from the hay and shook herself off, then turned

toward her teenage sister and crowed in glee at the
workings of the universe. Dian used to do that a lot,
Judith recalled, back when she was still called Lizzie.
Not anymore.

Judith let her eyes drop from the rafters and found
Dian gazing down at her, a faint trace of that long-ago
amusement on her face.

"Pleasant dreams?"

Judith flushed, but she did indeed feel refreshed,
whether because of the barn, the daydream, Dian's
presence, or the possibility that the invasion would
be harmless, she could not have said. She stretched
and picked up the water bucket that sat on one end of
the bench. When she turned back there was another
person standing there, a dark stump of a woman
whose head barely reached Dian's chest, scowl on
face and hands on hips as she glared at the stripped
horse.

"*Calmate*, Carmen," Dian began immediately. "*El
tenía una siesta larga abajo de un arbol* and then had
an easy twelve miles home. I never pushed him out of
a canter, and he positively begged to trot up from the
creek. *Te juro por Dios.*" She put her hand over her
heart to emphasize her honesty.

The horse had looked around at Carmen's silent
entrance and was now pulling against the immobiliz-
ing reins in an attempt to snuffle at her hands. He was
barely wet, in spite of the heat, and his neck and ears
moved vigorously, but still Carmen fixed Dian with
an eye filled with baleful threats and said nothing.

"*Mira*, Carmen, *siento mucho lo de esta mañana*,
what I did to Simon this morning. I hated to do it to
him, it hurt me to take advantage of his big heart, but
I had to. I hope he'll be all right?"

The compliment to her charge did it, and the horse-
woman allowed herself to reach out and make con-

tact with the horse's soft nostrils before snorting a brief forgiveness.

"*No fue gracias a ti,*" she grumbled at Dian.

"You looked at his off hind? I think I got the stone out before it bruised him, but—"

"Go teach your *abuela* to suck eggs. Don't you have anything better to do than stand around here jawing? Go get yourself something to eat. *Darte un baño, por Dios,* you're stinkin' up my barn. I'll finish him up. Got nothing better to do, hanging around here."

"Oh, Carmen, I can't let you care for a horse that I—"

"Shut up. *Vayate.*" She waved a dismissive hand at Dian, snatched the bucket out of Judith's hand, flicked the reins from the groove in the stanchion, and stalked off, muttering Spanish imprecations. The horse shambled after her, eager as an adoring puppy. Dian and Judith looked at each other, stifled laughter, and gathered up Dian's possessions.

... THERE WERE NO MALES AMONG THEM AT ALL,

FOR THEIR WAY OF LIFE WAS SIMILAR

TO THAT OF THE AMAZONS.

TWO

THE TWO WOMEN WHO EMERGED FROM THE BLACK cavern of the barn door were a study in contrast. One was a tall, loose-limbed woman closing in on thirty, killing weapons tucked easily under her right arm, left hand stretched down as if making ghostly contact with some hip-level object. She was dressed in a long-sleeved shirt and long trousers over tall soft boots; everything about her was the color of dust. Her wiry, scorched-looking blond hair was closely cropped above angular cheekbones, sun-dark skin, and intensely blue eyes, and she walked with the lithe economy of a distance runner. Dian had chosen her name when she attained her womanhood, in a self-conscious but determined evocation of the goddesses of war and hunt, for, even then, half her lifetime ago, she had known what her skills would be. Her contributions of game to the village's tables were regular, and she held a fanatic's eye toward the security of their boundaries.

The woman at her side, the woman she called sister, was a full head shorter, looked more than her eight years older, and moved with the more compact strength of a person whose muscles dig and lift and build. Her face was browner than the sun could dye it and broad across the cheekbones, set with eyes of the darkest brown and surrounded by thick black hair, glossy smooth in the sun with glints of white in the braid down her back. Her mouth was soft and smiled easily, although there was a long history of burdens borne in the lines beside it. She wore a loose, sleeveless yellow blouse, amateurishly embroidered with bright flowers, and rough woven shorts belted with a similarly colorful and badly woven sash. She had simple, thin-soled sandals on her feet, and she walked with that pelvic looseness peculiar to the last weeks of pregnancy, when ligaments relax and the center of balance shifts almost daily.

The two women, in fact, shared no known ancestors. They were adoptive kin only, milk sisters, Dian rescued and brought to the Valley by the person they both had called "Mother."

Judith was still smiling at Carmen's truculent generosity when they reached the corner of the barn, and Dian made to turn right, toward her quarters up behind the building. Judith stopped her.

"Come to the house," she suggested. "There's some lemonade."

"God, Jude, I would kill for lemonade. But I should go wash first—my clothes are filthy and there's probably ticks in my hair." The farmhouse, with its huge dining room and oversize kitchen, was the social and (if the word can be stretched to fit a community of 285 souls) political center of the Valley, as well as its lending library, town hall, records office, and savings bank. However, it was also Judith's home, and Judith was considerably more fastidious than Dian in matters of housekeeping.

"Don't worry about it," she replied, but added, "we'll sit on the porch."

They went around to the front, up the worn steps

where Judith had shelled the beans, Dian raising an eyebrow at the mess but refraining from comment. Judith scooped up the basket and bowl and pulled open the much-mended screen door, then continued through into the house while Dian leaned her things against the screen walls, her left hand unconsciously signaling to absent dogs that they should lie down, and eased herself into one of the shabbier chairs. She let out a deep breath at this first moment of peace she'd had in what had already been a long day and was far from over; then she put first one booted foot up on the low table, crossed the other over it, and closed her eyes.

Only to become suddenly aware of how very angry she was.

In an unknowing echo of Judith's earlier vision, the picture her sister had painted stood vivid behind Dian's eyelids: the Valley's residents racing round like frightened chickens, as open to invasion as a group of twentieth-century innocents. It made her feel like hitting something. She wanted to go out and shake Laine until the woman's teeth rattled—she was supposed to be Dian's second; why hadn't the damned woman just taken charge? Judith shouldn't have to do it all, she wasn't in any condition to carry that burden. Hell, Judith really shouldn't be here at all, she should be up at the caves with Kirsten and the others.

But it wasn't just Laine she was furious with, wasn't even stubborn Judith. *You stupid, stupid bitch*, she swore at herself. *You think you can go and have a camp-out any time you feel bored? What if you'd gone toward the sea like you wanted to? What if you hadn't just happened to wake up so early, hadn't had that headache, had gone downhill for firewood instead of up?*

Christ, you could have been counting waves and contemplating your fucking navel while the whole

Valley was being wiped out. You'd have come back and found burnt-out ruins and the buzzards picking over their bones, and how about boredom then?

Hey, a small voice objected, *if I hadn't been bored and gone out in the first place, we wouldn't have known the wagons were coming until the outer guards spotted them, and we'd be in no better a spot.* But she rode over her mind's objection, because she was frightened and furious and grave danger was coming wrapped inside two strange wagons, and there was not a thing she could do to stop it.

Luck alone had put her on that hillside at that time. She'd been bored because nothing had happened for so long, and now that something was happening, she wasn't ready. Of all the stupid, irresponsible things, to be off in the woods playing with the dogs instead of doing the job the entire Valley depended on her for. Only dumb, blind, terrifying luck had prevented those wagons from rolling into the Valley unannounced.

Dian was all too aware of the outsize role played by luck in the Valley's very existence: luck the place was overlooked by roving bands of Destroyers at the beginning, two generations ago; luck those raiders thirty years ago hadn't been better armed or more numerous; luck the people hadn't just quietly starved to death or fallen under some plague; luck they hadn't been twisted into brutal parodies of humanity like so many other communities. They were even fortunate in their fairly high fertility rate, and two of the boy children born in the last three years looked as if they might, please God, survive. Luck, too, in her own life: what but sheer chance could have brought the woman she came to call Mother to the crossroads just a few hours after a girl baby, not yet walking, had been abandoned? Sweat, and some blood, and more than a few tears had played their parts, but the potential catastrophes kept her sleepless as it was—and now her irresponsible inattention to the job had placed the Valley in jeopardy, dependent yet again on the whims of luck.

She gnawed a bit of rough skin from her knuckle and opened her eyes to the rich fields and the orchards beyond, to the smooth pond and the lush hillside vineyard and, rising dark above the far orchard, the protective curve of hills, clothed in silent redwoods. A pulse of some series of emotions seized her, something that for an instant brought her absurdly close to tears: love for those hills, that orchard; despair that she couldn't seem to be happy within those bounds like Judith; knowledge that somewhere—hidden deep, faintly felt, instantly suppressed, but nonetheless there—had been a tiny wistfulness at the idea of being free of the Valley, that finding the vultures squabbling over their bones would have been a horror but also *(don't even think it!)* a freedom.

Alone was a word with two edges.

The gentle sound of ice chips moving against delicate glassware broke her bitter reverie, startled her with a brief but vivid evocation of a string of naming ceremonies: Mother, Judith . . .

But it was only Judith, backing through the inner door, holding a laden tray with solemn attention.

"Both ice and the glasses?" Dian asked. "I don't know that the day calls for a celebration, Jude." Ice marked a social occasion, since the supply was limited to what one small freezer in the healer's office could produce and what the Valley had managed to store in the deep cave under sawdust. The glasses holding the ice were quite simply irreplaceable.

Judith set the tray on the table and lowered her bulk into the chair next to Dian's. She handed Dian a glass and held her own up to the light to admire the pale color of the liquid and the translucent slice of lemon, running her tongue voluptuously over the smooth edge before she drank deeply. She set the glass down with care on the table.

"I find them a comfort. Sometimes I get one out just to have a drink of water. It's like I can feel Mother's hands on them. And Father's too." Judith's father had died before his daughter entered womanhood, so that Dian had only a vague memory of him: neatly trimmed beard, strong arms, happy voice. One of his sons had lived, the pride of the community, Judith's big brother, Peter—hidden away in the cave now with the others. "I've gone ahead with the preparations we talked about. The sentries are set, the next ones should go out in about an hour; that's what Jeri said you wanted. I decided that you were right about wanting to keep the visitors away from the houses, but keeping them outside the Gates entirely seemed too blatant a message. They're hardly concealing themselves, after all. So I set Hanna and her family to putting up tables outside the slaughtering sheds, asked her to heat up the boilers. Did everything seem to be coming along okay when you rode by?"

Dian nodded. "Yes, it looked fine. I still think outside the Gates would be better, but even in the meadow I can put Laine and Jeri in the trees with their rifles, to cover us. What did you decide about Ling?"

"Dian, I can't send our healer up to the caves when there might be trouble."

"'Trouble,'" Dian snorted.

"For heaven's sake, she's been here ten years, plenty long enough to knock the aristocratic edges off her. And she never was as fragile as she looks."

"That's true," Dian admitted. The healer's delicate hands had never hesitated in that emergency amputation last year; her lovely Chinese eyes had not so much as winced away from the sight of the Smithy's bloodbath. The woman was an enigma—no family, no casual relationships, no reason to be here, as far as Dian could see. She'd just ridden in with Mother from a trip to Meijing nine and a half years ago and been here ever since. She'd come here to leave something behind, no doubt. Or someone.

Dian shook her head to clear out the extraneous thoughts and tapped the last precious chips of ice into her mouth, placing the glass on the tray with care. "I'd better go feed the dogs," she said, then paused in the act of getting to her feet. "Speaking of whom, how many of them do you think I should have down there tonight? I'm not sure I can control more than four at once if things go bad. I'd have to just turn them loose."

Judith looked at her grimly. "If things go bad, we'd want them turned loose. Bring five or six. You won't have any trouble with that many if things stay friendly."

"Right." Dian raked her long fingers back and forth through her hair, loosing a shower of dried leaves and dust. "Look, you asked me this morning if I thought there was danger. I don't know, but it doesn't feel exactly dangerous." Her hand moved to the back of her neck, and she stood, cupping the spot. "I wish I could pin it down, but it just feels like something very odd is going on. On the surface this whole thing is a straightforward problem, but I feel... prickly. And it's not just the foxtails in my shirt either!" She shot a glance at Judith, then sighed, gathered her weapons, and went out. Judith sat and looked at the sparkling, empty lake, her hands unconsciously traveling up and around the swollen globe of her belly.

The sun moved across the sky, the shadows began to lengthen. In the chapel, Judith recited the prayers she had learned at her mother's knee, then sat listening to

the polyglot prayers of those around her, from Latin
Hail Marys to half-remembered Nicene Creeds: the
age-old divisions between Catholic and Protestant
meant about as much now as the division between
MacCauley, the Valley's nominal owners, and Escobar,
who had begun as farm hands. Judith was both, as her
prayers were both Catholic and Protestant. In the infirmary, Ling the healer finished packing up her scanty
drugs, set another batch of bandages to sterilize, and lit
a stick of incense in front of her small Buddhist altar,
praying in fervent Chinese that her services would not
be needed. In the barn, Carmen, speaking her own native Spanish, reciting her own form of prayer, talked to
her equine charges, telling them what was going on and
that they shouldn't worry, before she went to help her
two co-wives with an early milking.

Not all the residents prayed. Dian finished doctor-
ing the paw of the young bitch, Maggie, who had
limped home during the afternoon, then went to look
for Laine and Jeri. She found her two lieutenants arguing over sniper positions among the trees and buildings, and settled it by telling them who she wanted
where. Before Laine could do more than bristle, a
rider cantered up the road with news of the wagons'
progress; she hesitated between Laine and Dian, then
to Dian's further vexation, gave her report to the
space between them. The report was brief; the rider's
relief at getting away from the two aggrieved women
palpable.

Others prepared for the coming invasion in a manner neither spiritual nor combative but merely practical. In the clear space between the sheds atop which
two snipers would lie, plank tables were being assembled, cook fires lit, beer barrels hauled, slabs of beef
laid ready, mountains of corn shucked.

Of all the residents of the Valley, perhaps only one
nurtured a degree of satisfaction: Judith's thirteen-

year-old daughter, Susanna, although as apprehensive as anyone else, was also gratified that she had been allowed to stay in the Valley instead of being hidden away with the men and the children. She pestered Dian until finally her aunt threatened to throw her bodily into the pond and sent her down to help at the makeshift kitchen.

And in the big cave, hidden deep in the hillside over the Valley, more prayers were said, another set of defense preparations was made, and old Kirsten prepared to tell one of her simple stories of Before.

KIRSTEN

Kirsten was old, had been old ever since anyone could remember. Ling, who in addition to being the village's healer was its unofficial historian, had long tried to pin down her age, with limited success, because the old woman made a game of keeping everyone guessing—even her granddaughter Judith didn't know for sure. The next oldest resident was about sixty-five, having been born during the final throes of what the West called "civilization." Pubescent when she had arrived, Ruby remembered Kirsten as being gray-haired even then; that would make Kirsten now in her late eighties or nineties; Ling would not bet that she had not passed her century mark.

Although her eyes had dimmed and she often slept now in the afternoons, Kirsten's hands and voice were firm, and her wits as sharp as ever. As she sat waiting for her audience to settle, the sunlight crept into the passageway that connected the cave with its entrance. The ancient eyes looked past the half-illuminated moving figures, past them and into a time long, long gone.

I am so tired, she thought to herself. I have seen too

much, fought too many battles, tasted more adrenaline than one woman ought. Long, long ago I was granted a few sweet years of childhood; then the Troubles began, with images burned into our minds: planes slipping into buildings with a bloom of fire; a city school dead down to the last classroom pet; a small town littered with corpses from a bioweapon. The vocabulary of terror—virus and nanophage, genetic modification and dirty bombs—causing the collective mind to wince back from the horrors, that grinding fear of crowds that seized us all, and our powerful mistrust of all but the simplest of technologies, followed finally by the Valley's retreat into itself. Riots raging Outside, and civilization's Destroyers—technophobia gone mad—at the Gates for our last male-fought battle, which saw three of our precious boys bleeding into the earth: my sweet Tony, little more than a child, pounding down the road with a gun in his hand, a David into battle. Only this Goliath killed his shepherd-boy before falling.

Too many sights, too many changes, too many years of chosen blindness—growing crops, raising children—and here we are, yet again counting our bullets and sharpening our arrows while old Kirsten keeps her people occupied and calm.

What pretty stories shall I tell you, my children? she mused. About my mother, maybe? First in her family to go to university (and last, it looks like, for a long time), fought her way out of a bad first marriage (No bad marriages now, are there, my children? We can't afford them) and through a male-oriented tenure system to establish a department of Women's Studies? There's a pretty story for the cave: the bitter joke of feminism, so many strong women fighting for so long to get the merest crust of equality, only to have the world turn around and shovel the entire feast onto our heads. Shall I tell you about equal rights, and we can laugh until our throats hurt?

No; all you want now, my children, is men's history.

Not the story of Alicia, for three years my very best friend, who came here from being raped by a mob, who whimpered whenever she saw more than two or three menfolk walking together, who finally hanged herself from the walnut tree when she was nineteen. And not how secretly glad it made me at first, for her sake, to hear that men all over the world were dying off.

Oh, my bones ache. How old does a woman have to be, to be allowed to vent her anger?

But they sit and wait, needing me.

No; when the time comes for you to hear those tales, when curiosity begins to unfurl like a fern frond out of a fire-ravaged hillside, you will begin to remember the books we all wrote for you, sitting on the library shelves, untouched and waiting. I won't live to see the day, but never mind.

For now it's a pretty story you want, my children, not something to trouble your sleep too much. Something to set the mood so we can pretend this is a party, a tale to take our minds off those approaching wagons.

Not a dark story, then. But because I am old and my bones do ache so, there may be threads of dark showing through the light. That I can't help.

The cavern had quieted, the faces were expectant. Kirsten's old lungs drew breath and she began obediently as she always began: *When I was young...*

"When I was young, the Valley belonged to my grandparents, and we always came up for the summer. When school stopped in June we would all come up together for a couple of weeks, before my father went back to work in the city. It took us half a day to get here. We would load up the car the night before—

you all know what a car was?" This was a ritual question, and invariably the children would demand to be told, and Kirsten would launch off into a description of the joys and terrors of the great, gleaming steel monster whose rusted shell now lay in the lower orchard, a home for mice and a beloved plaything for the children. "And once when I was a little older than Shawna here we had a car with a top we could fold back, and driving it over the hills to the farm the wind would grab our hair, and I remember how it felt to let my hair fly in the breeze, like some movie star." ("The movies" and "television" were two other favorite topics with her audiences, although it had been years since the last television screen had gone black, and the Valley's sole computer in Ling's infirmary was too valuable to spend on the few remaining discs.) "It took me two days to get the snarls out of my hair," she laughed a rueful chuckle, "and I cut it all off the following week."

"How many people used to live here, Grandma Kirsten?" prompted one of the girls.

"Well, let's see. My grandparents the MacCauleys lived in the big house, and the Escobars had the three houses at the far end of the Great Meadow—I married the son of one of them, Rosario, much later. So maybe twenty people altogether. Of course, when I was about, oh, ten or eleven maybe, my mother brought us up here for good, when the plagues began and the world began to go strange. By the time my womanhood came on me there were thirty-eight or forty of us here, almost as many men at first as women. My mother was here—my father was killed in one of the first Destroyers riots—and Grams and Gramps, although he died soon after we moved up. And of course my little sister and my brother Will. My mother's two sisters brought their families, and a bunch of Escobar relatives came, and some friends of both families came here too, toward the End. Now, who would you like to hear about?"

Voices called out names—"Gramps," "your father," "Aunt Eve"—but gradually the requests for "Will" won out. None of the children actually remembered Will, who had died ten years before, but they all felt they knew the irascible old man whose passion for gadgets and tinkering had given the community all of its most basic machines, from the heavy water-mill machinery to the much-repaired photovoltaic panels that powered Ling's computer and freezer, and whose stubborn refusal to be "coddled," as he called it, had driven the women to despair while setting a secret model in the minds of the young men.

"Will, is it?" Greeted with shouts of enthusiastic agreement, her old eyes glittered with amusement at their choice. "Ah, Will. He was a real rascal, that one. Always had bits of string and wheels and clock gears falling out of his pockets, always off somewhere in his mind. We used to tap on his head to get his attention—he'd never hear us otherwise.

"Will was a few years younger than me, and how he loved those early summers up here, more than any of us. It was safe here, you see, and he could run to his heart's content without fretting about the cars and crazies of the city. Starting at Easter time he'd begin making plans, sketches and drawings, books from the library, talking to Gramps on the telephone—you all remember what a telephone is?" Most of the women present had been to Meijing, but few would have actually used one of the city's telephones. To the rest it was another children's toy, a Remnant lump of colored plastic that they took on faith as a variation on the cup-and-string lines of the kids' forts; nonetheless, all nodded. "So, he knew weeks in advance what he was going to do, and just how long it'd take him.

"Then in the middle of June we'd set off, pack one

day and leave early the next morning. Once, when I was very young, it took only three or four hours to get here, but later the roads were bad, and bridges would go down, and toward the end we'd have to circle way south and then come up along the coast to avoid the crazies on the hill. We'd pack a lunch, and we'd drive and drive, and the sun would always be so hot, and the air-conditioning never worked—you know what an air conditioner was? No? You know the refrigerator in Ling's office, that she uses to keep her medicines cold? It was like that, only it kept a room or a car cool instead of just a box. An air conditioner. Anyway, it was always hot, and we'd sit and wait and fuss and ask, 'How long now?' about two thousand times until my parents were going crazy with it, and then finally, *finally* we'd come over the last hill and see the trees. We'd all shout and yell, even Mom, and when we got down to the creek at the bottom Dad would stop the car and we'd all spill out and run down to the water and splash for about two seconds, and then we'd all jumble back in any which way, and we'd start up the last hill, past the sheds and across the bridge, up the curve, through the orchard, and at last we'd pull up through the gate and under the walnut tree and stop at the house, and there would be Grams and Gramps waiting for us, and Grams would say, 'Oh, you must be fair parched for thirst,' and we'd all stretch and groan and go off to the veranda, but—who do you think had other things on his mind? That's right—Will. He'd jump out of the car holding the box of drawings and ideas he'd been saving up and shove them straight into Gramps's hands, and Gramps would push back his hat and scratch his head and say, 'Now, what have we here, young Will?' and the two of them would go off to the workshop back of the barn, heads together, Will's bobbing up and down and his tongue going a mile a minute, and the two of them would spend the next eight weeks in just that position, bent over Will's drawings for a new kind of gopher trap or building a wind-powered water pump, or a donkey-powered threshing flail, or any of a hundred other things. The rest of us spent the summer riding horses and swimming and exploring the hills, but Will spent it getting grease under his fingernails and bruising his thumb with the hammer.

"Sometimes, though..." The old voice faded for a minute and became reflective. "Did I ever tell you how this cave was discovered?" A few of the older women exchanged glances and shifted slightly in their places, but it was not a bad story, really, just... troubling. They did not interrupt. "I didn't? Will found it. Or maybe I should say, it found him.

"As you know, in those days, when I was young, men were very different. There were a lot more of them, for one thing, so they didn't have to be so careful. In those days my uncle and Gramps ran the farm, and Grams did the house and the garden. The menfolk made most of the important decisions and, more than that, they did all of the nasty, dangerous jobs, like digging up septic tanks and felling trees and running the farm machinery. Yes, Lilyanne, they did so. Boys ran wild, climbed trees, went hunting with rifles. Girls too, but boys more. Hard to believe, isn't it?"

Again there was an exchange of frowns above the listening heads. This was dangerous ground, introducing ideas that frustrated the boys and reminded the men of their impotence. All the women, including Kirsten when she thought about it, tried to avoid referring to the times when men were men and free to risk their feet with ax blades and their lives by traveling outside the Valley. Reminders made everyone uncomfortable, and there would be repercussions from Kirsten's suggestions—young boys up in trees, teenage boys with a gleam in their eyes. There was little they could do

about it at the moment, though, short of stifling
Kirsten's tale—and the long-term repercussions of that
would be worse. Better to let her go, and deal with the
masculine urges to adventure as they came along. And
have Judith give her grandmother hell tomorrow.

If there was a tomorrow.

"Anyway, Will had been reading up on bomb shel-
ters—they were very popular around then, places to
hide in case of a war—as if it did them any good when
it did come, trapped underground—but he decided
there must be caves up in these hills that we could
use. He was eleven, I think, the last summer before
we moved up here for good. He left after breakfast,
didn't show up at lunch, and by suppertime everyone
was out looking for him.

"I'll never forget that night. It was so hot, not a
breath of wind to stir the leaves and no moon at all,
just twenty or thirty neighbors out searching the hills
with lamps and torches and flashlights. We could hear
each other shouting out Will's name and crackling
through the bushes and calling back and forth, the
sounds bouncing around the hills and the lights flickering in and out among the trees, and the old farmhouse blazing with light in the center of the Valley.

"It was after midnight when Rosario's father found
Will, all day and half the night after he'd come across
this cave and the entrance fell in on him. Just there,"
she pointed, and the heads all turned as one to the raw
patch lit by the last of the sun, and stared in awe as at
the proof of a god's passing.

"They got him out and brought him down the hill on
a stretcher, a long line of men and women carrying
lights, looking like a lit-up caterpillar as they came. He
had a broken leg—that was why he always limped, you
know? It never really healed properly—and after the
doctor'd been and set it, after Will was asleep on the
daybed on the veranda, after everyone had been fed and

talked off the excitement and then gone off to their own homes, I saw my mother cry for the first time in my life. She was sitting next to him where he lay sleeping. She just sat there, holding her hands together in her lap, looking down at his face all scratched and bruised in the light of a candle, her tears just running helplessly down her cheeks and dripping onto her arms." Kirsten looked into the distance in silence for a few moments. "She lost two boy babies before Will, and one after. Not one of them got to his second birthday."

The cave was still, the faces ruddy now with the last of the sun's rays. The eyes were all focused at a mythic place long removed from sight, when men were free to travel without heavily armed guards, free to risk life and limb doing dangerous jobs, a barely conceivable time when a boy child might wander away from his caretakers long enough to get himself lost and injured. The younger eyes wondered at it, half disbelieving. Kirsten's hooded eyes watched the faces of the girls and the women as each took a deep breath, their minds coming back to this cave, and she saw how every one of them, every pair of female eyes present, glanced quickly at one or another of their twenty-seven males, from sturdy little Jonathan, asleep in his mother's arms, to Peter, his beard now more than half gray, and Anthony, ancient among the men at sixty-two. The same every time—a quick glance, a touch of pain, of love, of blessing and fierce protection bestowed. These twenty-seven were the most valuable possessions the farm community had, and also the most vulnerable.

Every person there knew that if the party on the road wanted anything, it would be the Valley's men.

It was nearly dusk when Susanna burst through the door of the veranda where Judith was trying to rest, to deliver Jeri's message that the wagons had cleared the

last hill before the Valley entrance. Judith pushed her
daughter gently back out the door and went to find
Dian, only to meet her halfway to the house. The two
women, walking shoulder to shoulder, came through
the gate beneath the walnut tree and made their way
down the once-paved road in the twilight. The noises
of the night were starting up, the whir of crickets filling the Valley; the sun's final rays were brushing the
tips of the highest trees on the cave's hillside. The
night air lay sweet and dusty and warm around them.
The dogs that flowed around the two women were attentive and glad for an evening out, knowing only
that some form of excitement was in the air. Dian
whistled them back from the millpond but let them
run on ahead to the lights and cooking smells that
waited on the other side of the bridge.

Culum alone stayed with Dian, walking at her hip
so her left hand brushed his massive shoulders. It was
their usual position, especially when something was
up, as if physical contact was a necessary element in
the partnership. Judith, glancing over at Dian's expression and then down at Culum's equally intent
face, hid a smile. The dog would not move from
Dian's side all night. Unless his teeth were needed,
she corrected herself, the smile fading. A hundred
eighty pounds of muscle, teeth, and brain made for a
weapon more effective than the bow in Dian's other
hand.

In the meadow, the lamps were lit and hung, the
big boilers gurgling to themselves. Dian checked the
defenses, adjusting the arrangements slightly to her
satisfaction: a half-circle of women with Judith in the
center, Dian and the other archers to the sides, the rifles above and behind. As she took up her own position to the right of the greeting committee, bow
strung and arrow nocked, she wondered if the others
were as conscious as she of the uncomfortable over-

tones of meeting here, in the ground where the messi-
est of slaughtering tasks were done. The echoes of pig
squeals and the whish of knives over whetstones
seemed to tremble in her ears.

Silence gathered and spread across the meadow. A
huge orange moon raised its head over the protecting
hills, lighting the road beyond the reach of the lamps.
The women took up their positions, the dogs arrayed
for maximum effect. The short wait began.

Suddenly the sound of harnesses and hooves rang
through the still air. As they drew near, Dian was hit
by a spasm of apprehension: they had made the wrong
decision—they should have remained in hiding until
these people declared themselves. Culum whined
softly, searching for the enemy she was feeling; she
nudged his side comfortingly with her knee and
fought the urge to step back into the shadows. One of
the women beside her had unconsciously moved until she was slightly in front of Judith, protecting her
and the life she carried. The strange outriders were
staying close to their wagons, although they could
undoubtedly see the lighted welcome party ahead.

Dian moved into the center of her dogs, the better
to control them. They were alert now, aware of why
they were here at this strange gathering. They sat on
their haunches, the five animals, and waited with
their humans.

The wagons were only a hundred yards away when
Culum reacted. Culum, who left Dian's side only
when commanded, who formed her other half, who
had not disobeyed a command since he was six
months old; Culum rose to his feet, hunch-shoul-
dered and intent, staring at the first wagon as if he
could see through its sides. His hackles bristled huge
across his shoulders and down his spine, and Dian
readied her bow: in a moment he would begin his
war-croon, and then all hell would be loosed, but

abruptly, with Dian's warning shout nearly to her lips, his head came up, his ears pricked, and his ruff began to subside; his tail even waved experimentally. Dian told him to sit. He twitched one ear and ignored her—*Culum* ignored her. And then, to her utter disbelief, the dog set off at a brisk, swinging trot down the road and got as far as Judith before Dian found her voice. Her outraged command cracked through the air like a whip.

Culum stopped, looked over his shoulders at her, and slowly, reluctantly, settled down onto his haunches, giving an audible sigh as he did so. He sat with one eye on her, head cocked, deliberate patience in every line of his powerful body. He was humoring her, she saw with amazement, putting up with her human shortcomings. Okay, he was saying. She had the right to order him around, but in his opinion she was being very stupid. Dian, meeting his gaze, only half-heard the approaching wagons. She had trusted Culum with her life before this; she would trust him now.

"Okay, if you say so," she told him. He stood with an air of satisfaction and trotted off eagerly to meet the strangers. Dian kept the other dogs where they were.

The first of the riders had come within hailing distance of the standing half-circle when her words of greeting were strangled by the sight of this huge animal trotting down the center of the road. Her horse shied and cribbed against the bit as Culum went past, but not until he neared the wagon did the rider reach with an oath for her rifle scabbard, then in the next instant draw back her hand and shout in an unnecessarily loud order to her people that nobody was to move.

Culum stared up at the now stationary wagon, completely ignoring the white-faced driver in his interest at what lay within. The woman nearly fell off her perch to the ground five feet below when Culum, tired of waiting, rose up easily onto his hind legs to rest his front paws on the driver's seat, peering into the closed canvas interior behind her. Dian had a moment to wonder at the woman's dedication to duty before a movement within shifted the wagon and caused Culum to draw back and thump down on all fours to the ground, looking up expectantly, tail wagging furiously. The wagon shifted again, and a low murmur came from within. Dian's nocked arrow raised itself marginally, and in the trees around her, the fingers on four triggers tensed.

One arm lifted the flap, and the driver hastily moved aside. The top of a glossy black head of hair appeared, followed by a large booted foot, a trousered leg, and a pair of startlingly wide shoulders. Then the rest of the figure emerged, unfolding itself until it stood upright on the front of the wagon, where it raised a face to the armed women and the lights.

A face that was dark with stubble.

"Holy Mother of God," someone whispered hoarsely into the shocked silence. "It's a man."

THREE

Dian stared with the rest of them at the sight, telling her eyes that she was indeed seeing a strange man climbing down from the wagon and gingerly patting the tawny head Culum thrust against his chest.

"They must be insane," she muttered. The only males she had ever seen on the road were the occasional lunatics such as Crazy Isaiah, the self-proclaimed prophet who usually spent some days in the Valley every spring on his southbound migration. She'd heard of large caravans of armed women protecting one or more men being transferred between towns or rich families, seen lesser versions on the safe roads near Meijing, but a male, apparently sane and whole, escorted by less than two dozen women through the wilderness? Unheard of.

And the shocks for the evening were not over. The man turned his back on Culum to reach up to the wagon. A small figure slipped through the canvas, helped by the driver to climb down into the man's arms. The child's features were delicate, but this was clearly a boy, four or five years of age. A beautiful, apparently healthy male child, smiling a bit dubiously at the hairy face of the dog that snuffled at his knee, extending a finger to touch Culum's prominent eye-brows.

The man, quite aware of the effect the two of them had on the women in the clearing, finally raised his head and looked around him. His eyes first sought out Judith, then went to Dian with the other dogs at her feet; when he spoke, his voice was as calm and anti-climactic as his words:

"My son seems to like your dog."

The words broke the spell that had held the meadow in stasis. A murmur arose from the women around Judith. The lead rider pried herself out of the saddle to walk stiffly forward. Although she did not appear to be armed, she sensibly kept her hands in clear sight and stopped well away from Judith.

"My name is Miriam," she began formally. "This is my brother Isaac and his son, Teddy. We come to you from the Oregon Territories, on a matter of great importance for both of our communities. I ask that we be allowed to impose on you, as uninvited guests, for a few days. We still have a fair amount of our own provisions, although we do have an urgent need for a doctor or healer, if you have one." Here her voice slid from its formality. "Two of us were badly wounded yesterday, and I'm afraid—" She caught herself, and after a steadying breath, continued. "We'll be happy to follow your requests regarding your security and will leave our weapons wherever you wish. I am sorry to have given you no forewarning of our arrival, but I think you'll understand why we couldn't when we have a chance to talk." She stopped, obviously so exhausted she could only follow a prepared text.

Judith turned to look at Dian, imperceptibly raising her eyebrows and pointing her chin in the direction of the main house up the hill. Dian looked again at the wagons, the ten mounted riders, the man, the boy, and finally at Miriam. She made her decision and lowered her bow to address the woman.

"If the wagons and weapons remain here, we would be happy to welcome you as guests." She watched closely for any sign of hesitation in Miriam's response, but saw only a relief so great it threatened to release her fatigue completely. Judith saw it too and stepped in.

"We have prepared food and drink for you. Would you like to take it here or up at the house?"

Miriam grinned, and Dian was suddenly conscious of the rich odors and long, laden tables; the strangers must be drooling.

"I don't think any of us craves a roof over our heads enough to wait while this is moved. We've had nothing but cold food for two days, for fear of stopping on that last part of the road."

"You were right to fear it," said Judith. "We never take wagons through there if we can avoid it. You were fortunate to have made it through with only two wounded, considering... considering the burden you carry. But here, have your riders turn their horses into the pen; Carmen will see to them. Our healer is on her way, so if your people would like to wash—there's hot water in there—and then to food and drink, we can see to your wounded."

While Miriam conferred with the man and gave orders to the women, Dian remained where she was and took it all in. The wagons were battered, of course, with the long journey and the attack, but beneath the wear they were well-fitted and sturdy, of clean craftsmanship without unnecessary weight or decoration. The same might be said of the people they carried—competent, healthy individuals beneath the weariness and the unusual circumstances. She watched the man and boy make their way to the wash building, all her dogs now accompanying them and the women beginning to fall in behind. She caught Judith's eye and shook her head in amazement.

"It's like something out of one of Kirsten's stories, men wandering around practically on their own. What can it be about? Well, let them eat and rest first. But I'm going to make the rounds of the sentries. It smells less and less like a trap, but my nose could be numb, following that." She jerked her head to indicate the two males and turned to watch the entourage disappear into the shed. She shook her head again and slipped into the night.

The second wagon had been driven closer to the lights, and when Judith went around the back she found a lamp hanging inside and Miriam and Ling, the healer, bent over a still form lying atop some blanket-covered crates. Even before she climbed in, Judith could see that the woman was seriously wounded; up close, her color was bad, her breathing ragged, and the blankets in which she was wrapped saturated with blood, some of it new and wet. The smell lay hot and cloying in the small canvas space. Another woman watched dully from under a bandaged head as the three of them grimly assessed the damage. Ling looked up at Judith.

"I'll have to take her up to the infirmary."

Judith nodded. "Get Carmen to drive you up, and take one or two others as well, to help you carry them in. She'll have to bring the wagon back down—Dian doesn't want it up there." She looked at Miriam, and asked, "You'll stay down here?" Seeing the woman's look of anxious indecision she said, "We'll join them within the hour if you feel all right about leaving her. Ling is a fully qualified healer, a very good one. She's from Meijing, and trained there."

"Yes, I thought so. I couldn't do anything for Jenn anyway, so, yes, I'll stay here."

"Do you know her blood type?" asked Ling.

"Type? No, but one of the others—"

"Find out. She could use a transfusion, and it'd save time if I didn't have to do a test."

"I'll go now," she said, and climbed out the front of the wagon. She was back in two minutes. "B positive, fairly sure."

"Good," said Ling, and to Judith, "I'll take Hanna and Kila with me; they can carry her in and stick around to be drained. Two of our B positives," she told Miriam.

"Take Susanna too," suggested Judith. "She'll be happy to help with the needles, and she can be your runner if you need anything."

"Fine. Let's go, before this woman turns white." Miriam bade a few hasty words of encouragement to the conscious woman before clambering with Judith out the back of the wagon. Judith rounded up the four individuals and sent them up the hill with the wagon, then gestured Miriam toward the sounds of cutlery and plates and the beginnings of conversation. Miriam glanced down at Judith's waistline and asked the question that spanned the ages.

"When are you due?"

"Another seven or eight weeks," she said, and continued with more information than Miriam would ask for. "This is my third time. You've seen my daughter, the girl in the wagon."

Miriam did not look surprised at this unwonted gift of intimacy, Judith noted, and she had manners enough not to ask about the other pregnancy: lost or healthy male, neither was her business.

"A blessing on your life" was all she said, a phrase that covered both Judith and the life she carried. Judith found herself warming to the woman.

The next hour was primarily a matter of fueling bodies and relaxing tense muscles, guests and hosts alike settled on benches before the long tables. An unstated agreement had been reached to set aside explanations and questions while more urgent matters were dealt with. Underneath, however, testing and probing was going on. Watching each other eat and drink and listening to apparently inconsequential talk made for the beginnings of understanding. Those seated near the man and boy, though too polite to gawk, nonetheless missed none of their words or gestures, and there was quite a bit of casual coming and going in the vicinity of that table.

By the time the guests reached their thick wedges of berry pie awash in equally thick cream, conversation was flowing more easily, helped no doubt by the mugs of beer that had gone down the thirsty throats. The moon lit the Valley and the lamps gave an air of festivity, and it was some time before Judith noticed Dian leaning against the shed with a plate in her hands, looking on as usual. Although, on closer look, she was alone; that was not as usual. Judith excused herself (her place across from Miriam was filled the instant she stood up) and went to join Dian.

"Where's Culum?" she asked.

"Lying on the boy's feet," Dian answered around a mouthful of food.

Judith looked more closely and, indeed, the table seemed to have been built over a pale boulder shape. "I hope he doesn't stand up under that table."

"Everyone has good reflexes," Dian answered. And the platters were nearly empty, anyway. "So, what do you think?"

"They seem a good lot. Exhausted, of course. My curiosity's killing me, but it's sure to be a long and complicated story, and Kirsten and the others will have to hear it too. I was thinking I might let Miriam off the hook tonight and set up a general meeting at the house first thing in the morning. Would that be okay with you?"

Dian grinned, her teeth dark with berries. "Of course not! I'll lie awake all night wondering, just like you will. But you're right, it'd be cruel to keep them up in the state they're in. In fact, I figured you might decide to put it off, so I asked Lenore to arrange for some beds. I thought Miriam and the man and boy should go in the big house with you, but I had them scatter our other...guests around, one or two to a house. I don't want them all together. And I'm also keeping the sentries at double strength for the next couple of days." She glanced up at a burst of laughter from the tables surrounding Isaac, and smiled wryly. "Just because we like them doesn't mean we should be stupid. Oh, yes—tell them they're all going to be searched before they go up. Jeri and Laine will do it. I've told them to be polite about it but thorough."

"If you think it's necessary. Where will you be?"

"Oh, around," Dian said vaguely.

"I can imagine. Anyway, that sounds fine. We'll probably finish here in about half an hour. I'm sure Miriam will want to check on her two wounded as soon as she can."

"Tell her that I helped Ling—and Susanna, so I'm sure you'll hear every detail—take out the arrowhead, and with the help of some of your precious ice we got the bleeding stopped. Ling was just starting a transfusion when I left. And I went up to the caves and let everyone know that they'd probably be able to come down first thing in the morning. Kirsten told them stories for a while, and they're settling down for the night—they didn't seem terribly disappointed that we weren't calling them back instantly. Can't think why."

Judith laughed, grateful for the relief of humor. It was true, the alerts that sent the people to the cave might be serious affairs, but the enforced leisure made it a social occasion as well, a dramatic break from the grinding toil of daily life. And as Dian had noted that morning, there was usually a higher than average number of babies born forty weeks later.

Judith went back to the table to reassure Miriam about her wounded rider and about her chances for a solid night's sleep before having to account for herself. The party broke up shortly after that, the participants trudging wearily up the road to their beds by the light of the swinging lamps.

Dian squatted in the shadow of the mill, her unstrung bow cradled loosely against her side as she studied the passing strangers. One of them looked in her direction, a small blond woman with the sharp features of a vixen—but when the stranger glanced away again, Dian decided that she'd just been curious about the mill itself.

No one else showed any interest in her, but she examined them closely, marking the great fatigue in their shoulders and awkwardness in empty hands accustomed to holding weapons. In Miriam she saw the beginnings of relief, as of one slowly straightening after setting down a heavy burden, and she wondered at it. In the man Isaac she noted again his awareness of the subtle currents around him and a calm acceptance of his place in those currents. There was also great affection in the way he held the now-sleeping child, chest to chest, one thin shoulder tucked under the man's stubbled chin, two sandaled feet dangling free. Judith's face she glimpsed in the wavering lamplight, listening to Miriam. Judith, too, looked relieved beneath her chronic look of strain, as well as preoccupied—no doubt speculating, along the same lines as Dian, how this group was going to affect the Valley. And finally, Dian looked at the dogs. She trusted her dogs as she trusted few humans, and the animals seemed to like these strangers. Culum especially had formed an immediate bond with the child, Teddy, which fact interested Dian greatly. Even now he walked at the man's side, so close that his rough coat occasionally brushed the boy's naked leg. She stayed silent and still until all the guests and the last of their escorts had disappeared behind the high corn, and then she stood, stretched her tired muscles, and walked up the solitary road in the moonlight.

The next morning dawned blue and gold, with a sure promise of heat. Those who had spent the night in the cave came down at first light, and the sun coming over the surrounding hilltops found them at chores and sitting down to early breakfast tables, chattering excitedly but at low volume, so as not to awaken these intriguing visitors. There were frequent glances cast up at the main house, in hopes of seeing the man or the boy, but as yet all was quiet.

By the time Dian came riding up the road, a large buck strapped behind her saddle, four rabbits dangling in front, and a pack of dogs ebbing and flowing around the horse's trotting hooves, most of the visitors had arisen and were at the tables of their host families, making the first awkward attempts at conversation. Dian had taken her dogs out well before dawn, both for exercise and to supplement the day's supplies. Despite the inevitable gore and violence of the kills, and despite not having been to bed that night, she returned refreshed, purified as always by the simplicity of death. As Dian passed the first houses of the Valley, she came across Carmen's oldest stepdaughter, Lupe, walking up and down the road, patting and comforting her screaming two-year-old sister. Lupe grimaced at Dian, and said in a loud voice, *"Ella no le gusta los estranjeros."* Dian nodded in sympathy; she might not go so far as to say that she didn't like them, but there was no doubt, fascination and fear would set the tone of the entire Valley for days.

Dian left the meat at the kitchen, then rode to the barn and rubbed down, watered, and fed her horse. When she went to the kennels to do the same for the dogs, she found Susanna in residence, sitting on the floor with the latest litter of puppies. The girl gave Culum a thump on his side by way of greeting and grinned up at her aunt, one puppy cradled to her chest and three more mock-fighting across her still-adolescent legs.

"Puppies have such a great smell, don't they?" she said. "It's like sweet and sour milk."

"You used to smell like that, mewling and puking at your mother's breast," Dian told her. "And your personal habits were every bit as irresponsible as these guys'." She laid the rifle, coat, and saddlebags on a table and went to liberate puppies and girl, brushing ineffectively at some of the more unsavory stains on her niece's clothing. After a minute she gave up, returned the puppies to their mother, and took her things down the hall into her quarters to see about her own breakfast. She called back over her shoulder at Susanna.

"What's your mother got planned for the morning?"

Susanna followed Dian into the house and helped her return equipment and clothing to their respective racks. "That's why I'm here—Mom sent me to fetch you. That woman, Miriam, wants to meet with you and Mom and Kirsten and a bunch of others, I forget who, as soon as you're ready. Why are they here? I was busy with Ling last night—did you hear that Jenn—that's her name, Jenn—looks a little better this morning, and Ling's pretty sure she'll live? Anyway, Mom wouldn't tell me anything this morning but to come here and wait for you, but I want to know what they're doing here. Nobody ever tells me anything. I'm not a child, you know. How can a man travel like that? Why did they bring the boy? What do they want?"

Dian laughed and placed both hands on the girl's shoulders, bending to look directly into the excited young eyes and saying clearly, "My questions exactly. And maybe if you'd let me get myself together, we can get them answered."

"Okay, okay," said Susanna. "I'll go tell them you'll be down in a bit. But there's breakfast there— Mom's even making coffee!"

"I'll be there as soon as I'm clean and the dogs are fed."

Half an hour later Dian trotted up the three steps to the kitchen door. Someone else had been up early, for there was a rich yeasty odor of fresh bread beneath the sharp tang of bacon. She followed the smells and the voices past dining room and library to the cool veranda. The veranda was large, wrapping around two sides of the house and fully ten feet deep, but this morning it was packed, with more people standing outside the screened walls—theoretically, one adult from each house, so all the forty-odd families might be represented, but it looked as if the entire population was here, even the babies.

Remnants of breakfast lay on the long table in the room just inside the veranda, and Dian paused to pick over what was left, peering into the empty coffee carafe with chagrin, then carried her plate to the door, where a couple of women shifted to make room for her. There was no sign of the man or his son, but Miriam and two of her women were sitting at the far end with Judith, Kirsten, and Ling. Peter was there to represent the menfolk, with Anthony, the senior male in the Valley. Laine sat in another corner and nodded to Dian, although there was no sign of Jeri, who had also been up all night.

Miriam was describing her band's trip through the destroyed cities on the other side of the hills; her narrative seemed to be drawing to a close. Dian watched her covertly as she ate, studying the woman's black hair and eyes and her strong, compact body. The stranger spoke with an air of authority and self-assurance, her voice quiet and even. Only her posture in the chair revealed her discomfort, as she sat stiff-backed in its softness.

"I'm very sure they didn't know that Isaac and Teddy were with us," she was saying. "If they had, they would never have let us get away so easily. They were just probing, and it was only bad luck that two of us got in the way of their arrows." She paused. "We had gambled on that, of course. We decided to send a small enough caravan that people would think us of little importance. As it was, we were almost too small."

That seemed to mark a good pausing place, for Judith stood up and began to organize a flow of dirty plates and utensils toward the kitchen. When most of the dishes were out, Judith looked down the length of the veranda at Dian.

"We wondered if you were going to join us."

Dian hastily swallowed her mouthful of sweet roll. "Sorry if I held things up. But you did get your revenge—to think I missed coffee because of a few lousy rabbits." General laughter was followed by shouts of triumph as Lenore came from the kitchen bearing a solitary cup of tepid, greasy-looking coffee and presented it to Dian, who held it up, sniffed it deeply, and finally slurped it with exaggerated appreciation.

"Ah, the nectar of the gods! Bless you, Lenore." She placed the coffee on the floor between her feet and wiped the last smear of egg from her plate before adding it to a passing stack of empty plates. She retrieved the cup and savored the contents while the room was settling down again. When it was quiet enough to hear children playing in the pond, she lowered the half-empty cup and looked across the intervening heads at Miriam. "I'm sorry I missed your story," she said in a carrying voice. "I was looking forward to it. Perhaps we can get together sometime, so I can ask you a few questions?"

Which was a roundabout way of asking, What do you want and how long are you going to be here?

Miriam looked down at her hands, fiddling with the narrow silver band around the ring finger of her left hand, then met Dian's question head on.

"I won't be staying for any longer than it takes to rest my women and patch up the lesser wounds. I may have to leave behind Sonja and Jenn, the two in your infirmary. I can't wait for them to heal; our village needs us back." Here she looked up to face Judith. "Isaac and his son will stay here, if you will have them. They are, to put it bluntly, a gift from my people to yours."

The silence was suddenly complete, breathless. Judith, who had also seen the woman's relief the night before and suspected the reason, was not taken by surprise, but with the closed expression of a seasoned trader she voiced the obvious question.

"Why? What do you want in exchange for your 'gift'?"

Miriam sighed gustily and said, almost as if to herself, "I'm really not the person for this. I'm a fighter, not a talker, and it's very likely I'll put my foot in it. But," she said, firming herself visibly, "our talker is in your sick house with blood leaking out of her shoulder, so—it's me or nothing." Her voice, too, grew firmer as she collected her thoughts.

"We come from a town in southern Oregon, near the Smith River, about three hundred miles north of here. It's a hilly area, mountainous even, with patches of decent farmland in isolated valleys. Like here, our communities tend to be small. At least, until recently. A couple of years ago a few of the more . . . unsavory communities joined forces with a leader from out of the north. They were then joined by others, and pretty soon there weren't too many left to oppose them. We are one group who does." Her voice stopped for a moment.

"Three hundred miles is quite a trek for reinforcements," Judith probed, "even if we could spare enough to make any difference to your safety. Surely you have closer neighbors."

"Yes. I mean yes, we have neighbors, but no, we are not looking for reinforcements. And it's not as simple as just fear of petty tyrants. There are things we cannot fight. You see, when our neighbors joined the northern group—the leader calls herself 'Queen Bess,' you may have heard of her? No? Well, you will. Anyway, they told 'Queen Bess' about a nearby cache of weapons and equipment from Before. Near as we can figure, the things were owned by a band of survivalists who didn't make it. None of the locals had been willing to touch the things, but Bess sent some of her people in for them. Most of the weapons were useless after all this time, but in grubbing about in the caves where the hell weapons were stored, her people set loose a plague." Miriam's face grew taut with the memory. "The first we knew of it were the dead fish in the river. Hundreds of them, stinking up the banks and bringing in every rat and dog pack for miles. Then we started seeing dead and dying animals. And then one day, seven of the women from a town upriver came into our village. They were all terribly ill, vomiting blood and losing great wads of hair. Our healer—she's only a doctor, but she spent a year in Meijing—she said they were not contagious, that it was radiation, so we let them in and tried to help, but there was nothing we could do. They died. All of them. One of them brought a small baby, who was still alive when I left, but our healer didn't think she was going to make it."

"When was this?" It was Ling asking in her light, accented voice.

"They came to us the first week of April. We immediately contacted all the friendly families around us, sent scouts to find out what was happening. That's when we heard about Bess and her part in it. By the first part of May it became clear that all the settlements along the river were threatened. Our drinking water comes from a spring, but our living comes from the river, and there was no group in the hills that could possibly take in all of us—there are more than a hundred of us. But, the poison upriver is moving down. Our reserves will see us through the winter, and when the river freezes it'll stop the spread—we hope—but next spring we must go. Or we will die."

Dian spoke up, her voice clear through the crowded veranda.

"And you want to come here."

Miriam's eyes swung to Dian as murmurs and gasps showed that not everyone had heard it coming. She nodded shortly, once, and turned to Judith.

"As I said, I am not the one who should be trying to put this to you, but, yes. We would like to propose that our two villages join forces. Not here, in your valley, but just outside it, where the water from your stream joins that of the other one. It is not ideally protected, but there's good land and plenty of trees for building with."

"Why all the way down here?" asked Judith. "There must be a lot of healthy places between here and there, without having to move three hundred miles?"

"Sure, there are healthy places, but they may not

be safe. It's Bess, you see. Even before the river poison we knew we'd have to do something, either go east into the desert or south into the protection of Meijing. Bess controls all of central Oregon now, from Portland on down, and she's starting to move. If we go south a hundred miles, we'll just have to face the same decision a few years down the line: join her or fight her. No village that's tried to fight has survived, and we're not big enough to consider it seriously. She's on her way to California, you can bet on it. If she keeps up at this rate—and there's nothing to stop her so far—Meijing will be the only one who can challenge her. The poison merely forced the decision on us. We chose you because of your location and because we thought you might take us."

Dian cleared her throat. "Who was your spy?"

Miriam opened her mouth to protest the accusation, reconsidered, then reluctantly answered.

"I don't like the word *spy*, but we were told to come here by the one who calls himself the Prophet Isaiah."

"Crazy Isaiah!" Dian gave voice to a roomful of skepticism. "You came hundreds of miles with two menfolk on the word of a madman?"

This time one of Miriam's two companions, a small blond woman named Anne, spoke up. "He's not as crazy as he gives out, not around us anyway. He—well, he's a sort of uncle. He winters with us sometimes. He was there when the poisoned women arrived, and it shocked him terribly. He lost his family in the same sort of way, years and years ago. After the women died he went silent for a solid week, just sat staring at the wall, and then he came to me—my family is caring for the sick baby—and told me that we all had to move and described this place. He was quite lucid and very definite that this was the only suitable place for us. 'The land is chosen' was how he put it."

"And so you came?" This time it was Judith who spoke the communal doubt.

"Well, no. Not right off." Miriam grinned, an expression as unexpected and appealing as it had been the night before. "We weren't that desperate, to have to take his word alone. We figured we had time enough, so we...well, we sent scouts. Syl, here, for one." She gestured at the third stranger, a woman with blond hair and a foxlike face, the woman who had appeared to notice Dian in the shadow of the mill. She was even smaller than she'd appeared in the darkness, shorter than Susanna. "She came down to see if he was right." Syl gave them a somewhat uncomfortable smile.

"How—" Both Dian and Judith began at once; after a glance at her sister, Dian continued. "How close did you get?"

Syl looked surprised that anyone should expect speech from her. She looked at Miriam as if for permission, then sat up straight in her chair.

"Not too close. Isaiah'd warned us about you and your dogs. I went up in a tree on the top of the next hill. Couldn't see too much of the valley, just enough to confirm that he wasn't talking nonsense. Took a look at the site the other side of the river. Was gone in a day."

"You must be very good."

"I was well taught," she said, with an oddly shy and secret amusement. Miriam moved briskly on, to defer any contemplation of the Valley's breached defenses.

"When she got back we immediately started making plans. At first we were going to send just a few down, to talk and discuss it. It was Isaac who proposed that he and Teddy be sent. As a 'gift,' he said, though I don't think he really likes the idea of being 'given' away. We—" She frowned and fiddled again with the band on her finger. "Our group is a little bit different from yours. For one thing, we seem to have a higher rate of survival for boy babies. Of a hundred and five in the village, twenty-eight—almost a third—are males." Miriam ignored the surprised noises that came from her audience. "And that's another reason we have to get away from the river. Of the four boy babies born in the last eighteen months, only one is alive, and he's the second youngest." She did not look at Judith, whose hand crept of its own volition to her belly. "Our doctor says it's related to the radiation plague that killed the fish and those women. We must leave." Her voice dropped to a whisper, pleading now. "We have to get out of there."

... THE NEXT DAY, WHEN THE CITY WAS

ON THE VERGE OF BEING LOST,

ITS SALVATION CAME FROM THE NEW DANGER ITSELF.

FOUR

THERE WAS LITTLE MORE TO BE SAID, NOT IN THE PRESence of the strangers, at least, and the meeting broke up shortly thereafter. Miriam and her women went to rest and heal their aches in the sunshine and prepare their equipment and stores for departure in a day or two. A general meeting of the community leaders was called for that night and everyone dispersed, talking intently in small groups, to whatever chores were too urgent to put off.

Dian and Judith split up, Dian to receive the reports of the women who had stood watch during the night, Judith to talk with the householders who had given the strangers beds. The two met up later in the morning with Kirsten, climbing to the old woman's sitting room at the top of the house. Kirsten and Judith sat, enjoying the breeze that moved through the attic rooms, while Dian stood at the window, looking down. In the road, some kids were playing Car Drivers, taking turns at Driver and Horse-Power (she could remember making that same mistake herself as a child—how can we have a car without a horse to make it go?). The boy Teddy stood to one side, holding his father's hand and watching the others play; at a distance adults and other children watched them in turn, the children in simple curiosity, the women with an interest rather more complex. Dian wondered idly if the little boy was always so shy, and tried to think if she had yet heard him speak. His father seemed to be telling him something; then the man turned as something caught his attention from behind the building. It was Peter. Judith's brother greeted the stranger, shaking his hand, and said something to the child, who answered by gluing himself more firmly against his father's leg. The two men stood talking for a moment. It was a lovely sight, to Dian and at least a dozen others: two men and a boy in casual conversation on a sunny morning. She ached at how natural and right it looked, until after a minute Peter asked Isaac something and, when Isaac shook his dark head, gestured and led the two new menfolk off in the direction of the pond.

From behind Dian came Judith's voice.

"What do you think?" The question was aimed at both her companions, but Dian turned from the window and took a chair facing the others. Her voice was sure.

"I think the woman, Miriam, is telling the truth—most of it, at any rate. Certainly the reasons for wanting to leave, that rang true. You agree?" This was directed at Kirsten, who dipped her white head in agreement, her gnarled hands busy with a piece of delicate needlework. "I also felt that the part about Crazy Isaiah, which sounded unlikely as hell, must be true. The only part I didn't like the feel of was when she referred to the males in her town. Not the numbers, though I do wonder if that could be an exaggeration—her calculation of percentage was a little generous, twenty-eight out of a hundred five isn't what I'd call thirty percent. You have to wonder if the numbers themselves are stretched. Our percentage is, what, twelve?"

"Twenty-four percent live birth rate, roughly ten percent survival at age three," Judith supplied evenly, and Dian kicked herself at the unnecessary reminder.

"Yes. But it was the other thing she said that struck me, what was it? 'Our group is a little bit different from yours.' That—smelled wrong. Tasted funny?" She searched for the right words, and ended up throwing up her hands in frustration. "I don't know how to say it, but she was hiding something, or rather avoiding bringing it up. Probably nothing important, but it was there." The three sat in silence, considering. Sounds drifted up from the road, the women and girls coming in from the fields across the road for their lunch.

"You are right," said Kirsten. "There is something unsaid. I wonder if we can get it from the man or boy, or from the two they will leave behind in the infirmary."

"Is there any reason we should say yes to this proposition?" Dian asked bluntly. "They're not our responsibility. Why should we risk our future on an unknown village hundreds of miles away? Why shouldn't we say no, very sorry, we don't want you on our doorstep?"

"I can think of any number of reasons," replied Judith. "Aside from the obvious humanitarian one. For one thing, what's to stop them from coming anyway? They could probably get here and set up for the winter without our help. What are we going to do, shoot them? Burn their houses down? They didn't even have to send these people to ask our cooperation at all—they could have just arrived. It would have been a gamble on their part, but then so is having what must be one in three of your adult women gone for two months. The fact that they didn't just drop out of the sky onto us makes me more inclined to listen to them seriously." Dian, reluctantly, had to agree. She picked up her sister's line of thought, musing aloud.

"Assuming for the moment that everything they've told us is the truth, and they've left out nothing major, I will admit that I like what I see. I like the way Miriam works with her people, and the way Isaac acts, both with her and with the boy. It gives the impression of a group of people we could get along with, disciplined but not oppressively so. It's even a manageable number, not so numerous (again, supposing we've been told the truth) that they'd threaten to overrun us, especially if they set up in the grasslands outside the Valley. They've got sense, they're well trained—I'd sure as hell like to know how that woman Syl got in and out like that without the dogs knowing she was there. And whoever organized this expedition has got sense and guts. Their horses are well cared for, their wagons and everything in them well made and carefully thought out."

Judith interrupted. "Did you spend *all* night going through their wagons?"

Dian gave her a tired smile. "Not quite the whole night. Enough to tell me about the minds of the people who own them. As for their bodies—well, still assuming we have the basic facts correctly—this sample of fourteen, roughly a tenth of their population, shows no signs of disease or malnourishment. They're intelligent, educated, and well made physically. Hell, if even one or two come up to the standard of the man, they'd be a prime asset." She stopped abruptly. Kirsten glanced at her with only a trace of amusement, but Judith stared, openmouthed.

"My God, Dian, you're blushing!"

Flustered, Dian stood up and went back to the window. The road was nearly empty now, and none of the strangers was in sight. She turned back to the room.

"Yes, well. Maybe we should say thanks but no thanks—his presence is already disruptive. The whole damned village is going to be at each other's throats over him inside of a week."

"We'll handle it," Judith said. "Personally, I think we'd be fools to pass their offer up. You have to admit, Di, that to have a friendly village next door would help defenses tremendously. It would give us a chance to expand out of the Valley without stretching ourselves—we've talked often enough about our overcrowding, and this way we could easily send six or eight of our families down there without leaving them or us too weak."

"Get rid of some of our troublemakers," Dian grunted.

"Not fair to use them as a dumping ground."

"We don't have anyone that bad. I just mean . . . there are those who might do better elsewhere."

"You're talking about Laine," Judith said bluntly.

"Laine needs more authority than I can give her," Dian said, trying to be fair. "She needs to stretch herself. Being in charge of the yearly trips to Meijing isn't enough." Not enough for Dian's taste, certainly—Laine was a constant thorn in her flesh, and she'd be happy to have the woman gone for months, not just weeks.

Judith heard the faint praise, but let it go without comment: Dian's woman, Dian's problem. She went on with her list of arguments. "A nearby village would also bring in a whole new set of genes. You know how Ling worries about the long-term results of intermarriage. We'd gain a lot, having them here, and as far as I can see without having to give up too much. And a one-to-three survival ratio—wow. If it's genetic instead of environmental, that would make another reason they would want to get clear of 'Queen Bess's' reach."

"All of which is assuming that Miriam is in fact telling the truth. And that there aren't any hidden traps. And, Jude, you know that's one hell of a big assumption."

"So what do we do?"

"Bamboo shoots under the fingernails, burning coals..."

"Di! Be serious."

"The other option is for me to go look. See firsthand how they live, what their problems are, what they aren't telling us."

"What, three hundred miles? Dangerous miles? You can't do that."

"Sure I can. It'd be great."

She had intended to be flippant, but her sister knew her too well and heard the yearning. Heard, too, how thoroughly Dian had thought about it.

"Kirsten, tell her she's crazy."

But Kirsten just let her hands fall idle, and after a minute she said, "Judith is right. We need these people. But Dian, you, too, are right. We must know what we are getting into before we allow these people to move onto our doorstep. Can you assure me that your women can handle the Valley security without you?"

Dian grimaced. "Considering the crap job I've been doing lately, it might be better without me. Laine and Jeri between them would tighten up discipline nicely."

"I don't agree that you have been doing a crap job, but I trust your judgment. However, we should also ask, couldn't Laine do the job of looking at the Oregon community as well as you could?"

The siren call of freedom wailed a protest in Dian's ear—why the hell should Laine get to go?—but she did her best to give an honest answer. "One woman by herself couldn't do it. Even two would be risky, so we'd have to send three or four, or else one and dogs.

We can't afford to have three women gone, and Laine really isn't very good with the dogs."

"So the question that remains is, when do you go?"

Dian leaned on the frame of the window and glanced at her sister. "After the baby comes."

"No!" objected Judith. "You can't wait that long; it'll be full winter by the time you're heading home. You can't travel in that kind of snow."

"Of course I can. You need me for the birth, Jude, you can't tell me you don't." Judith was silent, but looked stubborn. "And it's the only time that makes any sense. I can't go back with them; they'd be sure to get a message to their people and any dirt would be under the rug by the time we got there. I could follow just a few days behind them, but I don't know if it's fair to arrive when their town is still in a dither from these folk coming back. I should see them when things are as normal as they're going to be—like when winter is closing in."

"But winter will close in on top of you. What about waiting until spring?"

Dian stared unseeing into the brightness outside, thinking aloud. "We'll have to tell them I am coming, don't you think? They're going to expect us to send somebody to check them out—surely they won't believe we're going to accept them with open arms simply because they've brought us two menfolk. If we tell them I'm going to come in the spring, they'll either take it at face value or they'll suspect that we're being tricky and I'm actually going to be right on their heels. But nobody's going to expect me to arrive after the snows start in November. I'd have to be nuts." She turned to the room, a grin on her face. "So that's when I'll go."

"*Nuts* is the word. Kirsten, tell her she's crazy."

"She isn't, you know that, my dear. Your sister is

quite capable of sitting out a blizzard in the woods, particularly with her dogs."

"But what if something happened?"

"Something could happen a mile from home, or in the Valley itself," Kirsten pointed out. "I don't like it any more than you do, but it has to be done, and Dian is the one to do it. November or March, it's a dangerous journey, but she will be careful. Won't you, my dear?"

"Oh, yes," Dian said fervently. "Really careful." She didn't care if she sounded like a child begging Mommy for permission; her heart was beginning to soar. *Away*, she thought—*away!*

After a minute, Judith stirred. "I don't like it, but I guess you're right." She dredged up some humor and shook her finger at Dian, a gesture straight from their mother. "But if anything happens to you because you stuck around for the birth, I'll never forgive you."

"It's just possible you may find the storms are not quite so hard this year," said Kirsten mildly. Dian looked at the top of the white head, bent again over its work.

"Why do you say that? You been gazing in your crystal ball again, Granny?"

"Don't mock your betters, child. The winters are getting milder. You two are used to hard freezes and months of snow, but they aren't normal for this area. When I was a child we never had snow in the Valley. Sometimes on the higher hills, but not down here, and the pond never froze hard enough to walk across. It was after the Bad Times that the weather began to go crazy, killed the redwoods on the ridges, changed the birds we get. The last few years, though, they haven't been as bad. Remember last year, it was almost Midwinter before the pond froze solid? I can remember plenty of years we were snowed in by Thanksgiving." She bit off a thread and mused, "I wonder if it's possible that the earth is finally healing herself. Maybe she's going to forgive us after all."

In Judith a tiny warm hope kindled, unexpected against the cold of waiting for the birth, as if the possibility of the earth's reawakening strength was also her own. The three sat there in meditative, almost prayerful silence for several minutes, until Kirsten prosaically broke the communion.

"I'm sorry, girls, but my old bladder needs to pee."

The old woman and her granddaughters rose, and Dian asked one last question.

"Do you think anyone else should be told what I'm going to do? People will notice that I'm getting ready for a trip."

"Let's just say that Ling asked you to make a quick trip to Meijing for medical supplies."

"I'll have to tell Laine, but that can wait until I'm about to walk out the door. Okay? Now, I need to see if there's any lunch left. First breakfast, now lunch," Dian grumbled. "Hope I get one honest meal today."

Two days later Miriam rode off with her women, mounted for speed and leaving behind both wagons, the two injured women, Isaac and his son, and a lot of disturbing questions. The night before they left, there was a general meeting in the unfinished shell of the Great Hall. It lasted until late and was noisy with discussion and dissent, but in the end Judith's opinions were matched by those of the village: most of them liked these women and were impressed by the potential advantages of having them come. The opposition finally stepped down and the vote taken was unanimous for acceptance. This was not perhaps unrelated to Dian's movements during the meeting, her casual changes of seat and whispered conversations in a number of ears. Judith on the dais watched her actions out of the corner of her eye, knowing that once the dissenters were reassured that Dian would find out the absolute truth before the strangers came, their objections would be silenced; and so they were.

When she took the news of the vote to Miriam at midnight, Judith was amazed to see the woman come near to tears. Miriam covered her face with hands that trembled, and whispered "Thank God" to herself several times. When she rode off early the next morning, she looked like a different woman, now that her grinding worries had been lifted from her.

A small committee saw them off, including Judith, Dian, and Isaac. After the dust had settled, Judith glanced sideways at Dian.

"Well, back to work." She turned to Isaac. "I'd like you to wander around for a couple of days, to let you and your son get used to us. Let me know what jobs you'd like to take on—no," she interrupted him, raising one hand, "I don't want to know your work in Oregon. This is a new life for you, and I want you to be able to choose what you're going to do with it. God knows there are a million jobs that need doing. Find one you'd be interested in. Meanwhile, feel free to poke around and ask questions. Just, please, don't take any risks. Keep an eye on Teddy, don't swim alone, don't go out of the Valley without asking Dian or Jeri or Laine about it. You've come a long way to get here, and we don't want to lose you in the chaos of harvest. Okay?"

"I understand. Maybe I should start by helping with breakfast."

"Eating it, yes, but I don't want any work from you for at least two days."

"Right, if you say so. Visiting royalty, that's me." He grinned at Judith, nodded to Dian, and went off, whistling tunelessly, very aware of the two sisters' eyes drilling into his back.

"I do like him," said Judith.

"I saw him first," replied Dian.

"Did not."

"I did. His foot was sticking out of the wagon when I saw it from the hillside," Dian blithely asserted.

"Liar."

The two women walked arm in arm up to the kitchen to start the long day's labors.

ON OCCASION, THEY KEPT THE PEACE
WITH THEIR MALE OPPONENTS,
AND THE FEMALES AND THE MALES MIXED
WITH EACH OTHER IN COMPLETE SAFETY.

FIVE

ISAAC

THE FOLLOWING MORNING DIAN WAS WORKING WITH the dogs when Isaac and his son came around the corner of the barn, interrupting her drills on the "stay" command with three huge-pawed, floppy-eared puppies. When they caught sight of the two newcomers, the pups immediately made to hurl themselves in that direction, but at a sharp word from Dian they crept back, chastened, to their assigned spots.

"I'm sorry," said Isaac. "I didn't mean to disturb you. My son just wanted to see the dogs. Could we come back later?"

"It's no disturbance," she said, with one eye on the dogs. "Actually, the two of you could give me a hand if you'd like. I'm trying to get them used to working around strangers. And," she added, deadpan, "you have to admit that around here there's nobody much stranger than you."

Isaac looked at her sharply, then decided she had been making a joke; he gave her a polite laugh.

"If you and Teddy would like to just stand there for a few minutes, we'll see how undistractible these three can be."

For five minutes Dian worked her young dogs

around and between the two strangers, forcing them
to ignore the tantalizing nearness of new people.
They "came" and they "heeled" and they "stayed,"
and finally, when they had proven that they could indeed rise above temptation, she let them loose, and
all three raced to welcome their visitors.

Pats, praise, and caresses duly accepted, the three
animals trotted off to the livestock watering pool for a
drink, then flopped down in the shade in a tangle of
gangling legs, ridiculously long tails, and rotund
puppy bellies. Teddy followed them and stood watching their antics.

Isaac smiled; when he glanced at Dian, he found
her smiling too.

"Would you like some tea?" she asked. "Or cider?
Or there's fresh juice from yesterday's press."

"I don't suppose you have any of that drink we had
the other morning, do you? I could get to like that."

"Coffee? No," she said, shaking her head, "we only
have that on special occasions or for medicinal use.
One of the glass houses has coffee trees, and they give
us just enough to keep up our craving for the next
time. Probably be better for us if the damned things
died of some blight," she muttered darkly. He
laughed.

"I'd rather have something cold anyway. That's a
good juicing apple you grow here. Do you use the
same kind for cider?"

"The later apples are better for cider, along with
some ugly little ones that grow up the hill. It's good,
not too much alcohol in it, so you can drink it when
you're thirsty without getting too much of a buzz.
Would you like some of that?"

"I would, thanks. Can I help?"

"You heard Judith, you're not allowed. Pull that
bench around into the shade, I'll be back in a
minute."

A door slapped shut, and Isaac was alone. Really alone, he reflected—the first time since he'd arrived that he hadn't felt strange eyes prying at him, evaluating, speculating; without that pressure, he had to admit that this was a lovely place.

Emma would have liked it, he told himself.

He leaned back against the wall, listening to the morning, watching his son. The air was ripe with the smell of dogs—this was probably the kennels behind him. In a few minutes, Teddy grew tired of looking on and sat down in the middle of the three puppies, stroking various heads and sides, causing his father to smile at the similarities of the young, no matter the species.

Shortly afterward, Isaac was startled to hear Dian's voice coming through the window over his head, saying, "You have a visitor." He sat up straight on the bench—he'd heard the woman lived alone, but clearly she did not.

However, the person who came through the door with Dian had four legs: her big male, Culum, who paused long enough to acknowledge Isaac with a perfunctory wag of his tail before trotting briskly down to where the boy sat, half-buried in young dogs. Isaac had forgotten the size of the animal, or maybe his mind refused to believe its first impression, but it was true: the creature was huge. And it was heading straight for his son. Isaac jumped to his feet and took a step forward, but Teddy had seen the dog and scrambled to greet him like a long-lost friend; the boy's thin arms reached up to encircle the dog's massive neck in a hug, and Isaac subsided on the bench.

He cleared his throat. "Your dog certainly is, er, friendly."

Dian set down a tray containing a jug, three cups, and a bowl containing a handful of objects with burnt edges and unidentifiable lumps of something yellow, which Isaac assumed were meant to be cookies. She poured out two mugs of cider and absently held one out to him.

"Actually, he's not all that friendly—he's usually somewhat standoffish, unlike most of the others. For some reason he's really taken to your son."

Teddy was now fingering the tufts of hair that jutted out over Culum's yellow-brown eyes. Teddy's eyes were as dark as his father's, but there the resemblance between father and son ended. Isaac was thickset and muscular, slightly shorter than Dian, with a cap of tightly curled black hair and a heavy, four-day bristle already obscuring the brown skin of his face. His son was considerably lighter in color and slim, all knobby knees and elbows below his shorts and shirt, with wavy light-brown hair down to his shoulders.

"Your son is very quiet," Dian commented.

"My son is . . . different."

Isaac felt her eyes drilling into the side of his face. Different was not always a good thing for a boy child to be.

"Is there something wrong with him?"

"Nothing physical. He just doesn't speak. He can, and in fact sometimes he'll say whole sentences in his sleep, but he doesn't talk. It's . . . it's one of the reasons we're here, frankly. I thought a change might free him up. His mother died a year and a half ago, you see. He was never very talkative before, but after losing her, his voice just seemed to dry up. Emma, her name was. She was my wife," he added softly.

Isaac kept his eyes on the scene ahead of him, but he could practically hear the furious working of the woman's mind. He was, he knew, a rarity in many ways—a man who had lived in a city and in a small village, a man who'd made his own choices and acted upon them. He also knew that family structures in this place were about as fluid as anywhere else, including polygyny, serial monogamy, lesbian marriages, heterosexual marriages that their great-grandparents Before might even have recognized, and a lot of arrangements that they would not. He did not know precisely what this woman's bonds were, but he did know enough to see his way forward. His people—Emma's people—needed this place badly. He would do what he had to in order to give it to them.

Dian chose not to pursue the topic of wives.

"The boy seems bright."

"He is, very. He's reading already. He doesn't write, though he draws a bit. With me and a few others he's communicative, just not verbally."

Dian took a swallow of cider, watching boy and dog. They were now facing each other, eye to eye, the boy seated cross-legged with his elbows on his knees, Culum on his belly with his head raised. For a long time they just sat and studied each other, and then the spell was broken when Culum's long pink tongue shot out to lick half the child's face in one quick swipe. Teddy sat back abruptly, startled, then collapsed in giggles and threw his bony arms around Culum's massive neck. After a minute the child moved around next to the huge dog, who stretched out on his side with a sigh. The boy curled up with his head on the great rib cage, and in a few minutes they were both asleep.

Isaac looked to see what his companion made of the scene and found her shaking her head back and forth slowly, her expression indecipherable. She felt his eyes on her and presented him with a wry smile.

"I must look like a pendulum," she said. "It's just that I've never witnessed that before. I know it happens, but I've never seen it."

"What?" He was puzzled. "Don't kids and dogs usually get along?"

"Not like that. My dogs like children, but they

never consider any human an equal at first meeting. A bonding like that, instantaneous—it's very rare." She tore her eyes off the sleeping pair and faced Isaac fully for the first time. "I was almost certainly that way with the dogs." She stopped, as if that might be explanation enough; seeing from his expression that it clearly was not, she rubbed her hands over her face and reluctantly went on.

"I wasn't born here, in the Valley. Judith isn't really my sister. I have no idea who my actual parents were, except they were probably of a wandering band, most likely traders. Judith's mother was on her way home from Meijing when she found me at a crossroads. Not unusual, of course, lots of wrong babies are left to die, but with me it was different. For one thing I was older than exposed babies usually are—around seven or eight months, crawling pretty well. For another, there was no sign of anything wrong physically. Mother being who she was, she'd have stopped for me even if I'd had two heads, but she was struck by how strange it was to come across a perfectly healthy baby, just sitting there in the middle of the road bawling her head off. She was still in milk—she'd lost a baby barely six weeks before, had gone to Meijing to get her mind off it—and since it was obvious that I had been left there deliberately, she fed me and got ready to ride off with me. Just as she was about to mount up, her horse went skittish, and when she turned around to look, she saw standing less than twenty feet away a (as she described him) 'very, *very* large dog.' Luckily she had the sense not to reach for a weapon, because if she had he'd probably have taken her arm off. He wasn't exactly threatening her, just standing with his head down, staring at her and growling low in his throat. I don't suppose you've ever heard a wolfhound's growl, but it sure gets your attention. She stood really still and was trying to decide what to do when I turned

around in her arms, spotted him, and positively
shouted in happiness. I struggled to get down, so she
put me on the ground and I crawled right over to him.
He gave me a face bath, like Culum did to Teddy just
now, and then he looked up at Mother as if to say,
'Okay, I'm here now, let's go.' He had the stub of a
heavy rope around his neck, the end all frayed, and he
and I clearly knew each other, so she figured that
whoever had left me at the crossroads had tied up the
dog to keep him from following, and he had chewed
through the rope. As soon as he saw that she was going to be helpful to me, he was quite happy about the
arrangement. He came back with us and lived here
until he died, when I was seven. By that time Mother
had located two females of his breed, more or less—
they're related to the old wolfhound of Ireland—and
brought them here. The price must have been astro-
nomical, but they were the beginning. That dog was
Culum's grandfather. Those puppies are Culum's."
She studied the pair for another minute, but her mind
was already made up. "Your son needs a dog."

Isaac felt his jaw drop: a newcomer, and a child at
that, given one of the Valley's most valuable com-
modities? After a minute he turned thoughtful.

"Do you think a dog would bring him out of his
shell? Make him talk again?"

"That's got nothing to do with it," she said impatiently, and stood up. "It doesn't matter to me if he
ever talks again. Your son belongs with the dogs,
that's all. Pardon me, I have to get lunch for the
pups."

When she returned with three bowls of food, one of
the puppies was standing next to Teddy, sniffing at the
boy's ear with a wet nose. The child half-woke and
flung an arm around the puppy's neck. Dian gave a
sharp whistle between her teeth and put the bowls on
the ground, and the three long-legged, monkey-tailed

canines scrambled up the slope to their food. The boy and Culum trailed behind, one childish arm stretched up to rest across one massive back. Dian handed Teddy his cup of apple juice, then went inside for a platter of cheese and fruit to supplement the rocklike cookies. As they ate, Dian told the child a shortened version of the story she had given the father, in simple language but an adult voice. Eventually, when she was certain he understood, she came to the point.

"You know, Teddy, Culum doesn't act toward most people the way he does with you. He likes you a lot."

She had his full attention, and a look of pride was beginning to dawn in his face.

"You're going to be living with us now, aren't you?" she went on.

The boy cast a doubtful glance at his father, then nodded slowly.

"I'm glad about that, because I need someone to help me with the dogs. Would you like to do that?" This time the nod was fast and definite. "Well, I'd like you to come and help me feed them and clean their house. Maybe after school?" School would resume the following week, half-days at first. Another vigorous nod. "After you've helped me a while and learned how to take care of dogs, I'd like to think about giving you your own puppy. Once you've shown me you can do it. What do you think?"

The child's eyes went wide, and he looked at her with his mouth open. His eyes went to his father, then moved on to Culum and the three puppies wrestling in the dust, finally coming back to Dian. One slow, awestruck nod this time.

"Good. Let's say you'll work with Culum and me, or with Susanna whenever I'm away, and then next spring when we have more puppies we'll see if one of them suits you." She began to clear away the food bits and cups, then paused.

"One other thing. You don't have to talk, Teddy, to work with dogs." Isaac straightened up suddenly, but she ignored him. "We can find other ways for you to give commands, to tell the dogs what you want them to do. The dogs would like it a lot better if you did talk to them, because they love to hear their people's voices, but I want you to know that this isn't a deal, that you don't have to talk in order to get a dog. Understand?"

This time there was no nod, just a long and thoughtful look from his dark eyes. Dian broke it by standing up with the tray.

"I have to get on, there's work waiting for me in the orchard."

"Can we help there?" asked Isaac.

"Certainly not. Don't worry, we'll put you to work soon enough when your guest status lapses. I personally would recommend going down to the millpond for a swim, then up to the greenhouses. You'll find them interesting. Just follow the road to the end." She called the puppies in, holding the screened door for them to return to their kennel. "Come see us tomorrow, Teddy, and bring your daddy if you can."

A good-bye hug was administered to Culum, and the boy's thin hand slid into Isaac's. When they came to the corner of the barn, the boy stopped and turned around.

"Good-bye, Culum," said a high voice, thready with disuse. It took an instant before the realization hit Isaac like an electrical jolt: *Teddy!* And again it came: "Good-bye, Dian." He looked up at Isaac, and smiled like a cherub.

His father stared openmouthed at his son, then bent to snatch him up.

"That's right," he choked out, "it's Culum and Dian." Then, in sudden terror that making too much of the miracle would drive it away, he submerged his

... THEY KEPT ONLY THOSE FEW MEN WHOM

THEY REALIZED THEY NEEDED

FOR THEIR RACE NOT TO DIE OUT.

SIX

THE WEEKS THAT FOLLOWED WERE HECTIC FOR EVERY pair of hands in the village. The last cutting of hay was brought in, the walnuts harvested, wine grapes crushed and set to ferment, late blackberries picked and bottled, apples and grapes laid on grass trays to dry in the sun. It was a time of reveling in the earth's bounty, a time of aching muscles and sunburned skin and dusty, sweat-caked hair, of full stomachs and the intoxicating smells of summer from every corner. It had been a good season, and every pantry, root cellar, and storage shed was packed to its ceiling. Since the frost had left the ground the previous spring, all the Valley's efforts had gone into the earth, and those efforts, this year, were richly rewarded. Seven years before, people had died because the food did not last the winter. Three years ago the hay crop had been inadequate, and good breeding stock had been slaughtered. But this year (please God, bar disasters) there was plenty.

Then suddenly, in the last week of September, the major crops were in, the most urgent jobs done, and the children were back in the schoolroom full-time, fingernails still black from berries and walnut husks, minds grudgingly buckling under the demands of math and poetry, history and—Ling's task—rudimentary Chinese. With the greatest of pressures off, a half-day of semi-official lethargy crept over the adults, and Dian found herself sitting in the sun doing absolutely nothing.

The nights had begun to turn cold, so the sun baking her trousers and shirt was delicious. At the moment the only sounds were distant ones: kids at recess play behind the schoolhouse, hens clucking in the farmyard, the rhythmic mutter and splash of the windmill on the hill as it pulled water up into the small pond in front of her. The red of her closed eyelids and the unobtrusive sounds had a hypnotic effect, and she was half asleep when she heard Culum's tail thump on the dirt, followed by the distinctive creak of a body settling on the wooden bench beside her chair. She opened one eye, to discourage the intruder, and found herself looking into the trimly bearded face of Isaac. Opening the other eye, she studied him for a moment as he sat studying her and was visited by a vague and completely irrelevant thought.

"Did you shave your beard just for the journey down?" she asked idly. When he nodded, she closed her eyes again, saying, "It would take more than a smooth face to disguise you as a woman."

"There was some considerable discussion on that," he agreed solemnly. "I suggested padding a shirt with a couple of melons, but we decided I'd just have to go flat-chested and keep strangers at a distance."

Dian snorted, and then to Isaac's astonishment erupted into girlish giggles. When they had subsided a bit, she told him, "I was picturing you decked out like the Whore of Babylon, or one of those bizarre women from Kirsten's old books, a 'movie star' with tall shoes and painted eyes and rattly jewelry." She sat up to face the grinning man. "What can I do for you?"

"You can start by making me a cup of coffee." He cut into her protests. "Now, you can't put me off like you did last month. I know you have a supply of those beans, so don't give me any stories about medicinal uses and celebrations. Surviving this last month is celebration enough."

A number of times since Isaac's arrival, Dian had found herself on a team with the man, who had insisted on working on the backbreaking jobs along with the women. Some residents had found it disconcerting and protested that he shouldn't be allowed to put himself at risk of injury, but Dian thought it somewhat refreshing.

"You're a good worker," she said, and sat up. "Yes, let's have some coffee. I just hope no one else smells it," she said in a conspiratorial aside.

They went up to her house, stopping on the way to pay tribute to the younger generation of kennel inhabitants, who were not yet allowed free run of the village. Despite his protests that, really, cider would do, Dian threw a handful of kindling on the remains of the morning's fire and rummaged about for the ancient, blackened frying pan and the equally ancient grinder, the burrs of which were so worn that they would only accept one bean at a time. She and Isaac took turns stirring. The green nubs slowly browned and released their oils, but Dian and Isaac were half roasted themselves before the beans were done. As Dian stirred, wiping the sweat trickling into her eyes, she remarked, "Kirsten claims that Before they used to have a powdered coffee you could just stir into hot water. I wonder if it could possibly have tasted as foul as she says it did?"

Finally the handful of beans were shiny and black, and Dian dumped them onto a plate to cool, then replaced the pan over the fire with the water kettle, ducking her face under the faucet for a moment before screwing the grinder onto the table for the next stage. The crisp beans crackled through the metal burrs as Isaac worked the handle, a generous handful of chicory was added to the grounds to stretch them, and finally the drink was ready to assemble.

All in all it was a good hour before they had their mugs of coffee. Dian peered doubtfully into a lopsided and extremely ugly pottery jar and pulled out a handful of equally lopsided and rather well done cookies: these had brown lumps instead of the unidentifiable yellow of the previous batch. She carved off a few of the blacker edges into the slops bucket and told Isaac, "Susanna has decided that I don't eat enough, so she brings me these. They should go well with the burnt coffee, don't you think?"

Dian shoved her boot into the ribs of Culum, who had claimed the room's patch of sun, and when he had shifted over, she dragged up a pair of chairs. She and Isaac settled into the soft cushions, filled with a ridiculous sense of accomplishment and a pleasant feeling of easy companionship. They sipped the hot liquid and dutifully consumed a number of Susanna's cookies. Dian eased her head back on her chair, propped her heels up on Culum's side, and closed her eyes again, unaware that Isaac was watching her with a curious smile on his face.

"I'm not really just being lazy," she said. "I was helping out on the Hall roof last night. It was so nice and cool, and with the moon full, it's been easier to do it at night. I think it may be too dark tonight, though." She did not sound regretful.

"It's going to be an impressive building."

"Isn't it? Old Will, Kirsten's brother, laid out the plans nearly thirty years ago. We started it just before he died. Took us ten years just to get the material together. Have you any idea how long it takes to fell, haul, and mill thirty-eight sixty-foot eight-by-twenties?"

"I can imagine."

"Yes, you have done some carpentry, haven't you? In fact, didn't I see you the other day, working on one of the windows in the Hall?"

"You did. The upper half of the middle window on the east end is mine, all mine."

"I shall admire it when next I'm dangling off the roof attaching shingles. Is that what you've decided to do here, then? Carpentry?" As long as he wasn't felling trees, she added mentally.

"Some, I suppose. Actually, I've been spending a lot of time up at the greenhouses. We didn't have them in Oregon, but when I was a child the place I lived in had a big one. Not as big as the ones here, but to a child it seemed huge, a whole world filled with warm air and luscious plants. Orchids and ferns, mostly."

"Where was that?"

He paused, and then spit out his reply. "In a filthy pit of a place called Ashtown." The open loathing in his voice brought her eyes open.

"In Oregon?"

"Yes. Queen Bess has it now, I heard. Hardly surprising, they well suit each other. She wasn't around yet when I lived there, but I doubt it's changed much since I left."

"I'm surprised she wanted it, if it was that foul."

"You know what Ashtown is like? I found a dead otter on a riverbank one time. It looked sleek and alive from even a short distance, but when you looked underneath, it was all maggots and rot. That's Ashtown."

Dian thought it time to move to a safer topic.

"How do you get along with Glenda the Good?"

"Glenda...? Oh, you mean Glenn, at the greenhouses? She is somewhat otherworldly, isn't she?

Half the time she doesn't seem to know I'm there, unless I make a mistake, and all of a sudden she's standing next to me squinting down at this potential disaster, tut-tutting to herself. You know what she said to me yesterday?"

"That you need to learn some French songs to sing to the broccoli seedlings?"

"No, that was last week's lesson. Yesterday I was about to transplant some seedlings into two-inch pots, and I had an old broken spoon to move them with. I thought she was off in the next house, but just as I was getting ready to scoop a few out, there she was, laying a finger on my wrist." His bass voice changed, to Glenn's fluting whisper. "'Oh, no, Isaac, you must never use metal on these tiny babies. Violence against their roots at this stage predisposes them to receiving violence later in their lives, and they will call to themselves all the destructive pests of air and earth. Damp fingers on the leaves, Isaac,'" he trilled, "'damp fingers only, and they will give their best for us humans.'"

She watched Isaac's black bearded face relax from his pinched, thin-lipped, myopic caricature of the head gardener. He laughed, a deep, easy rumble, and she smiled, liking him. She let her head fall back again, enjoying the beat of the sun on her body.

"Yes, Glenn is a fine person, though, as you say, not entirely of this world. She's great with kids, though some adults find her difficult to work with."

"I don't. She's different, but not difficult."

"Are you glad you came, Isaac? From Oregon?"

"Yes."

"No regrets, no homesickness?"

"No regrets. I'm too busy to be homesick."

"And Teddy?" The boy talked to Dian sometimes, when Susanna brought him by the kennels. Not exactly conversations, but a few words now and then to let Dian know he was there.

"It's amazing, more than I could have hoped for. You and your dogs have done miracles—no, don't laugh. You didn't know him before. Up there, he had me and Mim—Miriam—and one or two others, but now he has a community. He talks. I will be forever grateful to you." He said this quietly, openly.

One corner of Dian's mouth twitched in a sleepy smile; her eyes had drifted shut; the sun was lulling her; she half-wished the man would leave.

"Dian."

"Um," she grunted.

"Dian, I need to talk to you."

His dead-serious tones ripped away her somnolent ease, and Dian sat up warily, lowering her boots to the floor.

"I'm sorry," he said, "I know you were up pounding nails half the night and I should let you have a nap, but this really can't wait much longer. I've been trying to see you for a week, but between the work and Teddy and your comings and goings, this is the first chance I've had." He stopped to peer into the bottom of his cup, as if to draw inspiration from the cracked glaze, and Dian braced herself for some disastrous revelation or request: that he was dying of some blood disease, perhaps, or wanted her to help him leave the Valley for greener pastures.

"Dian, everyone here has been remarkably generous with me, from the very beginning. You and I both know that Miriam would have given almost anything not to have had to take Teddy and me back with her. Another group might have demanded payment; Mim would have had to pay it. Instead, you welcomed me, accepted my problem son, and asked nothing of me other than not getting into trouble. Nobody other than Ling, who needed to know, even tried to find out why I left Oregon. I'd like to tell you."

"Why?" she asked bluntly, uneasy with the potential intimacy of this conversation.

"Let me explain first. It was partly because of Teddy that I made the break, in hopes that the change would do what in fact it has—freed him to make a fresh start. However, looking back, I suspect that a big part of Teddy's problems were my own. If I could have pulled myself together, I might have helped Teddy. I couldn't.

"You see, I loved my wife, very deeply. Too deeply, maybe, for this day and age. When she died I couldn't stand to look at anyone but Teddy, couldn't bear to touch anyone but him and Miriam. For months I simply couldn't function, not socially, and certainly not as a male. I have had two children by other women, but after Emma died the thought of sleeping with someone who had known her, who had grown up with her, made me nauseated—literally, physically, sick. Once upon a time, if a man didn't want to sleep with someone, he didn't. Hell, if a man didn't want to sleep with *anyone*, it was nobody's business but his own. Not anymore." His words were bitter, but his voice was simply resigned. "By this spring, Emma had been gone for a year, and some of the women started to get impatient. I understood it—really, what good is it if a man is fertile but won't do anything?—but when this trip came up, it was like a word from heaven. When I suggested to Mim that Teddy and I be allowed to come, as a kind of goodwill gift, I think the town was actually relieved to see me go. Being allowed to bring Teddy as well was a bit of a problem, but by that time he was so withdrawn he made them nervous, so between that and Mim's backing me, they gave in and let me take him."

"Why are you telling me this?" Dian asked again. "You should tell it to Judith, not me."

"Just, please, bear with me," he said, under a tight control that Dian could not fully understand and deeply mistrusted. "It has to do with the fact that, now the push of harvest is slacking off, there are a number of women here who are going to start getting impatient when all I do is transplant seedlings and haul firewood. It also has to do with the fact that, after being married for eight years, I know that I need a wife—one wife, some one person I can talk to and work with—don't interrupt me, damn it!—and sometimes sleep next to. It has to do with my wanting you to be that person in my life, here." His voice ran down and he sat, waiting for her response.

Dian sat gaping at him, and then a bark of involuntary laughter pushed its way out, a sound that distorted her face like pain. Isaac's brown skin flushed with anger.

"What the fuck are you laughing at?"

"Oh, God, not at you, no." She took a deep breath and scrubbed at her face with both hands, but it did not remove the twisted smile still pasted there—and really, there was undeniable humor in the situation, that the man would be so uncomfortable with the Valley's flirtatious women that he would come to her. "Isaac, you are ... well, I would be very happy to go to bed with you, but surely you must have guessed that I'm not fertile. Ling doesn't know why—perhaps they could find out in Meijing—but I'm not."

"Of course I guessed it," he said dismissively. "In fact, I asked Ling, and she told me."

"But ... I'm sorry, I don't understand what you want."

"To put it bluntly, it doesn't matter so much if you can't bear my children, not from the point of view of the Valley, because others will. Like I said, 'once upon a time' doesn't do it anymore; we have to be realistic: you have fewer than twenty adult males here, and half of them are somehow related. Ling put it rather clinically when she said that the gene pool needs expanding, and I am, to use her words, 'a resource that cannot be wasted.' A lot of men simply wander from one wife to another, or have several wives at a time, or just say the hell with it and let the healer do artificial insemination on whatever woman needs a baby, but I happen to be, basically, a strongly monogamous person. I badly need a home base. I am asking you to be my home base."

The smile on her face was no longer cynical, but it was weary.

"You haven't done your homework very well, Isaac, or you'd have found out that I'm not really the person for the job. I live alone by choice, and I can't cook much better than Susanna—hell, I'm not even home very much. There are plenty of women better qualified to play wife while you stand at stud for the village."

Isaac's face went instantly white, as if she had thrown a glass of ice water into it. He abruptly rose and started for the door, but she leaped up and got there first, jamming her boot hard against the base.

"Isaac, wait, stop—I'm sorry. I didn't understand, I am a stupid bitch with the sensitivity of a log, please don't go. No, look, I am really so very sorry, utterly, completely sorry. Please, forgive me?" She did not really know what she was apologizing for; she just knew that she could not let him leave like this. She reached out to touch his arm lightly, finding a surprising amount of muscle there, all of it rigid as a board. "Come back and sit down. Please?"

She thought that he would not and was stabbed by a sharp and unexpected sense of loss, but after a long minute, his shoulders sagged, and he turned away from her to drop back into his sun-washed chair. Dian picked up the carafe of coffee and went into the kitchen to rewarm it over the embers of the fire. She returned with it in a saucepan, to divide it between their cups, then settled back with hers into the chair facing him.

"Forgive me," she repeated. "I... Oh, Christ. Look, I'm sure you'll understand that I'm not exactly happy about being sterile. I mean, granted, I'm not a very maternal sort of person, but it would be nice to have had a choice in the matter. It was hard, when I realized that I'll never have children and therefore I have no real right to a husband. And unfortunately I'm not much of a lesbian—more by default than anything else, and that's hardly fair to a partner." One of whom had been, briefly, Laine, a moment of lunacy three years before that further complicated Dian's increasingly difficult relationship with her second-in-command. But perhaps it wasn't necessary to go into detail with Isaac. "So I live my own life, with my dogs and my friends and a night of sex now and then when I get hungry. I am... okay, I'm lonely sometimes, but that's life. And now out of the blue you come here and offer me the impossible."

She looked at him, and when her blue eyes met his, Isaac was rocked by three simultaneous revelations: Dian was younger than he'd realized, younger than he by a good ten years. She was also more vulnerable beneath her strength than he'd suspected. And third, he liked her, far more than he'd intended; that might make things easier in the short run, but it promised a load of hurt down the line. His simple plan threatened to become a lot more difficult. But it was too late to back away now, and Dian was already going on.

"It was a stupid joke; I didn't mean to hurt you. Although, I have to tell you, I really am a lousy cook."

She was gratified to see, after a moment, the corner of his bearded mouth give a brief quirk. "Can we just start all over with this conversation? Pax?" She held out her hand, and after a moment he took it, holding it an instant longer than was necessary. She sat back with her cup and cast around for a topic that might be safe.

"Would you tell me about your wife? Did you grow up together?"

It was the right approach this time, for both of them. The conversation that followed, a time of gradual exploration, laid out the first tentative threads of friendship. He told her about his beginnings, in the town where the adult males were kept in a pool, with the more powerful women getting the greater access and choice. When he was twelve, the last year he would be allowed to live with his family before being shut into the men's quarter, he was in the market with his sister Miriam. There they met some people from a distant village, come to sell their furs and dried fish; one of them was thirteen-year-old Emma. The three new friends ate lunch under the watchful eye of his guard, and talked. They talked for hours, and that night he and Miriam went through a back window of the house, over the rooftops, and down the city wall, to meet up with Emma's people on the road. Brother and sister were hiding in a hollow behind a waterfall when the town guards caught up with the wagons; from that niche they had watched the fruitless search.

"Ever since then, the sound of falling water has made me feel incredibly free. To tell you the truth, I think that's what decided me on this crazy trip, when old Isaiah said there was a waterfall at the foot of the Valley, above where they want to make their town. I took it as an omen." He smiled somewhat tentatively at Dian. She smiled back.

"I'm glad you came." She paused, studying his sunburned face, the short black curls, and the work-roughened hands, ending up by looking straight into his dark eyes with their frame of laugh lines. "If I'm to be your, er, 'home base,' does that mean you want to move in? I don't think there's really room for you and Teddy, although I suppose we could add on a room or two."

He laughed, and with that sound, the painful misunderstandings were set aside. "No, we're not about to move in on you. Teddy has adopted Susanna as mother/sister—she's made up a bed in the corner of her room where he sleeps sometimes. And I have my room in the big house, so I wouldn't actually move in here. I'll come here as little or as much as you wish, just so it's clear to the village that, for the time being at least, we are husband and wife, that I'm not free to move in elsewhere. Does that suit you?"

She looked at her hands, and answered him quietly. "It suits me very well."

"Shall I come tonight?"

"I think . . . All right."

He put down his cup and stood up, absurdly formal. "Thank you for the coffee."

"I enjoyed making it. Um, would you like to come for dinner tonight? I can actually cook, a little. Basic stuff, but you won't starve."

"I'd like that."

"Bring Teddy."

"Good. See you tonight, then."

"Isaac?" It was difficult to push aside this bizarre formality, but surely there ought to be more than this to what amounted to a marriage proposal.

"Yes?" His eyes were so dark, she felt herself falling into them.

"Isaac, I . . ."

"Yes, I know. It will be all right, Dian. It will."

His chest was broader than she had realized, his

hard arms gentler, his mouth cool and teasing. When the school bell rang, Isaac gradually pulled away, without reluctance. Dian stood at the door with a foolish expression on her face and watched his back until he disappeared. Then, whistling softly one of Kirsten's old songs, she turned toward the kennel door and went to teach her young dog Tomas how to fetch a horse.

... SHE SPENT THE WHOLE NIGHT TRYING TO DECIDE
WHETHER SHE WOULD UNDERTAKE THE VISIT
WEARING HER ARMOR OR NOT. IN THE END,
SHE DECIDED ON FEMININE APPAREL.

SEVEN

THE VALLEY'S HARVEST DAY REVELS TRADITIONALLY began around the first of October, two weeks before the day itself, when Judith went from house to house with a piece of paper and an ancient United States silver dollar, worn nearly faceless now but somehow more ritually potent than a coin minted in Meijing. When she got to the kennels, she found roof repairs under way, with Dian's feet and the bottom half of a ladder descending from a hole in the ceiling, accompanied by the sound of hammer and muttered curses. A cloud of dust and desiccated spiders had settled over Dian's boots, the rungs of the ladder, and the floor beneath.

"Sister mine," Judith called, and was answered by a sharp thud accompanied by a loud curse. The woman in the attic slowly extricated herself and came halfway down the ladder, where she stood rubbing her skull, the disturbed dust of half a century plastered to her sweaty skin and shirt. Dian swiped at her forehead with the back of one filthy hand and blinked at Judith from a black and now streaked face.

"Man or woman, heads or tails?" Judith chirped sweetly.

"Christ, Jude, you always cheat anyway," Dian said sourly. She hooked the claws of the hammer over the top rung and pulled her hand down into the sleeve of her shirt to wipe off the sweat from her forehead more thoroughly. "Why do you bother to pretend we have any choice at all?"

"Such accusations," said Judith indignantly. "It's completely random, entirely up to the coin toss. Come on, now: man or woman, heads or—"

"Man," said Dian. "And tails." It was the same call she made every year, since she generally preferred to take male costume and role in the Harvest Day dances. For the last four years, however, she'd drawn the woman's role; this year, all things considered, she would actually like to play a woman, so she chose the opposite to what she really wanted in an attempt to throw her sister off—that the dollar was actually given the power to choose was not a probability Dian put much store in. But Judith was not fooled.

The dollar flew glittering through the dusty air. Judith caught it and slapped it onto the back of her left hand, gave it a quick glance, and slipped it rapidly into her pocket.

"Sorry, sir, you're a man this year." She gave an evil chuckle as she wrote the result down on her paper. "Is Isaac here?"

"He's out back," said Dian, taking up the hammer again. "Look, next year I get to do the coin toss. You cheat."

"I never," Judith protested, all hurt innocence with a gleam of mischief in her eyes. Dian climbed back up into the hole and a few minutes later looked down to see Isaac's puzzled face staring up at her through the rungs.

"What was that all about?" he asked. "What does she mean, I'll make a lovely woman?"

Dian swore an oath and scrambled up into the attic to stick her head out of the hole in the shingles.

"Cheat!" she shouted at Judith's back, but she was answered only by a demure wave over her sister's shoulder.

Harvest Day was the highest point on the Valley's calendar of events. Even in a bad year, when the prayers were fervent and anxiety lay beneath the feasting, the day was more joyous than Christmas, more intense than Planting Day, wilder even than the Midsummersnight celebrations held on the Fourth of July. Food, games, and dance were the order of the day, and the coin toss to determine each person's gender—men and women alike, everyone over the age of ten—contributed its own mad hilarity to the proceedings: costumes were required, with the half designated "men" wearing vestigial neckties and sturdy trousers while the other half, the "women," wore dresses. A pregnant "man" partnering a bearded "woman" was a commonplace Harvest Day sight.

For Dian, the day was a time when she could both see and demonstrate the growing skill of her pupils in the martial arts, to show off the Valley's strength and, in a more practical vein, to lay bare the areas in need of work during the winter months. Bullets were, unfortunately, too expensive for a marksmanship competition, but archery and hand combat filled the day. So, as harvest slowed and hours became free, she increased the time spent with her students, in preparation.

The first sign of trouble came like a distant rumor of thunder from a clear blue sky, on the Wednesday following the coin toss. Dian and Jeri were on the green in front of the growing Great Hall with five senior girls, age fifteen to nineteen. Around them lounged half a dozen mostly somnolent dogs and a handful of younger competitors hanging about, ostensibly to pick up tips but actually to admire their seniors and root for them. Jeri, slow, good-natured, a born second-in-command and of incalculable value to Dian, was fending off the attacks of three girls with deceptive ease and teasing them into a state of red-faced, half-laughing fury. Dian was with the other two girls, both of whom wore padded helmets, demonstrating in careful movements the potential in seven feet of oaken staff. In a deliberate, formalized dance she swung and met, whirled and showed the use of the end and the power in its length.

After running through the motions several times, she called Jeri over, tossed her a helmet and buckled one on herself, and the two women squared off. Jeri was well suited to the staff, placid and deliberate and instantly unforgiving of error, and Dian rarely came away from a bout unbruised. Today it seemed particularly difficult to pay attention, and Dian attributed the first hard crack across her leg to the distraction of the hammers nearby (although those seemed to taper off after a few minutes), and the second one she put down to the lack of sleep engendered by taking Isaac to her bed, or perhaps the anxiety about Judith, or—and, whack, came a third bruise, on her shoulder—to the upcoming trip, when suddenly all the alarms in her head burst out as if she'd heard the bolt slide on a rifle, and she dove and rolled and came up with the staff ready, a huge surge of adrenaline jangling her nerves. And there was nothing there, nothing but the startled dogs, on their feet and growling questions at one another, and Jeri lowering her own staff in puzzlement, and the astonished pupils and the audience drawn by the impromptu bout. Dian searched wildly for the source of those internal alarms, as startled as the others and nearly as bewildered—then abruptly she whirled around and found herself looking into the brown eyes of Miriam's wounded guard, Sonja.

Sonja was not armed. She was just leaning casually against one corner of the Hall with her arms crossed. The intense warning bells lessened somewhat, now that the object was in sight; in the stillness Dian straightened, loosed the buckles on the helmet, and let it drop to the grass. She leaned deliberately on her staff, facing the newcomer.

"Afternoon," she said.

Sonja did not respond, merely stayed holding up the wall as she ran her eyes over the students, the dogs, Jeri, then back to Dian. Finally she spoke.

"Are you practicing a folk dance with those things, or would you like to learn how to fight with them?"

Jeri shot an apprehensive look at Dian, who was trying hard to control the wave of anger brought on by the taunt lashing her already charged nerves.

"You being something of an expert, I take it," she said, politely scornful. She knew immediately that she wasn't handling this at all correctly, but she could not seem to regain her balance, could only react and bristle like some untrained and brainless dog.

"Around here, I suppose I am," said Sonja flatly.

"Then it's too bad about the head injury. Otherwise we might have to ask you to demonstrate your skill."

The barb hit home. Sonja stood away from the wall, her hands dropping to her sides.

"There's nothing wrong with my head. Let me have one of your staves."

"Oh, no, not without an okay from Ling," Dian said firmly.

"She'll pass me. Ask her." Sonja stared at Dian, daring her.

"Right," said Dian. "I'll talk to her about it."

"When?"

"When I see her."

"You're afraid. You know I can beat you."

"You had a bad injury," said Dian, trying for reason, struggling to keep a lid on the temper this woman seemed intent on setting off. "Nobody comes back into competition without the healer's approval."

"Won't hurt to ask her." A breath of interest ran through the onlookers, and Dian decided to end it.

"I'll ask her. Okay, girls, we're wasting time here. I want you to practice your rolls, as long as we're here on the nice soft grass. Jeri, hold your stick out at about hip level. Now, I want you each to go over it, land at a roll, and rise in one movement. Fifteen times should do it. And, yes," she held up her hand to Sonja, "I'll go find Ling and see what she says." It was the best job of defusing she could manage at the moment, and if Sonja was unsatisfied, or if she suspected that Dian might have some say in the healer's decision, she had no chance to protest, for Dian turned her back and walked off.

The hammers had started up again before she reached the infirmary. The healer was not there, but Dian traced her to Judith's house and waited on the veranda until Ling came through the door. Dian explained the situation to her, but the healer was shaking her head before Dian had finished.

"Absolutely not. After a bang like that she shouldn't do anything strenuous for at least a couple more weeks, and certainly not something that could mean another crack on—" She stopped, cut short by Dian's upraised hand and expression of alarm. "What's wrong?"

"The hammers," Dian said, and then she was running, slamming out the fragile screen door and pounding toward the silent Hall.

Ling followed and arrived to see Dian kneeling beside Jeri, who lay crumpled, white-faced, and clutching one leg. Dian rose and took a single step toward Sonja, and a chorus of voices broke out, proclaiming that it was an accident, that Sonja didn't mean—that Jeri fell across—that she couldn't help—Ling ignored them all, crouching down beside the woman on the ground.

"Is it your leg or your knee?" she asked Jeri.

"The leg, I think," Jeri said through gritted teeth. "It was my own damn fault."

"Are you sure of that?" Dian's tight voice came from above Ling's shoulder. Jeri grimaced up at her.

"I'm sure it was, Dian. I was just clumsy, and she'd already started her swing—"

"There's time for this later," interrupted Ling. "Consuela, run down and bring my bag, it's on the table just inside my front door." The girl sprinted away, and Ling spoke to two of the women. "Get the stretcher from the back of the Hall, would you, and a blanket."

Two hours later, with Jeri drugged and splinted and settled in the infirmary bed, Dian went looking for Sonja. She didn't have far to go. The woman was sitting right outside the healer's door and rose at Dian's stormy appearance.

"Is she going to be all right?" she asked immediately. "I'm really sorry, I misjudged her movement—I guess it's been so long since I went up against someone new that I forgot I didn't know how she was going to move. Is she okay?"

Dian was nonplussed. The woman seemed genuinely concerned, and her words of apology and explanation tumbled over one another in their haste and relief, yet she continued to radiate low, steady waves of threat. Could it be an act, this contrite face? If so, what kind of game was she playing?

"Okay," Dian said finally. "We'll treat this as an accident. But I'll be watching you." She walked off down the road, and a dozen steps away she whirled about and saw what might have been a look of amusement snatched off Sonja's face. The woman's expression remained open, even relieved, but a spark of disdain reached Dian, and the unmistakable sense of menace.

Over the course of the next two days, Dian talked with a number of people about the incident. Judith looked thoughtful and shook her head decisively at Dian's self-doubt. Isaac looked dubious, and said that Sonja was aggressive, but he didn't think she'd deliberately try to cripple someone. Kirsten pursed her lips and said she was not surprised, but would not elaborate. Ling looked worried, although whether her concern was with Sonja or Dian, the latter could not tell. Laine, who was present when Dian was closely questioning Jeri, kept her thoughts to herself, but then that was hardly unusual.

All in all, there was little Dian could do aside from keeping an eye on Sonja, which she did, in between the hours of drilling her students and preparing for her trip, and helping with the late harvest and the Hall, and being with Isaac. Sonja's compatriot, Jenn—the talker, as Miriam had called her—took Sonja aside for a long conversation, after which the newcomer seemed to make more of an effort to fit in. She began to build a clique for herself—true, among the more dissatisfied women—walking and working in innocent accord with her new neighbors.

Innocent but for the vague aura of threat that surrounded her, of which only Dian was aware.

Dian was aware of many things, those first weeks of October, intensely so, as if the tough outer layers of her skin had been stripped away. Had early fall ever smelled so sweet, the heady perfumes of earth and apples, the air heavy with cooking blackberries and the first fermentation of the wine vats, the soft aroma of sun-baked dust and the tang of newly cut firewood and the rich musk of human sweat? Why had she never noticed before how gently the wood smoke hung in the morning air, how all-pervasive was the flavor of the honey-scented candles as the evenings drew in? And the nights, the indescribable beauty of those nights, the odors of the cooling Valley through the open windows, the breath of cedar from the blankets newly taken from their chest, and the salt and the heat and the intoxicating maleness of the man in her bed.

Within a week Dian had discovered how troublingly addictive Isaac was. She had never before realized how powerful, emotionally and physically, the male of the species could be, since the only man in the Valley with a build similar to Isaac's, namely Peter, was forbidden to her as a brother. But Isaac—Isaac was big and solid, he could be pummeled and wrestled with, and sleeping with him was like sharing the covers with an affectionate bear. He was patient and intelligent and imaginative, he paid attention, and he cared. He cared.

All of which, while Dian's body fervently appreciated it, made her increasingly nervous. She wasn't altogether comfortable being cared for, and she certainly had no intention of becoming dependent on him—she couldn't afford it.

But Isaac stayed just this side of pushy, and demanded little from her. If he'd told her he loved her, she would probably have laughed and afterward seriously considered throwing him out—love was more than she had bargained for. However, he did not tell her; he simply showed her affection, passion, and friendship, and let her get on with her life.

Of the three, she told herself, it was his friendship that she valued the most. The looming problems of what to do with the dogs during her absence simply faded away under the knowledge that Isaac and Teddy would take over, that she would not have to worry about their care under a distracted Judith or an unwilling Laine, because Isaac would care for them. Beyond that, his friendship gave her a sounding board, a place to dump her frustrations and irritations that would not burden the already overladen Judith or prompt well-meaning questions from Ling. His intelligence meant that she could consult him, bring him her problems, and ask his advice, and gradually, without realizing it was happening, she began to give him her trust.

The affection strengthened her, and the wrestling and breathless laughter were glorious, but for his honest, solid friendship she was humbly, profoundly grateful. Her happiness was not all-engulfing: she was constantly aware of Judith's tension, like a minor chord playing in the back of her head night and day, and she continued to worry about Sonja's unpredictable behavior. Even the upcoming trip, which at first she had seized like a child grabbing a present from under the tree, now brought mixed feelings, because she would be leaving Isaac, and she suspected that when she returned it would not be quite the same. There was a bittersweet edge to the weeks, but the sweetness was all the greater against the bitter knowledge of its brevity.

Harvest Day dawned, cold and clear and bursting with the essence of autumn. Dian woke to the sound of voices and feet heading toward the cooking pits, but instead of planting her dutiful feet on the cold floorboards, she turned luxuriously over against Isaac's furry bulk. She woke again an hour later to the incredible, tantalizing fragrance of coffee and something sweet and yeasty and toasted. Isaac was just getting back into bed, a cup in one hand and something brown in the other, which he proceeded to dip into the cup and stuff into his mouth.

"What have you got there?" she demanded. "How long have you been up?"

"Oh, hours. I roasted the coffee and made doughnuts. I hope you like them." He took a large bite and chewed in an extremely self-satisfied manner, scattering crumbs across his luxurious black beard, which was matted on one side from the pillow, and into the curls of chest hair that sprang from the inadequate robe he wore.

"It smells like heaven."

"Yours is on the table."

"I must have been sleeping like a rock not to have heard you." She reached across him for a brown circle and examined it, first with curiosity, and then with suspicion. "Wait a minute." She sat up and pawed through the plate of doughnuts; they were all either half raw or half burned. "You didn't make these, you liar, Susanna did! Why, you—"

"Watch out! My coffee, don't—"

"You don't deserve any coffee, deceitful man. I suppose you took all the edible ones too."

"Each one of those is at least half edible. Susanna guaranteed it."

"So I have only a fifty percent chance of being ill today. Maybe I'll just stick to the coffee."

"Suit yourself." Isaac deposited a black section on his plate and reached for another mottled round. He held it up thoughtfully.

"She is talented, that girl. It's not easy to burn just part of a circle of dough in a pan of liquid fat. Takes considerable attention to detail, it does."

"She is indeed talented. Thank God she wasn't allowed to make the coffee."

"You don't think she did?"

"Oh, no. This is Lenore's coffee, no mistaking it."

"You may be right."

"I'm always right. Hand me that one on top, would you?"

. "That one's raw on the other side, try this one. And kindly don't spill your coffee in my ear."

"Sorry. You know, they're better than they look."

"My ears?"

"The doughnuts, idiot. So, have you decided yet whether or not to compete today?"

Isaac drained the last vapor of coffee from his cup, sighed regretfully, put the cup on the table, and punched up the pillows behind him. Dian finished her doughnut, leaned across him again with her bony elbow in his stomach to sip her coffee, and on her return cuddled into him and rubbed her face across his chest. He put his arm around her back and looked down at the top of her head with a curious expression of affection and longing and an exasperation that verged on resentment. Dian saw none of this, and when he sighed, she took it as a sound of simple contentment.

"Well?" she said.

"Well what?"

"The competitions. Are you going to compete?"

"Ah, yes, the games. Tell me again the events of the day," he requested.

"I've told you."

"Say it again."

"All right. Breakfast, which we've just had. Then the rest of the morning to lay out the preparations. We do the foot races, followed by lunch. Following that we do the tug-of-wars and the athletic events, then a siesta—"

"Hey, I'll enter that. I'm good at siestas."

"You'll like the next event too—dinner. After that the kids do something, a skit and recitations usually, and Kirsten says a few words, then there's dancing and enough beer and new wine to make your head pound for a week."

"I'm exhausted just thinking about it. Actually, I was asking about the competitions themselves."

"A bit of this and a bit of that. Half a dozen divisions of tug-of-war, the races that go from sack race to a five-miler, then hand-to-hand combat and finally archery."

"I think Teddy and I are entered in the three-legged race. I'll need another of these, don't you think, to give me energy?"

"Turn to lead in your belly, more likely, but I'll cheer you on and bring a wheelbarrow to the finish line and fetch you back home. Anything else?"

"Teddy's entered in the archery."

"I didn't know he could shoot," she said, surprised.

"He's pretty good for his age. Are you competing in anything?"

"The five-mile race. I'm judging the fights. Is there any more coffee?"

"One cup. I'll split it with you. No archery, then?"

"I suppose so. I tried not to enter last year but they made me. I thought they'd like to see someone else place first, but I guess not."

"Perhaps this year you'll find the competition's improved," he said mildly, and carefully clawed a blob of raw dough from his mustache.

"In archery? Not likely. Laine's my equal with a rifle, but not a bow."

"Too bad you can't dig up some of the old flintlock rifles, make your own bullets. Not really appropriate, I guess, doesn't go with the rest of the things. I wonder why you do your competitions on Harvest Day? We always did ours on Midsummer's."

"I don't know," she mused into his chest hair. "I

never really thought about it. We always have. I should ask Kirsten."

"Makes sense, in a way. It's all about strength, isn't it? Strong bodies, the strength of the earth in harvest. Your hair smells nice," he added. "Is there any hurry to be up?"

In answer she pulled the covers up over their shoulders and pressed herself against him. "Apparently there is," she noted.

"I WILL NOT ENTER THE LISTS AGAINST SUCH A
MAN WITHOUT FIRST SEEING HIM
AND SPEAKING WITH HIM."

EIGHT

DIAN AND ISAAC EMERGED EVENTUALLY TO LEND THEIR hands to the communal effort. Teddy spied Isaac and came shrieking down the hill to snatch him away for the exciting hanging of lamps from the raw rafters of the half-finished Great Hall. Dian continued on to the kitchen, took her turn at the spit and hauling beer kegs, setting up trestle tables and stealing savory bits from under the cooks' noses, then went up to the green to supervise the demarcation of the fight circles and pacing off the archery targets.

At eleven o'clock the foot races got under way. This was one area in which the boys did well, so that five of the eight races were won by boys, including the tightly contested struggle up the final hill from the mill in the five-mile race. Dian was definitely over the hill for the straight slog and came in behind most of the eighteen-to-twenty-year-olds, and a fair number of the younger teenagers as well. Red-faced and panting, she staggered over to where Isaac and Teddy stood and collapsed at their feet. Isaac sneered and walked off, but Teddy dropped to his knees, looking worried.

"Are you okay, Dian?" he asked. She sat up briskly, breath miraculously restored.

"Sure, Teds. But," she said to Isaac, taking the cup of cider he had actually gone to fetch, "I'm getting old. Twenty-eight's no good for that uphill sprint. Time to change the rules—over a longer distance I'd take them all. Say, ten miles. Down to the new village site and back, that should do it."

"There's nothing more obnoxious than a bad loser," Isaac commented primly, and hauled her to her feet. "Come on, it's time to root for your menfolk."

Susanna's team placed first in the egg race. The wheelbarrow relay was called on account of cheating. Teddy and Isaac came in dead last in the three-legged race.

At midday the bell rang and the entire village, with the exception of the poor souls standing sentry, gathered at the outdoor dining area and helped themselves from heaping trays of bread, great wheels of cheese and slabs of ham, bowls of pickles and preserves and fruit. The big kegs were tapped, a thanksgiving prayer and a toast were given, and the Harvest Day festivities were well and truly under way.

Judith sat on a stool away from the crush, short of breath and sore of back but well content with the two hundred and seventy-odd men, women, and children before her. There had been years when the groaning board was approached with hesitation, when the adults (all too aware of the scant hay in the barn, the previous summer's droughts or untimely rains, or the spring's late freezes) thought twice about filling their plates and satisfied themselves with their children's leftovers. This year, however, the stores were full and, bar disaster (pray God), Planting Day would find them strong.

Lunch hastily swept away, everyone made their way to the green and the length of thick new rope that stretched nearly from one side to the other. To allow the meal to digest before the serious competitions, and to start the afternoon with simple amusement, the tug-of-war was held right after lunch. School classes competed first, then one end of the Valley against the other, and finally all the "women" at one side against the "men" at the other—lacking the formal costumes of neckties and frills that would appear in the evening. Dian took her place among the designated males and found herself but two away from Sonja. The newcomer gave Dian a nod, spat on her hands, and took up the rope.

The "men" won, in a heaving pile of uproarious bodies.

After a pause to refill beer mugs, the white-limed circles took center interest. Dian never entered the fights as a contestant, although before Jeri's "accident" she and Dian had planned a demonstration with the staves. Now, however, Jeri was set to judge, along with the newcomer Jenn, whose injuries still gave her trouble. Dian stood behind the judges for the first few fights and was pleased at the considerable potential of feint and flurry. There was a boy entered this year in the seven-to-ten-year-old level, and Dian watched with an uncomfortable mixture of relief and shame as his heavier opponent pulled her punches a bit and pinned him gently to the ground, as she had been instructed. It had cost Dian much effort to convince the others that boys needed to learn hand combat, and an injured boy at this stage might have meant the end of it; still, the disappointment on his face was hard. She went over to him and hugged him across the shoulders.

"Great job, Tonio. I'm proud of you." She pretended not to see the quick swipe of an arm across his eyes before he looked up.

"I lost, Dian."

"Good heavens, that doesn't matter. I hope you're

not going to kick yourself for not being a superman against a girl who has ten pounds, two inches, and three years' experience on you? I never won anything until I was a lot older than you." This was an outright lie, but it did the trick, and after one mild suggestion and two specific compliments on moves he had made well, she sent him away, if not happy then at least encouraged.

The other fights went well. Dian was peripherally aware of Sonja prowling about in the background, watching her as much as the contestants, but the woman did not approach her, not even to demand that she be allowed to enter the ring. Dian was uneasily aware that she would soon have to do something about the chip that rode the woman's shoulder like a familiar spirit—but not today. During the "knife" bouts, with stubby lengths of dowel dipped in ochre that left painted "wounds" on the fighters' skin to help the judges, Sonja watched, still and intent, but she vanished after the last of these. Then came the archery, and Dian was too busy to look for her.

Archery was the foundation stone of the village defenses, and it was assumed that every able body could use a bow in a pinch. The boys threw themselves into it with all their hearts, for it was one of the few activities that was both essential and permitted them, and Dian, amused, fostered the determined rivalry of her twelve young men against the girls. The war between the sexes was far from dead, and knowing that all the really top archers in the Valley were women rankled at the men.

Competition began with the youngest kids, with diminutive bows and the targets barely a stone's throw away. Warily regarded arrows flew wildly—with a couple of exceptions. One of those was Teddy. She went to stand behind him, took in the tight-lipped concentration, his expert position, and the bow three inches longer than anything she would have given him; when the arrow hit just a thumb's breadth from dead center, she raised an eyebrow and looked around for Isaac. He smiled modestly. She stalked up to him.

"Give me your hands," she demanded.

"My hands are yours," he said, and held them up. She examined them closely. The left hand was inconclusive, but the right—She ran her thumb over the ends of his fingers and muttered to herself.

"Why didn't I notice these calluses?" and to him, accusingly, "Do you shoot?"

"I've been known to shoot occasionally, yes."

"Mr. Humility, eh? Do you win competitions?"

"I've been known to win, yes."

"Right, these boys can use a good model. Find a bow, I'll put you in the adult group."

"Oh, I don't know, Dian, I'm really out of practice," he began, and was interrupted by a snort of laughter, quickly stifled, coming from behind them. Dian looked around to see Laine's rapidly retreating back, and when she returned to Isaac, there was a definite twinkle in his black eyes.

"Do I sense a conspiracy here?" she said slowly. His smile broadened, and he winked.

"Look to your laurels, my dear. The competition has improved."

Sure enough, when the time came to shift the targets back for the adult heat, there was expertise in the way Isaac strung his borrowed bow and great familiarity in the fingers he ran over the arrows. He noticed her watching and grinned a doggy grin; Dian decided then to pay a bit more attention to accuracy than was normally required. Just in case.

He was good. He was, in fact, very good. In the middle distance his scores jockeyed with those of Dian and Laine as they left behind Carmen's eldest daughter

Clara and a vastly improved young man named Salvador, who had come in tenth last year. As the distances increased, so did Isaac's scores, possibly, Dian told herself, because of the edge his superior chest muscles gave him. The final scores in the stationary shoot put Isaac at the top, by two points. It was the first time a man had placed first in more than twenty years. The young men looked immensely smug, and the betting on this event, for years the most predictable of all the competitions, heated up.

The moving targets were next. While the course was being cleared, Dian went for a drink. She talked to a few people, drank her cool water, refilled the cup, and took it over to Isaac. His new admirers drifted off, with sideways glances at Dian, and she handed him the cup. He thanked her.

"Sneaky bastard," she told him under her breath. "Hiding your fingers. I hope you get blisters." He laughed politely as if she had made him a compliment, and poured the water down his throat.

With his first shot at the wheeled target, the odds offered against him dropped still further. The others held on, and Salvador staged a valiant rally that put him three points up on Clara, but eyes were on the trio of Dian, Laine, and Isaac. Wagers climbed—three cords of split wood, two Meijing silvers, half interest in a pony. The target seemed to pull Isaac's arrows like a magnet, whereas Dian had to work for her bull's-eyes; Laine began to fall behind, point by point, through inexperience and nerves and an unfortunate breath of wind. At the end of the round Isaac, cool, unblistered, and three points ahead, turned to Dian and half-shouted at her over the tumult of a hundred and more adult voices:

"Are you pleased with your competition, then?"

It was all very well and good to provide a thrill for the onlookers, but this was getting serious. To lose to a man, even Isaac, was unthinkable. Dian pushed her way to the trough to wash her face and have another drink, then went back across the green to see to her horse for the third round. There was a crowd gathered under a tree, at the center of which was Jeri, leg in plaster and a slate propped on her other knee.

"What's up?" Dian asked, craning to see the slate.

"Bets," she said succinctly, and wrote down the name of the woman in front of her, followed by the words *3x4 ft. window.*

"Oh. What odds?"

"Three to one."

"What? You really think Isaac—"

"Oh, no," Jeri said quickly, and tugged on Dian's arm in order to speak into her ear. "I'm betting on you. I've seen Isaac ride." She shook her head and took the next wager, and Dian walked off grinning to herself.

Jeri, as it turned out, was one of the few who was totally pleased with the final result of the day. Isaac, indeed, was no horseman, and whereas Dian cantered past the target like a centaur, sinking her arrow cleanly into the bull's-eye all six times, Isaac only made the center once out of three left-hand passes, and on the awkward right-hand tries failed miserably, once nearly missing the edge of the target entirely. Laine caught up with his score on the third pass and surpassed him by the end.

He seemed content with his third place, however, and the only ones who did not call out with full-voiced appreciation were those women—and, most especially, men—who were faced with the sudden improvident debt of pairs of boots, fur coats, bits of their houses, and long-hoarded silver. Isaac surrendered his horse and bow to their owners and walked up to shake hands with the victors.

"Well done, Laine," he said. "You were absolutely right about the lessons. Next week?"

"As usual," she said, then laughed and elbowed him in the ribs at the look on Dian's face before turning aside to talk with Carla and Salvador. Silence fell as Isaac formally took Dian's hand.

"And you, Dian. I hope you are well pleased?"

"You gave me a run for my money, I'll give you that." She hesitated, and then, in public view and with nothing held back, kissed him full on the mouth, to a surge of whistles and hoots.

Later, as they were making their way down the hill to a pre-siesta swim, Dian fell quiet, barely acknowledging the remarks of passersby. Eventually she said to Isaac, "That was very interesting, that was."

"What? Beating me? Or almost losing?"

"Neither. Or both, I guess—more the reason you lost. You would have won if it hadn't been for the ride-by. I'm going to have to talk to Judith about giving the boys more riding experience."

"Oh, look, I only let you win because I knew you'd be such a witch if you lost."

"What! Double bastard!" she cried, and whacked him smartly on the back of his head. "Let's see how fast you are on your feet," and she took off sprinting down the hill to the pond. He glanced around to make sure Teddy was with Susanna and set off after her, to the joy of the dogs giving chase. He hadn't a hope of catching her, though, and by the time he lumbered up and flung himself into the millpond, she was halfway across, floating nonchalantly on her back.

Twenty minutes later, clean and refreshed, they walked together up to her quarters for a siesta, which, though not precisely restful, was certainly relaxing. When Isaac had fallen asleep, Dian slipped quietly out and went for a round of the sentries. They had drawn lots for the duty, and the losers this year were prom-

ised next year free, so there was not too much resentment. She told each of them about the competitions,
assured them they'd be relieved by the night sentries
in time for dinner, and went back. She was just tying
her necktie, a gaudy strip of orange and pink silk from
some distant fashion era, when the big bell rang, a
thing it usually did only for emergencies. Isaac shot
up in bed.

"What was that for?"

Dian reached into the closet and plucked out the
frilly gown that was his lot for the night, and tossed it
lightly into the air so that it came to rest in a cloud of
pink across his head.

"Come along, Miss Isaacs, enough beauty sleep.
Time to prettify yourself for the ball."

The prettification took somewhat longer than Dian
had reckoned. They were late for the beginning
speeches and missed Judith's invocation and half of
Kirsten's talk. The acoustics in the big wooden hall
were surprisingly good, even without a finished roof,
and from her place on the stage Kirsten's thin voice
carried to all corners. As Dian and Isaac came up on
the porch, they could hear her clearly through the
doors and the open windows.

"...a number of bad years, it is true. There were
years without babies, years when we had to kill the
milk cows for food and gather acorns for our bread.
There were years when late frosts took the seeds and
early frosts took the crops. One terrible year we had
no wine whatsoever, except for medicinal use." A
light wave of laughter flickered through her listeners.
"Come to think of it, even that was a blessing in disguise, because the wine tasted so bad nobody would
admit to an illness that whole year." Chuckles rip-
pled through the hall, and the old woman smiled
down at them. "We give thanks to God for the fine

weather, for the blessings of healthy bodies and strong muscles and clever minds. We give thanks for another year of protection from enemies, from pestilence, from disease. We give thanks for this good land and its riches that give us life." She held a moment of silence, broken only by baby noises from the back, and then her quavering voice began slowly to sing, to be joined quickly by over two hundred others:

> *Praise God from whom all blessings flow,*
> *Praise God all creatures here below,*
> *Praise God above, ye heavenly host,*
> *Praise Father, Mother, Holy Ghost, Amen.*

Old Kirsten's face crinkled in a loving smile, touching each person with the love and approval of ages past. "You have worked hard, my children. Tonight you must play hard. You will excuse me if I don't join in all the dances?"

She moved to leave the stage, and cheers erupted. It took several minutes before Ling, the master of ceremonies, could be heard.

"Just a couple of things," she shouted, repeating the phrase until relative silence fell. "Thank you. Just a couple of things. Dinner's nearly ready, and after everyone's been served we'll have music and the kids with their readings and this year's play. After that, it's dancing 'til the cows come home, or go out, I suppose. Does the patient first want to work up an appetite? One dance before we eat?"

A roar of approval again smothered her voice but gradually submitted to her raised hand. "One more request, from your medical personnel. Please don't take off your shoes to dance—we haven't managed to finish the floors yet, and I for one don't want to spend the night in the infirmary digging out splinters." The laughter was lost in hoots of appreciation as the musicians and dance caller climbed up onto the stage and arranged their chairs. The caller would use a megaphone later in the evening, but for now she stood up and bellowed.

"Take your partners for the Virginia reel!"

The "men," some with carefully painted mustaches and all wearing something resembling a necktie, lined up facing the "women," who were in a variety of flounces and frills. Isaac's furry, heavily muscled torso strained against a lacy pink maternity negligee, one of the few things Dian could find that he could breathe in without ripping the seams. Susanna had trapped him as he came in the door and attached several pink bows in his beard and hair, and as Dian looked down the line she saw that Judith's brother, Peter, had a beard carefully plaited and tied in a dozen delicate crimson ribbons, to match the lace on his skirt. Two years before he had also been a "woman" and appeared in a stunning emerald number, but this outfit had obviously come under Susanna's influence, because she was dressed as his twin. The loud voice from the stage called for the "ladies" to curtsy to their partners, and the lines of dresses bobbed down and up, led by husky Peter's deep knee dip. Dian was not the only one to collapse onto the floor, holding her sides and risking splinters with the tears running down her face as the caller shouted for order.

The Virginia reel was a rout before it had begun, and in good-natured disgust the caller sent everyone out to the food.

The legs of the trestle tables pressed into the ground under their burden. Juicy roast pig, bloody beef, fried chicken, tamales, crepes, and cheese tarts, three kinds of egg, five vegetables (the ears of corn dripping with butter), eight kinds of salad, and more desserts than even eighteen-year-old Salvador could sample.

Afterward, those who had not cooked did the cleaning up, and Dian, up to her elbows in suds, listened to Ling's string quartet, the village band, and the smaller school band. She slipped in next to Teddy in time for the last of the recitations, and then came the annual school play, written each year on some classical theme or current event in the life of the village. Two ten-year-olds carried out the title board, turned it around, and Dian sank down slowly into her chair. It read:

THE BONDING OF ISAAC
A COMEDY IN THREE ACTS

The giggles and glances had just begun to subside when Teddy, beginning reader that he was, piped up.

"That's your name, Daddy!"

Dian glanced at Isaac and saw that he had gone bright red; they did not look at each other until it was over.

A wooden wagon pulled onto the stage, and from it appeared an immensely hairy figure at least eight feet tall (she had seen the children practicing hard with stilts over the last month, but had thought nothing of it) who pounded his chest (to the accompaniment of a drum offstage), flung his immense horse-tail beard over his shoulder, and shouted gruffly at the assembled womenfolk (one of whom appeared to be pregnant with quintuplets), "Take me to your she-der!" In act two he proceeded to eat everything in sight and carry entire (papier-mâché) trees in one hand, followed about by an equally hairy and rather bewildered toddler. (As the child was being led across the stage by his elder sister for the third time, Teddy finally got the joke and tugged at Isaac's pink skirt with an excited, "Is that me, Daddy? Is that me?") In the third act, a last-minute addition had the hairy giant splitting three arrows in a bull's-eye before pounding his chest and carrying off a fainting female with a puzzled but amiable Culum on a rope. Dian and Isaac laughed politely and clapped, and wished fervently for the dancing to begin.

"ON ACCOUNT OF YOU,

THE ISLAND WILL CHANGE THE STYLE OF LIVING

IT HAS OBSERVED FOR A VERY LONG TIME."

NINE

MIDNIGHT CAME, AND WENT. MOUNDS OF BLANKET-draped children lay like so many uneven boulders set down against the walls. The original beer kegs were long gone, the current one was running low, and about an hour ago jugs of a remarkably powerful spirit had begun to circulate. The band had got its second wind a short while before, no small thanks to the jug beneath the fiddler's chair, and those men and women who were still upright and coordinating were being whipped into a positive frenzy of sweating activity.

It was a polka at the moment, and Dian was steering Isaac through the thinning crowd. The pink ribbons had long since fallen from his hair, the seams of his dress were giving way, and neither of them was entirely sober. It took Dian a moment to grasp that the second, beardless Isaac hanging on her arm was in fact Susanna, urgent and intense. Dian stopped, and the odd trio promptly became the stationary target for careering pairs. She hustled her two partners into a quieter corner.

"What's the matter, Suze? Is your mother—"

"No, there's a fight going on outside. I think you should stop it."

Dian strode out of the Hall with Susanna and Isaac on her heels, in their wake a handful of others who had about reached their fill of the dance. It was immediately apparent what Susanna had meant: under half a dozen lamps hung from a tree, a fight circle had been set up. It held, almost inevitably, Sonja and Laine. Dian pushed her way through the excited onlookers. The fight had obviously been under way for a good few minutes, and although neither of the women was drunk enough to have it affect her coordination, both were sufficiently anesthetized that they had no inclination to pull their punches.

They were using the dowel "knives," Dian saw, but the dark stain on the tips was not entirely paint, and both women, stripped to the waist, were bruised and bleeding and grinning ferociously at each other in the uneven light.

"All right, that's enough for tonight," Dian said firmly. Neither Sonja nor Laine seemed to hear her but continued circling each other until Laine feinted left and then rushed right. Sonja dodged and kicked out, and Laine's roll was awkward. She staggered to her feet and turned toward Sonja, dowel held out.

"That's all," Dian ordered more loudly. Laine's eyes flicked to her, then back to her opponent.

"Oh, back off, Dian. Harvest Day's supposed to be fun, isn't it?" She jabbed at Sonja playfully, a blow that would have ruptured something had it connected. "One day in the year you can enjoy yourself." Another jab, easily avoided. "Old stick-in-the-mud Dian (jab), let's-keep-things-tidy Dian (jab), never-take-a-risk Dian (jab)." Her tongue flicked out, savoring the taste of the blood on her split lip, her eyes locked on Sonja's, and she bared her teeth again. "First time I find me a girl doesn't mind playing rough, old Mama Dian comes along. 'Time to put your toys away, children, before you get yourselves dirty (jab).' Why don't you just piss off, Dian? Go play with your doggies (jab). Your new pretty boy (jab). Just leave me for Christ sakes alone."

Throughout this speech Sonja's guard had dropped more and more, as none of the jabs were seriously meant, and when she glanced up on this last word to see how Dian was taking it, Laine hurled herself forward. It might have succeeded had not Sonja's hand, stick firmly grasped, come around with the full force of her body behind it and met Laine's forehead with a solid crack. Laine collapsed as instantly as a scissored marionette, tumbling into a limp and sprawling tangle on the grass.

The first thought that flashed through Dian's mind was, *That's both of my right-hand women down*, and the second was, *I'm going to have to shoot her like a mad dog*, before the necessities of action brought her to attention, made her stop the crowd's *(crowd? Where did all these people come from?)* automatic surge forward and fill her lungs to bellow hugely for "LING!"

"I'm here," said the voice practically at her elbow, and the healer bent over Laine, pulling back her eyelids, feeling at her wrist. "Will somebody get the stretcher and a blanket from the Hall? We seem to be making a habit of this," she commented emotionlessly.

"Keep her here," Dian ordered, to no one in particular but everyone in general, and helped carry the stretcher down the hill. No one needed to ask which "her" she meant.

In half an hour Dian was back, Culum locked securely away, Ling's phrases "mild concussion" and "hell of a headache" ringing in her ears. Sonja had regained the sleek black suit she'd been wearing and stood leaning against the tree, ignoring the people around her as if it were the most natural thing in the world to do at half past one in the morning. She did look up at Dian's reappearance on the scene.

"Is she...?"

"No thanks to you. Why are you doing this to us? It wasn't enough to break Jeri's leg? Won't you be satisfied until you kill off all my best women? What do you want?" she demanded ferociously, and Sonja, whose face had grown more closed with every word, stood silently with her chin up and a half sneer on her lips, as superior and unreachable as a resentful teenager and every bit as infuriating.

At the sight of that incongruously adolescent expression, Dian's hot anger suddenly shifted, becoming cold as the water under ice. Her blue eyes narrowed, but her shoulders and fists relaxed and her mouth slid into a grin of her own—but where Sonja's expression was a shout of rebellion, Dian's bore the lazy pleasure of a hungry shark.

Without taking her eyes off Sonja, Dian shrugged off her tweed jacket, tugged the absurd scrap of orange silk from her collar, and thrust both garments at the nearest bystander. "Come on, girl," she coaxed in a voice that trickled fear down many of the nearby spines, "you've been picking fights for two weeks. Well, now you've got one. Why settle for second best when you can have me?" She took two steps forward, that ominous grin plastered on her face, then shot out one swift hand to slap a stinging and contemptuous blow onto Sonja's cheek.

It was no fight; Sonja was no match for a roused Dian. She tried, but Dian was her better in skill and experience and had two inches' reach on her. For every blow that Dian failed to dodge or block, three or four hit Sonja, all of them slaps, all to the face, and increasingly hard. Sonja's nose was soon bleeding, her lips broken, her cheeks flaming even in the lamplight, her eyes watering from the blows and from tears of frustration and rage at the scornful precision of Dian's blows and her refusal to fight properly, and every time Sonja tried to rush forward and seize hold, Dian either faded away or tripped her, and always there came the contemptuous slaps, the pleased shark's grin.

Dian found no relief in the violence, no satisfaction in the blood that had begun to flow freely down Sonja's chin and into her mouth. Each sting across her open palm served only to deepen her fury, each jolt along her arm fed the frustration and rage she hadn't known was there; by the time Sonja had been rendered to a swaying figure trying only to keep her arms in front of her face, all Dian wanted was to reduce her to a pulp. One final, brutal backhand dumped the woman to the ground, and Dian stepped forward.

"Dian!"

The shocked exclamation hit her like a bucket of cold water, and the half-begun movement of Dian's foot stuttered to a halt. She pivoted, and there stood Judith in her night robe, huge of belly, huger of eyes, her mouth pulled back in a grimace of disbelief, her head shaking a slow and jerky denial: disapproval personified. She held Dian with her eyes for a long and breathless minute, Dian slowly becoming aware of others looking on as well. She closed her eyes briefly and a hard shudder ran through her; when her eyes opened she had regained control. Chest heaving with exertion, she drew her hunting knife from its sheath and dropped to one knee beside the half-stunned Sonja.

"Dian," Judith demanded, but this time Dian ignored her sister. She placed the honed point of her knife under Sonja's chin and forced the woman to raise her head, to meet Dian's eyes through her own single unswollen one. A new rivulet of blood started down the woman's rigid throat. Neither of them noticed.

"Do I have your attention now, you stupid bitch?" said Dian in a voice like Culum's growl, low, focused, and crawling with threat. Sonja blinked her white-surrounded eye in affirmative, did not move her head. "It's decision time. Not next week, not tomorrow, now. What will it be: go, or stay?"

A faint motion of the lower lip bared Sonja's teeth a fraction, but even without this slight movement Dian could read the answer in the woman's eye. She was taken aback but hesitated only an instant before bringing her face down so close she could feel Sonja's breath.

"Stay it is. But you hear me, bitch, and I'm only saying this once. I'm here, I'm gone, it doesn't matter. I will always, *always*," she repeated, poking the knife a fraction in emphasis so that the trickle of blood thickened, "be back. And if I find out that you've stepped one inch out of line—one inch—I'm going to cut off your fucking head." She waited to see the *yes* in the woman's eyes before she withdrew the knife. She stood over Sonja, wiping the knife on her trousers and fighting the urge to kick the woman. Instead, she retrieved her jacket and necktie and walked away into the night.

Once away and safely hidden by the dark, she stopped by the horse trough, trembling. It seemed a very long time before the reaction passed, and when it did it left her feeling ill and so tired she wanted to weep. She bent down to wash the blood off her face, oozing from a blow to her eyebrow. She took out her handkerchief and pressed it to the cut and sat on the edge of the trough. After a few minutes she became aware that there was someone in the darkness behind her. Yes, she had expected her sister to come.

"I'm sorry they woke you up," she said. There was no answer.

She turned and saw, not Judith, but Teddy, small

and solitary behind a post of the Hall's porch. Half of his face was visible in the lamplight from the window behind; it looked as empty as a marble statue. As empty as it had the first days after his arrival. She turned back deliberately to the trough and washed her face again, ran her fingers through her hair, and went to sit on the other side of the post from where the child stood. Blood continued to seep down next to her eye, and she held the handkerchief back up to her face. She couldn't see him, hidden on the other side of the massive post, but a minute later a feather touch brushed across her damp hair, then retreated.

"Nobody got hurt, Teddy," she said into the night. "Laine will be fine in a day or two, Sonja's bruises will be all gone in a week, and my cut barely hurts at all. Faces bleed easily, it's nothing to worry about. I'm afraid I spoiled the shirt, though." She leaned back to look around the post at him, taking the cloth from her face for a minute to reassure him. "See?" He seemed to have lost his words, and Dian cursed herself furiously.

"You saw it all, didn't you?" He nodded. "It's scary when grown-ups get really angry, isn't it?"

Ah, yes, that was the crux of it. He looked away, looked back, studied the dark stains down her white shirtfront.

"Oh, Christ. Teddy, I'm sorry. You're right. I was mad at Sonja because she hurt two of my friends. They're two people the Valley depends on when I'm gone, but it was wrong of me to hurt her in return. Tomorrow I will go and apologize to her. I promise. Is that better?"

He nodded, and then to her astonishment he stepped around the post and put his arms around her. She folded herself about him and held him close. Many long minutes later, she looked up, and saw Judith and Isaac standing in a patch of light spilling from the Hall, watching. After a long moment, she nodded ruefully at their wordless comments, and stood up with Teddy in her arms to join them.

LAINE

The next day the Valley was restless and ill-humored and generally hung over, and chores were tackled with grim determination. Dian went to the clinic three times to check on Laine before she found her at the door, arguing with Ling, an argument Laine won by the simple expedient of walking down the steps and away. When Dian fell in beside her, Laine glanced down at Dian's knee, which looked naked without Culum attached to it.

"How's the head?" she asked Laine.

"It's been better."

"Eyes focusing okay?"

"They've been better, too. What do you want, Dian?"

"We've got to have a little talk."

"Last time we had a little talk, you ended up kicking me out of your bed."

"I didn't kick you—"

"Di, my head feels like crap. What do you want to talk about that can't wait?"

"I wanted to say I was sorry."

"For what? *You* didn't knock me silly."

"For riding your ass like I do."

Laine had no comeback for that.

"Laine, you're good, and you work like the devil, and I never tell you how much I appreciate that. Half the time I treat you like some raw beginner. You've got every right to stand up to me."

"I know I do," Laine replied, but the assertion was more automatic than heartfelt. "Was that all?"

"No. About Sonja."

"What's left of her." She bristled again.

"Oh, come on, Laine, I didn't hurt her that bad."

"You would've, if it hadn't been for Judith."

"Yeah, okay, I was pissed at her."

"Hey, I'm the one she hit! I'm the one who should've been pissed."

"So why weren't you?"

"Because I was unconscious, for shit's sake!"

The two woman stared at each other; Dian's eyebrows rose, making her look so remarkably like Culum that Laine began to laugh. Dian joined in, but Laine stopped, putting her hand to her forehead.

"Jeez, that hurts."

"Sorry. Laine, honest, what's going on with you two?"

"What do you think?"

"Are you in love with her?"

"She's been here for five minutes, Dian."

"Yeah. So, are you in love with her?"

"In lust, sure. And I like her."

"She's dangerous."

"Not to me. Not to anyone else in the Valley."

"Just to me, you mean?" Dian's voice was sarcastic.

"Well, probably, yes."

Dian narrowed her eyes. "Does she know about us?"

"I told her, sure."

Dian's gaze went far away, as if she was trying to fit together the pieces of a mental puzzle. Laine gently massaged her temples, trying to shift the ache, until Dian stirred. "You're saying this whole thing is jealousy?"

"Dian, let's say things just got a little out of hand. I mean, put yourself in her shoes—she's scared to death what might be happening to her people without her; she hates that she's left behind. She was important there and is less than nothing here, and you've made sure she knows it. And she's never been surrounded by strangers before, never. She overreacted. And, maybe she's showing off, just a little."

"To you?"

"Why not?"

"I can think of a lot of reasons why not."

"She got drunk, she blew off steam, end of story. Just because you never let off any steam..."

"Not like that I don't."

"Not like anything. Hell, even in bed you're always thinking about where your damned dogs are."

"Yeah, and the one time I don't think about where they are, my partner finds a cold nose up her ass."

Laine's eyes snapped open in surprise and she erupted in laughter, then clutched her head, moaning. "God, don't make me do that. Christ, I'd forgotten—what a shock that was. Oh, that hurts."

"I had to scrape you off the ceiling." Dian grinned at the memory.

"You nearly had to scrape Culum off the floor. Talk about rude awakenings."

"Laine, look, I have to tell you something, but you can't pass it on to Sonja, not yet."

"Trust being your strong point. If this is going to take much longer, can we sit down?"

They climbed gingerly onto the low split-rail fence surrounding the cornfield, well experienced with splinters.

"Laine, I mean it, you can't tell her. This is about security, not about you and me."

"What is it?"

"This trip I'm taking as soon as Judith's given birth? It's not just to Meijing for supplies. I'm headed to Oregon. I didn't think it was a good idea to wait until spring."

Dian explained: her reasoning, the arguments put

by Judith and Kirsten, the decision. Laine listened without comment until Dian had finished, then asked, "Jude and Kirsten are the only ones who know?"

"And Ling. And now you."

"Not Isaac?"

"So far, Isaac thinks I'll be back in a week with Ling's medicines. I'll tell him just before I go."

Laine raised her eyes to Dian's without hesitation. "Okay, I won't tell Sonja until you leave. But I swear to God, you can trust her."

"I'm going to hold you to that, Laine. But you've got to watch her. She could do a lot of harm here."

"Does Judith feel that way too?"

"Jude's undecided. She's more willing to wait and see."

"Well, since you're going to ask me, then no, Sonja hasn't said anything about any secret they're hiding."

"Would she have?"

Laine had to think about that for a minute. "That I honestly don't know. If it was something she'd sworn to keep silent about, then probably not."

"Still loyal to Miriam."

"Wouldn't you be?"

Dian didn't answer. She didn't really have to. "You'll consult with Judith, all the time?"

"Dian... Ah, hell. I've been a bitch. I'm sorry. It's just, you just have a way of getting under my skin. But you have to believe, I would never do anything that put anyone here in danger. And all right, that includes taking my eyes off Sonja. You can go off to Oregon without worrying. I give you my word."

And it seemed that Dian was satisfied. When she left a short time later, Laine pondered the meaning of that: Dian trusted her. Who'd have thought it? Maybe they'd just been too young. Or she had been—Dian was six years older, she should have known to keep an infatuated kid at arm's length.

But that was years ago, and Dian wasn't as exciting as she'd thought. Sonja, on the other hand...

Judith and Kirsten were strolling arm in arm back from the high orchard when they saw two women meet in the middle of the millpond bridge: Dian, heading downhill with three young dogs bouncing merrily in front and Culum fixed to his mistress's side, and Sonja, coming the other way. Sonja hesitated for an instant when she noticed Dian, then squared her shoulders and came on. When their paths intersected, Dian nodded briefly, Sonja responded with an equally curt phrase, and they continued on their ways, Dian's left hand coming out to soothe the fur on Culum's ruff. Kirsten shook her head and started walking again.

"Too many alpha females around this place," she said as if to herself.

"Dian came to see me early this morning," Judith told her. "To say she thought she shouldn't go north, that we needed her here."

"And you said?"

"To tell you the truth, I was torn. Watching her with Isaac yesterday, I couldn't stand the thought of breaking them up so soon. Did you see the way she was laughing? God, I haven't seen that since—"

"You didn't tell her that?" Kirsten said sharply.

"Almost, but in the end, no, I didn't. You sound like you think I shouldn't have."

"It would have been a great mistake. The only reason Dian is allowing herself to be with Isaac is because she's convinced it's temporary. And she's right—when she comes back, even if they stay together, it will not be at all the same."

"Why not? There are others coming, and if one of

the women wants a baby by Isaac, artificial insemination is easy enough."

"Which is what they may decide to do, but it will still be different, for Dian. So what did you tell her?"

"I told her not to be a fool, that the best thing for everyone was for her to get out of the way for a little while. To let Laine try out her leadership wings on her own, without Dian to second-guess her."

"Hard words," said Kirsten calmly.

"I tried to soften it. I'm worried about Dian. She takes too much on herself, tries to do everything on her own, and then blows up when she finds someone slacking off. She doesn't lose her temper often, but when she does—God, last night I thought... She could have hurt Sonja badly."

"She intended to: Sonja was a catalyst, although it remains to be seen what the results of that reaction might be. I wish we knew something about your sister's biological parents," the old woman said, not for the first time. "There's a vein almost of madness running through the girl. But even without the genetics, you can see where her pressures come from. She started life knowing that her mother considered her unfit to live, but she was raised here, lavished with love and respect, by people who saw her quirk as a gift and not a sign of being nonhuman—trust and betrayal, love and abandonment. Everything to Dian is Us-and-Them, and when she sees a threat to her people, she goes wild."

"She was telling me a while back about raising dogs, how if you beat a dog, it learns not to trust. But if you take a beaten dog young enough, and offer it affection and protection, it's your slave for life, blind to your faults. When I thought about it later, it seemed to me she wasn't really talking about the dogs."

"I think you're right."

"But, Grans, I don't think Dian's happy here anymore. I think . . . Sometimes I get the feeling that what she really wants is to pull up roots and become a Traveler." It clearly hurt Judith to say this, but she pressed on. "That if it wasn't for thinking that she'd be abandoning us, she'd take off in a flash."

"Her compulsion to loyalty is indeed excessive. It blinds her. I fear someday it may get her into real trouble."

"As far as the rest of us are concerned, it's been a blessing."

"I hope the poor child realizes that, while she's beating herself up."

"I made a point of telling her."

"Wouldn't hurt to tell her again," the old woman said.

Later that afternoon Dian came looking for Judith and found her on the veranda piecing a quilt. She sat down, shaking her head at Judith's offer of a drink, and watched her sister's hands at work. One of the snippets of fabric she recognized from a length of cotton their mother had bought from a trader just inside the gates of Meijing, fourteen years before.

"How are you feeling, Jude?"

"Bloated. Stretched. Tired. And yourself?"

"Like a damned fool."

"And hung over."

"Is that what it is? I suppose so. I had a talk with Laine," she said abruptly, and got up to peer out the screen at nothing in particular.

"And?"

"I apologized."

"To Laine? Why to her?"

"For riding her. I come down on her too hard, too often. It's no wonder she gets so wild. I told her that. And, it seems that she and Sonja are together."

"I know."

"Did you? I didn't. It's too bad, in a way."

"What way?"

"She should get pregnant—Laine, I mean. It might slow her down a bit. Teach her caution."

Judith dropped her work into her lap and laughed. "That one, cautious? She'd be climbing a rock face during the contractions, don't kid yourself. She's just like you."

Dian turned around, surprised. "Like me? Old stick-in-the-mud? Old—what was it—keep-things-tidy?"

"It's been forced on you."

"Well, maybe a bit of responsibility will force it on that girl too," Dian grumbled, overlooking the fact that Laine was only half a dozen years younger. She ran her fingers through her hair, and for once neither twigs nor hay fell out. "I told her that if she's going to be in a position where the Valley depends on her, she's going to have to watch what she's doing, not to be so utterly careless of herself. I told her that she wasn't immortal. You know, I don't think she had the faintest idea what I was talking about. I swear," she said with a sigh, "she makes me feel positively circumspect."

"She makes me feel old," said Judith.

BOOK TWO

THE ROAD

IF THEY BORE A FEMALE, THEY KEPT

HER, BUT IF THEY BORE A MALE . . .

TEN

JUDITH'S LABOR BEGAN A WEEK AFTER HARVEST DAY, on what proved to be the last day of the year's Indian summer. She came awake long before the dawn, restless despite the cool night, to lie staring up into the silent house, feeling the carefully constructed walls of her own defenses beginning to crumble, to bulge and crack with the force of the horrors the next months could hold. Again. Dear God, she prayed without hope, let this baby be a girl, a safe, dull, uneventful girl baby, so my biggest worries will be diaper rash and colic and teething pains. Even now her mind's barriers would not let Judith squarely confront the terrors a boy baby could bring, the fear at every cry and the gut ache of tension over the months and years of greatest vulnerability, when every runny nose could be followed by death, when every quiet night might be the last. The fear which could not be faced battered and pried at her until, in a spasm of claustrophobia, she flung aside her blankets, threw on some clothes, and scurried barefoot down the stairs toward the back door and air.

In the kitchen she paused just long enough to scribble some explanatory words on the message slate, grabbed some fruit and bread to drop into her pockets, then lunged for the door.

Judith stood on the top step and gulped in the clean predawn air like a surfacing diver. The baby responded, moved heavily within her with a surge of tiny heels that kicked against her heart and lungs and robbed her momentarily of breath. Soon now, it would be very soon, but the urge to be out of the house was powerful and immediate. She stepped into her shoes, turned toward the upper fields, and quickly left the village behind.

All morning she worked her slow way up the path alongside the stream, the faithful, clear water whose presence made the village possible. With each step in the quiet woods her mind calmed, her panic retreated. By the time the sun had cleared the eastern hills, she was on the knoll that overlooked the Valley, where she sat on a long-downed redwood to eat her pears and the brown roll. From her isolated perch she could see all the Valley from the water tanks down to the Gates; impassive as a god, she watched her people go about the day's work, saw the children spilling into the yard of the schoolhouse, the brilliant glare of reflected sunlight from panes of the distant glass houses, the proud gleam of new wood that was the growing Great Hall. The only sound that reached her was the faint rumble of the mill wheel, grinding grain or running one of the tools. She could pick out figures, though, and as she watched from her high seat Dian appeared with a swirl of tiny dogs, a miniature doll with a cluster of pale ants. The woodpecker that drummed on the dead tree a hundred yards away seemed considerably more real than her sister below.

Motionless, with the rough, soft bark beneath her thighs, she could feel the energy rise in her belly, the still-sporadic hardening of the powerful uterine muscles as they flexed, and let her go, and flexed again. In part of her mind she knew that she was foolish to spend her energies on a strenuous climb, and she had not intended to go farther than this knoll. However, another part of her was badly in need of the strength only this walk could give. Her body and spirit felt the pull of the spring on the hill behind her. She rose and stood for a moment, undecided, kneading at her lower back with both hands and surveying the miniature world far below. She took a deep breath, exhaled it slowly, and set her face again to the source of the waters.

It was nearly noon when she finally entered the ancient circle of trees from whose base rose the spring. She paused on the thick black duff, the decayed needles of millennia, and listened to: silence, broken only by the scold of a squirrel, the creak of a branch high overhead, and the gentle mutterings of water moving down the hill. She stood, scarcely breathing, for a long time, so long that she began to think it was no longer there, that the remembered sound was a construct of her imagination, and then suddenly she heard it. It lay below the silence, not a sound, but the impression of a sound, a rhythm, a hum too low to register on the ears, like the working of a distant hive of bees only far, far greater, infinitely more powerful, eternal, untouchable. This was the voice of the redwood cathedral.

Judith sank awkwardly to her knees, plunged her hot face into the small, deep pond that was the spring's open mouth, and drank deeply from the earth's icy water. She rose with an effort and brushed the strands of wet hair back from her face, and then she turned to seek out the fallen tree among whose roots she had sat both times she had come here before. Her first visit had been when she was thirteen and the blood of new womanhood had come upon her. The other time she had come followed the death of her tiny son. She had spent a week here then, and even now, eighteen years later, she remembered clearly how her breasts had ached, had swollen and hardened and ached and leaked and finally begun to dry up, and she had gone back to her life. And now, this late, unlooked-for pregnancy, another cycle of flinging herself into the jaws of the Fates, offering up her body and her mind in exchange for the chance of a new life. She sat, quietly watching the clear water well up into the pool and slip over the moss-covered rocks, and soon, with neither surprise nor consternation, she felt her own waters break and drip into the ground, to be absorbed by the earth below. Cradled by the soft ground and the mass of roots, Judith slept.

Some time later, probably no more than an hour, Judith woke to the gradual realization that there was another person in the grove. She opened her eyes and saw first the horse, nibbling on the bush to which it was tied, and beside it the dog lying patiently with its chin on its paws. Judith turned her head and looked up into Dian's face, which was without expression but for the faint smile lurking behind her blue eyes.

"Have I given you enough time?"

"Oh, yes, I suppose." Judith looked wistfully over at the bubbling black pool and felt the first true stirrings of her labor. She smiled back up at Dian. "This baby's not going to wait forever," she said, and started laboriously to rise.

"No, just sit there a minute. I'll bring the horse up here." Dian walked swiftly through the trees to unloop the reins from the branch and led the bare-backed old mare to the fallen tree, pausing at the spring to fill a jug with water from the deepest part of the pool. She pushed the cork in firmly and handed the jug to Judith.

"You might want this in a while."

She helped her sister climb onto the mare's broad

back and sit sideways, then she, too, mounted, her arms draped loosely around Judith's swollen torso. With her sister's head resting on her shoulder, Dian turned the mare down the hill by the pressure of knees and feet. Culum led the way.

By the time they passed the lookout knoll, Judith's contractions were strongly established. When they reached the first fields Dian was having to help her control her breathing, and when the mare's even steps stopped outside the back door, Judith had begun to sweat. Her breaths came fast and sharp, alternating with periods of rest. Ling was sent for. Peter and Lenore helped ease Judith down from the horse. Clutching the water bottle and stopping once on the stairs to breathe through contractions, Judith reached her room.

Darkness came early that night, brought on by the gathering clouds. While the rest of the house met over a dinner that was both subdued and excited, while the first drops of rain in six months pattered onto the dust, Dian and Ling lit the lamps upstairs and helped Judith in her work.

It was a steady labor, now that Judith's mind was not fighting the birth, for her body was healthy and her muscles strong. Susanna came up after dinner to walk with her mother and wipe her sweating face with cloths dampened in the spring water. Dian and Ling breathed with her, talked to her, encouraged her, and rubbed her back. After the downstairs dinner, David, the child's father, stopped in and exchanged a few optimistic words with Judith, then left, saying that he would be back after the little kids were in bed. He and Judith had an affectionate relationship, but their love had no great depth to it. She found some of his mannerisms vaguely irritating, and he knew it and was sensitive enough not to stay with her during the whole labor. After he left, Judith sat down on the bed.

"He's a good man," she said absently. "I think I'll lie down for a while."

Judith's labor went on, grew, built, expanded, took her over. By ten o'clock she was engulfed by it, aware of nothing but the endless waves of almighty contractions, one on top of another with barely time between them for her breath to return to normal. Dian was behind her on the bed, her arms and back burning with fatigue from the effort of supporting Judith's half-upright weight, her throat hoarse from the hours of murmured words. Susanna came and went with containers of water, her hands raw from wringing out hot towels for her mother's lower back. Ling checked her instruments for the seventh time, particularly the frightening ones in the sterile package sitting outside the door. She'd used those only five times over the years and was greatly relieved that Judith's progress, though slow, was normal, that surgery did not seem to loom large tonight. She went to scrub her hands yet again in the basin, Susanna pouring the water, when her ears picked up an odd but expected sound: after hours of even rhythm, Judith's great breaths had caught, faltered, and then resumed.

Ling finished washing her hands and went to examine the birth's progress. In a minute she stood up with satisfaction.

"You can push when you want to."

And push she did. David arrived again to take Dian's place at Judith's back, and the two women, the man, and the young girl all poured their energy into Judith. In half an hour the black wet hair was crowning. Three more pushes and Ling was saying, "Hold it, hold it, don't push, let it come gently," and a squashed, straining red face emerged, followed by the shoulders, and then in a rush the slippery purple body of a perfectly formed new boy baby came into the world.

Ling ran her professional eyes and hands over the soft, hot little person before placing him on his mother's chest for warmth. His bright dark eyes seemed myopically to study his surroundings. He blinked once at the lamplight, and then he and Judith were looking into each other's eyes.

"Your son, Jude," said Dian. "He's beautiful, he's strong, he's your boy baby, and he needs you."

"I know," whispered Judith. She closed her eyes and began to shiver despite the warmed blankets they were wrapping around her, then, as Ling cut the cord, placed her hands on her son's body and touched his wet hair. "I know. God give me strength."

Dian and Ling left an hour later, after Judith had curled up into an exhausted sleep. The house was asleep as well, even Susanna in her room with Teddy, but as Dian looked back into the room before closing the door it was not Judith she saw, but David. The young man was sitting in the rocking chair, the chair in which Kirsten had nursed Judith's mother, holding the old woman's new great-grandson in his arms. Dian could not read the expression on his face as he studied the sleeping features of his son and delicately stroked the thick, soft hair with his thumb, but she thought he was not far from tears. David had three daughters, but none of his sons had lived to walk.

The following morning Judith woke slowly, aware immediately of the gurgle of rain in the spouts and falling onto the veranda roof below. Then she felt the baby nestled to her side and came fully awake. When she opened her eyes she found Kirsten seated in the comfortable chair near the window, knitting some dark red wool by the thin light.

"Good morning," said the old woman. "I came to see my newest baby. Let me get you some tea first, though. Someone has been crashing about in the kitchen for an hour; she ought to have a kettle hot by now."

She returned in a few minutes with the hot, sweet tea and set it within reach of Judith's hand, then closed the door firmly and settled into the chair with her own cup to study Judith's expressionless face. The rain continued to drip outside. Soon the baby stirred, seeking touch and nourishment and comfort. Judith put her cup on the table and brought him to her breast, still impassive, not looking at the baby her arms held.

"You don't have to keep him, you know."

Judith looked up, startled.

"You've been through this once before, and lost. You don't have to do it again. He would be welcomed, cherished, by several good women I could think of."

Judith looked down in silence at the fuzzy head. A minute passed.

"If you would rather, I could even place him outside the Valley. I know women outside, including a few in Meijing, who would care for him well, and you would not have to see him and have him near you."

Judith still did not answer. She drank her tea, and after a few minutes shifted him to the other breast, without raising her eyes to Kirsten's. The old voice went gently, affectionately, inexorably on.

"If you cannot give yourself to him, then you cannot. It does not reflect badly on you. It is not your fault, it is not a weakness or failure, it is simply the way things are. But you must not keep him with you if you are unable to give him your love. That would be unfair to him. It would be like a mother without milk in her breasts insisting on nursing her child—no fault of her own, but another source must be found or the

child will die." Kirsten moved over to sit on the bed
next to mother and son and caressed the tiny ear with
her gnarled finger.

"A boy baby has a hard enough time, in this day
and age. We cannot allow him to have anything but
the best possible beginning. It is true: this one may
die," she said, with love and brutality. "You know it. I
know it. He may even know it. And we owe it to him,
as a small human being, to make what days he has as
full and as comfortable and as filled with love as we
possibly can. If he lives, that love will make him a
better person. If he dies, it will come near to killing us
too. I know. I lost four sons, remember. But we can't
do it any other way. Not for his sake, we cannot. Or
for ours."

She rose and looked down at Judith's stricken face.

"You think about it. If you need to give him up, do
it soon, child, before he becomes a habit."

Before she went out of the room, Kirsten turned
and looked back at the figures on the bed. As she
watched, her granddaughter's tears began to come,
her arms rising to curl around the small figure of her
sleeping son. Now, Kirsten thought, they would stay
there. She closed the door quietly with a curious expression on her face, a mixture of triumph and self-
contempt, and picked her cautious way down the
stairs for her breakfast.

SEEING HERSELF SO AFFLICTED, SHE REALIZED THAT, IF
SHE SOJOURNED THERE ANY LONGER, MORE DIFFICULTIES
MIGHT DAMAGE HER GREAT FAME AS A MANLY KNIGHT,
WHICH SHE HAD WON BY OVERCOMING SO
MUCH PERIL AND TRAVAIL.

Eleven

THE THREE DAYS FOLLOWING JUDITH'S BIRTH WERE A strange time for Dian, when the mad rush of last-minute preparations alternated with leisurely visits to Judith, Kirsten, and Isaac, with no transition between the two states. The rest of the Valley still thought she was simply going to Meijing, but Isaac now knew the truth. She'd told him the morning after the birth; he'd taken the news quietly, and although Dian could see it was troubling him, she really had no time to spare for his feelings. One minute she would be in her rooms, searching her drawers for socks without holes while throwing Isaac tips on dog care, making notes for Jeri about winter defense and lists of things that her pack of supplies was missing, when suddenly she would remember that she had told Judith she'd join her for lunch. Off she would run, sloshing through the storm to the main house and into a world of new mothers and old women, a world dominated by the need for quiet rest and a rapt attention to minutiae. She would sit in this atmosphere, eating an unhurried and undemanding meal and making gentle conversation, then eventually step out the door remembering that she had to tell Isaac what to do if

Rosie came into heat early and that Jeri should be asked to check the list of ammunition Dian might bring back from Meijing and also be reminded about the family of foxes that had moved in over the hill.

On the afternoon of the second day she staggered into Ling's front-room clinic, deposited her dripping rain gear at the door, and dropped into a chair amidst the jars of herbs and the sterile tools.

"If I think of one more thing to remind anyone of, my head will burst," she declared. Ling took off her glasses and looked at her dubiously. Dian sighed, sat up, and said more calmly, "You had some things you wanted me to bring back from Meijing?" The last trading trip had been just months before, with pack-loads of scavenged valuables, intricate winter needle-work, and tanned furs exchanged for medicines and manufactured goods, but a trip Outside would never be wasted on one purpose.

"You do look tired," Ling said affectionately. "I think you'll find the trip itself more restful than the preparations, when you finally get away."

"If I ever get away."

"You will. Thank you for sparing me the time," she added, and reached over to the central drawer of her rolltop desk for two envelopes. She handed the smaller, unsealed one to Dian. "This is your introduction, so you don't have to convince them who you are. I've asked my relatives in Meijing to give you hospitality and help you with your shopping list. I made a copy of the list in English for you—yes, go ahead and take it out. As you see, the top part is urgent, all small, mostly medical and laboratory supplies but also an assortment of things like violin strings and pieces for the photovoltaics. The second section is bulkier necessities that you can bring if you don't mind burdening your horse. The last part is up to you, if you feel like bringing back a packhorse. Anything you can't carry this time, they'll hold for us, and we'll get it in the spring. Give the list to whomever you're staying with on the way north; they'll have it waiting when you come back through."

"How on earth do I pay for all this?" Looking through the list, she saw a number of rare and therefore expensive items, goods that had not been manufactured since Kirsten was a girl. And although she would be taking some small goods and a parcel of completed needlework, it was only a summer's worth of trade.

"No need to pay, we have a lot to our credit with them, from my last trip there." Ling's expression was a bit too bland, but Dian shrugged.

"If you say so—but this amounts to a hell of a lot of furs and embroidery."

"I know, but you'll have no problem. And this," she said, holding the thicker envelope out, "if you'd give it to the same person. Sorry about the weight; it's notes and the results of a project I'm working on with one of the healers in the City." Dian took it curiously. It was more of a parcel than a letter, a bulky rectangle encircled with ribbon and sealed with red wax bearing Ling's chop.

"Look," said Ling before Dian had a chance to comment, "you must be cold. I was just going to make myself a cup of tea. Do you have the time? Good." Dian followed her into the kitchen and planted her backside against the stove while Ling bustled about with sticks for the fire and water for the kettle.

"Ling, I'd like a traveling kit from you. The usual first-aid stuff, a couple of water-purification tablets if there are any left, that sort of thing. I won't need a snakebite kit this time of year, but I would like some internal tampons, if you could make me up a dozen. There are times in the woods when it's best not to give off any blood smell."

"Happy to; I'll bring it all by in the morning." Ling turned to the cupboard and took down the pot and a tea caddy. She bent over the leaves with unnecessary concentration, to speak over her shoulder. "I should tell you, one of the things in that letter concerns you. I told my friend that you might want the Meijing specialists to examine you as to your fertility, and I suggested areas they might explore. If you don't want it mentioned, I can remove it from the letter without difficulty." She turned with the pot in her hands and looked at Dian, who was studying her own long fingers intently. "I just thought, with Isaac, you might be interested."

"That's good of you, Ling, very thoughtful. I doubt that I'll want to do anything about it, but leave it in anyway. I may change my mind." Ling nodded, seeming relieved at Dian's easy response.

They drank their tea and talked of this and that, of Teddy and Judith and Sonja. Ling listened to Dian's description of breakfast with Judith and her baby and suggested that Judith's acceptance of her son was due to Kirsten, who had spent a fair amount of that first morning with Judith, but whoever was responsible, it was a blessing, both agreed.

They were interrupted by a noisy entrance and stepped out into the hallway to see one of Carmen's sisters being helped out of a rain cape, her face pinched and white and one finger jutting out at a very wrong angle. Dian gathered her things to leave.

"Thanks for the tea."

"Anytime. I'll bring the kit by tomorrow. Oh, here—I wanted to give you this." Ling paused in the act of settling her patient into a chair to fetch an object from her desk. It was a waterproof neck bag made of heavy plastic, only mended once; she slid the letter and list inside and worked the fastener, dropping the cord over Dian's neck. "That will keep your papers dry even if you go swimming."

"Which, from the looks of it, I may," Dian said with a glance at the window. Ling laughed and waved her out, and turned to speak soothing words. Dian shrugged into her stiff, clammy waxed-cloth raincoat and closed the door on comfort, to splash away into the dark afternoon, her mind already racing ahead.

The following day, the last before she rode north, Dian took Isaac out of the Valley. The storm had cleared during the night and left behind it a day of intoxicating freshness and clarity, when even the autumn-dark leaves of the orchard took on a final sheen of beauty before falling victim to frost. They trotted down the puddled road with five of the dogs, crossing the bridge and passing the sheds, hearing ghostly whispers of that August night when the wagons had come. They were nearly to the Gates before Dian had Isaac dismount, and they led the horses down a narrow track toward a steady, growing thunder.

The trees fell away abruptly, leaving them standing on a sandy bank looking up at a thick sheet of brownish water that shot out of the hillside fifty feet away to plunge into one end of a pool, which was at the moment the color and probably the consistency of thin mud. Isaac stared, openmouthed.

"Well, there's your waterfall." Dian had to shout into his ear to be heard. "Fancy a swim?"

His answer came as a loud hoot and an assortment of clothing flying into the air. He raced naked across the narrow strip of sand and plunged into the deep, cold pool, and came up gasping for breath and bellowing at the top of his lungs.

"God, it's cold! My God, it's cold! Come on, Dian—it's perfect! Oh, God, it's freezing!"

The row of dogs stared aghast at the man's swift

and inexplicable lapse into madness; when Dian saw
their expressions she began to giggle. She looped the
reins over a branch, took off her clothes, and folded
them into a neat pile in a relatively dry spot out of the
reach of hoof and paw, then walked up to the water,
steeled herself, and dove cleanly in, coming to the
surface halfway to the center of the pond. With a
tremendous effort she did not scream at the shock of
it but instead shook the liquid mud out of her eyes
and trod water, and controlled her chattering teeth
long enough to bellow at Isaac, "What's wrong? Too
cold for you? I guess they make them soft up in
Oregon. Why, you think this is cold—I've swum here
when you had to break the ice to get in. I've swum
here when the snow—" Isaac came after her with a
roar of mock anger, and she slid away from him to
swim, invisible, over to where the falling water boiled
back up from below. The noise was deafening. She
looked around for Isaac's blue, drowned-looking face
and mouthed, "Coming?" Without waiting for an answer she clambered up the rocks and around to the
not-so-secret niche behind the wall of water and sat
in the little cave, shivering hard and hunched over her
knees.

In a few minutes Isaac ducked through the sheeting
water, hair, beard, and body hair plastered down and
one knee bleeding from a gash. He sat down beside
her.

"Warm enough?" he shouted politely.

"I could be warmer," she admitted. "I don't think
I've ever been this blue before."

Isaac turned his attention from the sheet of water
in front of them to examine her skin.

"It's a very attractive color," he said. "However
shall we warm you?"

"Oh, I can think of one way," she replied.

It was some time before either of them noticed the

cold again, but eventually they burst out of the hidden cave and began leaping about vigorously. The dogs, who had more sense than to venture into any such inhospitable body of water if they did not have to, lay on the far bank and watched them grimly: the man's insanity was obviously contagious. The two humans ran along the edge of the pond, splashed through the outgoing stream at the far end, and ran back to their horses and the wary dogs. They dressed quickly, or, rather, Dian did. Isaac put on various odd bits of clothing as he found them, but it was a good quarter of an hour before they discovered his second shoe in the branches of a tree.

They climbed back to the road, mounted, and continued out through the Gates. The shoulder of Isaac's jacket, which had come to rest in a puddle, steamed gently in the warm sun. The dogs flushed a hare out of cover, but Dian called them back, partly because a hunt would change the tone of the outing, but mostly because she didn't want to give Isaac any ideas about hunting that he might decide to follow up after she had left. They rode for half an hour, to the top of a rise overlooking the stream where it joined another, larger creek, and there they sat and ate sandwiches and drank cider beer, and talked. They decided that Crazy Isaiah had a lot of sense after all, for this place where Miriam proposed to build a new town was a good one, easily irrigated and not impossible to defend. They decided that Isaac should choose three or four of the most promising boys and work on their skills with the bow and arrow. They decided that white clouds were a perfect complement to sky that particular color of blue. They talked of things unimportant and of things vital, and for a while they lay back on the damp hillside and talked of nothing. Isaac broke the silence.

"Why dogs?" he asked.

"Sorry?" He might as well have asked, *Why air?*

"It's just, when you and Teddy are together with the dogs, I sometimes feel like I'm tone-deaf, or color-blind. I mean, I like dogs, and I can certainly see how useful these of yours are, but it almost seems like they're more...real to you than half the people around you."

"They are more real. They're my life. They're my partners, my friends; they make me laugh, they challenge me. They keep me honest. Training a dog is like growing a new limb, one that you weren't born with. Before you grow it you couldn't imagine much use for it, but after you have it, you can't imagine doing without. When I train a dog, part of what I'm doing is training myself to listen to that dog, to understand its own individual way of looking at the world, what that dog needs to enable it to come into full awareness of itself as my partner. When you partner a dog, you become that dog, and it becomes you. Otherwise it's all bullying and bribery. You can force a dog to obey by bullying and bribery, but there's no honor in it, and that dog will almost never give you its all."

Dian dug a smooth stone from the ground at her feet and rubbed it around in her hands. She called Culum and let him see it, then flipped it off down the hill into the grass. He plunged happily after it. She went on talking.

"That's why I wanted Teddy to get involved with dogs. Not only does he have that amazing rapport with them, but he badly needed to get outside himself." Culum arrived back with the correct rock, which he dropped into her hand. Dian thanked him and threw it again. He plunged off into the brush after it, with a fraction less enthusiasm this time, it seemed to Isaac. "I didn't think it all out that first day, not so clearly, but it just felt right then, and still does. Something about the way he looked, really looked at

Culum was different from the way he looked at anybody else, except you. He was paying attention to Culum." The dog returned, this time depositing the rock
at her feet, but still within the acceptable limits of
"fetch." Dian, immersed in her thoughts, absently
reached for it and threw it off again down the hill.

Culum, head lowered, studied her through his eyebrows for a long moment, and then trotted off dutifully down the hill.

"You know, Kirsten found me a book from Before
about how they used dogs as a kind of therapy when
they were dealing with criminals or sick people or angry kids. They found that these damaged people
would respond to dogs when they wouldn't to other
humans, because the dogs seemed to be so undemanding. Dogs wouldn't insist that the person shape
up but would just accept them as they were." Isaac
was somewhat surprised to see Culum returning with
the rock, for he had half-thought the dog would quietly fade away, bored with the game. But, no, here he
came, looking if anything even more willing than he
had been at Dian's first throw. His tail was up, eyes
alert, and he positively galloped up the hill to his pon-
tificating mistress.

"The funny thing was, though the book didn't
seem to notice it, in the end the dogs would be more
demanding than all the human counselors. The dogs
would act as if their human was a truly noble being,
worthy of partnership, and—to the amazement of the
various authorities—the human came out of herself,
or himself, long enough to begin actually to act nobly,
and often never really went back in." Culum stood
before her now, rock in mouth. Dian absently held
out a hand for him to deposit it into. "Not, of course,
that Teddy was that disturbed, but—What the hell?"
She stared at her palm, where the rock had turned
into something else, a lump that suspiciously resem-

bled a petrified clump of old deer droppings. "Culum!" she shouted in outrage.

Good heavens, thought Isaac, that dog's laughing at her, and he was, standing there, tongue lolling, grinning from ear to ear at the effect his clever trick had on his mistress. Dian threw the lump of turd at him; it disintegrated off his head, one segment landing neatly in Isaac's cup, then she launched herself down the hill after the rapidly accelerating, and still laughing, dog. The other dogs leapt up enthusiastically to join the chase, and there was soon a tide of dogs washing around Dian, each of whom would nimbly lay on just enough speed to scoot out of her reach whenever she reached out to catch them. Culum abandoned the game of tag and came to sit next to Isaac, and the two of them looked on from their viewpoint of lofty masculinity.

By the time Dian returned to Isaac, her chest was heaving and her face was red with effort. Culum retreated in dignity a few yards up the hill, just in case. She gave him a dirty look and dropped down next to the still-grinning Isaac.

"Okay, okay, enough said about the relationship between dogs and humans. I'm sure you got the point," she said.

"Oh, I got the point, all right. In fact, it's right there in my cup."

Dian peered in and saw the dry turd floating placidly in the cider, and snorted. That set Isaac off again, and the two of them leaned against each other, shaking with laughter.

"Oh, Isaac, I'm going to miss you," she said, and as if the sun had gone behind a cloud, the easiness of the afternoon shifted.

I'm going to miss you, Dian had said, surprising herself. She hadn't intended to say it, hadn't realized the depth of its truth until the words were in the air between them. What had begun as a somewhat bewildering but highly pleasant interlude was now something else entirely, something with roots that screamed at the threat of being pulled up. She loved Isaac, sure, but she'd never bargained on being *in* love with him. She had never intended anything but easy affection followed by fond memories and a degree of relief when she was allowed to go her way. But that was something very deep that had spoken: I am going to miss you.

I'm going to miss you, Isaac heard, and the longing in her voice slipped into his heart like a knife. What had begun as a deliberate bid for shelter (and be fair— he had told her) for himself and Teddy, a move to defuse the growing tensions over his availability by making his own choice, had grown considerably more complicated. And he couldn't have known that his chosen bond would be severed so quickly—when she'd told him the morning after Judith's birth that her trip north would be immediate, his first thoughts had been a tumble: *Shit, there go my plans* and *Thank God it won't get any deeper* and *Couldn't she have warned me?* and *Who would I have chosen instead, if I'd known?* When she told him she was going, he'd very nearly unloaded all the secrets onto her—but he didn't, because Emma's people were his, and he'd given his word. And anyway, where would he begin? How to say to these people that the thing that terrified them the most was part and parcel of their future neighbors' daily lives? He'd even played with the idea, briefly, of injuring Dian in some way to delay her, of having a quiet word with Sonja that would result in some minor but incapacitating broken bone....But Judith would just have sent someone else instead, and he thought that, of all people here, Dian was the one whom he might trust to make a judgment based on her eyes, not her habits of thought.

"Can I ask you something?" he said, more to break the dangerous intimacy than because he wanted an answer.

Dian seemed relieved at the diversion. "Of course."

"Why, honestly, are you making this trip? Do you think Miriam and I and everyone else are lying? I mean, not you, but I think I should know if the Valley sees me as a potential enemy within the gates."

Dian looked at his dark eyes, seeing her own reflection there. "No, I don't know of anyone who seriously suspects you of deceit. I'm going north because I made a promise, before we voted to accept you, that I would check with my own eyes to be sure that everything was as it was presented. It's my job to guard the safety of my people here, even when the enemies are only in our imagination." She smiled ruefully at him. "I trust you, I hope you know that. I would trust you with my life. But I cannot extend that to the whole village. I have no right to lay two hundred eighty lives at your feet. It would be irresponsible of me. Surely you can see that."

The word *trust* twisted the knife deeper into his heart, and he wanted to cry out for her not to go, wanted to tell her what she would find and why it did not matter. But trust worked on other levels, and he had given his word. No, he would say nothing. She would go, as she clearly longed to, no matter how much she would miss him; she would travel free and unencumbered with nothing but her dogs, and she would see what there was to see, and she would have the return journey to think about it and decide for herself that it did not matter.

Whether on her return she would trust him again was an entirely different matter. And she was studying him now, her eyes narrowing as she tried to see why he was hesitating.

"Yes," he said, and leaned forward to kiss her

lightly. "Of course you have to go. Just come back safely. Please?"

They were late returning home, and by the time Dian had sluiced off the dried film of grit from her body and arrived at the main house, dinner was just being laid on the table. Lenore looked up as Dian came through the kitchen door.

"Oh, good. Judith said you'd eat with her tonight, and I told her I'd bring hers up so you could talk without having to shout over the rest of us. Do you want to grab that tray there, and we'll take it up?" Dian followed her up to Judith's room, half-listening to Lenore's chatter about the Meijing markets and half a dozen things she hoped Dian would look for, all of which were already on Dian's list. Lenore knocked at the door before she opened it, and laid her tray on the table near the window. After greeting Judith affectionately and going over to look at the sleeping infant on the bed, she kissed Dian good-bye and left. The sound of voices and of cutlery on plates cut off sharply as the door closed behind her.

Judith joined Dian at the table, sitting on a thick cushion, and began to remove the covers from the steaming bowls.

"You're looking well," said Dian.

"I'm feeling great. I've been going downstairs for meals, but I wanted you to myself tonight." She looked up guiltily. "It's good of you to come—I'm sure you'd rather be with Isaac or getting packed."

"Everything's ready to go and I spent the whole day with Isaac. I want to have a nice, relaxed dinner with my sister and talk to my nephew, so don't fret."

Lenore's dinner was, as usual, good and plentiful, and included a couple of Dian's favorites. She commented on Lenore's generous nature and Judith agreed.

"She is very fond of you. I should tell you, I think,

that she has done a great deal to calm down the women who were upset about you and Isaac. There weren't a lot," she said, seeing Dian's face. "Just a handful, but they resented it a bit until she talked to them about you. And reminded them that we'd have a whole new bunch of menfolk in the spring."

Dian's need to respond was cut off by an abrupt piglet grunt from the bed. Judith went over to fetch him, came back and settled him at her breast, and picked up her fork to finish her dinner one-handed. At the end of the dessert she sat back, switched sides, and looked down at the downy head cradled in her hand.

"I'm calling him Will," she told Dian. "He looks like old Will a bit, Kirsten says, though I can't see it. Maybe around the eyes," she amended, studying the lids intently.

Dian looked over her cup at mother and infant, nourishing each other, and wondered if Isaac's wife, Emma, had looked like that, nursing Teddy. Without considering what she was doing, she began to tell Judith about Isaac's past, about Ashtown and Emma, his escape and what his wife's death had done to him. It did not take long, and at the end she sat and listened to baby Will's suckling noises, slowing now.

"I don't know why I told you that," she admitted.

"Actually I knew the outline of it already. Ling told me a few days ago. Oops, toss me that cloth, will you? Thanks." She wiped the stream of milky drool from her son's slack mouth and positioned him on her shoulder.

"I gathered he and Ling'd had a couple of heart-to-hearts," said Dian. "I'm glad he feels comfortable talking to her. But I wanted to make sure you knew, because you'll be the one who'll have to deal with it while I'm gone, and especially if I don't come back. No, let me finish, Jude. I'm not expecting any danger, and before you ask, no, I don't have any of those 'feel-ings' you're so fond of. I fully expect to have a high old time between here and Meijing, and a nice quiet ride north, after which I'll turn around and be back here by Christmas. Just let me say this and then you can for-get it.

"If I don't come back from this trip, I want you to protect Isaac. He's a lot more vulnerable than he seems, and something is troubling him, although I don't know what it is. Just make sure that everyone gives him time to look around and decide, like you did when he first got here. He's intelligent and reason-able. He'll make the right decisions, given the chance. If he's bullied and badgered, he could easily do some-thing really...really stupid. Protect him. Promise me?"

"I have no intention of having to do anything of the sort, so, yes, I'll promise. Here, hold this man-child for a minute while I go to the toilet." Judith trans-ferred the baby into Dian's arms and left them. Dian held him and looked into the dark, wise, focused little eyes and felt his tiny fingers wrap firmly around her finger. She talked soft nonsense to him and drank in the new, warm smell of him, the perfection of his fin-gernails, the whorls of hair on his head, and told her-self fiercely that she was content with her life.

She was also content to hand the now-damp baby back to his mother and stand up to go. Dian did not want to say good-bye to this woman, her sister, who faced what might be a lengthy period of grinding anx-iety. She wished she could give Judith a talisman against the fear, or at least give her strength to face it, but instead she was forced to take refuge in a stream of inconsequential words.

"Good-bye for now, baby Will. You'll be a big boy when I see you again," firmly not mentioning other possibilities. "Take care of your mother, let her sleep—which is more than I've done. You look tired, Jude. Good-bye, sister mine. I hope to be back by Christmas, if the snow isn't too bad. Just call me Santa Claus, arriving through the snow with a line of packhorses behind me!" She embraced Judith and Will gently. "Good-bye, sweet sister, lovely baby. Eat a pie for me at Thanksgiving."

Dian's chatter stopped suddenly. She had frozen with her right hand cupped around the top of Will's head, looking past Judith's shoulder at his drooping eyes, her head tilted slightly as if she were listening to something far away. After a few moments she spoke, her voice thoughtful and slow.

"He's going to be okay, you know, Jude. He doesn't feel...unattached. Temporary, like Carmen's boy felt." Carmen's strong-looking son, born eighteen months before, had died in his sleep at ten weeks. "He's well named. He'll be here when I get back." Her gaze stared through him a bit longer, then she blinked, met Judith's startled eyes, and looked down at her hand curiously. She jerked it away from Will's head and rubbed her fingers together as if she had burned herself, and to Judith's amazement she flushed. "I'm sorry, Jude, I didn't mean to do that. I—I'm tired, I guess."

Her sister put her free arm around Dian and held her close, then freed her. "Take care, Dian. Have a safe journey, come back rested. We'll pray for you every night. Oh, I nearly forgot. Stop by Susanna's room, will you? She has something for you."

"Cookies, no doubt," sighed Dian.

Judith's eyes twinkled. "No, something a bit more useful. And you don't need to worry about it. Lenore and I 'helped' her with it. It won't fall apart on you."

"Thanks. I'll go up and see Kirsten first." Dian climbed the stairs to say good-bye to the old woman, whose footsteps she had heard outside Judith's door a while before. When Dian came down ten minutes later, the light under Judith's door was already out. She tapped softly on the next door, which belonged to Susanna, and went in. The girl—no, Dian thought, nearly a woman now—sat reading Teddy a story. She got up quickly and came to hug Dian.

"How's my favorite niece?" asked Dian fondly. "Your mother said you wanted to see me."

Susanna's eyes sparkled as she twirled and went eagerly to her closet to pull a cloth bundle down from the shelf.

"We made this for you, Mom and Aunt Lenore and I. I collected the feathers—Teddy and I did, didn't we, Teds?—and helped spin the lining, Aunt Lenore wove it, and Mom and I sewed it. Do you like it?"

There was no need to feign enthusiasm.

"Sweetheart, it's beautiful!" And it was, one of the finest sleeping bags Dian had ever seen. The outer cloth was as tightly woven as anything Lenore had ever made, and Lenore was the best weaver in the Valley. The inside material was softer but also tight, and the down filling was thick, yet the whole pushed into a relatively small roll, as Susanna demonstrated. She and Teddy transformed it several times, from fluffy tube to taut roll, before Susanna tightened the drawstring and placed it in Dian's hands.

"It was going to be your Christmas present, but you might not get back in time, and Mom figured you could use it on your trip."

"I sure can. My old one was getting pretty flat." She took the child into her arms, kissing the top of her head in a rare display of affection, and released her. "I'm not going to be able to look down at you for long, the rate you're growing. Thank you so much, Susanna. It's a lovely gift, one of the nicest I've ever had. I'll think of you every night when I climb into it." Teddy was watching her uncertainly, so she sat down on the bed and gathered him up too and gave them both a hard squeeze. "And you too, Teddy Bear. You two are going to be so busy while I'm gone, taking care of Teddy's dad and Susanna's mom, and each other as well. To say nothing of the dogs. I'm sorry to leave you with my jobs on top of your own, but I'll be back as soon as I can. I love you both. I'll miss you very much."

It was as much as she could stand. Once downstairs she opted for cowardice and avoided the still-crowded family room, creeping out through the veranda and closing the screened door quietly behind her.

...BUT IF THEY BORE A MALE,

HE WAS IMMEDIATELY KILLED.

TWELVE

SO IT WAS THAT FOUR DAYS AFTER LITTLE WILL'S BIRTH, Dian left on her trip north. She slipped out long before first light, with the stars still sharp in the cold black sky and most of the Valley's buildings invisible in the dark. The milking shed glowed with the light of lanterns, but the women there had their heads up against the warm flanks of the cows and saw nothing. Four people alone watched her go.

Isaac was the first. He rose with her, cooked her a breakfast, and went with her to saddle her horse, saying little all the while. When all was ready, he wrapped hard arms around her, his thoughts a turmoil of exasperation: longing and affection riding on a powerful undercurrent of guilt tinged with apprehension, all the contradictions of his life here coming together but finding expression only in the fervency of his embrace. Dian read an entirely different message in the strong grip that held her a few moments longer than necessary, and put her toe into the stirrup with something close to relief. Isaac rested his hand on her booted leg, then stood away and let her ride off.

Old Kirsten, awake at her attic window, was the second witness. She heard the muffled sound of a horse's hooves on the damp road and leaned forward to see. As Dian paused in the dim shaft of light thrown down by the old woman's lamp, Kirsten pressed a thin hand against the cold window pane, a gesture of farewell whose intensity did not penetrate the glass. Dian waved a casual hand and rode on.

And at the base of the Valley, her last greeting party waited. As she approached the narrow passage known as the Gates, Dian wasn't altogether surprised to hear Culum's brief warning grumble, indicator of a person nearby who wasn't a clear threat. She reined in, and said into the darkness, "Couldn't wait to see me go, huh?"

Laine answered by striking a light and setting it to a small lantern. She was sitting on one of the rocks brought to reinforce the natural outcrop, the butt of her rifle resting on the ground, but beside her stood Sonja, rifle half-raised, clearly startled at Dian's appearance.

"I see you didn't tell her," Dian said.

"I told you I wouldn't."

"Tell me what?" demanded Sonja.

"The little trip Dian's been getting ready for? It's going to be a bit longer than some of us thought. She'll be gone at least a couple of months."

Sonja frowned, taking in Dian's laden pack and the two dogs at her feet; then slowly she began to smile. She said nothing, simply lowered the butt of the gun onto the ground and stood there, as if claiming possession of the rocks on which she stood.

"I meant what I said, on Harvest Night," Dian told Sonja, in a voice that made Culum stir with unease. The woman's sure smile faltered, but so, yet again, did Dian's resolution. Maybe she was wrong to go. She'd felt this woman as a threat; yes, those feelings had faded, but what did that mean? And sure, Judith had sworn she would watch Sonja, but Judith's concerns were elsewhere, and Kirsten was too old, and Ling not strongly enough attached to the Valley's security. And as for Laine, where did her loyalties really lie? Maybe she should turn the horse back to the barn and put this off until she was absolutely certain. Sonja was hiding something—as Isaac was, she realized, and maybe it was the same something.

Which gave her two options: she could get down and pull the Valley's three newcomers apart until she found out, or she could go to the source. Forcing a showdown would be very ugly. Dian might get her answers, but there was no doubt in her mind that Laine would leave the Valley as a result, and she would take others with her, not the least of whom would be Isaac. And Teddy would be torn from the dogs.

What did she have to go by, anyway, that couldn't be explained by her dislike for this woman? Normally, Dian would have trusted her feelings; now she trusted those of Judith, Laine, Kirsten, and everyone else.

She took up the reins and urged the horse forward, out of the Valley.

By midmorning the sun had taken the frost from the leaves and the horse's breath no longer came in clouds. Dian stopped at a small stream and let him loose to graze on the greenery along the water's edge. The grass on the hillsides had not had time to sprout up after the rains, although the sere brown of summer seemed softer somehow. The dogs splashed into the cold water to drink, then flopped down in the sun. She glanced over at them as she fished out the makings for tea and breakfast from her bags, and decided that she had made a good choice. She had originally thought to bring Culum and his mate, Rosie, because they worked together so well, but had reluctantly discarded that idea for a number of reasons, not the least being that Rosie was due to come into heat in about two months and Dian really didn't want to deal with every pack of wild dogs for miles. The other was the temptation a mated pair of hounds might be to the packs of human scavengers. She didn't imagine that two of her trained dogs could be taken against her will, but she also didn't want to present an irresistible temptation. And then there was the undeniable fact that Rosie worked well with Laine, two contrary personalities that recognized something in the other. That alone would not have had her leave the female dog behind, but it nudged her over into decision.

So she had brought Culum's son, Tomas, instead, despite his youth and incomplete training. Culum liked Tomas, he worked well with him. The older dog would provide the experience, and Tomas would grow into his half of the partnership rapidly. She hoped. It was a bit of a gamble, but even though he was barely out of puppyhood Dian could feel his potential. Dogs, like people, rose to meet the demands made on them. She could only trust that the demands made on Tomas during the trip would not outpace his capacity to grow into his new role.

Her horse pleased her as well. She had managed to talk Carmen into giving her Simon, fully recovered without harm from her cruel use of him on that long-ago summer's morning and as big of heart as ever. He was not the fastest thing on four legs, and he was extraordinarily ugly, but he had intelligence and stamina, and those were things of greater value on a trip of this sort than looks and speed.

And with each mile she had ridden that morning, Dian had grown more reconciled to the decision made before the Gates.

She found her pan and went to the stream for water. On the way back she kicked Culum gently in the ribs. "Hey there," she said. He opened one eye and peered out at her. "Go get yourselves some breakfast," and at her whistled command for the hunt, Tomas leaped to his feet. Culum thought about it for a minute, then stood up, stretched, shook himself, and trotted off into the field with Tomas at his heels.

The pot came to a boil, and just as Dian took it from the fire and reached for the tea herbs, the two dogs reappeared, each carrying a large hare, which they dropped at her feet. "Oh, well, done, gentlemen," she told them, and they sat expectantly as she pulled her knife from her belt and swiftly cleaned each carcass of fur and bones. Her dogs never ate uncleaned kill. Not only was such a thing contrary to the principles of the partnership they had with their human, it was also just asking for a perforated intestine.

Dian let them have the bulk of their meat, holding back two of the legs to grill over the coals for herself. She went over to the pack and fished out the two extras she had allowed herself to bring. One was an ancient steel thermal jug with a new wooden stopper, carved complete with threads by Isaac. It was ridiculously heavy and covered with dents and scrapes, but its marvelous efficiency enabled her to have a hot drink without having to stop and build a fire. The other luxury was a large chunk of crystallized honey, to be sucked or put into hot tea when she felt the need for fast energy. She took the jug now and filled it carefully from the hot pan, straining out the majority of floating leaves with a twig. She started to screw in the top, then stopped, reached over and broke off a small piece of the honey, and dropped it into the tea.

"What the hell," she said to the dogs. "If we had some of Judith's glasses to drink from, we could have a real party." Her companions licked their chops and did not comment.

The exhilaration of being out under the open sky persisted throughout the day, and as darkness fell she chose a spot hidden from view and collected wood for a fire. Wrapped in the thick down bag that her family had made, she fell asleep thinking of the prayers they were saying for her and slept dreamlessly, as she had not for many months.

The portion of her trip from the Valley to Meijing would take four days, three of which would be in the hills. It was the longest she had been away from people and houses for over a year, and when she awoke the following morning the ropes that bound her to the Valley seemed but gossamer, dispersed on the faint breeze that moved against her face. Her heart sang. She burst out of her sleeping bag with a roar and pounced on Culum, who scrambled to his feet and bounded away, then bounced back and responded with mock roars of his own. The two of them wrestled as Tomas stood barking violently and the horse snorted nervously, until finally Dian collapsed panting on the frost-rimed grass. Culum came to her and shoved his head hard into her chest, and she seized his ears as handles and shook his massive head back and forth vigorously.

"God, isn't this fine?" she asked him, and seriously he agreed that, yes, it was.

Her breakfast was a stale sweet roll and some of last night's tea from the flask, and it filled her mouth with more flavor than anything she'd eaten for a long, long time. She packed her things away with automatic precision, mounted up, and rode off in the first slanting rays of sun through the trees, singing under her breath one of Kirsten's old songs about black being the color of her true love's hair. The dogs trotted and sniffed and held their tails high as they investigated the bushes. Squirrels chattered at their passing, jays gossiped cheerfully, a hummingbird flashed past Dian's nose. Even the normally phlegmatic Simon picked up his shaggy feet with more bounce than usual.

All that morning they followed the ridge of the hills, riding a wide circle around the village whose arrows had wounded Miriam's people two months before. By the time they entered the small road, little more than a pair of tracks worn by the wheels of wagons and carts, the dawn's exhilaration had settled into a quieter, more businesslike satisfaction. They were more alert now that the possibility of meeting someone was greater, and when a rabbit burst across their path she let Culum take it but put it into her catchbag rather than stopping to feed the dogs.

By the late afternoon, Dian was just beginning to relax, knowing that they were unlikely to meet other travelers now, when suddenly Culum stopped dead twenty yards ahead of her, ears pricked and tail rigid in his concentration. Tomas slowed, then he, too, came to a halt with his head up, listening. Dian immediately slid off Simon and led him into the bushes. She tied him to a secure branch, slid her rifle from its scabbard, and silently signaled the dogs to her. Well off the road, they made their stealthy way forward through the undergrowth.

In a very few minutes the sound the dogs had heard reached her ears as well, a sound for all the world like the cries of a small baby. Culum whined softly in his throat. Dian put Tomas on a "down, stay," and went ahead with Culum to a point where she could see the road.

Just ahead lay a crossroads, where the cart track she'd been following met a larger road that had once been paved. The crossroads was marked, as usual, by a herm, in this case an upended slab of concrete, ragged on this side and with dried tufts of fern fronds growing out of its cracks. The sound came once again from the other side of the herm, then stopped. Nothing moved.

She and Culum picked their way in a cautious circle around the crossroads, but the only signs of life were drying horse droppings several hours old. Culum gave no indication of any waiting humans. It was not a trap. She stepped onto her original road and walked forward to the standing stone, which remained silent. The stone was taller than she was, buried deep into the ground, with a crude ithyphallic figure gouged into its surface. She gestured Culum to a halt behind her, and as she moved around to the back side of the herm, small bones crunched beneath her boots. She put her head around the stone, and looked down at a sleeping baby.

It was a girl baby with white-blond wisps of hair, lying naked on a small rag of faded yellow blanket as if to protect her delicate skin from the hard ground until her end came for her. Dian had been exposed like this, not because of any physical abnormality, but due to her strange and unnatural closeness with a dog. In this child's case, however, it was immediately apparent why she had been left: both feet had six toes. She was less than a week old, for her cord, though dry, was still firmly in place.

Dian's first impulse, immediate and shameful, was to walk away. No one would know, no one would criticize—except Mother: that look of withering disappointment that made a person instantly want to do better. Except Dian herself: the infant might be her.

Less than two seconds of hesitation, then self-contempt washed over her and sent her forward to kneel at the infant's side. The tiny chest rose and fell, the translucent eyelids twitched.

"Okay, Culum," she said quietly, so as not to wake the child. He came forward to stand beside her; the big dog, father of several litters, looked worried, and she muttered, "What are we going to do about this, huh? We can't leave her here, especially not if her feet are all that's wrong with her. She's a pretty little thing, aside from those. I might persuade someone along the Meijing Road to take her; they're not so damned paranoid closer in to Meijing. Maybe in Meijing itself? They might not keep her—there's sure as hell no Chinese blood in that head of hair—but surely they'd care for her while I'm up north, if I agreed to take her away with me when I come back down. Jesus, I can just hear Judith—my first trip to civilization in fourteen years and I have to bring home a baby. What do you think; shall we take the thing to Meijing with us?" Culum wagged his tail in agreement with whatever she said. She studied the blue-veined eyelids, the pursed pink lips. With a pang she noticed the tiny blister at the point of the upper lip: the baby had been suckled. With the scrap of blanket, evidence pointed to a mother who had hoped the verdict would not go against her new daughter. "I wonder," she mused, "how difficult it can be for Meijing healers to remove a toe? If they could do that, nobody would ever need to know, would they?"

Culum wagged vigorously at the decision in her voice, and the baby jerked back into screaming awakeness.

"But Mother of God, what will I feed it until I can get some milk?"

By the time Dian had cleaned the infant with an unsoiled corner of the rag and taken off her own warm sweater to wrap it in, the child had cried itself back into exhaustion. She mounted up gently, with the light bundle tucked into the crook of her left arm, and rode away from the crossroads for nearly an hour before the baby roused again. Half a mile farther on, Dian spotted a cluster of boulders, among which a small fire would be invisible from the road. She set some water to boil with a chunk of the honey and a pinch of salt. It took forever to boil, during which time she plugged the cries with a reasonably clean finger. The mixture took even longer to cool, but she could trust neither the water nor the raw honey in the system of an already weak infant, so she blew at the steaming liquid and walked the screaming baby up and down in a fruitless attempt to soothe.

Finally, the sweet mixture was cool enough to offer, and Dian dug a square of sterile bandage cloth from Ling's first-aid kit and dipped it into the warm honey water. To her vast relief, little Sixtoes sucked at it greedily. Mother's milk it wasn't, but it had calories and it would keep her alive for a day or two until Dian could get something better. The infant took the better half of a cupful, burped loudly, and twitched off to sleep. Dian emptied the warm pan of honey water into her thermos flask and let the fire die out.

Her own dinner was a cold one, eaten by feel. The stars were hard and bright and normal to the west, yet nearly invisible to the east, where an eerie glow rose from the sleepless Meijing Road—as if some enormous forge had been banked up for the night. Or as if the land there was radioactive, poisonous, and foul. How had people Before lived under that endless light? No wonder they went mad.

The baby slept with her, inside the warm bag, and woke three times during the night to be fed. The second time Dian came abruptly awake from a dream about warm rain to realize that what went in must also come out and that a baby couldn't go too many hours wrapped in the same sweater without creating a flood. She jerked the dripping little body out of the beautiful new sleeping bag, and the sudden movement with the shock of the night air had the obvious result: the miniature lungs burst forth in outraged shrieks that echoed through the trees and brought both dogs to their feet, growling.

"Oh, God, shut up!" Dian whispered desperately, searching in the dark for the wide-stretched mouth to put her finger into. This time the baby was too upset to fall for that ruse, however, and her screams became even louder. "Sweet Jesus," she hissed, "you'll have everyone in ten miles at our necks!" In desperation she yanked up her shirt and pushed the rigid, wailing, sopping-wet infant up to her breast. The result was nothing short of miraculous. The earsplitting yells immediately cut off, turning into little searching grunts and then hiccups of satisfaction as the mouth latched on. It did not seem to matter that there was no milk, because after a minute of suckling the child gave a deep, shuddering sigh and relaxed. Dian did the same, her ears ringing in the silence. The dogs lay back down. The night sounds gradually came back.

With the baby still attached, Dian felt around for the thermal jug and cup, and when the cloth was wet she worked it into the join of mouth and breast. The child latched on to it without hesitation. Dian fed her and changed the wet sweater for the shirt off her back and sometime later drifted off into a fitful sleep, the child cuddled to her chest, the sleeping bag's cold wet patch under her shoulder, her heart filled with a profound sympathy for her own mother.

THE BEAUTIFUL BLACK DAMSEL, WHO WAS

VERY MAGNIFICENTLY ATTIRED . . .

THIRTEEN

BY THE FOLLOWING AFTERNOON DIAN WAS GROWING desperate. Her nipples were chafed raw by the baby's fruitless comfort-suckling, her cake of honey was nearly gone, and she had nothing else to use as swaddling clothes. Two rinsed shirts were draped over her saddlebags, drying slowly in the chill air, both of them decorated with unsavory and apparently indelible stains—she had briefly eyed the bundle on the back of her saddle, but firmly decided that her shirts were a more reasonable sacrifice than Lenore's fine weaving or Kirsten's intricate embroidery. The tied-together legs of her long woolen underwear made a sling, to leave her hands free for riding, and every time the baby peeped she put something in its mouth to forestall noise. She hadn't really slept the night before and now twitched nervously at the slightest noise from the woods. The baby was fine—warm, dry, fed after a fashion, and rocked by the horse's motions—but Dian was a wreck. The two dogs kept their distance and would not meet her eyes. They looked distinctly embarrassed.

She was glad for their sakes that they met no one along the way, not even when their ridge track

dropped into the larger road that connected the ocean
with the Meijing Road. This east–west road was fairly
well kept up, though its use was largely seasonal,
mainly by vacationers and pilgrims heading for the
sea or the healing springs at the foot of the hills.
She, however, was going east, where in about three
hours she should reach the Road and an inn for the
night and, please God, milk (human or otherwise) for
Sixtoes.

The baby woke as they reached the base of the
hills, so she stopped near the long shadow of a Remnant to feed her. As the baby sucked at the wetted rag,
Dian's eyes followed the tremendous sweep of roadway that curved gracefully off the hillside behind her
and swung around in a powerful arc far above her
head, only to end in a truncated tangle of concrete
chunks and frayed metal rods. Suddenly she realized
that she had sat at this precise spot before, with her
mother, on their trip to the City when Dian was fourteen. Dian alternately dipped and fed, and she was
visited by the ghost of that good woman who had rescued her, describing the purpose of the roadway over
their heads, the immense speed of the cars being so
great that these massive artifacts had come into being
just to save the machines from having to slow down
as they changed direction. There were not too many
of these raised roadways left, Dian remembered her
saying. The explosion that had reduced the end of this
overpass to rubble had apparently also killed a number of the people setting it, so this section had been
left standing by default. Dian didn't know which was
harder to understand—the people who had built this
magnificent piece of basically useless architecture, or
the people who had come along later and destroyed it.
Compulsive construction followed by compulsive destruction. It was all rather hard to believe.

Sighing, Dian looked down at her trousers, wet yet

again with a combination of spilled honey water and leaked urine. Little Sixtoes slept happily through a change of shirt-diaper, and Dian grimly stuffed the old one into the bag she used for game the dogs killed on the way. She would need to buy a complete change of clothing in the Meijing markets. Fitting the baby back into her makeshift sling, she mounted Simon and rode tiredly down the hill toward the Road.

It was almost dark when she came upon the first cluster of inns, little more than shacks. She rode past those, giving wide berth to a larger one with a drunk and violent party that had begun to spill out onto the road. The buildings grew more substantial, the businesses around them more securely established, and she slowed to examine them hopefully. One inn she rejected because it was too big, another because its painful neatness did not seem to bode well for her peculiar needs, and a third she rode past for some vague and indefinable reason. Finally she was nearly onto the Road, and there she looked up to see a sign declaring this to be *The Black and Beautiful.* The inn's name was picked out in fresh gold letters beneath an imaginative depiction of the lovers from the Song of Solomon. Electrical lights shone out of the windows, the door was set in a wide porch scattered with comfortable-looking chairs, and the whole place appeared well cared for without being fussy. Dian dismounted and ordered the dogs to guard the horse, then she settled Sixtoes in her sling, squared her shoulders, and went up the steps.

Anticlimactically, the desk just inside the door was unoccupied, although there was a great deal of activity going on. A pair of dining rooms opened off the entranceway, each with its own fire, its complement of happy but well-behaved diners, and its serving women scurrying in and out. One of these came out of a pair of swinging doors with a laden tray, nodded at Dian before disappearing into one of the dining rooms. In a minute she reappeared with the empty tray tucked under an arm. She betrayed no emotion at Dian's looks, just a professional welcome.

"Are you wanting dinner?" she asked.

"And a room, if you have one. Are you the inn-keeper?"

"I'll get her, if you'll wait just a minute." She went back through the double doors, and after several more tray-laden women had scuttled through, the doors opened to emit the tallest, blackest human being Dian had ever seen, drying her hands on a flowered apron. The woman's liquid black eyes went immediately to Dian and Sixtoes, but as she moved toward them she also took in the progress of the diners, the fact that a lightbulb was burnt out over one of the tables, and that a woman at a table next to the front window was missing a spoon. She stopped one of her women with a raised finger and pointed out these flaws, then came up to Dian.

Dian was nearly six feet tall herself, but she had to look up into this woman's eyes, dark and proud over high cheekbones. Her willowy frame was both flexible and hard, her skin exactly the color of the polished ebony carving on a shelf in Ling's clinic, in this case topped with a magnificent head-wrap of gold and black cloth. The woman politely overlooked Dian's derelict state—stained clothing, makeshift sling and shirt-wrapped baby, uncombed hair and unwashed smell—and spoke in a deep voice that managed to be both warm and businesslike.

"What can we do for you this evening?" she asked.

"Pretty much everything," Dian blurted out. The woman raised her eyebrows at the thin note of desperation and relief, and ran her eyes across Dian, withholding judgment.

"Looks to me like you could use some help with your baby."

"Well, that's the problem," said Dian carefully. "She's not mine. If she were, I could at least feed her, but I found her at a crossroads in the hills and I don't have anything but honey water to give her, and I've run out of things I can use as diapers."

The innkeeper stifled an automatic step away, her eyes flicking in the direction of the nearby tables. "What's wrong with her?" The key word in what Dian had told her was *crossroads*: nobody would abandon a whole, healthy child at such a place.

"As far as I can see, the only thing wrong is an extra toe on each foot. She's not sick, and there's certainly nothing wrong with her appetite—or her lungs." Dian smiled at her feeble joke, but the woman was not distracted and stood eyeing the bundle on Dian's chest. A sudden waft of air brought the most delicious odors to Dian, onions and meat and yeast bread that caused her stomach to cramp in desire. She swallowed, and met the woman's eyes. "I couldn't see that her having twelve toes rather than ten was a good enough reason to leave her for the coyotes. I'm taking her to friends in Meijing," she added, to serve notice of her disguised respectability—anyone who could claim friends in Meijing was a person to be reckoned with. "I won't be there until tomorrow, though, and she needs food now. I could try cow's milk, or goat's, or if you know anyone with a baby who would be willing to feed her up. I can pay," she hastened to add.

The impenetrable brown eyes studied the baby, and Dian braced herself for a refusal. However, the innkeeper said only, "Unwrap her."

Dian laid her burden down on the floor and peeled back the various pieces of wet cloth. Once naked, the baby reacted with the closed-fisted arching typical of the very young infant and began to cry. When Dian

looked up she noticed several small dark faces peering
at her from the break in the swing doors. She squatted
next to Sixtoes, resting her hand on the infant's thin
belly, and waited. Most people would have nothing to
do with a baby once she had been exposed at a crossroads, and an innkeeper was vulnerable to the opinions of her clients. The woman stood and looked
down at the squalling mite with the queer feet, and
made up her mind.

"Yes, she deserves a chance. Damn these supersti-
tions, anyway." Dian exhaled gustily and started to
gather up her charge, but the woman's powerful arms
came past her to scoop up the baby with a practiced
ease. To Dian's surprise she loosened her shirt and put
the child to her own breast before she turned to the
doorway, pausing to kick the sodden and soiled remnants of Dian's wardrobe to one side with her foot.
The faces in the doorway vanished.

"Come on in here," she threw over her shoulder.
Dian obediently followed her toward the door which
led to the kitchen. She glanced at the table of diners
closest to the door and was relieved to see them smile
at her in a friendly fashion. She wouldn't have wanted
to hurt this woman's business any, but these customers didn't seem to mind having an exposed baby
brought in.

The kitchen was a big bright room with a long
plank table running down one side, the wood pale and
soft from frequent scrubbing. Five used plates were
clustered at one end, where the children had abandoned their nearly finished meal. One place was still
occupied, by a toddler who looked up interestedly at
Dian, absently massaging a fistful of unidentifiable
food into the wispy black tendrils that stood out on
its head. The occupants of the other four places stood
watching their mother expectantly. The innkeeper removed a pan one-handed from the stove and turned to

the children, who were lined up in front of her like four steps.

"Wilama, you run and fetch me a diaper and one of Aisha's nighties. There are some soakers on the line in the boiler room—bring me one of those too. Mbeke, set a bath to heating for this lady, and then go next door and borrow one of Fayola's shirts and a pair of trousers—she's closer to this lady's size than I am. Omo, you show the lady the stables for her horse. And, Chinua, you can lay a place for her in here. Is that okay with you? And what's your name? I'm Jamilla."

Dian, watching children scatter with clear purpose in various directions, realized belatedly that this last was directed at her. She hastily introduced herself and agreed with everything, and was fascinated to see the woman, with Sixtoes at her breast gulping greedily, turn to the sideboard and use her free hand to dish out several large servings of a fragrant apple crumble. She plunked a large pitcher of thick cream down next to the bowls and without apparent effort picked up the heavy tray with one hand and thrust it into the hands of one of the women who came through the door.

One of the children had moved to the door leading outside, where she stood waiting with exaggerated patience for Dian to take notice of her. Eventually Dian did so and, tearing herself away from the intoxicating smells and the flurry of activity, followed Omo out the door to the stables, where she settled Simon on clean straw, gave him hay and water, and closed Culum and Tomas in with him for the time being. Back at the house she was given over to the care of ten-year-old Mbeke, who handed Dian a pile of clothing and a large towel with her eyes cast down to the floorboards, escorted her to the bathroom, and carried away Dian's own clothes, held well away from her body. Dian felt they really should be burned, but

Mbeke glanced into her eyes for a brief instant and pronounced with all seriousness her judgment that they would be clean in the morning. Dian had her doubts, but the shirts and trousers that were given her the next day, while not exactly pristine, at least were no cause of embarrassment to the dogs.

It was one of the most satisfying baths she had ever climbed into, and it washed away much more than mere dirt. When she walked downstairs in the borrowed clothing—short in the leg and tight in the shoulders—she felt truly herself for the first time since Culum had heard the cries at the crossroad. Only yesterday?

The daughter who had been sent scurrying for a diaper was sitting at the foot of the stairs, playing with a kitten while waiting for Dian. She looked to be about six, and despite her deep skin color she reminded Dian of Susanna at that age. Unlike her older sister, this one was not in the least bit shy and chattered at Dian with Susanna's liveliness and that same twinkle of mischief hiding in the back of her too-innocent brown eyes.

"I gave your dogs some food, but they ate it awfully fast, so maybe they want some more, but Mama said I should ask you first. They sure are big. What are their names? Can you ride them? Do you want some supper? Is that your baby?"

Dian gravely answered the barrage of questions on the way back to the kitchen, which population had increased by two dogs, a mountain of dishes, several more children, and three adults, one of them a man, all of them darker of skin than anyone in the Valley. The man was sitting with a completely limp Sixtoes cradled to his chest: she looked as pale as Dian felt, although no one else seemed too concerned about skin tones. Introductions were made all around, and a laden plate was slapped down in front of Dian.

Dian dove into the food that she'd been smelling for what seemed like hours and said not a word for the next fifteen minutes, by which time the mountain of dishes had been transformed into so many neat stacks of clean plates and the voices from the dining rooms had all but disappeared. She came up for air to accept a third helping of sweet, cream-drenched apple, and then blushed mildly when she saw the expressions on the gathering of small faces across the table from her. She ate the last dessert anyway, and enjoyed it, before finally pushing back from her plate.

Fayola, the neighbor whose shirt was on Dian's back, hung up a damp towel on an already buried rack near the stove and came to the table with a cluster of mugs and a gigantic teapot.

"Well, if you didn't have enough to eat, it's your own fault," she told Dian, and handed her a cup of tea.

"A full stomach, a clean body, and a quiet baby—what more could a person ask for?" Dian asked rhetorically.

"What's her name?" asked the woman, nodding at the baby. Dian stared at her blankly, and the expression on her face was too much for the row of children. They began giggling and had to be threatened with expulsion by Jamilla before they went still, but their eyes continued to laugh at Dian.

"Don't you call her something?"

"Well, no. I mean, I guess I think of her as Sixtoes, but that's not a name." Actually Dian had thought of her as an awful noise and a gigantic problem, if she'd had a moment to think of her at all. Seeing her properly dressed and with a belly full of real food, she seemed much more of a person, even asleep. "I haven't had time to think about it, I guess. What do you think?" She addressed this to the room at large and was met only by a thoughtful silence. The object of their concerted gaze slept beatifically in the man's arms.

"What did you say your daughter's name was?" she asked Jamilla, gesturing at the six-year-old diaper-fetcher with Susanna's eyes and Susanna's questions.

"That's Wilama. She's named for my grand-aunt," said the innkeeper.

"'Wilama,'" Dian said thoughtfully. "You know, I have a new nephew named Will, born last Tuesday. That makes him and, er, Sixtoes nearly twins. What if we gave her a name somewhere between Will and Wilama. Willa?"

Wilama would have turned scarlet had she been the color of her namesake, but as it was she just grew a bit darker and collapsed into another heap of giggles with her sisters and friends.

Jamilla grinned widely and untied the apron from her waist. "Past time for bed, all of you. Kiss your new milk-sister good night." She shooed her kids out the door, lifting the sticky-haired toddler whose milk supply Willa was sharing and carrying her off upstairs after the others. Dian accepted a refill of her cup and settled down for a delicious long talk with the remaining adults, a chance to catch up on the news of the world. The Valley was very remote.

The noises from upstairs gradually subsided as the various sets of feet were put to bed in the part of the inn directly over the kitchen. Willa began to stir, nuzzling hopefully back and forth in the man's neck. When Jamilla came back in, dropping into an oversize rocking chair with the heartfelt sigh of a long day's labor behind her, she accepted baby, mug, and a chair for her feet.

The talk went on until what seemed a very late hour. Tea was exchanged for thick glasses filled with a powerful cherry-flavored liqueur, and the talk turned from gossip and business to criticism of Meijing and the future of the Bay area, which might have been useful for Dian had she been able to remember the details the next day, or indeed been able to understand the conversation. As the evening went on, the formal English gave way to a more colloquial dialect, accented in a way she wasn't used to and which occasionally rendered key words incomprehensible. She did pick up that the man, whose name was Yusuf and who was clearly Fayola's husband, seemed to be the father of two of Jamilla's children as well. And by the evening's end, Dian was relatively certain they worshiped some African deity named 'Nyame.

It was all terribly interesting, but eventually the neighbors drained their glasses and began to gather up their sleep-sodden children. There seemed to be one too many children for adult arms, so Dian, checking first that her feet were steady on the ground, offered to carry one. She came back a few minutes later to find Jamilla still at the table, feeding Willa yet again, looking amused at the tiny pale head nestled into her large black breast. Dian rinsed and dried the used glasses, and then stood uncertainly. Jamilla turned her smile upward to Dian.

"I'll take the little one in with me tonight, if you don't mind. That way I can feed her without waking up the whole house. Tomorrow I'll give you the names of some friends on the Road north who'll help you. I know everyone on the Road, pretty near, and it seems like half of 'em have just had babies. Your dogs can go up with you, if you want. Just keep them off the bed."

Dian assured her that she would, turned with barely a glance at Willa, and went off to a very welcome and beatifically undisturbed night's sleep.

...THE ISLAND HAS BEEN ISOLATED

FROM MEN FOR MANY AGES.

Fourteen

Dian rose, as usual, before the sun. She dressed in her borrowed clothes, took the dogs out for a run, checked on Simon, found Jamilla up to her elbows in flour and arranged breakfast for Culum and Tomas, asked after Willa and received news of her peaceful night with gratitude, snagged a mug of hot chicory-coffee laced with cream, and returned with it to her room, where she went back to bed for nearly two hours, reading a frayed and unintelligible novel involving a wealthy male detective, his dauntingly competent manservant, a naked male body that appeared mysteriously in a bathtub, and a bewildering array of other male personages. Under other circumstances this reminder of other times, free from cares and free with menfolk, would have been disturbing, but today it could not touch her, and she lay with the smell of coffee in the room, listening unconsciously to the sounds of feet that grew, reached a peak, and gave way to relative silence. She felt like a queen.

Luxury palled, though, and as there were no signs of servile maids, or competent manservants, staggering in under laden trays, she put her boots back on and went down to appease the empty hole within.

Once downstairs she hesitated. The voices of children came from behind the swing doors, but in the front dining room a dozen women sat with their plates, talking volubly. Gossip, or responsibility? Or was she even invited into the kitchen?

Her dilemma was taken from her when a younger, lighter-skinned version of Jamilla backed through the doors, made a graceful pirouette with twenty pounds of food on her tray, and gave Dian a smile like warm honey.

"Mornin'," she drawled. "There's a chair for you in here, next to the fire. Can I bring you some coffee, or tea?"

Extravagance won.

"Coffee, please. And I hope I'm not too late for breakfast."

"Never. What would you like?"

"Whatever you have, and lots of it. I just like my eggs soft and bacon crisp."

"Be right with you."

And she was. With eggs two degrees from liquid and a tangle of salty bacon that crumbled on the tongue, with two slabs of some soft stuff, neither bread nor pudding, that had been fried crisp on the outside and drenched in honey, with a plate of fried apple slices that tasted of a mysterious aromatic spice and a basket of warm muffins and a plate of buttered toast and more coffee than Dian had seen in a year, until finally Dian admitted defeat and pushed her well-used plate away from her. The woman came and looked down at the debris.

"I thought you said you were hungry," she said in mock disappointment.

Dian groaned, and allowed her to refill the cup. When the table had been cleared, she sat looking at nothing in particular and bent her ears to the conversations around her. One trio was talking family—a new husband, healthy babies, a house. On the other side of the fireplace, two overdressed women with hungry faces and flabby bodies were trading business stories—a market cornered, a new product brought north, the coup of outsmarting a group of Meijing traders. Their conversations wove in and out, but the one that most intrigued Dian came from the five women seated around a farther table, women who did not have the look of people who would pull out a sheaf of family photographs, who did not have any spare flesh or rings on their fingers. Women who bore the clear stamp of Traveler.

Their talk was difficult to hear over the family and business noises, but after a few minutes one of the women noticed Dian's intent gaze and tipped her head in an amused invitation. Feeling like a peasant invited to dine with royalty, Dian took her cup over and pulled out a chair, added her name to the brief introductions, and sipped her drink while the conversation resumed. It seemed to concern a bridge being rebuilt, and from there the road north and the possible markets opening up along the northern California coast, a place now of silent desolation, impossibly cold in the winters, shrouded in fogs all summer. Talk moved on to the inland valleys, to the gradual reopening of the abandoned but safe delta lands under the auspices of Meijing. Two settlements had been established, northeast of the City, and three more were planned. This would mean growth along the line to the north, the string of small cities that led eventually to Portland.

"Yeah," said the oldest Traveler, whose eye folds indicated Meijing blood. "And sooner or later Meijing and Portland will be forced to lock horns. God help us then."

"Is that because of Queen Bess?" Dian asked, eager to demonstrate that she was not entirely without knowledge of the world. But the older woman snorted.

"Oh, honey, they won't wait for her to get involved. Ashtown'll take on Meijing all on its lonesome."

"Ashtown?" Dian said. "I know someone who spent some time there."

"She was smart to get out," commented Rhoda, a burly woman in a plaid shirt who was missing half an ear.

"It's a he."

"Even smarter, then."

"What do you mean?" protested another woman, a lugubrious blond woman with the unapt name of Merry. "Ashtown's a nice place. Clean. Honest. Quiet as a graveyard, sure, but nightlife ain't everything."

"Graveyard's the name for it," muttered Rhoda.

"What's wrong with it?" asked Dian. Rhoda frowned into her cup, clearly not wanting to answer, but eventually she looked up and saw all their waiting and curious eyes. She laughed uncomfortably.

"I dunno. It's all right, I guess." She shrugged, although it seemed to Dian halfway to a shudder. "Place gives me the creeps, is all," she said defiantly, and after a moment the talk moved on.

It was technical talk, of good inns and friendly towns and the places one had to watch for traps and ambushes laid, of where along the Meijing Road to get the best bedding and pans that wouldn't lose their handles, and who had flints and fuel for lighters, and an expensive but efficient little hand-crank dynamo lamp for those nights with more hours than a person cared to sleep. Each of these Travelers had a home, a place to retreat to and play at being part of a family until the days began to lengthen and the feet began to itch, but none of them talked about those places in other than an oblique manner. Dian did not again mention Isaac, or anyone in the Valley.

Dian's cup was long empty and her bladder becoming uncomfortable when a strange noise began to build in the background. She looked out the window but could see nothing. The noise grew, punctuated by a raucous cry like a flock of geese all honking at once, and she got up and leaned up against a window to peer down the road. Children, horses, and chickens began to scatter from the path, and suddenly a gleaming scarlet monster came racing down the rutted roadway. Honking and roaring, the anachronistic monstrosity flew past at the speed of a gallop, turned onto the main road, and vanished, leaving behind it a cloud of dust and the visual impression of five haughty sets of shoulders and heads within.

She turned to the woman next to her, one of the proud-family group. "Do you get many cars along the Road?" she asked. She had seen several on her trip with her mother, and they had made a deep impression on her, not entirely favorable.

"Nah, Meijing's tight with permits. There's maybe one or two a day go past down here, more as you get closer to the City. A family about five miles south has a whole bunch, lined up and waiting for fuel permits. Dream on—they're just for officials and medical use. Although my sister got a seat on one a while back. It was expensive." Her voice was wistful.

"I'm surprised the people put up with them. I'd have thought they'd throw rocks, or shoot at the drivers."

"They do if the cars go outside Meijing's borders. But as far as Meijing is concerned, the owners are welcome to a few gallons of gas a month if they're willing to tinker with them."

Dian shook her head at the noise and at the smell that drifted in through the half-open window. "I'm glad I don't live near them," she grumbled, and went to take her leave of the Travelers.

She then searched out Jamilla, finding her in the kitchen, nursing Willa while watching with a gimlet eye a young woman rolling out pie crusts. Jamilla glanced up as Dian came in, and then went back to her scrutiny. The apprentice seemed oblivious, and Dian gave her full points—she knew that she herself could never have stood there with that particular pair of dark eyes waiting to pounce on a mistake. The young woman was either nerveless or half drunk.

Jamilla took up two pieces of paper from the table and held them out to Dian. The first was only a scrap, with three names and directions to businesses on them.

"Those are friends along the way who'll help you with Willa. If they're not there for some reason, ask a neighbor for help, but they're almost certain to be there." Dian nodded and folded the paper into her pocket and turned to the other one, her itemized bill. She stifled a wince at the price of her two meals, but otherwise it was very reasonable. With one exception.

"Why didn't you make any charges for Willa? She kept you up half the night and used a fair number of your diapers."

"It wouldn't be right. That's the kind of thing that can't be paid off in money. You help someone else in need; that'll pay off the debt."

"You drive a hard bargain. All right, I'll accept, on one condition: that you accept a gift for your kids." The big woman smiled at this and took her eyes off her helper for an instant to seal the agreement with a glance. Dian mentally added a large percentage by way of a gift, counting out from her purse the coins minted in Meijing.

"Baby Willa and I—" she began.

"Now, watch out, girl," Jamilla broke in. "You're getting all crooked, and you'll have a handful of scraps left over. Aisha could do it better," she scolded. The young woman's brown skin turned pinkish—she was not as phlegmatic as she had appeared. Dian overlooked the interruption.

"Baby Willa and I will try to stop in on our way back down, so you can see how she's doing after the start you've given her."

"Now, that'd be nice," said Jamilla. "All right, Tamma, just trim off the edges and I'll do the rest. You did fine." She disengaged Willa, checked that the diapers were dry, and stood up. Willa did look better, less gaunt than she had been the evening before, more like a baby and less like a starving animal as she lay in the crook of Jamilla 's strong arm and squinted at the morning light. Dian was amused at the picture they made, the tall black woman and the tiny, pale, white-haired piglet of a baby.

"You make a fine pair," she told Jamilla.

The other woman smiled down fondly into the eyes of the small person she held. "She's a good baby, this one. With what she's been through I expected her to be all tense and anxious, but she's not. As soon as she got some food into her she calmed down, like she knew she had people caring for her and the world was all right. She's a bright one, she is. Aren't you?" she said to the serious face, and then looked up at Dian. "You go get your things together, I'll bring her out front."

A short time later Dian led her saddled horse to the front door of the inn. The clear weather was holding and gentle ripples of steam rose where the sun touched the frosted shingles. The dogs snuffled at the enthralling odors along the road, their noses catching up on the local news and gossip.

Jamilla came out the front door under the sign. Dian studied it for a moment by daylight, then shook her head.

"The painter didn't do you justice," she told Jamilla,

who only laughed. Dian swung herself up into the familiar smooth shape of the saddle and reached down for baby Willa. She was sound asleep with her belly full of warm milk and didn't stir when Dian settled her into the new, proper sling (bought by Jamilla and added, along with the price of five new diapers and a soaker cover, to the bill). Jamilla's son Chinua and the toddler Aisha were on the top step watching the dogs, the other three girls having left for school some time before. Dian sat for a moment looking down at the warm, shrewd black face at her side.

"'Thank you' is not enough. I am in debt to you, and I don't think I'll be able to pay you back."

Dian was amazed to see the face break into an expression of pure mischief.

"Oh, no, you're not. No sirree. I gave that debt to 'Nyame, and 'Nyame charges interest. The only way you'll work it off is to find somebody with an even bigger problem and help her with it. Or him. That's the only way you'll cancel that debt." She looked smug at her cleverness, and into Dian's mind came an image of Susanna's face when she had tricked Dian in a chess game and beaten her for the first time.

Dian chuckled and took Jamilla's hand, squeezing it tightly.

"As I said, you drive a hard bargain. I'll try my best to work off the debt, but thank you anyway. I hope to see you in six or eight weeks. Give my love to your kids. Especially Wilama."

Jamilla's hand slapped the horse's smooth flank as Dian turned away toward the Road, whistling her dogs to her. She rode off into the clear morning, gentle snores coming from the warm body cradled to her chest.

Dian had one piece of Valley business before the day was her own, and she found the broker just two miles up from where the side road entered the main thoroughfare. The woman had actually been born in the Valley, moving into town as a teenager when her mother fell ill and stayed on. She was trusted, so that the haggling Dian did was perfunctory—the prices the broker got for Lenore's fabric were higher than anything Dian could have arranged, and the woman positively crooned over a pair of Kirsten's pillow covers. Laine had sent a handful of sparkling jewelry, which she'd found on an overnight trip—best not to ask where, Dian had decided—that, once tested, fetched a startling sum. When business was over, Dian answered her questions about the Valley—Judith's birth, Kirsten's health—then signed the chit with her name in English and its Chinese equivalent, accepted a purse with some of the proceeds in cash, and rode away. Willa hadn't even peeped.

Dian felt like a two-year-old in front of a Christmas tree as the Road opened up that morning, her jaw hanging down with the splendor of it. She saw more strangers in the first ten minutes than she had in the last ten years: women washing their shop steps; women driving animals and carrying loads of colorful wool and jangling pans; women pedaling rickshaw carts filled with produce and clothing, old machines and new shoes; women opening shops that sold jewelry and pots, hats and boots, vast gleaming heaps of tomatoes and oranges and eggplants and onions; shops with meat and shops draped with the carcasses of chickens, ducks, and geese, and some shops that Dian was not sure exactly what they were selling. One of these had a small window displaying half a dozen pictures of scantily clad men, and a stout door. Did it sell photographs of men? Did the shop act as a broker of some sort among groups who wished to trade men? Did it—appalling thought—sell actual men? Dian could not imagine that Meijing would tolerate such an activity in its area of influence, but what did the pictures signify? Dian looked back over her shoulder at the—shop?—and nearly rode into the wedge-shaped gap between a warehouse and a large wagon from which two heavily muscled women were pulling hundredweight sacks of rice and grain. She excused herself, extricated Simon from the trap, and nodded red-faced at the two workers. Laughter followed her up the road.

She had forgotten the rhythm of the Bay Road, but it soon came back to her. Every eight miles a Meijing sentry box and approval station spawned a cluster of shops, inns, churches (or mosques or temples), and services. Each cluster would begin with a sprinkling of flimsy, sometimes portable stalls among the roadside farms, the first of them selling the produce grown behind them, the next selling cooked snacks and knickknacks. Then a few houses would offer rooms, and finally came one or more true inns, large or small. In the midst of the inns would stand the sentry box, not a box at all but a tall, sturdy building capable of housing, and defending if necessary, a dozen or more Meijing guards. North of the inns came the shops with their endless variety of wares, and in their midst would be the approval station, where buyer and seller could come for arbitration, testing, and currency exchange. Then a few more, rougher-looking inns, more flimsy stalls, and a patch of increasingly sparse housing where the fields could be seen, occasionally coming down to the road itself, before the next center—and more stalls and inns—began to creep up on the traveler.

The morning remained crisp and clear. A salt tang drifted up from the waters of the Bay, and the colors and smells of harvest shone from the stalls, intensified by the oblique angle of the autumnal sun. Traffic was well under way, the clop of shod hooves on the well-patched hardtop followed by the burr of rubber tires or the rumble of iron and wood wheels, the whir and warning bells of a thousand bicycles and rickshaws, and twice the thunder and stink of a combustion engine that cleared the road and made Dian's horse shy and the dogs' eyes show white. Once she thought she saw something in the sky over the Bay, a squat dragonfly shape that looked like what the old books called a *helicopter*, but there were too many sounds around her to hear any motor, and the thing's mottled blue-gray coloration made it hard to see. When she looked up again after negotiating a narrow patch, it was gone—if it had been there in the first place, and was not a figment of her overstimulated imagination. Might as well think she'd seen a dragon.

Dian had been looking forward to this part of the journey for weeks, ever since it had been decided that she would go north, and Willa's presence would make no difference. Today the riches of northern California were laid out at her feet, awaiting only the reckless use of the heavy pouch of coins at her belt, and she intended to take full advantage of it.

She bought a few utilitarian necessities: fifty rubber canning rings, a box of assorted nuts and bolts, eyeglass lenses in half a dozen magnifications, lengths of the rubber tubing useful for everything from drawing blood to making slingshots. And she bought gifts: two dozen graduated embroidery needles for Lenore, along with a rainbow of silk floss. For Ling she found a flute made of cherry wood with a mouthpiece of walrus ivory, for Judith a trio of silver bangles such as their mother used to wear. Peter she decided would like a piece of magnificent red silk fabric that Lenore could sew into a shirt, and Kirsten would treasure a set of four ivory double-pointed sock needles. An ivory-handled folding knife for Laine, a beautiful palm-sized leather-bound book of poetry to satisfy Jeri's secret passion.

Susanna was more difficult, caught between child-hood and maturity. She saw a pair of silver and abalone earrings and matching necklace, but the price seemed low, and the shopkeeper was reluctant in al-lowing Dian to take them to the approval station. When she insisted, taking care to speak to the guards in Chinese like a civilized person, her suspicions were confirmed by the station's Geiger counter.

"Ah, crap, that's barely a reading," the would-be seller protested—in English. "Look at that, you could wear them twenty-four hours a day for ten years and not get so much as a rash," but Dian had already dropped the offending jewelry in the woman's hands and left her to explain to Meijing's representatives why she was selling goods from the contaminated zone.

Two miles later Dian was looking in the window of another, more reputable silversmith and spotted the ideal gift. It was a tall, slender silver mug, etched with a double line of domestic animals around the base. It proved clean, if expensive, and joined the other ob-jects in her bags.

Despite the delays, Willa was still deeply asleep when Dian reached the first of the three stops Jamilla had suggested. It was off the road but easily found ("Follow your nose," the innkeeper had said), a fra-grant and immaculate bakery. A bell tinkled over her head as she went in, and a round, glowing pink woman greeted her from where she was rolling out pie crusts on a vast marble slab.

"Good morning," said Dian. "Are you Paula? My name is—"

"You're Dian," the woman said briskly. "I had a message from Jamilla a couple of hours ago. Is the baby hungry?" She dusted off her hands on a towel and came around the counter.

"I guess not." Dian looked down at Willa's completely slack face. "She's fast asleep. Do you think I should go on? There's another woman two hours north..."

"That'll be Deirdre. No, she'll be hungry long before that. I'll wake her up and feed her in a bit, as soon as I get my pies in the oven. I hate to leave pastry rolled out. You probably want to wander around, though." Before Dian could protest, she raised her voice and called out, "Candace! Come here a minute, will you?" A younger, rounder pink woman appeared from the back, holding an apple and a paring knife. "Candace, this is the baby Jamilla sent up. Could you hold her for five minutes while I finish the pies? The lady wants to do some shopping." Candace's eyes lit up and she went to the sink, washed her hands, removed the sticky-looking apron, and came to take baby Willa from Dian.

"My daughter Candace," the woman said unnecessarily, picking up her rolling pin. "Come back in forty-five minutes."

Before she quite knew what was happening, Dian was standing outside the shop. She was surprised at how much she resented being pushed away from the child and wondered, somewhat glumly, if this was the stir of some unsuspected maternal impulse. But still, it was a pleasant side street, quiet after the bustle of the Road, with a number of large trees dropping their yellow leaves on the ground on the lawns around three tall wooden houses from Before. Suddenly the noise of the Road seemed too much, and the fields at the far end of this street beckoned as a place free of sly merchants, hungry babies, and noise. She slipped the rifle from its scabbard, left both dogs to watch Simon, and strolled up the quiet street toward the hills.

In a few minutes the sounds of the Road had faded to a muted rumble. The street ended abruptly and a footpath entered somebody's market garden, lush with the last remnants of the summer tomatoes and green beans, the ready fall crops of lettuce and peas, and the beginnings of the winter's root vegetables. Dian let herself through a gate in the high deer-proof fence that surrounded the oasis of greenery, and found herself on the edge of grassland with oaks and an occasional outcropping of concrete chunks to mark the passing of a building. Cows grazed among the remains of foundations and chimneys. Overhead, three small birds dove at a hawk, driving it off armed with nothing more than agility and determination.

Dian walked out into this landscape, as foreign in its way as the Road was, and settled in the shade of a sprawling oak tree. Twenty feet away, a ground squirrel eyed her nervously, unwilling to venture far from its pile of concrete and twisted steel bars. A sentinel quail atop a chimney two hundred yards beyond too-hooed to its flockmates. The breeze brought the baked smell of dry grass. Around the base of the next tree several black and white cows lay ruminating, their jaws moving steadily, tails flicking. A memory tickled the back of her mind as she watched the cows, a memory of another hot day, other cows. And Kirsten, a Kirsten with still a faint touch of brown in her hair.

"When I was young," she had said, as always. They were sitting on a fallen log in the upper pasture, watching the cows, and the sweet perfume of warm blackberries rose from the baskets at their feet. "When I was young—very young, I think—we went to visit a house down near the Bay. It was a big, crazy place, all twists and turns and doors that went nowhere, carved stairways that climbed up and ended at blank walls. It was beautiful, in a bizarre way, filled with lovely glass windows and fine workmanship. It made a deep impression on me—for a long while I wanted to be an architect when I grew up. I even remember the cock-and-bull story the guide told us about how the woman who built it was haunted by ghosts and believed that so long as she kept working on the house she wouldn't die. Oh, she was haunted, no doubt, but not by anyone else's spirit. She was the daughter of a family of gun makers, the Winchesters —they built the rifle that 'won the West' in the nine-teenth century. She was a rich, lonely old woman who was obsessed by the thought of all those souls torn from their bodies by the weapons her family had made a fortune on, and she kept herself busy by exer-cising her creativity and money on this endless, empty, beautiful house." Dian saw Kirsten's hands reach for a gentle handful of the soft berries and pop them one by one between her already purple lips. "The image of that house comes back to me at odd times, that poor woman making a thing of crazy beauty built on blood. What Ling would call 'working off her karma.' It's a good parable for what we used to call 'Western civilization,' which was of course nei-ther particularly civilized nor peculiarly Western."

The harsh scree of an overhead hawk scattered the ghost of Kirsten's rich laughter from Dian's ears, and when she looked again at the hills around her, she re-alized that it must have been very near this place that Kirsten's father had died. Perhaps those massive foun-dations and blocks on the next rise over were where his ashes lay, mingled with the ashes of a million cre-mated books. The University library, according to Kirsten, had taken a month to burn.

Not that the precise site mattered. This entire area—say, a fifty-mile radius around this spot—lay drenched in blood, condemned to infamy in whatever history was left to the world. It was here that the movement that was called Destroyer was born, the final synthesis of sophisticated technology and reli-gious fanaticism, a synthesis of knowledge turned against itself that literally blew the foundations out from under humankind and caused the world to collapse in on itself. It was a few miles to the east, across the deceptive, clear, blue, sparkling waters of the still-toxic Bay, that Joseph Walker had invented his kitchen-cupboard explosive, so beloved of the low-budget radical groups, that had set the world to flames and rubble in a few short years. It was just north of here, where live oaks now took root and deer came to graze, that one of those fanatical groups had set their homemade bomb in the University, aiming at the library, ending up in the laboratories, and thereby loosing, inadvertently or by intent, the swamp of manmade viruses that had swept away half the world's population within three months, and half of the remainder before the year was out. One of those viruses had proven to have a lasting affinity for the male genetic structure. No, Dian thought, getting up and brushing the leaves from the back of her trousers, this was not a happy place to pass through.

She made her way back to the bakery, telling herself that she was not exactly eager to see the infant, just concerned, but when she got there she found Willa in a state she'd not seen her in before: calm and alert. The child lay on Candace's lap, examining the young woman's face. Paula was taking some pies from the big oven, filling the air with spice and apple, and Dian went to stand behind the baker's daughter to witness more closely this amazing spectacle of Six-toes awake and not screaming.

"What did you do to her?" she asked. "She's quiet!"

Paula looked at her oddly. "Fed her, burped her. Changed her diapers. Why?"

"I've just not seen her so . . . content before." Dian leaned down to look into little Willa's face, and the wise gray-blue eyes shifted to gaze into her own. The two studied each other for a long minute, then the small face turned red and a muffled explosion came from below. The laughter of the three women startled her, but before she could screw up her face to cry, Dian scooped her up out of Candace's arms, thanked her benefactors, and went to find another diaper in her saddlebag.

ON THIS ISLAND CALLED CALIFORNIA,

THERE WERE MANY GRIFFINS,

BECAUSE THESE BEASTS WERE SUITED

TO THE RUGGEDNESS OF THE TERRAIN.

FIFTEEN

THE ROAD'S TRAFFIC WAS THICK NOW, BOTH FOOT AND wheeled, and the dust and noise rode heavy on the air. The fields receded, giving way to neat rows of squash and corn and later to small flower gardens, before disappearing entirely behind fences and walls. Grand houses began to appear—or rather, their high and solid perimeter walls began to loom over the public way, laced along their tops with wicked shards of glass and broken by iron gates with guards wearing uniforms of various colors and decorations. The shopkeepers' wares became more gleaming, despite the dust, their smiles broader, their hands more clever. Culum and Tomas grew increasingly edgy, and twice Culum showed his teeth at riders who pressed too close. The second time disturbed even Simon, when they were all crushed between an unexpectedly swerving coach-and-four and a high wall topped by jagged bits of glass. Dian cursed the driver loudly, to no response, and turned off abruptly into the next lane, which led east to the Bay.

She sat for half an hour atop the long, high ridge of gathered rubble that kept the Bay from the Road, sat and threw rocks and allowed the dogs to run after birds and the horse to crop at the stubby grass. It must have been beautiful once, she thought, when the Bay was alive, with tule rushes and seabirds and sailing boats. And oil spills and the haze of automobiles, she reminded herself. But before that, before the universities and their libraries filled with clean, proud students, even before gold's siren call pulled in the miners' thousands and the camp followers' tens of thousands, back when Richard Henry Dana had spent his two years before the mast and sailed into the pristine Bay, looked with amused disdain at the dingy settlement around Mission Dolores, and left for his aristocratic home in Boston—then it must have been a glory.

What would Dana have thought if told that two hundred years later the children reading his book in a remote one-roomed schoolhouse would be no more technologically advanced than he was? And for that matter, what about his mighty Boston? Was it still a city? Or had it, too, slipped back and become a dingy settlement with subhuman primates skulking in the debris? Boston was somewhere near Washington, if she remembered those long-ago geography drills, and as far as she knew that city still existed in some form or another, the nominal capital of what some might still call the United States. There had once been a President there. She wondered if there was today, if anyone bothered, and then she noticed that Tomas was venturing too near the water and whistled him back.

It was all too remote to matter, Presidents and a theoretical, three-thousand-mile-wide nation. Meijing mattered. The world knew that history: nameless home to generation upon generation of fishing peoples, later named Yerba Buena by the Spanish fathers who built their adobe Mission of Sorrows, then known as San Francisco, under which name it was transformed first by gold, later by trade, only to have its high towers and busy streets abandoned in the panic of the Troubles, leaving behind the inhabitants of its most crowded sector. Meijing, now the greatest remaining city for a thousand miles in any direction.

Meijing was not the seat of a great empire or military power, although her hold over the area was complete, her authority as yet uncontested. Meijing kept the peace, it was true, but only as a peripheral function to her main interest: trade. She had a port, the biggest, most reliable port along the whole West Coast short of Seattle, and through her wharves flowed a constant stream of goods, thick furs from the north and exotic foods from the warm south, scavenged Artifacts and recently manufactured machines, luxuries and essentials and the ten thousand things that kept the darkness at bay. She also controlled the only dependable north road, for the land east of the Bay was contaminated clear up to the foothills of the great mountain range. Common knowledge had it that the land was filled with monstrosities and barrenness and death, and certainly travelers desperate enough to chance it had not been known to return— although whether that was because the land was toxic, or because the Destroyers ruled there, no one could tell. Rumor had it that Meijing had launched airplanes out over the area, which had never been seen again. What the truth was, only Meijing knew, and Meijing with a secret made one of its stone Buddhas look garrulous. Like the ancient maps used to say, *Here Be Monsters*.

Rumor was changing, though. The Travelers' talk at Jamilla's had included vague references to returning life, in the northern reaches of that land across the Bay, anyway. Time would tell. In the meantime, there was only Meijing, its road, its port, and its ferry.

A large part of Meijing's power was due to the chance of her location astride the only remaining north–south road, but Meijing's greatest asset, the thing that her people nurtured and used and occasionally abused, lay in neither port nor road. Her strength and authority lay in her preservation of a hundred thousand facets of a civilization now dead, her hoarding within her walls the techniques and instruments produced by humanity at its technological peak, now lost to the rest of humankind. Her power was in her knowledge, and her knowledge was immense.

People came to Meijing with their unfixable machines, their incurable illnesses and irreparable injuries, their unanswered questions and unverifiable theories, from all the reaches of the habitable world. The gadgets, illnesses, and questions were brought to Meijing's walls, taken inside, and returned for collection at a specified later time, at a specified price. Few, very few outsiders were given leave to enter, most of those on a limited training program such as Dian's mother had gone through. Meijing was inviolate, and the outside world knew little of what went on within her walls. Dian would be one of those privileged few, not through any virtue of her own but because she was the daughter of a woman who trained there and the friend of a woman actually born there. She would have to watch herself carefully, so as not to betray that trust. She looked down at the fuzzy head nestled to her chest and not for the first time was assailed by doubts as to the wisdom of her impulsive humanitarian action. Perhaps she should—she couldn't abandon Willa now—what if in Meijing they—but surely they were too civilized to—

Dian rose, distracted if not exactly soothed by her sojourn beside the waters, and put her troops back on the Road.

Her second stop was to be at the workshop of a carpet weaver named Deirdre. Shortly after midday the tide of the traffic ebbed and began to turn, and where in

the morning she had been caught up and pulled along
by the northward flow, now the trickle of carts coming back from the city began to grow, until the wrong-
minded types like herself were crowded to one side.
About one o'clock she paused for a breather and a
drink, and a strange thing happened: she was approached by a man.

He came up to her as she leaned against the
gatepost of the small café, a mug of beer in her hand
and one eye on the animals to make sure they didn't
overfill their bellies at the water trough. He was a tall,
cadaverous male with wild hair and a yellowed beard
trailing down his chest in matted ropes, wearing the
standard dust-colored robe and carrying the requisite
staff. This one had neither sandals nor rucksack. He
leaned over his staff, fixed her with a fanatic eye, and
waited.

Dian pulled back slightly and tried not to breathe
in too much of his accompanying effluvium, and
racked her brain for the ritual words. What the hell
were you supposed to say? Mother had done this that
time—oh, yes.

"Greetings, Brother."

"I greet you, sister."

"Whence do you come, and where are you bound?"

"I come from nowhere, I am bound toward salvation, for I move on a holy quest." The words came out
in a bored mumble, all the syllables strung together.

"What seekest thou, Brother?"

"I seek the forgiveness of mankind and offer myself
up as a sacrifice to the living God." These were the
only variable words of the ritual but seemed no more
his own than any of the others. He looked at her impatiently, and she finally dredged up the closing
words.

"It is a just cause, Brother, and may the Heavens
bless it. Please permit me to offer you refreshment to

strengthen you on your way." He turned away before the word *refreshment* had left her mouth and was already standing at the café's serving hatch. She leaned past him to put a copper in the woman's hand, and when the Pilgrim gave a snort of incredulous disgust, dug a second one from her pocket. She drained her mug and left quickly. Granted, becoming a Pilgrim was one of the few options open to males who would or could not live under control, but they made her nervous. Even Crazy Isaiah, though relatively harmless, she found an uncomfortable reminder of the occasional inhumanity of modern life. To say nothing of the fact that Pilgrims on a holy quest had a distressing tendency to go berserk and kill themselves and others if they thought they were about to be taken captive. All in all, it was best to submit to buying the man a quick meal and get away from him.

She found Deirdre's carpet-weaving shop half an hour later in one of the largest of the eight-mile centers south of Meijing, hedged in on one side by a painfully gaudy building—covered in various oranges, yellows, greens, reds, and several pounds of gold leaf—whose sign, visible a mile down the Road, declared it to be the Church of Understanding, and on the other by a tawdry cinema house whose advertisement of *moovies, 3-D, and videos* was almost obscured by photographs of polished-looking men in a variety of unlikely poses, all of whom seemed to have artificial teeth. She tore her eyes from this array of amazingly identical yet apparently distinct males and reined Simon to a halt.

In her fascination with the cinema kings, she had not registered the vehicle in front of the shop, but now she did, a gleaming maroon and silver closed carriage pulled by a matched foursome of equally glossy black geldings. Tied alongside were six saddled horses, the entire equipage blocking a fair amount of the Road and looking out of place in front of the unassuming whitewashed shed whose small sign said only *Weavers*. Two armed women in unnecessarily ornate maroon and silver uniforms blocked the door of the shop. Dian dismounted slowly in front of the "moovies" shop and looped Simon's reins to the post ring provided, studying as she did so the extraordinary photograph before her, that of a cinema king—a movie star!—threatening passersby with an unwieldy, thrusting black weapon. Most amazing of all was the movie star's costume, which looked remarkably like human skin but bulged in an exaggeration of masculinity, veins popping, sweat gleaming, muscles writhing across his chest and shoulders. It was a clever enough joke, she supposed, then paused to reflect on the oddities of humor, that what former peoples had apparently thought highly amusing, from her point of view should only appear grotesque. She shook her head, told the dogs to stay on guard, and left her rifle on the saddle.

The two uniformed guards immediately moved away from the building, bristling like a couple of strange dogs, their gun barrels down but very ready. Dian glanced up and down the road in hopes of seeing a Meijing guard, belt bristling with all those unidentifiable shapes, but there were only civilians. So she repeated her "stay" gesture to Culum and Tomas and, touching the firm little shape in the sling for confidence, walked up to the women. She stopped ten feet away.

"I'm looking for Deirdre," she said politely.

"She's busy," the older one said curtly.

"Yes, I thought that might be the case. Can you tell me how much longer before she's free?"

"No, I can't."

"Can't, or won't? Ah, never mind. She is expecting

me, I'm afraid, so if you would please just give her the message that Jamilla's friend—"

"No message. You'll have to wait." The woman had a lumpy face and small eyes that gave her a stupid, bitter expression. The younger one was tense, bony, and spoiling for a fight; for an instant Dian was tempted, but the warm burden that began to stir on her chest made her clamp down hard and keep the politeness in her voice.

"Well, I'm really sorry, but this baby is going to start yelling her head off in about two minutes, and Deirdre is the only one who can do anything about it. It may disturb your employers, but that's up to you." She bared her teeth in a smile, and Willa obligingly let out a first, questioning bleat. To her apprehension Dian saw the younger one react, even more aggressively than she had anticipated. The woman's hard, narrow face looked almost happy as the tip of her gun came up from the ground. Dian's hand shot out to her side, palm down stiffly, and a sharp command rang out.

"No!"

The woman was startled by the unexpected movement and the command, which had not actually been directed at her. Dian continued more quietly.

"Please don't do that. My dogs really don't like it when someone points a gun at me."

The two guards looked past Dian at the vision of three hundredweight of muscle and teeth, crouched quivering where Dian's hand had frozen them as they moved apart and toward the women who threatened their mistress. She could see the women take in the eagerness, the shoulders huge with hackles, the yellow eyes locked on to prey, white teeth beneath the lips; both guards seemed suddenly less interested in dominating Dian. The tableau held for a long moment, all of them oblivious to the traffic and noise a few feet away, until it was broken by the shop door opening. A woman not much older than Dian, dressed in the maroon uniform and with a handgun strapped to her hip, stepped out and ran her eyes over them all, stopping on Culum.

"What is going on?"

"This woman was trying to get in—"

"A woman with a baby and no gun? And you decided to push her around."

"No, we were just—"

"I've warned you two before about this."

"But she—"

"Shut up." Quiet, light, and dangerous. "We'll talk about it later." She met first one set of eyes, then the other, and both fell away. She glanced at Dian. "There seems to have been a misunderstanding here. May I help you with something?"

"It's all right, no harm done. Yes, I need to speak with Deirdre. I have a baby she's due to feed shortly. Do you know how much longer she'll be occupied?"

"They're nearly finished. Perhaps five or ten minutes. Shall I tell her you're here?"

"Yes, please. Tell her it's Jamilla's friend."

"Just a minute." She went in without looking at her two subordinates. They in turn studiously ignored Dian, who walked over to the dogs, smoothed their fur to gentle them, and sent them back to their positions near the horse. Willa stirred again, and Dian jiggled her.

When the woman came back, her jaw was clenched and her mouth tight.

"They want you to come in."

"Who is 'they'?"

"My, er, employers."

"And Deirdre?"

"She's with them. They want to see you, and the

baby." The idea appeared to make her unhappy; Dian thought she could guess why.

"Ah. Menfolk?"

"Yes. Three."

"I see." Dian tried not to look amused at the impossible situation this woman had been put into. She turned to speak over her shoulder. "Culum, Tomas, guard. Willa, come and meet your new admirers."

Under different circumstances she might have helped the woman out, offered to disappear quietly or at least shed her weapons, but it amused her to pretend she did not see the consternation it caused when she walked in with a large, well-worn hunting knife on her belt and God knew what else hidden on her person, the guard knowing that there was nothing she could do to stop her. Even when they were inside, the woman was thwarted at doing her duty, for when she would have taken up a position just inside the door so as to keep an eye on the potentially hazardous Dian, the youngest of her charges waved her out with a flip of his bejeweled fingers. She protested in strangled tones, but the oldest one looked at her.

"It'll be all right, Brigit," he said. "This woman isn't about to murder us or kidnap us. Are you?" he asked Dian.

"No, sir," she said. "I already have more than enough to keep me occupied, without more worries."

"But, sir—" Brigit said without much hope.

"You can wait outside the door, Brigit." She left, shoulders rigid and an expression on her face that said this would not be the end of the matter, that she would see that her ultimate employers, the women whose menfolk these were, would know the details.

The youngest of the men did not wait until the door closed to laugh derisively, arrogant in his ephemeral power. He was perhaps nineteen, a blonde with elaborately coiffed hair, wearing a sort of doublet and hose affair in brilliant green silk and velvet, his eyes painted black and green with makeup, a ring on every finger. The brown-haired man next to him, about thirty years old, wore more ordinary clothes, less flamboyant in blues and reds but of superb quality. He had faint pocks on his cheeks, and his nose and mouth were pinched as if to keep a bad smell from entering. He dismissed Dian from notice with impersonal distaste, his eyes on Willa as if she were some strange, misplaced, and faintly repulsive specimen of the natural world, a slug on his lettuce or a damp salamander in his shoe. A huge diamond on his left hand pulsed and sparkled in the bright workshop, and Dian reflected that if Laine's scavenged necklace had increased the Valley's credit as much as it had, the jewelry in this room would probably buy the entire place, and half its people as well.

The third man seemed positively plain in his brown jacket and trousers and a snowy white shirt. His hair was peppered with gray, his eyes dark, mustache neat. He was sitting next to a slim, brown-eyed woman who wore a simple long dress of some soft burnt-orange fabric with a drape like a painting. He glanced at Dian with polite interest, although as he took in Dian's rough hair and rougher boots and the delicate head grizzling and rooting in her arms, his expression turned to amusement. The woman seemed lost and glanced around for some clue as to how she should respond. She half-stood to welcome Dian, sank down, plucked at the seams of her skirt, and smiled uncertainly.

"You're Jamilla's friend?" she asked, in a voice that was less womanly than Susanna's. "And the baby. Good. We, uh, we were just finishing up, if you'd like to—"

"Let her sit down." The oldest man's suggestion was a command. The other two tucked their sleek,

tidy feet under their chairs and shifted marginally
away from Dian.

The oldest man turned back to Deirdre to continue
their interrupted discussion, which seemed to concern the colors of a carpet she was doing for him and
its relationship with some existing furniture, particularly an ancient Chinese painted screen. They pushed
through a great heap of multicolored threads on the
table between them, extracting a few, discarding others. Deirdre was so distracted as to be fluttering, the
man seemed determined to continue, the other two
men started to talk about a horse race, Willa grew increasingly restive, and Dian tried to push away her irritation.

No introductions were made, of course. The horse
race talk evolved into ribald speculations concerning
the sex life of the jockeys. Five skeins of thread were
laid out on the table. The man continued to rummage
through the others in a desultory manner, as if he,
too, had only half a mind on the business at hand but
was for some reason loath to let it go. He did not look
again at Dian or the baby but held Deirdre's attention
with details that even Dian could tell were needless,
and when Dian realized what he was doing her mild
irritation boiled over.

This bastard was not in the least interested in talking about yarn samples; he wanted only to manipulate the three females into a state of complete
frustration, for his own entertainment. She stood up
abruptly and, at the looks on their faces, knew she
had overreacted; well, the hell with it. She smiled
what felt like a snarl and jiggled the startled Willa.

"I am terribly sorry," she said to the man. "The
child is hungry and seems to be interfering with your
discussion. Perhaps I ought to remove her, so you can
finish without interruption." It was a hint not even

he could ignore, but she was not prepared for the twist he put on it.

"By no means. If the child is hungry, let it eat," he said, and waved regally toward Deirdre and sat back in his chair.

From the look on her face Deirdre had not actually lived with men for a long time, and nursing a baby around strange males was an unfamiliar, and not entirely comfortable, experience. Nonetheless, after an initial hesitation she reached gamely for the baby and set about putting the strange armful to her breast under the gaze of three absorbed sets of eyes. Eventually, after what seemed a long time, Willa was suckling.

"I thought yours were older than that," commented the oldest man. Deirdre looked up.

"Oh, this one isn't mine," she said. "I'm just helping out until this woman can find a wet nurse."

"Why?" interrupted the man in green. "What's wrong with her?" He nodded at Dian, who caught his eye and held it.

"Not that it is any business of yours," she answered deliberately, "but the child is not mine either. I found her, abandoned, at a crossroads. Exposed." The young man jerked upright, started to rise, caught himself, and looked apprehensively at the nursing pair. The man with the diamond ring had no such compunctions, or pride; he was already on the other side of the room with his hand on the doorknob.

"What's wrong with her?" the young man again demanded.

"Absolutely nothing," Dian answered blandly. "Just an extra toe or two."

The man's eyes went to Willa, as if he half-expected an octopus's tentacles to squirm out from the wrappings, but he relaxed slightly in his chair. However, the man at the door would have none of it.

"Come on, Hari, it's time to go. We said we'd be back by one."

The younger man stood up in agreement.

"Daren's right, Hari, and I've got things to do before the party. Let's go."

"I'm not finished," the oldest man said flatly, but Deirdre spoke up, hesitantly.

"Really, Hari, there's not an awful lot more to do right now," she said. "I'll work up a sample with these colors, and after that you can tell me what you think. But that's going to take me at least two weeks. I'm grateful you could come down and see me." It was as close to a dismissal as Deirdre was capable of giving, and although Hari did not like it, Dian could see him decide that it was better to accept with grace rather than make a scene. He stood up, nodded to Deirdre, and swept out without further acknowledgment of Dian or the baby.

The door shut behind the men, and Deirdre blew out a sigh of relief. She shook her head ruefully at Dian.

"I'm sorry about that," she said. "The family is one of my better customers, but there are times when I wonder if they're worth it."

"I hope I haven't chased them away permanently."

"Don't worry, they're not that easily put off. Sad, really, all that energy and money, and being men they have nothing to do all day but indulge themselves. Hari's really very clever with colors, he does a lot of designing. He's all right. In small doses. Sit down," she added, and, "Can I get you something to drink?"

"No, thanks, I had something a little while ago. Do you mind if I take a look at the workshop?"

"Not at all. Here, I'll come with you, just let me switch her over—what's her name?"

"Willa."

"Willa, that's right. Little ones like this are so easy

to handle, once they get the hang of it." And so saying she tucked the child more firmly against her body, straightened her dress, and led Dian out of the office space and into the workshop. It was a bright, noisy space, with seven or eight women, two of them slim brown-skinned figures dressed in the brilliant wraps Dian thought were called *saris*. All of them were talking happily over the clatter of their looms while half a dozen children played around their feet.

"Which one is yours?" she asked, nodding at the pile of multicolored kids.

"None of that crew. Mine are taking a nap—they're twins, fifteen months and all mischief, but thank God they're good sleepers. Do you weave?"

Dian was grateful the woman had not asked, Do you have children?

"No, but I have a sister-in-law who does beautiful work. She'd love this."

"This is the lighter stuff in here, for curtains and upholstery to go with the carpets. My part's through here," and she ducked through a draped doorway into a smaller shed behind the main one. Five huge frames held works in progress, and three women looked up at their entrance, their flying fingers not even pausing. A fourth woman knelt on the floor atop three hundred square feet of spectacular, sinuous gold and scarlet dragon on a rippling background of blues and greens, a pair of sculpting shears in her hand. Dian went to stare at the carpet and make noises of unfeigned appreciation. Deirdre brushed them aside.

"It's all right. Nothing very challenging, aside from the size, but they tend to like traditional designs in Meijing. Boring, but it pays the rent."

"How much would something like that cost? If that isn't—"

Deirdre casually named a sum that made Dian blink and clear her throat.

"And a small one, maybe by one of your apprentices?"

"For you?"

"A gift. For a man."

"What kind of thing does he like?"

Dian was at a loss.

"I don't really know. I mean, he likes the sorts of colors you were laying out for those gentlemen, but he hasn't been around—been with us—very long. He's quiet. Funny. Strong. He likes waterfalls," she offered a bit desperately, and Deirdre laughed.

"A strong man who likes waterfalls. That should be fun," and then she paused and her dark eyes began to focus far away. "I wonder," she said, and a minute later, "That might do it," and still later she dragged herself back and smiled absently at Dian. "I was going to do a small sampler for Hari, perhaps I'll do an actual carpet instead that would do for your—what's his name?"

"Isaac. His name is Isaac. I could pick it up in six weeks or so, if you've got it finished—I'll be coming back through around then. Or if not, maybe next spring, someone from my family will be coming up then."

"Six weeks should be good. Isaac, you say. And waterfalls. Hmmm."

Ten minutes later Deirdre put Willa back in Dian's hands and waved away her thanks. When Dian turned in the doorway, Deirdre was already bent over a large sheet of paper on the worktable, a bristling cup of colored pencils pulled up in front of her.

Dian's last stop before reaching Meijing gleamed at her from several miles down the Road, a dazzling white-walled hacienda atop the last set of hills before the city. Three hours after leaving Deirdre's shop, she turned Simon's head to follow the insignificant signs pointing to *cantina* and entered a maze of alleyways

that stepped and twisted and finally fell away respect-
fully a distance from the inn's perimeter wall, whitewashed and laid with a businesslike icing of broken
glass and wire along the top. She dismounted and led
Simon through the massive black gates. Once inside
they were pounced upon by a silent brown child who
looked remarkably like a miniature Carmen; she
tugged at the reins until Dian relinquished them.

"I'm not staying," she told the child. "I'll be here
less than an hour. *Yo estaré aqui menos que una
hora,*" she called, shrugged, and sent Culum and
Tomas off after them. The woman who appeared from
the inn's doorway sent a rapid fire of choppy syllables
rattling against the back of the retreating child, who
merely hunched her shoulders another fraction of an
inch and continued walking. The woman, all squat
browns and blacks, looked a question at Dian.

"My name is Dian," she started, but got no further.
The woman bundled her inside, conjured up another
of herself, twenty years younger and forty pounds
lighter, who tugged the baby, carrier and all, from
Dian's arms with the same single-mindedness that the
stable girl had shown, bustling off again into the dim
and fragrant depths of the inn. Dian's flustering guide
completely ignored Dian's attempts at both Spanish
and English but shooed Dian ahead of her through half
an acre of glossy red-brown tile floors, massive black
beams, and rough, spotless white plaster walls.

At the end of their travels the innkeeper, or her representative, shoved Dian out into a courtyard, a huge
sun-washed area broken into intimacy by a number of
half-walls, four enormous spreading oak trees, and a
meandering and apparently unplanned watercourse
with three ponds, a dozen changes of level, and a
soothing trickle of water from the wall to mark its
beginning. There were two cooking pits, each large
enough for half a cow, half a dozen potbellied clay

fireplaces, strings of colorful hanging lamps waiting for night, countless flowerpots blazing with marigolds and zinnias and asters, four large bamboo cages of songbirds, a pair of somnolent orange cats, and an incomparable view of the walls of Meijing, that massive silver snake that rode the hilltops and protected the last city in the West from overview. Dian was the only human being in sight.

She walked aimlessly around the courtyard, admired the view and the goldfish in the ponds and the birds in the cages, and had settled into a disconsolate chair to await Willa's return when the door from the cantina burst open and a third black-clad, tightly bunned woman stormed out with a red-enameled tray laden with a large bowl of crisp brown corn chips, three smaller bowls containing dips, and a large blue-glass pitcher filled with a dark brown liquid topped by a thin layer of finely textured froth. She dumped the tray in front of Dian, miraculously not spilling a drop from bowl or pitcher, seized the jug, and paused.

"*Bebe Usted cerveza?*"

"*Sí, señora, con mucho gusto.*"

The woman nodded brusquely and dashed the liquid into a tall, narrow blue glass, slapped the pitcher down, and stalked off. The seemingly careless service had resulted in a precise measure of beer with a head of caramel-colored foam that blossomed one half inch above the glass, then subsided without so much as a dribble. It was a beautiful beer, cool and heavy and sweet against the warm, salty chips and the fire of the thin red-brown dip, the tang of the lumpy red one, and the creamy rich garlic of the green one.

All in all, Dian was well satisfied with what she took to be her dinner. Then the other trays arrived. Three of them, carried by three more women (no, surely not three more of these phlegmatic Hispanics?), who marched across the red tiles and dealt out bowls, plates, and baskets with a verve that should have sent each object spinning to the ground but somehow did not. Dian tried to dredge up some appropriately appreciative phrases, but was not fast enough off the mark and could only fling various forms of *gracias* at the black backs.

Bowls of beans and rice, succulent prawns in a *piquante* sauce and chicken *mole*, the chocolate sauce so thick it swallowed the chicken, and flaming *chile verde*, along with a basket of fresh hot tortillas, a platter of *flautas* topped with sour *crema*, a plate of tamales, and—Dian groaned, knowing she could never eat it all, and knowing she was going to make herself ill trying. The sun inched across the tiles, the shadows grew long, and finally Dian sat back, stunned and pop-eyed and incapable of movement. She rested her head against the convenient chair back, and in two minutes she was asleep.

She woke to find a cat in her lap and the sun in her eyes and the table as clear as if the feast had been but a fairy dream. Except for her stomach's evidence—she felt like Judith had looked last month. She pried the disgusted cat from her thighs, got to her feet, and went to find Willa.

There were people in the inn now, perhaps a dozen figures scattered across one corner, as dark and quiet as the rooms themselves. Dian waited for a brusque figure to materialize, and as her eyes adjusted to the low light she realized that three of the seven people sitting at the large corner table, drinking *cerveza* and eating tortilla chips with satisfied, tired movements and low voices, were men, and that the other six women, sitting at three surrounding tables, were guards, their eyes on Dian and their still hands hidden beneath the tables. Dian nodded easily to them and walked off at an oblique angle toward the kitchen smells.

Before she could lay a hand on the doors, they flew open and there stood the first of the black-gowned women, framed by a square of light and an almost tangible air of chilis and grilling tortillas and voices. She had Willa in her hands and thrust her out, carrier and all, toward Dian. Willa had been out of the carrier, though, Dian noted as she buckled it on: the baby was now wearing an allover shapeless garment of scarlet cloth with a flock of tiny, bright-colored birds in flight across the sleeves and down the front. She exclaimed over it, received no reaction from the authoritative figure standing arms akimbo before her, and was seized by a flare of irritation.

"I would like to say thank you to whoever fed Willa," she said firmly.

"*No es necesario.*"

"*Para Usted, señora, no es, pero para mí, y para este bebé, y*"—she pulled out her trump card— "*para mi amiga Jamilla, sí, es necesario.*" Her Spanish was that of a child, Dian knew, but the message was unmistakable: kindly move out of my way, old woman, before you piss me off. The woman wavered, took half a step back into the busy kitchen, and halted again as the sound of a child's wordless voice rose above the babble. Dian relented slightly.

"*Por favor, señora,* my mother raised me to have good manners, and she would be upset if I walked away without saying *gracias* to the woman who gave this baby suck." As Dian had suspected, the woman's English was up to this, because in a moment she nodded shortly, gestured Dian to stay put, and leaned back to shriek into the kitchen. Voices cut off, pans stilled, and a beautiful young woman, almost a girl, came to the doorway wiping her hands on a towel. The *señora* assaulted her with a string of words unintelligible to Dian, and they both turned to look at Dian, one suspicious and the other smiling happily.

"I was happy to help you, *señora*," she said to Dian. "It is a pretty child, although the toes, they make my grandmother worried."

"They make me worried too," Dian told her, "though probably for different reasons. I appreciate your willingness to have her in your house. And for the red suit. Can I return it...?"

"Oh, no, it is not new, my...my child has grown out of it." Dian interpreted the hesitation in light of the grandmother's obvious reluctance to have her in the kitchen and the sounds of the child on the other side of the door.

"You have a son?" The grandmother made as if to push Dian out the front door of the inn, but the young woman only dimpled.

"Yes. He is almost two. I have a picture," she said, and fished a much-handled photograph of a sturdy child from the pocket of her apron. The subject of the studio portrait shouted loudly twenty feet away, but Dian would not have asked to see him for the world. She admired the image (thinking privately that the bright pink tinting on the child's cheeks made him look like a doll) and thanked the women again before taking her leave.

The stable girl was there waiting with Simon and the two dogs, perched on the edge of a hitching rail with the reins in her hands, communing with Simon and completely oblivious of the dogs. She seemed reluctant to give over possession of the horse, ignored the coin Dian held out to her, and slouched off to await her next equine visitor. It was as well, Dian thought to herself as she checked the girth and mounted, that some people's passions were fulfilled by their environment.

"TELL THEM A FOREIGN DAMSEL WISHES TO SEE THEM;
AND ASK THEM IF THEY WANT TO SEE ME
INSIDE OR HERE WHERE I AM."

SIXTEEN

ALL AFTERNOON THE FOG HAD BEEN SPILLING OVER THE tops of the hills from the sea, soft waves that dissipated before they reached the ground. Now, however, the sun's heat was no longer enough to keep it at bay, and it was tumbling over the top of Meijing's walls like an immensely slow tidal wave.

The wave broke over the travelers a mile from the city gates, and the world closed in, clammy and dim. In the half-light the city walls lost their glow and were only gray and very solid. At the city's gates, streamers of fog blew across the huge archway and gave for a brief instant the impression that the city itself was sailing briskly through a stationary cloud.

Dian rode through the gates and dismounted inside the courtyard, which was even more enormous than she remembered, its farthest reaches only a series of glowing lights through the damp. The courtyard functioned as between territory, separated from the interior by the same sheer, high, windowless walls that the city presented to the rest of the world. A person in the Court of Traders might be technically within Meijing's walls, but she was emphatically not within the city.

The courtyard was emptying rapidly in the early dusk; most of the smaller stalls were already boarded and padlocked. The Approvals building here was the great-grandmother of the individual units along the Road, an eight-hundred-foot line of interconnected cubicles, no more than twenty feet deep and studded by dozens of evenly spaced doors alternating with windows. Both ends of the building were dark, but toward the middle quite a few of the cubicles were still fully lit and bustling with desperate energy as the soon-to-be-benighted traders hurried to have their last-minute purchases weighed, tested, and analyzed by the technicians and their gleaming, mysterious array of equipment.

The courtyard had not actually changed much in fourteen years, Dian saw. At the far right end of the Approvals building was the same stretch of unmarked wall with its insignificant door, which according to her mother was one of less than a dozen points of access to the city. She pulled the waterproof neck pouch from under her shirt, took out the letter from Ling, and made for the doorway.

Before she had covered half the distance, a tall Chinese woman in the dark green uniform of the Meijing guard intercepted her. The woman was everything Meijing represented: sleek and strong, her belt strung with compact devices whose purposes Dian couldn't even begin to guess, although all of them looked scary.

"That door is not open to visitors," the guard said firmly but politely; out of the corner of her eye, Dian saw a figure atop the long building shift her attention as well.

Dian signaled the dogs to relax and, careful to make no rapid movements, held the letter out to the woman. The guard did not reach for it but instead, unfailingly polite, asked Dian to open it. Only when it was free of its envelope and the page unfolded did the woman take it, stepping away to read Ling's delicate characters. When she had done so, she looked up thoughtfully at Dian, her dogs, and the baby who was beginning to stir against her chest.

"You will have to wait a short while out here. I am sure you understand, I must give this to my superior."

"I understand, but if you will be very long, do you think someone could arrange some food for the baby? She will be hungry soon and I have no milk for her."

The woman looked a bit nonplussed at this, but she merely nodded and tipped her head to speak a few words into the air. Dian started to look and see who the guard was talking to, then caught herself—she was speaking into a shoulder radio, although the device itself was hidden. After a moment, the invisible colleague must have responded, because the woman turned and disappeared through the door, which, oddly enough, did not seem to be locked. Dian left the dogs with Simon and, conspicuously leaving her weapons on the saddle, took the waking baby for a stroll. Whispering soothing nonsense in a singsong voice and jiggling her up and down, Dian stopped to peer in the windows of the Approvals building. In this lab she could see a white-coated woman, her glossy black hair bent over a microscope while a trader waited impatiently on the other side of the counter. In the next cubicle another technician was holding a long strip of paper up before a group of five people, two of them men with heavy beards and bright, elaborately wrapped turbans on their heads. Further down she could see what she took to be a Geiger counter, though it was much larger than any she had seen before. In that stall also there was a pair of women in travel-stained clothing, only these two were shouting at each other in silent pantomime behind the glass. The technician in this cubicle looked on apprehensively, a pile of heavy, gleaming, very old silverware on the counter in front of her. As Dian watched, one of the women threw up her hands, shoveled the forks and spoons roughly into a cloth bag, and slammed out the door.

By now Willa was beginning to tell the world of her hunger, to the curious looks of some of the women remaining in the courtyard. Dian was just starting to wonder if she might be able to find some goat's milk outside the gates when the small door opened and the tall guard came out, followed by two others.

"Would you come with me, please?" she asked. Dian gathered up Simon's dangling reins and glanced up at the rooftop figure, of whom she had been very aware for the last ten minutes. That woman held a wicked-looking black shape in her hands that looked like an old semiautomatic weapon. She nodded politely at Dian as she passed, following the guards through the door, which was just tall and wide enough for a laden horse. The dogs followed, alert but controlled, and Dian entered the forbidden city of Meijing.

Walking down the narrow labyrinth to the echoing clop of the horse's hooves and Willa's sporadic protests, one guard in front and two behind, Dian saw through two sets of eyes. One set was hers as she was now, a woman familiar with the strategies of defense, who knew herself to be the equal of most of the women guarding this city. The other eyes belonged to a gangly adolescent with a new name and a new body, brought from a remote village to this hidden city whose very name evoked its magnificence.

They were now passing doors, some of which had half-recognized characters painted onto them (one something to do with soldiers, another with food requests—Dian kicked herself for not going further with Ling's Chinese lessons) and others which were unmarked. One entrance was obviously the hospital for the area's ill and injured, the doors broad and ramped, the air outside it smelling of drugs and pain. Shortly after the hospital, the roof gave way to open air. An overhead row of electrical lights flickered on, showering a harsh blue illumination onto the passageway and causing Simon to snort and toss his head.

Then the walls turned a sudden corner and ceased altogether, and she was startled to find a view of inner Meijing rolled out before her—she'd only expected to be given access to the walls, not the inner city itself. But here it was, lit by the last rays of the sun that slid underneath the fog, turning the silver walls to a warm rose color and making the world stop to catch its breath at the serenity and perfection within.

All the bustle of the city's business was conducted within the actual structure of the perimeter wall itself. From outside Meijing, the wall seemed only a monolithic barrier, but on the inside there were great variations in depth, with balconies and roof gardens and thousands of windows to overlook the great uneven parkland that was the city, the sweep of countryside meticulously natural and unplanned in its heights and hollows, grassland and lakes, forest groves and tidy orchards and flowering shrubs. When she'd been here with Mother fourteen years ago, it had still looked raw in places, the new hills formed of rubble recently planted and containing unfinished patches; now it seemed that the last of the tarmac and concrete had been hauled off to the walls and the Bay, and under the softening, roseate fog, it looked like a young Eden.

"You are seeing it at the proper time of day," spoke a quiet, precisely accented voice from Dian's elbow. "The other side of the city is best at dawn, but from this side, dusk is better."

Dian turned to the tiny figure standing at her side.

The face was tantalizingly familiar, but who...? The woman smiled.

"You do not remember me?" she chided.

The smile brought back a flood of memories, among which was a face much younger and not so amazingly small.

"Jung Xiansheng! But you're so—" She stopped, not wishing to cause offense.

"Old, I know. And you have grown half a foot I think since my student your mother brought you here. The news of her death saddened me, but your presence brings me happiness. Come, let us refresh you, and your child. Your milk has not come in, I was told?"

Dian's laugh roused Willa. Raising her voice, Dian said, "She isn't mine. I rescued her at a crossroads, a couple of days ago. A simple birth defect, nothing contagious." The older woman raised one eyebrow and nodded, then turned to Dian's three escorts with a stream of Chinese too fast for Dian to follow, though she caught a few words, such as *horse* and *mother* and *tea*. One of the women bowed and marched back into the wall passageway. Teacher Jung spoke to Dian, loudly enough to make herself heard over the vigorous little set of lungs, "You will I think want those two monsters with you?" and nodded with a twinkle at Culum and Tomas.

"If it would not trouble you, please. They have excellent manners. I need only my saddlebag, if you wish to take the horse," she said to the tall guard. "And you would probably be more comfortable if you searched me here, would you not?" Dian transferred the squalling Willa to Teacher Jung's arms, where the infant calmed somewhat. She took the hunting knife from her belt and the narrow throwing knife from the top of her boot and gave both to the guard, who put them into Dian's saddle roll. Dian then held her arms out for a brisk pat search, waited while her bags were examined, and returned the guard's bow. The woman bowed low to Teacher Jung, then nodded to one of the others to lead the horse away, and followed. Jung sighed.

"Mai is a little overzealous in her duties, but a good girl. She is my number-ten grandchild." She took Dian's arm and started off at an angle across the parkland, talking about her family. An onlooker would have thought that she walked in the park every evening on the arm of a towering, disheveled blond woman with stained clothing, a howling infant tucked into her other arm, and a pair of dogs, either of whom easily outweighed the old woman, sauntering along behind.

Their path soon reached a magnificent freestanding building in a grove of timber bamboo, which Dian took for a temple until excited children of various sizes began to spill from within, chattering wildly at Teacher Jung and only just controlling their obvious desire to gawk at these huge, light-haired creatures (both two- and four-legged). An adult followed, and Jung placed Willa in the woman's arms with brief instructions. Cries of starvation trailed off through the house until they were abruptly cut short. Food had been provided.

Meanwhile, Teacher Jung was making solemn introductions, and Dian bowed formally to each child and promptly forgot the names.

"Now," said Teacher Jung, slowly and in English, "That is enough for tonight. Miss Dian will be here tomorrow. She will talk with you then. Did you understand, MeiLan?" The smallest tot looked puzzled until an older sister translated for her, and then she presented Dian with a smile of angelic sweetness, bowed with the others, and back they poured up the steps into the temple-house. Teacher Jung watched them go with a grandmother's pride.

"I hope you will pardon their manners," she said. "They are young and inexperienced."

"Their manners are beautiful," Dian said in an unnecessary protest. "I hope I will be allowed to talk with them."

Teacher Jung nodded complacently.

"I very much hope you will stay some days with us. Ling said in her letter that you are on your way north to investigate a group of potential immigrants to your valley, but she thinks you may not be overly pressed for time." It was a question.

"I'd love to stay for a day or two, but I'm afraid that you may not find us the easiest of guests."

"Nonsense. But the baby—oh, goodness, here I criticize the children's manners! You are weary from the road and I make you stand and chatter. Come, one of my granddaughters will show you to your rooms, and when you have refreshed yourself you will come and drink tea with me, and we will talk. First, however, I think Ling will have sent a small parcel for me?"

Dian pulled the thick envelope from her bag and with both hands gave it to the woman, to her evident satisfaction.

"Very good, thank you. Ah, here is CaThai, she will take you upstairs. When you are rested, come down, and someone will bring you to me. There is no hurry, we will not take our meal until eight-thirty."

Dian bowed and followed the tiny trouser-clad woman upstairs, where she was shown a small room with three comfortable chairs around a burning fire, with an adjoining bedroom, complete with two large furry pads on the floor for the dogs and a spacious bathroom whose tiled tub stretched fully six feet long. She thanked CaThai, who giggled as she left. When Dian was alone, she introduced the dogs to their beds, dropped her grimy saddlebags onto the floor, and went to soak the smell of horse, dog, and dust from her skin.

The water was murky by the time she'd finished, so she fiddled with the control to the shower, a mad arrangement of five spray heads, and when she had finally found how to make it neither scald nor freeze her, nor puncture her more tender parts with streams like needles, she figured she was clean enough and shut it off.

The towels, all four of them, were warm from a loop in the hot-water supply. She wrapped one around her, began to walk out of the steamy bathroom toweling her hair with another one, then came to a dead halt at an absolutely horrifying thought.

"Oh, shit," she said to Culum, lying in the bathroom doorway with his chin on his paws. "I forgot to buy myself a shirt."

Here she was, about to go to dinner with her mother's honored teacher, head of one of the most powerful families in Meijing, and the only clothing she owned was crumpled and permanently stained, thanks to Willa. And the shops around the gate would be shut by now. Perhaps she should plead exhaustion? Impossible to do so without causing offense. No way around it, she would be letting her family down badly this evening, confirming all Meijing's worst thoughts about the peasants living in the country. Damnation.

She slowly rubbed the towel across her scalp, stepped over Culum, and her eye was caught by a flash of color from the bed. A shimmering blue-on-silver-shot silk tunic and trousers with a two-inch band of embroidery, also blues and silver, around the collar and down the front. She held the tunic to her chest with the sleeve stretching down to her wrist; the trousers, too, reached her feet. She shook her head in wonderment: With fifteen minutes' warning, the family's guest had been provided with a warm room, beds for two hulking dogs, and clothing suitable for a misshapen barbarian. They'd even managed to come in and out without alarming the dogs. No wonder these people controlled the world.

The silk was cool and heavy, disturbingly sensual against her skin, but the clothes might have been tailored for her, and there was even a pair of soft cloth shoes, snug but not impossibly so. She went into the bathroom to see if her hair was anywhere near presentable, decided it was hopeless but at least clean, and spent ten minutes trying to decipher the labels on a collection of cosmetics, gadgets, and bottles she found behind the mirrored cabinet. In the end she settled for some nice-smelling face crème, rather than risk the spectacle of childishly applied makeup.

She was prepared to ask at the base of the stairs for directions, but just outside her door stood a casual cluster of children, laying in wait for the privilege of escort duty. As the procession went down the stairs, one of the bravest girls reached forward and gently squeezed Culum's tail. This reduced half the crew to shrieks of laughter, and they remained behind, huddled together on the carpeted staircase and exclaiming wildly, but Dian managed to gain Teacher Jung's office with her remaining three bodyguards.

Jung called for her to enter, but she barely looked up from the papers on the desk in front of her.

"I do not like to be discourteous," she said, "but I think it best that I finish reading this before we talk. Please take some tea, and feel free to browse through the books."

Dian took her cup to the shelves, where a gold-lettered spine caught her eye, and she sat down with the book of photographs of San Francisco—all from Before, of course—and drank her flower-scented tea. Ten or fifteen minutes passed before Teacher Jung stirred, tapped her papers together into a neat pile, and came to take the chair across from Dian. She was wearing gold-rimmed glasses.

"Thank you for waiting," she said. "Ling's words had some bearing on our conversation. But first, tell me more about finding the child."

Dian explained; to her surprise Jung pressed her, most knowledgeably, for further details: Where precisely had Dian found her? Was that the second or the third crossroads along that length of roadway? Had she kept the scrap of blanket? No? Pity, it might have helped to identify the group. Abandonment is a serious crime. And the names of the women who nursed the child? Yes, she knew of Jamilla, and Deirdre, although she had not had the pleasure of meeting either. The woman at the cantina was not identified? It should not prove difficult.

"But, surely," she said finally, "you do not intend to take the child with you on your northern journey?"

"It would be a bit difficult," Dian agreed. "I thought I might ask you for advice on arranging a dependable wet nurse and have her care for Willa while I'm gone. I can pay, that's no problem. I also wanted to ask you about her toes."

"Certainly the toes can be dealt with, and at the price of some physical discomfort now we can save her a lifetime of mental agony as a pariah. There will be no trace by the time she begins to walk. As to the other, do not be ridiculous. You are Ling's family, therefore you are ours, and we take responsibility for one of our own. She will be cared for by us until you return."

"Thank you, Jung Xiansheng. That's a burden off my mind."

"Good. Would you care for another cup of tea? No? Very well." She peeled her glasses from her ears and fixed Dian with a speculative gaze, then seemed to come to a decision. "My dear," she said, "I would appreciate it if you would consider spending four or five nights with us and allowing me to perform some tests upon you. I do not mean physical tests," she said quickly, seeing Dian's reaction. "Ling says in her letter that you may wish a detailed examination, and I would be happy to arrange for that if you so choose. Perhaps on your way back down. I mean psychological ones, or perhaps *parapsychological* is the word I want. Let me explain." She poured herself another cup of the pale tea and took several sips as if to strengthen herself, then placed the cup decisively on the enameled tray and began.

"To much of the outside world, we in Meijing are a cross between traders and sorcerers—highly successful, disgustingly wealthy traders with a mania for privacy, sorcerers holding an uncomfortable familiarity with technology. Those who know us better are aware of the responsibilities we take on. The military police are the most visible, and therefore most controversial, but even our critics give us credit for schools and health care. We are a small population within the city, and yet we try to keep the population under our influence not only safe and free from disease but also mentally healthy. All of the children in the Bay Area are educated to the age of twelve, and nearly all citizens can read and write, at least in English. Citizens who are talented, whether they are Chinese or not, we nurture and educate further. We train and encourage not only scientists but musicians and artists, we establish libraries, even run film and video centers for entertainment.

"Gradually, carefully, we reintroduce the more useful machines, the more vital medical procedures, pushing back the darkness one step at a time. It is a good metaphor, for we often feel as if we were holding a small candle in a large and drafty space. For some time our success was questionable. There was a period of half a dozen years when I, for one, believed that we were playing a fool's game, that the light would go irretrievably out and humanity would be left in the black night, alone and without comfort until such time as it reinvented fire. And the future—who knows what it will hold? You may have heard of our neighbors to the north?"

"Queen Bess?"

"Her, and her liege cities where feudal tyranny is termed freedom, where slavery and perversions are matters of daily life. Bess and her ilk worship the dark and are most persuasive in convincing the ignorant that it is light. She is the reason we do not trade certain otherwise harmless goods that can be converted into arms.

"However, I am raising an umbrella against tomorrow's rainstorm. For now we have succeeded, by many harsh and selfish acts, in building a shield around our own flame, walking a narrow path between those who would have us share all our knowledge this very moment and those who would see us willingly burn our books and settle into the nineteenth century. Our behavior has at times appeared nearly as shameful as that of Ashtown, even to us, but I believe that time will reveal our ruthlessness to have been justified. All around us other lights guttered and died, but within the shield of these walls, ours survived.

"I wax too poetic, perhaps. I see you are amused. However, it is difficult to contain my enthusiasm and joy when I see what is happening in the world around me. For, to continue with the metaphor, we have found other souls in the darkness, and in passing our flame on to them, we strengthen the light for us all." She paused to sip from the cup, and then continued.

"Your mother, the woman you call your mother

and whose maternal surname you took, was one who came to us from out of the edges of darkness. We shared our flame with her, and she took it back, and your Valley became an outpost in the darkness. She also took with her one of us, my granddaughter Ling, who chafed beneath the restrictions placed on her here, who looked for a view beyond the walls.

"Ling writes to me regularly. With, I hasten to say, the knowledge and approval of first your mother and now Judith, as well as old Kirsten, whom I shall never meet but feel as if I know as a sister. If we are to help to spread the boundaries of civilization, we must have knowledge of the conditions of the people. I know your Valley well, thanks to Ling's reports. I feel as if I could walk into the big house and lay my hand on Lenore's shuttle, I could tell you what book Judith and Susanna are reading now in the evenings, where Lisa's new henhouse will go, how far Carmen has gotten with the new saddle she is constructing. Yes, you are astonished that I know so much. You have a spy in your midst, unsuspected and all-revealing. It is an uncomfortable thought for you.

"And now I am going to make you even more uncomfortable. I am going to ask you to go one step further and reveal to me, not the workings of your Valley, but of your own inner self.

"I acknowledge that I have no claim on you, that I have no right to this. If you refuse, there will be no penalty. I will only say that I do not ask it lightly or for the sake of the meaningless curiosity that was endemic in the times Before. I ask because there are faint intimations that this massive trauma humanity has suffered in the last three-quarters of a century has encouraged the development of certain previously rare and fragile abilities, the very existence of which was in times past seen through superstitious eyes. We would like to know if these nascent abilities are uncontrollable flukes or skills that might be encouraged and developed.

"And that covers what I wanted to say to you. Please think about my request; I do not wish an immediate answer. Tomorrow would be fine. Do you have any questions of your own before we go in to dinner?"

Dian wrenched her mind off Jung's words and came up with the question that had been bothering her ever since Ling refused to answer it.

"Yes. About the list of things that Ling asked me to bring back? Some of the things on it were expensive...."

"If you are asking, does your village pay for it all, perhaps inadvertently through Ling's reports, the answer is no. We regard you, as I said, both as family and as an outpost, and therefore in need of certain assistance. Not to create dependency, for we do not wish to create colonies, but because you cannot yet afford them yourself without endangering your future through overspending your resources. We do not send food, or we have not in the past, but machinery, medicines, and the skills to enable you to live with greater productivity than mere subsistence—those we provide freely. Soon we would like to establish a communications system. If you are asking if this will become niggardly or stop were you to refuse my tests, that answer, too, is no. We are not petulant children here, and I have to assume that if you refuse me, you have good reason."

"I am not—I don't intend to refuse, but couldn't they wait until I come back?"

"I would very much prefer that they not be put off, for two reasons. The obvious one is that you may not come back. You know as well as I that you are going into a highly dangerous area, and I am not talking about the four-legged animals. Beyond this, it would be helpful to have the results now, so that if we need to confirm any speculations or hypotheses that arise, we can do that upon your return."

"I see. Well, in that case, yes, let's do it now. Or to-morrow, I mean. Whenever you like."

"Good. Very good. I thank you in advance. And now the others will be waiting for us. I trust you are hungry?"

...SHE CONCEIVED A DESIRE TO SEE THE WORLD.

SEVENTEEN

DIAN WAS IN MEIJING FOR FOUR NIGHTS AND THREE full days, but afterward, within a very few days in fact, her time there became timeless, a period of dreamlike insubstantiality, of vivid vignettes unconnected by any logic of cause and effect. This may have been a side effect of the mild hypnotic drug administered each morning before the tests began, but secretly Dian thought it was due to the otherworldly nature of Meijing itself and her basic inability to comprehend its structures, goals, and techniques of learning. The only clear times in her mind were the last day, which she spent largely in conversation with Teacher Jung, and the first evening, although even that was fuzzy around the edges.

Other than those two periods, there were rooms—three different rooms—two of them with huge banks of blinking, muttering computers that made Dian somewhat queasy until the technicians brought in some bamboo screens to conceal them. There was floating relaxation in her memory of those rooms, with a curiously repugnant flexible tube placed over one hand and a heavy snug helmet like a balaclava strapped to her head. Teacher Jung had been there, asking questions and making suggestions, along with an indeterminate number of white-coated women and men who came and went and spoke snatches of half-understood conversations in Chinese and English: "Clear signs in adolescence...." "Pity we can't find the biological parents...." "Dogs? Old Kirsten's influence....threat....fear response....alpha and delta waves..."

Only twice did Dian feel, or later remember feeling, the unmistakable foreboding of a source of potential menace. The first was mild, from an innocuous-looking man in a white coat, around whom she could neither sit still nor concentrate, nor would she allow him to move out of her sight. The second time she could recall no specific source, just a wild rise in the level of excitement among the white coats.

That must have been late on the second day, because she could remember being tired but unable to fall asleep until late. But the very first evening in Meijing, before the tests began, she remembered clearly—most of it, anyway. Dinner was a simple family meal that included a handful of the older children, twenty-five adults, and as many dishes (as a primitive, and hence of uncertain manners, she was not forced to endure a formal banquet—for which, having heard her mother and Ling laugh wryly over such an ordeal, she was extremely grateful). Afterward she had come to be in a room so luxurious she was afraid to move lest her sleeve brush some precious and fragile object from a table or spill wine on one of the carpets, which were as colorful as the one she had seen in Deirdre's work shed, so thick and firm underfoot that if she closed her eyes she felt she was standing on the floor of a redwood grove. The dogs were there, and she was in an agony of anticipation at the potential disasters in their waving tails—but that must have been the following night, surely, when they were clean from their baths? Yes, that's right, Culum's ruff was damp, and once he and Tomas had made the rounds and presented their compliments to their amused hostesses and hosts, she ordered them to lie down in front of the fire and took her own chair in relief.

That first evening, then, was in the smaller, quieter room, with no dogs and fewer people, three of them men. The wine was stronger than she realized, and she remembered talking about herself rather more than was likely. At one point she found herself kneeling in the cool silk trousers on an inch of carpet pile, drawing rough diagrams of Old Will's watermill machines with a gold-nibbed pen on the same smooth, thick paper that Ling treasured for her most intricate ink sketches and brush calligraphy, paper Ling doled out a sheet at a time to the most prized of her pupils, paper taken tonight from a desk drawer in a casual stack by the young man with the inquisitive eyes and set before Dian as if it were a mere slate. She looked at the paper for a long minute before she realized that her audience was waiting, and realized also that it would be an act of intolerable rudeness to let these people know how intimidated she was by this unintentional demonstration of supreme wealth. She pulled herself together and touched the nib to the silken page.

However, she was reasonably certain that it was late on the second night when her door opened, to the conspicuous absence of any protest from Culum and Tomas, and the smooth, slim young man whose interest in the Valley had prompted the desecration of the fine paper with her childish drawings entered her room and her bed, asking polite but merely formal permission and slipping out before dawn, leaving Dian with the vaguely unclean sensation that she had been used to satisfy a faintly perverse taste for the bizarre. Yes, that was definitely the second night, without a doubt, because the following evening she had gone to her bed apprehensively and not fallen asleep until midnight had passed and she knew the visit would not be repeated.

There were two days of the tests. On the third day Teacher Jung sent for Dian after breakfast, and when Dian appeared, she stood up.

"Now, my child, we have locked ourselves inside the laboratories for too long. I believe we deserve a reward. Come, bring those monstrosities of yours and we shall take them for a walk."

The dogs did little walking. Rather, they pounded up and down the hillocks and through the groves at a hard gallop while Dian and Teacher Jung made their more leisurely way toward the tallest hill in sight and started up the side. Dian hid her surprise—she had tended to think of Teacher Jung as venerable and frail, because of her size and the formality of her speech, but she had no trouble keeping up with Dian's long stride, and when they halted it was as much to admire a prize view as it was to rest. Only toward the top of the hill did Jung loop a hand the weight of a songbird's foot through Dian's arm, and even then the touch felt more like one of the truth machines in the laboratory than a bid for support.

They spoke of nothing in particular, the easy conversation of long acquaintance. Teacher Jung commented on the antics of the dogs and asked curious questions about breeding practices (she sympathized with the problem of inbreeding and agreed to keep an eye out for compatible stock to trade for some of the Valley's pups, and if the old trader asked if Dian had considered the potential market for those pups in Meijing, it was without pressure). She was interested in Dian's methods of communication with the dogs, trying to imitate Dian's piercing whistle and laughing at her own failure, and she asked about Ling, of whom she had been very fond and missed still: even detailed letters left out the important things. Using the subject of the Valley's healer, Jung worked her way around to what she had come here to say.

"I only regret that it is such an arduous road between Ling and us here in Meijing. I fear each time she comes will be my last opportunity to see her. Every three or four years is not enough. But she is happy, I think. She is needed in your valley and does not feel closed in. There are always those who need to be stretched, to feel that they live on the edge of a desperate situation, and she is one of those. A pioneer, I suppose. It is hard on those left behind, though. Her cousin talks about her a great deal, reads all the parts of her letters that I allow him. That was why he was so terribly interested in the mill machinery the other evening."

Dian stopped. "That was Ling's cousin?" Teacher Jung's hand fell away and she continued walking. After a minute Dian followed her to the top of the diminutive mountain, on which had been placed a tiny pavilion of exquisite simplicity and an elegance even Dian recognized. Teacher Jung lowered herself gratefully onto a bench and patted the seat beside her. Dian sat.

"It is the most beautiful of all views, this one," she noted. "Made only more lovely by the labor in its approach. Yes, he is Ling's young cousin. He craves nothing more than to follow her out of the city, a chance to perform actions more dramatic than the small and delicate nudges we perform here. You know, I think, that Ling met your mother on one of her visits here and was fired with a sort of missionary zeal. We could not stop her from leaving, of course, but I could not have foreseen how well it would work out in the end."

Dian, however, was still thinking about Ling's younger cousin. "Do you like to kiss?" he had asked her; his mouth had tasted faintly of anise, his skin of salt and incense. "I..." she began, and stopped, unsure of how to put it. "He...came to my room the other night."

"Yes, I know. I thought, however, that a repetition might not be for the best, although if you do not agree, you are most welcome to approach him. You have had quite an effect on our young men. And young women, in a slightly different way." She shook her head sadly. "You blow into our careful warm nest like a gust of mountain air, whispering of wide horizons and barely glimpsed potentials of the human spirit and the strength to be found in simplicity. Here, if you will permit me another metaphor, we spend our lives nurturing the more exotic breeds of vegetation, the delicately perfumed tiny flowers and the subtly lovely species of bamboo. You are as unlike bamboo as it is possible to be, and to be near you is to breathe the heady air of another world. And you wonder that our young men find you attractive? It will take weeks to make them forget you. Some of them will find that you walk their dreams forever."

"I...Oh, Jung Xiansheng. I'm sorry. I really shouldn't have come."

For the first time Jung showed Dian a face other than the one of gentle good humor, and for an instant her old eyes snapped in something close to anger.

"Do not say that. You must never apologize for being what you are. Had I not wanted you here, not wanted the young people exposed to you, I would not have permitted you beyond the walls. Your being here has taught us all a great deal, about the world for which we take some responsibility, and about ourselves. Knowledge is never to be spurned, particularly self-knowledge, though it be painfully gained. You remind us of our duties, of the impossibilities of our task. We who have all the weapons we could want, all the skills and technology in the world, need to be reminded what it is to be an unprotected human in a dirty, nasty world. The last days have not been easy ones for you, and I thank you, humbly, for the effort you have made. I am grateful you came. And," she added with a sly and wistful smile, "I am not entirely sorry you are going."

"I, too, am grateful to be given entrance. I cannot even begin to thank you for having me here."

"And now it is time to start back down this hill that gets just a little taller each time I come. Mai wishes to see you again—you remember Mai, the guard who brought you to me? I told her she could have you for lunch and afterward you might put on a small demonstration with these dogs of yours, if you do not mind. She is interested in the potentials of such animals. She is another one who feels the call of the horizon and works it out by the intensity with which she does her job." Jung sighed again. "Perhaps it is time we thought about making a few small holes in the walls that we so laboriously built. It will not be easy, when the time comes to remove them. Many of us are struck down by spiritual agoraphobia at the thought of living unprotected."

It was nothing, Dian carefully did not say, to the growing claustrophobia she felt at being hedged in by this golden and exquisite prison.

She spent the afternoon with Mai, ate lunch in a rooftop café atop one of the fingers of building that jutted out from the main wall, and went downstairs afterward to meet Mai's husband and two co-wives and their aggregate five children, none of whom were boys. The dogs behaved beautifully, Culum as usual and Tomas because he'd spent the morning running off his energy, and when the heat was out of the autumnal sun they all went outside and she demonstrated how the dogs could be controlled over great distances with whistles. The children were intrigued with the fetch command—"Culum, fetch the ball." "Culum, fetch the knife." "Tomas, fetch the horse" (borrowed for the purpose). Seeing their delight, Dian brought Culum over to where she and Mai stood, squatted down, and whispered in his ear the syllable of the guard's name while pressing his muzzle against the woman's leg. She then sent him off on another command while she casually walked thirty feet away from the guard. When he returned, she gave him another command.

"Culum, fetch Mai." He looked at her, eyebrows peaked, tail stirring uncertainly. She repeated the command a couple of times until, just as she was about to give up, he understood and bounced across to where Mai stood. There he stopped. Fetching horses or sheep was easy, but this Mai had no reins, and one simply did not nip at friendly humans. He started to take her trouser leg in his teeth, only to be put off by her startled step back; finally he just walked around behind her and leaned. With considerable authority. The children were ecstatic.

The following morning brought a light tap at the door soon after what would have been dawn had it not been raining. Dian told the dogs to stay where they were and raised her voice. "Come in."

The door opened to admit one of the household's children, balancing a small tray with a cup and teapot on it. Carefully closing the door, the child, who looked about nine, walked over to place the tray on the table next to Dian's bed, then stood back to address her in careful English.

"Grandmother asked me to tell you that the first ferry will go in three hours, and we will eat breakfast in one hour if you wish to join us."

"Thank you, I would enjoy that. Um, could you remind me of your name? I'm afraid I can't keep track of all the new people I've met."

"My name is Jian."

"Oh, yes, of course. Jian, thank you for bringing me a cup of tea." The child stood there hesitantly as if she had a question on the tip of her tongue. Dian reached over and poured herself some tea. "Is there anything I can do for you, Jian?"

The child was silent for a moment longer, then blurted out, "How did you get those scars?" She pointed to the puckered skin on Dian's shoulder and the thin jagged line that ran down over her ribs, and rather belatedly Dian realized that perhaps she should have covered herself before inviting the child in. She wasn't even sure this person was a girl, after all. She reached casually for her shirt.

"A wild boar." She looked at the expression on the small face, the lips forming an *o*, and burst out laughing. "Sounds exciting, doesn't it? Actually it was stupidity. Most injuries happen because of stupidity. It's true I was chasing a wild pig, but it wasn't the pig itself who did this. He doubled back quickly and my horse dodged and I fell off into a tree. The branches were sharp. I was fifteen, but I should have known better than to chase a pig through the brush. That's what the dogs are for," she said, and gestured at Culum and Tomas. The ruse succeeded in distracting her examiner, whose disappointment at the lack of romance in Dian's story was patent. The curious black eyes studied the dogs, who in turn were watching her (him?) with equal interest. Another question was bubbling up, though this one burst without any nudging from Dian.

"May I touch your dogs?"

"I'm sure they'd love to say hello to you. In fact, would you like to take them downstairs and let them out for a while? Perhaps your grandmother would let you feed them too. She knows what they eat."

Her offer was greeted with great enthusiasm, and the door closed carefully behind the wagging tails.

Dian listened to their noisy progress down the stairs, but she was sure that even Tomas would take care not to knock into a person who weighed less than half what he did. The sounds of children's voices grew at the window and then faded as Jian showed off her—his?—living trophies to various small relatives.

She sat back against her luxurious pillows and laughed ruefully into the empty room. Ladies and gentlemen! She walks, she talks, she reads and writes and drinks from a cup. She even eats with chopsticks! Presenting, for your delight, the Wild Woman from Borneo! Dian sipped her tea with pinkie raised, to the acclaims of imaginary thousands, then went off to take what she suspected would be her last decent bath for a very long time.

Breakfast was, as usual, tea, fruit, and a simple, sustaining rice porridge, in marked (and necessary) contrast to the sumptuous evening near-banquets. After she had finished, she took her leave of Teacher Jung and found herself touched to damp eyes when the old woman kissed her as a daughter. Then, feeling faintly ridiculous, she went to find Willa, and although the child was more interested in her breakfast than saying good-bye to her rescuer, Dian picked her up when she came up for air and kissed her sweet-smelling, pleasingly rounding cheeks, then gave her back before her protests could develop.

"She is looking very beautiful," she told the woman who was acting as wet nurse.

"She very big," said the woman. "Very, so very big."

"And getting bigger. Thank you."

"Very big."

Mai came for her and took her on a perfectly terrifying ride on the electrical train that ran, unseen and unsuspected, along the top of the wall. Mai bemoaned the lack of view, but Dian found the sheer walls an arm's length from the windows quite thrilling enough, and when they passed another train going in the opposite direction her heart nearly stopped. The wall fell away at irregular intervals, offering brief lightning flashes of life inside the wall that were more tantalizing than illuminating. Several held nothing more than groups of people, quickly glimpsed before the vision flicked off and the wall was back before her face. Once she glimpsed a concrete canyon strung with what looked like a thousand wash-lines, comforting in its homeliness; her next vision, so brief as to seem hallucinatory, was less reassuring: a courtyard filled with heavily armored vehicles, surmounted by three of the blue and gray dragonfly shapes that could indeed only be helicopters—her sighting along the Road hadn't been imaginary after all.

The dogs, oddly enough, were unfazed at this novel method of travel. Not until the end of the quarter-hour ride did Dian think to wonder if Simon was hidden in one of the other cars, but when she tottered out on uncertain legs he was there, saddled and waiting under a long shed roof on the ferry quay. She ran her hands over his familiar sides, let him snuffle hopefully into her cupped hand, and threw her saddlebags over his back. An official led him off through the wet morning to the livestock hold, after Mai assured her that her possessions were completely safe and guarded, then the two women went up to the snug cabin. There were tables there, with benches, but Dian went over to the rain-swept window, trying not to think how very dreary it was going to be to ride through the stuff. The ferry cast off for its short trip across the Gate, and she looked up in silence at the Remnant of the great bridge overhead, that magnificent reminder of the abilities of a race gone by, the patchy orange towers balancing what remained of the cables and roadway—and then Dian's eyes narrowed.

"Do I see people working on it?"

"Yes, didn't you know? Three years ago the Council decided to repair it. We should have it open in another ten years or so." Her pride and her love for the bridge was apparent in her voice and eyes. "And look, this will also be new since you were here."

Mai pointed across the cabin to the eastern side. "We are making a shrine out of the Rock." The island's ugly concrete Remnants were gone; in their place lay a wide, flat stone platform centered in a green park, with a huge shapeless framework of beams and posts woven on top. "The workers are nearly ready to start covering the frame," Mai told her. "It will be a Buddha, one hundred feet tall and covered in gold leaf. We've been collecting jewelry for twenty years!" she told Dian happily.

Dian pictured the impact of sailing in from the ocean, beneath the restored bridge, an immense golden Buddha in front and the austere walls of the city rising on the side. "It will be magnificent," she agreed, and felt more of a barbarian than ever. Ah, well, perhaps Willa would drink in some culture during the next few weeks.

"Would you like to show me the route you propose to take?" Mai asked. A neatly folded map had appeared on the table, as an offer rather than a demand for information. Dian did not hesitate to join her to pore over it.

She traced her finger along the dotted line that indicated where the highway Remnant ran, noticing two bridges that her own map said were still standing but on this map were marked as down. She sighed, thinking of the additional scrambling and backtracking ahead. Mai leaned intently over her finger, giving bits of information such as, "That village is best avoided," and, "The schoolteacher in this town is very helpful." When they had finished, Dian folded the map and made to hand it back, but Mai shook her head.

"It's yours, if it is helpful."

"Thank you."

"I remember your mother," Mai said unexpectedly.

"Do you? When did you meet her?"

"Nine, or was it ten years ago? I believe it was her last trip here. She was a fine woman."

"She was."

"She would not be happy at your venturing north."

"You think not? She was happy enough to take first Judith and then me to Meijing, and that ninety miles is by all reports more hazardous than the two hundred ahead of me."

Mai studied her, and smiled. "You're probably right. Too, she would not have encouraged timidity in her daughters. But still—you must promise me that you will go no farther into Oregon than your friend's small village."

"I intend to turn right around and come back."

"Good. There is . . . ugliness to the north."

"Ashtown? Some people were talking about it."

"And their allies. You do not want to be within their grasp."

"I promise, I have no intention of sightseeing beyond Isaac's village."

They were nearing the dock on the other side when Mai reached for her bag, drew out two small parcels, and handed the first one to Dian. "Grandmother asked me to give this to you." Dian curiously unwrapped the parcel and held up a folded sheet of slick, thin, clothlike stuff. Her bewilderment must have showed as she thanked Mai, because the woman picked it out of her hands to shake it out and drop it over Dian's head.

"It's a rain poncho, from a waterproof cloth called nylon we've just started making. It seems to work very well, though we're not sure how many years it will last before the waterproofing wears off. At least three, anyway. It's both lighter and more dependable than the waxed cloth you wear."

"And to think I was just dreading riding in this drizzle. Thank Jung Xiansheng for me, would you please?" She examined the odd cloth closely, then looked up to see Mai holding out the other package.

"And this is from me. I thought you might find it useful." She watched Dian unfold an unadorned pale brown shirt, as lightweight as the raingear but far more elegant. "It's silk, and I know it feels delicate but it's really very strong, much tougher than cotton. And, it doesn't have any diaper stains on it yet." She cut off Dian's protests with a friendly but firm look. "We cannot have it known that a guest was allowed to leave without the proper equipment, or even a clean shirt, now, can we? Bad for our image."

Dian decided that it was at least partly a joke, so she chuckled. Mai smiled back at her.

"I know you feel you will have to repay us, but please don't. You are family, and families help each other. Perhaps, if you need to repay us, you could consider allowing one of us to come visit your home one day."

"No need to consider, I'd love it. So long as it's you."

"It would be a great privilege to be chosen. I have never been more than twenty miles from here." Mai studied the runnels on the window wistfully. "I would like to see how free people live, before I am given so much responsibility that I am unable to leave."

Mai's remark gave Dian much cause for thought as she joined the boat's exodus on the northern shore, and over the next days as well. On the whole, she eventually decided, given the choice, she'd rather be a barbarian.

Before the end of the first day, Dian had shaken off the remnants of civilization and cultivated farmland to disappear into the unfamiliar hills and woodlands north of Meijing. She soon grew into the dreamlike rhythms of moving through complete wilderness, of going a day, two days without seeing a creature that walked on less than four legs; she rediscovered the sensation of being the head of a corporate animal composed of herself, the large and powerful partner beneath her, and two sets of sensitive, roving eyes and noses around her, which at a gesture transformed themselves into jaws and teeth. She moved beneath the trees and the sky, she went hours, an entire day, without using speech, she forgot the words to Kirsten's songs. One night, awakened by the rip of a cougar's voice, she found herself wondering if the Valley really needed her back.

Whether it was the climate or a particularly bad dose of the epidemics, human beings had become nearly extinct along California's northern coastline. Villages clustered at the edges of what had been mid-size towns, and although the inhabitants were gentle people, probably due to a combination of poor nutrition, ill health, and the depressing squalor of their surroundings, she found herself avoiding them. Cities had become villages, towns were inhabited only by ghosts, and after she saw a green sign with still-visible white letters saying **Welcome to Ukiah, pop. 15,297** being used as the roof of a communal henhouse surrounded by a group of a dozen tin shacks in the middle of a log palisade, she left the road entirely and took to the hills.

The first snow met her in Crescent City, and on a

whim she stopped at an inn that reminded her of
Jamilla's, neat and unpretentious. A barely legible
sign was hung carefully beside the door, the original
bed-and-breakfast sign, with the subscript: *est. 1987.*

She stayed an indulgent two nights there, getting
clean, eating absurd quantities of food, sleeping, and
on the second afternoon walking down to the smithy
and spending an enjoyable couple of hours there gos-
siping while Simon was being shod. When she left
town in the morning the ground was white, and the
dogs bit at the snow happily and Simon snorted and
blew. They rode north awhile, crossed the river, and
turned inland, making for the hills. She figured that,
riding cautiously, they would come to Miriam's village in four, maybe five days.

She was wrong.

BOOK THREE

ASHTOWN

... SO VIOLENTLY THAT SHE WAS FORCED TO DROP

ONE KNEE TO THE GROUND.

EIGHTEEN

THE ATTACK CAME WITHOUT WARNING. EVEN THE dogs were caught unawares, and Dian's growing sense of unease she had put to the threat in the sky. As the afternoon's first flakes began to fall, her mind was preoccupied with the question of where to hole up in strange terrain, and her eyes had been studying the cliff that rose from the frozen stream she was following, in hopes of seeing an overhang or cave. So it was that the silent arrow flew against the wind into their midst. An instant too late, a blinding alarm shrieked out in Dian's head and she threw herself to one side, so the arrow that was aimed at her belly sank instead deep into the side of her upper thigh. The combined zip of the passing arrow beside his nose and Dian's sharp move on his back startled the placid Simon into a shy, tumbling Dian headfirst and uncontrolled out of the saddle. The last thing she knew was a brief blur of dogs, Culum and Tomas launching themselves downwind with the roar of battle beginning to break from their chests; then the rocks rose up to meet her, and she knew no more.

She came back slowly, reluctantly, perhaps an hour later. Her first dim awareness was, ironically, one of comfort, of being warmed and protected from the elements. Gradually some less pleasant sensations intruded. The rock jabbing her left cheek brought her up closer to consciousness; as she began to stir, she became aware of the deep ache in all the parts of her that were not so warm, parts that were in fact deadly cold. Her eyes fluttered open and gazed in dull incomprehension at the tawny field that dominated her vision. Her eyes had no inclination to focus, but as she lay thinking muzzily about what her current state might mean, she eventually decided that what she was seeing was fur, light-brown fur dusted with flakes of snow. She lay with that fact for nearly a minute, incurious, before her sluggish brain dredged up a degree of awareness. This was Culum's neck. It was Culum nestled into her belly. There was also warmth and motion coming from her back. Something told her the warmth was unlikely to be Isaac. Tomas? Yes, Tomas was lying against her spine, his deep chest filling rhythmically with air and pressing regularly into the middle of her back. She thought of this, and a trickle of uneasiness entered her heart, a sense of wrongness that went beyond her lying on a cold, hard surface. Tomas's breath against her back. Culum's neck in front of her. Culum's still neck.

Realization exploded in her mind. The horror, the impossibility of Culum's stillness drove her to stand and look, to prove herself wrong, to pummel him back into breath and warmth, but at the first whisper of movement her thigh came awake. The breath was driven from her lungs, and her throat emitted, not the shriek that reverberated within her, but a queer breathy moan, oddly like the sounds Judith had made in the final stages of her labor. She lay very still, trembling, and the arrow in her leg grew and burned there until it felt like a firebrand being ground into her flesh. The pain pounded in her ears, made her dizzy, and then well-meaning Tomas stirred from his place along her spine and stood up. That added jostle pushed her over the edge, and she blacked out again.

This time she emerged more quickly and aware of where she was. The cold was penetrating, now that Tomas was gone from her back, although she could feel his nose and breath on the nape of her neck. Keeping her muscles absolutely lax, the arrow's burn was manageable, and she forced herself to think. The temptation to sleep was immense. Particularly when, after a few minutes, she knew what she would have to do in order to leave this place.

There was no shelter here. Therefore, she had to get on the horse. To get on the horse, the arrow would have to come out, or the moving point was going to mangle her until she either bled to death or would never walk normally again. If it was barbed—and by the looks of it, it would be—there were two ways to remove the thing. One was surgical, to slice her own flesh open with her knife, dig out the arrowhead, and bind the terrible wound—without passing out forever. The other was to treat it like a fishhook (and for a moment Ling was there, the black cap of her hair gleaming in the summer sun as she bent over the hook embedded in the web between Susanna's thumb and forefinger, Ling's voice in the mutter of the iced-in stream, saying, "Better an inch of clean cut than half an inch of carnage"). An exquisitely cautious exploration with her fingertips told her that the arrow was buried in the strong muscle along the back of the upper thigh, having caught her just as she threw herself sideways. It had missed major blood vessels and skimmed past the bone, but it felt to her well and truly sunk in. On the other hand, it was aimed at the back of her thigh, not toward bone or artery. No choice, then—but, oh, God, she wished Ling were here.

She pulled the heavy, razor-sharp hunting knife from its sheath with frigid fingers. Trying to jostle the shaft as little as possible, she set her thumb and the knife blade on opposite sides of the wood and squeezed. Her arm shook with the effort, but the sharp steel cut its way through the hard wood until it was nearly at her thumb. She slid the knife back in its sheath and reached down to break off the arrow, a small twinge that made her body go rigid from toe to scalp. Sweating freely now and panting with apprehension, she held out her arm until the callused palm was just brushing the splintered break, then lay completely motionless for a time, trying to brace herself against what was to come. Suddenly, with a cry and a sharp spasm, her hand slapped down flat against the front of her thigh, driving the vicious barb out of the back of her thigh. Thin, keening moans filled the creekbed, joined by the whines of Tomas. After another minute her shaking fingers crept around the bloody trouser leg until they encountered the protruding steel, and with exquisite care explored the object as if it might just fall out on its own. It did not. With a sob of anticipation, Dian arched her back, wrapped her hand around the shaft, and jerked. Blood flowed thickly from both ends of the arrow's path, and Dian leaned forward and vomited onto the ground in back of Culum's head.

For several minutes she could only lie there, sobbing freely. When the first insult of pain had retreated a fraction, she whispered into Culum's back, "Tomas." His cold, worried nose removed itself from her neck, and she knew he would be watching her alertly, craving the reassurance of a command, any command. She cleared her throat. "Tomas, fetch the horse." No movement came from behind her. She prayed silently and gave the command again, trying to summon a firm, clear voice as if this were only a training session, with all the time in the world. "Tomas, fetch the horse."

He stood up. She heard his claws dig into the hard-frozen sand as he stretched luxuriously. He moved around into her view, sniffed once at Culum's dead ear, and wagged his long tail, looking down at her expectantly.

"Yes, you're a good dog, but I'm going to bleed to death here, boy. Tomas. Fetch the fucking horse!" She had to get her leg bound up, and the cloth she wanted was in her saddlebag. If he wouldn't bring it, she would have to remove her coat and sweater to get at her shirt.

She closed her eyes and snapped at him through gritted teeth. "Damn it, Tomas: fetch the horse!" And to her vast relief she heard him move away. She raised her head, and sure enough, he was trotting over to where Simon was trying to graze. The young dog seized the dangling reins between his teeth and backed up with them, tugging the horse along. Simon was amenable to the familiar exercise, and in a very short time Tomas stood before her proudly, tail wagging.

"Yes, you are a good and clever dog, Tomas, and if we're very lucky we may get me out of here alive." She reached for the reins and looped them around her wrist, for the smell of her blood would make even Simon nervous and Dian knew that Tomas would never catch him if he actually bolted. The saddle looked a long, long way up from where she lay.

She made it upright as far as the saddlebags, where she found a bandage to bind around her thigh, then loosed the sleeping roll and tossed it over Simon's neck. She was then faced with the obstacle of actually getting up onto the horse. She was half-tempted to take off the saddle completely, both for the ease of getting onto the smooth back and because a small

voice told her that it would be easier on the animal if
he were not burdened with the saddle after his rider
had fallen off and died. On the other hand, once up
she could tie herself to the saddle, and that might give
her a greater chance of finding help. Besides, the effort
of going around and uncinching the girth was just too
much. So, standing on the wrong side and scrabbling
to hook her good left leg over the horse's back, biting
back curses and cries of pain so the already agitated
creature didn't bolt entirely, she somehow made it
into the saddle and lay her swimming head against Simon's neck so she didn't faint again.

When the blackness had retreated, she took out her
knife and hooked its point into the fabric of the precious sleeping bag, slitting the bag straight across the
bottom and halfway up one side. Down cascaded
across Simon's shoulders and onto the creek bank to
mingle with the snow, but the chambered construction of the bag would keep most of the feathers in.
She worked the resulting tube over her head and
draped it across the top of her legs. The cold embrace
of the storm retreated a step, and she blessed Susanna
and the child's mother and aunt from the depths of
her heart.

It took her a few more minutes to bind herself onto
the saddle, hands clumsy with cold. By the time she
had caught up the reins, cursing with the effort of
leaning forward against Simon's neck, there was a
small red icicle hanging from the corner of her stirrup, and the light was beginning to leave the sky. She
could see Culum, though, all too clearly. In death, his
huge body looked almost small, a limp pile of fur with
an arrow sticking from its broad and noble chest.

"Thank you, my friend," she whispered. "Go with
God. I will come back and bury you if I can."

She turned upstream again. There was no point in
turning back—the nearest friendly people were two

days behind her, and she had seen no likely places to take refuge along the way. In the unknown ahead of her there could be help, or at least an abandoned shell of a house. Her attacker, slumped in a heap with a broken neck, was obviously not from the area, judging by the amount of equipment her horses carried. She only hoped that the woman had been alone, and that the next face she saw asked questions before shooting.

Within the hour Dian knew vaguely that she had made a mistake, but by that time she was in no shape to do anything about it. Once darkness fell there was no way to see shelter unless she fell headlong into it, which was not likely with Simon and Tomas in charge. I should have taught him to fetch a house, thought Dian idiotically, and after that lost track of the world. There passed a time of darkness with great soft pieces of snow slapping against her face, and occasionally branches, and twice she would have been swept off but for being tied. Once she saw Tomas, or rather his outline, white and frosted against a piece of dark ground, and once a pale owl, startled from a low branch. Hours later she had a lucid patch and became aware that the stream had disappeared, that they were climbing now, through trees. Oddly, it seemed that Tomas was nipping at the heels of the tired horse, driving it up the hill. Dian knew then that she had to be dreaming, and laughed weakly. "You're not a herding breed," she told Tomas mildly, and fell back onto Simon's neck.

It was pitch black and still snowing when Dian woke to realize that they were standing still. Tomas was barking, for some reason, though it didn't sound like his fighting bark, which confused her. It confused her even more when there came a sudden shaft of light from out of the darkness. Tomas went quiet. Something touched her knee, a pair of hands swam

CALIFÍA, DRESSED AS A WOMAN IN THE

VERY BEST OF EXOTIC RAIMENT...

NINETEEN

THE ARROW CAME ON THE SEVENTEENTH OF NOVEMBER. For the next six days, Dian lay in the grip of blood loss and fever. Looking back, she could never decide whether she remembered the period as a myriad of tiny days or as one endless one, for she had no clear time reference in which to lodge her memories. Those memories were many and elemental: light and warmth and comfort and pain and fear. The strong hands and placid, ugly face of her rescuer—whom she slowly grew to recognize as a stranger, and a woman, not Isaac—were a constant presence, although for one period they were inexplicably absent. The renewed terror and loneliness and pain of Culum's loss overwhelmed her, but at last the half-familiar hands and the warm, bittersweet drink returned, accompanied by a voice that told her over and over that Culum was safe now, safe and cleanly buried and sleeping content in the knowledge that she was well, and Dian allowed herself to be soothed, even though she knew he was not safely underground, knew that he would never be, for she had abandoned his bones on the banks of the stream.

It was the dreams she remembered most clearly, after her mind had cleared. The visions of Culum's

beloved and traitorously abandoned body torn by
crows and coyotes haunted her and made her rage, until Tomas and the strong hands returned to calm her.
Faces came and spoke to her, though she could hear
no words. Isaac came—the real Isaac, not this caring
stranger, and Miriam, and Peter, and Carmen came to
unsaddle her horse and Teddy sang her a voiceless
song. She waited for Kirsten and Judith, but they remained hidden, until she wondered if she had angered
them. She called to them, begged them to forgive her,
for leaving Culum and for destroying the beautiful
sleeping bag, but they stayed away until the seventh
night, the night the fever reached its climax.

Kirsten and Judith came together, sitting on the veranda in the warm sun of a summer's afternoon. They
both looked young and happy and smiled at her with
love, although something about them made her feel
uneasy. She started to tell them how glad she was to
see them, but Kirsten raised her hand to stop her.
Kirsten started speaking, and to Dian's relief, this was
one voice she could hear.

"When I was young," Kirsten began, and smiled
again. "When I was young, there was no death in the
world. Nobody I knew had died. I did not know that
anybody could lose a child." She stopped, and she and
Judith sat beside each other, gazing calmly at Dian,
who knew then what was wrong: there was no baby
in Judith's arms. She cried out, but the old woman
again held up her hand, and continued. "Death came
when I grew older, when I grew old enough to begin to
understand what it took to make a life." Her eyes
grew sad, and her face began to fade. "Some of us who
are given great pain are given the ability to know
great joy as well." She looked intently at Dian, then
the vision faded completely, leaving only an echo:
"Take care of yourself, child. We need you here."

They were gone, and Dian dropped into the first true sleep she had had in many days.

Late the next morning Dian's nose woke her. Her body lay on its side, limp as an old dishrag, but when her eyes opened, they joined her nose in rejoicing at life, even though what dominated her vision was completely unidentifiable. The object before her looked like the wool duster Judith used, a brown fluff on a stick, except that this one seemed to be rattling. Dian regarded it blankly for a couple of minutes and had just become aware of a faint trickle of puzzlement when the brown fluff rose and turned to look at her. A cat, of a most unusual shading, light body and black boots and eyes almost as blue as her own. And it was indeed rattling, for the noise it made could hardly be called a purr.

Feeling reassured that neither the universe nor her sanity had changed too drastically, Dian looked beyond the odd cat into the room. Although she had been there for some days, this was the first time she had seen her surroundings with lucid eyes. After studying the room for a few minutes, however, she wondered if she was indeed fully lucid. The room...sparkled. Not that it glittered—far from it, the furnishings were simplicity itself. There were chairs with cushions, a low wooden table, a brown and gray rug on the floorboards, a fireplace with carved mantelpiece, curtains on the windows, and a black pot near the fire from which came the marvelous smells that had awakened her. None of this was the least bit showy or out of the ordinary. The room sparkled because of the perfection of each object, how it was placed in relationship to the others, the way the colors blended to form a whole. She drank it in for several minutes, this woman who rarely noticed the ropes of cobwebs and mismatched oddments of furniture in her own house, and then closed her eyes. She must still be feverish, she thought.

The next time she was awakened by her ears. A rustle and thump came from behind the door. When it opened, Tomas bounded into the room, pausing to shake a small snow drift from his fur before he crossed the rest of the room in one great leap that sent the cat flying for high ground. He thrust his big head gently into Dian's chest, and when she started rubbing his ears he shut his eyes and crooned with pleasure. It took several minutes to relieve him of the most urgent messages of greeting, but when she weakly gestured for him to lie down, he flopped down on the floor next to her bed and sighed gustily with pleasure.

Dian's rescuer had come in behind the dog, dressed for the outdoors in jacket and gloves, a pistol on her hip, and her arms filled with a variety of leather pouches, reed baskets, and unglazed pots. She leaned against the door to shut it, her eyes lighting up when she saw her patient's response to the dog. She turned to unload her burden carefully on the table, talking over her shoulder in that husky voice that had soothed Dian's dreams.

"It's good to see you awake. I thought you might be joining us today." Her arms free, she unfastened her deerskin jacket and the belt of her holster and hung both near the door, took off her gloves, and paused beside Dian's bed to rest a cool hand on her patient's forehead. "I'd like you to have something to eat, then later on I'll help you get clean and clothed. All right?"

Dian nodded, distracted by the intoxicating smells. The woman went over to the fireplace and pulled the pot from its hook, which loosed billows of fragrant steam into the room and set Dian to swallowing, although whether from residual queasiness or hunger she could not have said. The woman spooned some of the pot's contents into a small bowl and picked a spoon out of a drawer under the table. At Dian's bed-side she hesitated, put bowl and spoon on the wooden stool previously occupied by the cat, and went through another door, which Dian had not noticed. Returning with an armful of pillows and quilts in au-tumnal colors, she inserted them behind Dian's shoulders and head. When she was satisfied with the angle, she took up the bowl, sat on the stool, and be-gan to feed Dian.

The first mouthful confirmed Dian's suspicions that she was still feverish. It looked like gray gruel, but it hit the tongue like a taste of paradise and set-tled her stomach instantly; Dian thought that she could eat it forever. She had no idea what it was, other than something with the texture of mealy porridge, but the exquisite salty–sweet flavors filled her with well-being, and she felt like a charged battery, tin-gling with energy down to her toes. It was the most completely nourishing food she had ever tasted, and even as the woman was removing the supports from her head, Dian slipped into a sound, dreamless sleep. And woke an hour later with two questions pressed against the front of her mind: Who was the woman, and did she have a toilet?

When Dian's eyes came open this time, the cat was gone and the woman was sitting in front of the fire, sewing together the bottom of Dian's eviscerated sleeping bag, strong fingers working the needle with ease and precision. Looking at her, remembering her first sight of those hands by lamplight, Dian could not imagine why she had mistaken her rescuer for Isaac. Granted, this was not a pretty woman, although her smooth skin was a beautiful coppery brown and her eyes were dark and compelling. Her body was too thick and muscular to be considered graceful, her face disfigured by a long scar that ran from forehead to

chin, narrowly missing her left eye. Dian later found
that it had been left there by an enraged mother bear,
many years before.

In spite of her outer ugliness, the woman was possessed of an air of self-assuredness, of quiet strength
and balance. She sat there like Kirsten, or like Ling after one of her meditations, in the hold of a serene cen-
teredness. Dian wondered if her fever was rising
again.

Then the woman looked up from her work, and her
eyes crinkled a welcome. She pushed the bag off her
lap, picked up a cup that waited on the hearth, and anticipated Dian's questions, both of them.

"You probably want to know who I am. My name
is Robin." She came to sit next to Dian, holding her
patient's shoulders up so she could drink from the
warm cup. Again, that wash of marvelously right flavors. Did fever affect the taste buds, or was it just that
she hadn't eaten in so long? When the cup was empty,
Robin put it on the small table.

"I'm sure you'll need a toilet fairly soon. I could
bring you the pan, or if you feel up to it I'll take you to
the toilet. Do you think you could manage a bath?"

Dian became immediately aware of how very dirty
she felt, despite the numerous sponge baths she
vaguely remembered over the past days.

"I must be getting better," she told Robin with an
attempt at humor. "I feel filthy." She started to sit up,
and stopped abruptly as the pain shot up and down
her leg.

"Don't you dare break open that hole of yours. I'm
nearly out of things I can use for bandages." The
woman pulled the covers back from Dian's body,
which, the invalid noticed for the first time, was covered only in a long, soft, sleeveless shirt. With care
and apparently no effort, Robin lifted her from the bed
and carried her through the cabin, past a closed door-

way, and into a small bathroom. "Relax your leg muscles completely," she ordered, lowering Dian onto the ancient, cracked, but apparently still functional porcelain throne. "Don't try to get up. I'll be back in a few minutes."

She reappeared through the doorway a discreet minute later with two large pails of steaming water, which she emptied into a large, half-filled tub in the corner of the tiled room. She went out and returned with two more steaming containers, emptying them, too, into the standing water. When she was satisfied with the temperature, she turned to Dian.

"Ready?"

She lifted Dian, steadied her, and helped pull the shirt over her patient's head. Looking down, Dian was shocked at the state of her body. Her right leg was swollen and discolored from hip to knee, an ugly purple-green with the remnants of dispersing blood. The entrance wound was red and angry, and trails of blood seeped down her leg when the bandages were eased away. Her hip bones jutted out under the pale skin like those of an ancient cow, and an assortment of half-healed scrapes and bruises on her arms and, her fingers told her, her scalp and face showed where she had fallen.

"Mother of God," she muttered.

"It's actually looking a lot better." Robin's eyes crinkled again at Dian's snort of disgust, then she added seriously, "The fever's gone, but the infection isn't. I want you to get in this bath and soak. It'll hurt, and it'll bleed, but we've got to get the poison out." She watched Dian for a moment to make sure her patient's good leg could hold her, then went over to a shelf that held the baskets and pouches she'd carried in that morning. She took a handful from two and a smaller amount from a third and piled the various leaves and twigs into a square of white cloth. She hesitated, bent to look more closely at the oozing wound on Dian's leg, then added two or three other bits before tying the cloth up and dropping it into the water. The air was instantly filled with the heady fragrance of a wooded stream. She turned back to Dian. "Now, for you."

The tub was long enough for Dian's leg to remain relatively straight, but the process was still torture. Robin kept coming in with yet more hot water, until Dian felt near to passing out, but then her torturer returned with a cup of hot, sweet liquid with a familiar bitter undertaste, and the dizziness retreated.

She soaked until her fingers puckered, and Robin washed her body and hair and finally lifted her out onto a towel. Dian could barely stand, leaning against Robin's vastly reassuring shoulder with passive tears leaking from her eyes. She did not notice the clean sheets on the bed, barely felt the gentle hands that wound a fresh dressing around her upper leg. When Robin had finished and pulled the blankets up around Dian's shoulders, Dian was already asleep.

Twelve hours later, when the watery morning sunlight slanted through the cabin windows, they did it all over again. And twelve hours later, with darkness long fallen, again. This time Dian lay for a moment, looking ruefully up at her rescuer.

"You were probably looking forward to a nice peaceful winter, and here you are using all your firewood to heat water and watching your supply of food go down my throat."

Robin gave Dian her eye-wrinkling smile. "There is all the time in the world for peace and quiet. And there are more deer than anyone knows what to do with in this part of the world; provisions are no problem."

"Well, just be sure you don't starve to feed Cul—to feed Tomas. He can hunt for himself, although it's a good idea if you take the meat off the bones for him."

"I've been doing that. Although it took me a while to figure out why he'd bring me rabbits and just stare at them, salivating furiously. I think your dog considers me a slow learner." Then the wide face grew serious, and Robin rested a hand on Dian's shoulder. "I buried them, you know. Your other dog and the woman. I didn't want to leave you alone, but your mind was so troubled, you couldn't sleep, so I rode back along your tracks and found them. I dug two holes, one for each of them, well away from each other, far above the water line, and brought the woman's two horses back here. Your dog is safe now."

Dian closed her eyes and felt more weak tears, these of mourning, dribble down her temples into her hair. "Thank you," she whispered. "Thank you." She turned on her side, and the tears came more freely, and she sobbed quietly. Robin's hand continued to smooth the damp hair from her face until Dian twitched and passed into sleep.

Robin studied the face of this unforeseen guest, a threat in so many ways, then with a sigh stood up and went to finish the day's long-delayed chores in the greenhouse.

ROBIN

Cat was quite the best conversational companion Robin had ever found. She listened attentively, rarely interrupted unless it was with some essential comment on the weather or the presence of some small mammal, and seemed as willing to listen to silence as to words. Even when her eyes drifted shut in the midst of one of Robin's monologues, she was polite enough to appear attentive.

She did not, however, much care for the presence of a large dog in her domain and had taken to spending her days in the greenhouse. Robin, in recognition of the hardship this extra human in their lives was creating, stoked the small wood-burning stove just a bit higher by way of compensation. Cat was now settled contentedly on the shelf above it, prepared to carry out her half of their conversation.

"Yes, I know," Robin said, "the dog's a pain in the ass. You'd probably move out if I got one permanently, but I have to warn you, I'm thinking of it. Just thinking, so don't worry yet. What do you make of the woman?" Cat yawned, and Robin took up the tiny paintbrush and went to see if there were any tomato blossoms that needed fertilizing.

The greenhouse was well worth the mountain of firewood it ate up over the winter. It not only made for a start on the growing season come spring but, with some imagination, provided a year-round supply of fresh vegetables. Robin had discovered it five years before and spent an entire summer dismantling it and transporting its awkward triple-layer plastic panes across fifteen miles of countryside, then spent another three months rebuilding it against one side of the cabin. The small cast-iron stove that burned day and night had come from another abandoned homestead, and Robin had needed two weeks dragging it on a sledge (and nearly breaking a leg in the process) to bring it here. But those January salads made every step, blister, and limp worthwhile.

"Aside from the dog, I mean," Robin resumed, head-deep with a lamp among the tomato vines, "what do you think about her? Should I be working harder to get her out of here? She really is alone—she can't have been lying about that, not as sick as she was, and I did bury her dog. And she says no one's coming to look for her, but still. Should I bundle her up and take her somewhere? She says she's headed for that village up past the sinkhole, the one where Syl lives. You remember Syl." Cat kept an eye on the twitching vines but said nothing. "Of course you do, she brought you those fish. And, yeah, I know, Syl never said anything, so why should Dian? Still, I don't like having her here. I mean, I do like having *her*, but having anyone here, it's not safe. But, hell, it'll be a while before she's fit to travel anyway—I'm not about to kill her by strapping her onto a horse. Although that would take care of the problem, true. Cat, I really wish you were more help here."

But Cat said nothing, and Robin was left to work it out alone.

HENCE, ALTHOUGH SHE HAD NEVER BEFORE BEEN

CONQUERED BY ANY GREAT FORCE OF ARMS... SHE

WAS AS SOFTENED AND WEAKENED BY THE VISION...

AS IF SHE HAD RUN A GAUNTLET OF IRON MALLETS.

TWENTY

THE FOLLOWING DAYS WERE A ROUND OF EATING AND
sleeping, Dian's strength seeping back with each cup
of broth and bowl of food. She ached all over, was
brushed by odd moments of queasiness or shivers,
and had less strength than a newborn, but three days
after the fever had broken, she sat in the chair in front
of the fire for nearly an hour before Robin had to help
her slump into her bed.

On the morning of the fifth day she woke to an urgent desire to be outside. Soothing and harmonious
the cabin might be, but she had not seen the sky except through glass for nearly two weeks and her lungs
thirsted for unheated air.

Robin had fashioned a pair of crutches to help take
the strain off the torn muscles, and after breakfast
Dian fit them under her arms and hobbled awkwardly
out through the mudroom door and onto a wide,
roofed-over porch. Robin made no attempt to help
her, though Dian knew that her progress was being
closely watched. Once safely out, she whistled to let
Tomas know he was welcome to join her now, then
pushed the door shut after him. She leaned on the
armrests, feeling her face go taut against the cold,

drawing in great drafts of the frigid air. The low sun on the side of her face held about as much heat as moonlight, but it was one of those brilliantly clear, biting days that follow a storm, and the ground was gloriously white after the dim warm colors of the cabin. Dian spotted a rough bench next to the door and edged the crutches cautiously over the wet boards to it, lowering herself down with gritted teeth and breathless oaths.

Gradually, one muscle at a time, she relaxed. A minute later the door opened and Robin came out. She dropped a moth-chewed blanket across Dian's knees, then buttoned her jacket (cut large, Dian noticed, to accommodate the gun she wore always) and headed out across the snowy expanse to the barn, with Tomas wading companionably after. Robin's boots squeaked deliciously in the dry powder, her breath rose in clouds, only to be obscured in a greater cloud when she pushed open the barn door and the building exhaled into the morning. She pushed the door closed again, shutting the warmth inside and Tomas out. He continued on to snuffle at the heap of snow that was the woodpile, pawing from time to time at promising areas of scent.

Dian shook out the blanket and wrapped it snugly around her, then let her head rest back against the cabin wall, only her eyes moving. Tomas reappeared with something in his mouth, something fist-size and hard—a fir cone, she saw when he tossed it into the air then plowed through the deepest available drift to pounce on it like a puppy. He had never seen snow this deep before. For that matter, neither had Dian. The hard serenity of it was oddly soothing, seated as she was with a toasty cabin at her back.

Robin's voice rose and fell inside the barn as she talked to the horses. Like Carmen, Dian thought, although the two women did not resemble each other in anything other than equine conversation and the close proximity of their skin color. If anything, Robin persisted in reminding her of Isaac, although for the life of her she couldn't have said why; Robin's posture, maybe, or her attitude of quiet certainty? And their hands. That first night, some similarity in the blunt shape of Robin's fingers had planted in Dian's fevered mind the idea that she was being rescued by her faraway lover. Something of that delusion had clung, attaching a degree of her feelings for Isaac onto Robin. The two might be brother and sister, or maybe cousins. Except that they looked nothing at all alike.

She did wonder why the woman lived out here on her own. Wondered, too, if she might have had relatives in Ashtown.

Dian retreated into the house before the weakness could catch up with her, navigating her crutches with care through the door and settling into the soft chair in front of the fire. She dozed on and off during the rest of the morning, dimly aware of Robin coming back inside, smelling of barn, and of Tomas dropping with a breathy thump onto the hearth rug. Dian extricated her foot and eyed his ribs critically. He'd put on weight since leaving the Valley, all of it muscle, and although she'd thought he was at his full height, he seemed to her a fraction taller. Not yet as big as Culum—but Dian caught herself: not as big as Culum *had been*. Still, Tomas was shaping up to be an impressive dog.

Robin's voice startled her from the kitchen corner. "Is he getting enough to eat?"

"What? Oh, sorry, didn't realize you were there. Oh, yeah, he's fine. In fact, I was just thinking that he's grown, even with the hard work of this last month."

"Do they get much bigger than that?" Robin paused

in the act of laying a bowl on the table, sounding almost apprehensive.

"Couple of inches. You saw his father."

The dog Robin had buried had indeed seemed a great deal of deadweight, but the corpse had been in no condition to measure.

"Do you have very many of these immense creatures?"

"Six—five adults and a litter of pups, with maybe another litter by the time I get back."

"And do they eat a cow a day?"

Dian chuckled. "Just about. We do a lot of hunting—and I have to tell you, I wish we still had your deer problem down there."

"You're welcome to as many as you can herd south. But in the meantime, why don't you come here and help me eat this one?"

After lunch, Dian retreated to her bed and Robin to the greenhouse, but this time Dian's nap was shorter, and she rose, navigated to and from the toilet on her own, and in passing the window saw movement behind the glass. She found the door on the other side of the fireplace and stepped cautiously down into the thick bark that carpeted the glass-house floor. Robin glanced up from a cluster of tiny clay pots, fine-nosed tweezers in one hand, magnifying glass in the other.

"You want me to bring you a chair?"

"No, I'll stand for a minute, thanks. What are you doing?"

"Trying to sprout fern spores. I dabble in useful plants—some ferns have roots that are medicinal, plus I happen to like the look of them. But they're so tiny, it's like planting dust motes."

"I'll try not to sneeze."

Dian looked around in admiration. The greenhouses at home were utilitarian affairs ruled with an outwardly gentle but ultimately iron hand by Glenn.

There, pots were arrayed in regimented lines, weeds banished before they got in the door, and mere flowers given grudging space at the coldest corners. Robin, on the other hand, had arranged this small space as if it were a natural grotto. Lettuce in various colors made a pattern beneath a tree fern, whose trunk in turn was studded with the leaf clusters of epiphytic orchids. Small purple flowers sprang from between bright spinach leaves, and up one wall grew a tower of bean vines with lavender flowers.

"How much wood does this place burn in a winter?"

"Oh, not as much as you'd think. The walls are triple-glazed and heavily caulked, and there's a foot of bark insulating the floor."

Still, Dian noticed, that hadn't exactly answered her question. Then again, she hadn't exactly answered Robin's question about the demands of her dogs for meat either. Fair enough.

"Do you have problems getting the flowering vegetables to ignore the fact that it's winter?"

"Sure. I'd get more out of them if I could light the place, but that's beyond me. Even with the short growing season, each plant begrudges me a few tomatoes or beans before turning up its toes in disgust. Pollination is tricky—I once tried to put a hive of bees in here, but they weren't at all happy. So I just go around with my paintbrush, for those that need it."

"I wish I could help you weed or something."

"You can scrub and chop carrots for dinner, if you need something to do."

"Scullery work I can do, although anything more complicated, you might rather stick to raw vegetables."

"Not much of a cook, huh?"

"You might say that."

"How are you at making snares?"

"Snares? Like in rabbits?"

"Like in rabbits. I have a great desire for a new fur bedcover."

"I make absolutely first-class snares. Although I can't see me getting out to set them anytime soon."

"You make them, I'll set them."

"You got yourself a deal. I'll even skin them for you."

And so it began. Dian made snares, Robin went out twice a day and brought the bodies back for Dian to skin and clean; they all ate a lot of rabbit, and the square footage of stretched skins in the barn grew.

Still, Dian found the healing excruciatingly slow. Half a dozen times a day she would peer at the soft scar tissue, poke it experimentally and twist her torso around to see the back of her leg, then limp off to ask Robin if there was no way to hurry the process. At first, Robin simply gave her packets of herbs to soak in and hauled unending buckets of hot water to the bathtub, but after a week of this, and after Dian had twice interrupted the task of moving the infinitesimal sprouts of fern spore with the aid of the tweezers, Robin laid the glass down and looked at her.

"Dian, it won't get better any faster with fussing. It was a very bad infection—you're lucky you didn't lose the leg. Why are you so jumpy, anyway? You have months to go and see that village and get home, don't you?"

"Well, yes, but . . ."

"But what?"

"But I shouldn't impose on you any longer. And I'm not even doing any work to help out—if I make any more snares you can go into the snare business, and in another week you'll have enough rabbits to carpet the house."

"Ah. I make that two 'buts.' My answer to the first one is this: Dian, it is rare for me to have someone to talk to besides Cat, and I find, somewhat to my surprise, that I am enjoying it. To the second I say, if you're bored with resting, find something else to do."

"But I'm not good at anything you need! I'm a lousy cook and a worse seamstress. I can't knit. All I can do is outdoor things, and my goddamned leg will barely get me to the barn and back."

"Will it get you to the barn and back?"

"Well, yes."

"Then go say hello to your horse. He's forgotten what you look like." Robin lifted the tweezers and went back to her work. Unexpectedly, the thought of Isaac returned to Dian's mind. What had he said once, about greenhouses? *When I was a child the place I lived in had a big one, a world filled with warm air and luscious plants.*

"Have you ever been to Ashtown?" Dian asked idly, but at the final word the woman across from her dropped the heavy glass into the soft planting medium. With a curse as vulgar as it was unexpected, she bent over with the long tweezers to salvage the infant plants.

Dian took Robin's silence as a hint that it was time for her to leave. As she clumped through the cabin on her crutches and worked to get herself dressed for cold, she considered Robin's reaction. It had, she decided, looked very much like a flinch at the name of Ashtown.

Yet another point of similarity with Isaac.

It turned out that Dian could indeed make it to the barn on crutches. It was a lot smaller than the Valley's huge building, more of a work shed with a stall in the back—one stall and a makeshift pen to hold the three newcomers. Four horses where Robin usually had one made the interior nearly cozy, but the stack of hay overhead looked woefully inadequate to Dian; Robin would have to find a buyer for the dead woman's pair, or else turn them loose to fend for themselves.

Shelves below the hayloft explained Robin's collection of herbs. Dried branches, pots, and a hundred baskets looked like some pretty serious medicinal "dabbling" to Dian. On the other wall Robin had hung the stretched rabbit skins accumulated over recent days, and Dian went to check their condition, one at a time. Some she thought too coarse, or in too patchy a condition, to be used for anything but lining boots, but even without those, Robin would have a fine bedcover. When she had finished looking the skins over, she gave Simon's shaggy sides a thorough brush and did the same for the others, then sat down for a while, gritting her teeth until the protest in her leg had settled down.

When she let herself out of the barn, her eye caught on the chopping block near the snow-shrouded woodpile. The heavier logs and the big ax would be beyond her, but surely kindling... She found the cedar logs, tested the blade of the hatchet, and set about reducing a tree round into a heap of thumb-size sticks. Then came the problem of hauling the kindling to the cabin. The crutches got in the way, and even when she improvised a sling, the weight of it banging her crutch nearly had her down twice and left a trail of cleanly split sticks across the snow, but she refused to leave the fetching to Robin. The third trip over, and the third load lost, she threw the left-hand crutch in the direction of the porch and hobbled the rest of the way on the right one. To her surprise, it was more satisfactory. More painful as well, but the tidy pile of firewood was well worth the price of a few hard twinges.

She wrestled the wood through the door and arranged it in a neatly ostentatious pile near the fire, then collapsed, shaking with exhaustion, onto her bed. She didn't stir until Robin woke her for dinner; neither of them mentioned Ashtown again.

The following day, Dian conceived the idea of running a deer past the cabin porch and picking it off with an arrow. It took three days for her to coax, cajole, bully, and flatter Tomas into rounding up a small herd and flushing it in her direction, by which time her leg was nearly good enough to have done it herself, but when it actually happened, when Tomas got the idea and pounded off in the direction of the creek, the venison was no longer the point. Between them, woman and dog, they did it, and in a manner that, Dian knew, Culum himself could not have done much better.

That venison tasted sweeter than anything Dian had eaten for a long time.

A day or two later, Dian was sitting in front of the fire working her way through a pile of some local bark that Robin said would be best for tanning the rabbit skins. The bark chunks were hard as rocks and had to be shaved down finely with her knife into the basket in her lap—mindless work, conducive to thought, and, as usual, Dian's inner gaze turned south. Baby Will would be smiling now—assuming her dream had been just the fever—charming all. And in Meijing, Dian's white-blond foundling, Willa, would be freed of her extra toes, firmly on the road to a normal life.

And Sonja. Dian was not much of one for prayer, but she hoped Someone was watching over the woman, keeping her from doing too much damage. Laine . . . Yes, she realized, I trust Laine. She irritates the hell out of me, but I know her, and she will make the right decisions. I was right to leave her.

Ah, but Isaac. Even more fervent were her wishes for protection over him. Which was funny, when she thought of it, because he was one of the strongest men she knew, and not only physically. Fragile, perhaps, but with Teddy there to need him, Isaac would stand firm.

She missed him—missed them all—but not as much as she had anticipated. He was too distant, and in sadness, Dian knew that she did not expect him to be there for her again when she returned. As a friend, yes, but possibly nothing more.

Was that why Robin reminded her of Isaac? Dian was not in the least attracted to the woman, but then, Isaac seemed to be shifting in her heart as well, from lover to something less intense. A brother, perhaps, as Robin was sister.

The warmth and the musings and the dull job proved too soporific. The knife slowed, jerked once or twice as she dragged herself back from the edge, then her hands were resting on the soft pile of shavings as she drifted away.

She only half-woke when Robin came in, hung her jacket on its hook, and walked into the kitchen to fix lunch. Watching her movements through sleep-clouded eyes, Dian's thoughts looped back to where they had been before she fell asleep: onto Isaac, onto Robin. Idly, she watched as Robin stretched to the shelf for a pair of mugs, as she took the bowl of greens from the sink, then came over to stir the venison stew; as Robin moved around the cabin, going about actions she performed a dozen times a day, Dian's gaze slowly sharpened, coming awake in a way it had not before. Her eyes locked onto the shape of the woman's shoulder; when Robin stood and turned toward the table, the throat that rose from the open neck of her shirt seemed to travel slowly past Dian's vision. Memory stirred, sensations from the time of fever: the feel of Robin's body, the power behind those lifting arms, the very smell of her when she came inside from a session cutting wood...Dian's breath caught, and she came upright, staring in fascination at the way Robin's spine and hips merged.

Robin turned to set a loaf of bread onto the table and glanced up into Dian's eyes. Time froze for an interminable instant, until Dian tore her gaze away and cast it toward the fire, a fire that was by no means close enough to account for the burn rising in her cheeks. Tomas, on the hearth rug with his head between his paws, cocked one bushy eyebrow at her. Dian sat stiffly and tried to breathe normally, but she heard Robin lay down the bread knife, then walk over to sit on the stool that functioned as a second chair.

"Go on, ask your question." Robin's voice was calm as always, but was that an undertone of humor?

Dian looked up guiltily into Robin's face; she saw apprehension there, but also, yes, a degree of amusement. Dian opened her mouth, couldn't think what to say, and shut it again.

Robin's broad face relaxed into a wry grin. "I can see I don't need to wear my vest indoors anymore," she said, and to Dian's amazement stood up to unbutton the plaid shirt and tug it out of the waistband of her trousers. Beneath it she wore a snugly fitting vest; this she also unbuttoned, removed, and tossed onto the kitchen table. With it went her breasts.

The Robin standing in front of Dian was now, without a doubt, not a she. This Robin was a stocky, smoothly muscled man, who stood scratching his ribs through a thin undershirt. What had once been a husky female voice was now that of a man, frankly laughing and saying, "Ah, Dian, your face is priceless. I really didn't know my sex change was so believable, but I was beginning to wonder." He walked over and flicked the curtains shut across the two windows, then hung the padded vest on a hook between the deerskin jacket and the revolver.

"Jesus Christ!" Dian finally got out. "Why?"

"Why the act? Or why the act with you?" He smiled gently, shaking his head as if she were a disappointingly slow child. "Surely you can't imagine that a sane and healthy man would be allowed to live out by himself in the woods? I do have the occasional visitor, you know, especially during the summer. There's even one or two who know who I really am—one girl in the village you're heading for, in fact. She came across me in the woods without my shirt, stupid of me, and blackmailed me into teaching her everything I know about tracking. But if word got out that I wasn't just a crazy old woman living off by herself, I'd be locked away in some town in no time. I've had that. I would honestly rather be dead." Even through her astonishment, Dian heard the lack of bitterness in Robin's voice and body, simply a matter-of-fact acceptance of the way things unfortunately were.

"But...how could you keep it up all this time? With me here, I mean? How could you stand it? You must have wanted to throw me out into the snow!"

"Well, no. Actually it was kind of fun." He stood up and went back to the table, taking up the knife to slice the bread, paying close attention to the precision of the act. Dian heard surprise and a bit of wistfulness creep into his voice. "I found that I really enjoyed being a friend, being another woman who didn't make you feel uncomfortable when I put you in the bath or brushed your hair. I'm sorry, in a way, that you realized the truth, because now you're going to feel uncomfortable around me."

And he was right. The thought of the routine intimacies he had performed on her body during the illness made Dian feel—uncomfortable was a vast understatement. Appalled, perhaps. Even more so, the realization that she was in a cabin, an isolated cabin, with someone who had been suddenly transformed into a strange man—the thought and her reaction to it confused her, flustered her, so that she plucked the first thing that came to mind and threw it out.

"Did my monthly period come while I was sick?" The thought was intolerable, she did not want to think about it, wanted to snatch back the question.

"No. And it won't for some time either." Again that amusement beneath the calm voice—was he laughing at her discomfort? If so, this person's change of persona was not limited to the merely physical, but he did seem to be enjoying her confusion. She seized desperately onto a discussion—any discussion, to give her mind a chance to settle.

"Because of the injury, you mean, shock and blood loss. I remember the last time I was injured this bad, it took about six weeks for it to come back."

"Oh, I think you'll find it takes somewhat longer this time," he said, his voice muffled from where he was rummaging in the bin under the sink for an onion.

"Do you? How long, then?"

"I'd say about another eight lunar months." His head reappeared, and Dian wondered how she could ever have mistaken those crinkling eyes for a woman's.

"Eight—but why?"

"Because, my dear, you're about seven weeks pregnant."

Stunned as a bird against glass, Dian stared open-mouthed at her companion for so long his amusement faded and began to be replaced by concern.

"It is all right, Dian. Babies are great."

Seven weeks. Mid-October. When she and Isaac—and for a moment, her thoughts froze: Would the child have Asian folds over its eyes? Surely not. Oh, why hadn't she allowed the Meijing doctors to do the physical exams Ling had suggested?

"I'm sterile," she protested numbly.

"I assure you, you are not sterile." He was dead serious now, and starting to look worried.

She did not doubt him, not for a minute. Now that he had told her, her body shouted its agreement. She hadn't thought about her periods, and since the accident she had been too ill to notice the telltale signs of tender breasts and occasional queasiness, but now she could even feel the presence of another human being within her. And that knowledge contradicted everything she was.

She stood up and stumbled to the door, oblivious of the pain in her leg. Then Robin was by her side, supporting her. She would have fallen down the two front steps, one wood, the other raw stone, if he hadn't held on to her with hands that were both welcome and utterly repellent. She pushed away from him and walked out into the knee-deep snow, thinking of Isaac until the bright snow faded in her eyes and she collapsed.

She woke hours later, the cabin lit only by the fretful light of the fire, her bed warm and safe and her leg hurting abominably. She shifted to ease it, and Robin's voice came from nearby.

"If you need something for the pain I'll give it to you, but I'd rather not carry it on too long, because of the baby."

"Pain isn't the only thing I'm going to have to put up with," she said, a bit grimly.

"Is the baby not wanted, then?" he asked, without any trace of criticism.

"It's not that," she said. She shifted again, and winced. "No, it's not that it's unwanted. It's just that, on top of everything else, it was a shock. Not even a bad shock, just a big one. And I'm not really feeling up to any more, please?"

"No more shocks today, no," Robin promised. Silence filled the cabin, broken only by the fire and little huffs and whimpers from Tomas, dreaming by the fire.

"I left home sterile, and I'll return with one baby in my arms and another one in the works." She shook her head. "Lord Almighty, as Kirsten would say."

Robin stood up, smiling to himself a little sadly as he went to assemble dinner. She had taken both pieces of news well. This was a fine woman. If he'd known one like her twenty years ago he might never have moved out here. Not by himself, anyway. He hoped this man Isaac was a worthy partner for her.

If Dian had been told that she would be living in close proximity to a strange man and think nothing of it, she would have laughed in disbelief: she'd known so few adult males in her life—the number she'd lived with could be counted on her fingers—that a new one was not something she could simply overlook. That Robin was a man she did not doubt—she had met a few eunuchs, wandering as Pilgrims or sheltered inside Meijing, and Robin was not one of those. Yet as the days passed, she did indeed simply think less and less about it.

He was, in effect, the brother she had never known. Once she thought of him as such, their relationship fell into place, and she thought no more about it.

She did, after much deliberation, bring up the possibility that he might go back with her to the Valley. His vehemence was all she had expected.

"Absolutely not. I'll miss you when you leave, Dian, and I'm sure your family are all lovely people, but I can't be locked up. It makes me go crazy. Thanks anyway."

"Robin, look, I wouldn't want to leave here either, if I were you. But, please, just think about it—think about three things. One, you wouldn't be locked up. There's a lot of space there, and nobody would force you to come in if you didn't want to. I give you my word. And two, down there, with Meijing's backing, what you call 'dabbling' with herbs could go far. I've heard you grumbling about not being able to tell precisely what this leaf and that mold do—well, our healer would love to give you a microscope and glass dishes and books and anything else you need and let you get on with it. And third, to be realistic, you may be forced to make a move within the next few years anyway. Even if the radiation poisoning or whatever it is doesn't spread into this watershed, Queen Bess will. And you can't count on her missing the fact that you're a man living alone. You'll be inside one of her towns before you can blink."

"Not for long," he said grimly.

"Robin, please, think about it?"

His jaw worked as he stared out at the snow, and then nodded curtly. "I'll think about it. But I'll tell you now, I won't go. As you said, this is my home." It was all she could do, and she let it go.

December wore on, and she began to venture further out into the woods, began to run the nearer trap lines herself, then all of them. The stack of rough-cured skins grew. They ate very well. And she was much taken aback one day when Robin asked how much longer she was thinking of putting off her trip to the village.

"Oh. Well, I don't know, I still don't have much stamina. . . ."

"Nonsense, you've been out for five hours today, and you're barely limping. You have plenty of stamina

for four days on the horse and a couple miles' hike."
He looked more closely at her face. "You don't think
I'm trying to push you out, do you? Hell, I'm not letting you go until I get my rabbit-skin blanket. I just
thought, if you went fairly soon, maybe you could be
back in time for Christmas dinner."

"I AND MY FORCES SHALL TAKE THE
VANGUARD IN THIS BATTLE."

TWENTY-ONE

SO DIAN SET OFF ON THE FINAL MILES OF HER JOURNEY, five weeks late and with her troop diminished by one dog and a load of strength on the part of its leader. Simon was in great shape, and Tomas was ecstatic to be on the road again, but Dian's thigh did not like being in the saddle, and she was not looking forward to the demands of even this short trip. She did not look back at the cabin, since she would feel silly if Robin had already gone back inside, and even sillier if she found him standing on the porch to wave good-bye. She told herself firmly that everything would be fine; she'd be back in less than a week and they would stuff themselves to a stupor with Christmas cheer. And after that she would keep at him until he gave in and decided to give the Valley a try, and they would go south together, and she would be home long before Easter.

On the second day out from Robin's cabin, Dian became aware of a familiar itchy sensation, like the restless onset of a fever but accompanied by vivid images: the slaughtered Smithy village; an arrow flashing at her out of the snow; the back of Culum's lifeless neck. She had never put as much store in what Judith called her "Feelings" as others seemed to, but she did know that when she felt this way, something was wrong somewhere. She kept Tomas upwind of her and watched closely the ground on the other side, but the hours passed and she saw nothing, heard nothing. By noon on the third day, her skin was crawling and she twitched at every small and natural noise, and still nothing had happened.

She found a sheltered grove near a frozen stream and there she unsaddled Simon, feeding him and fastening a blanket over his back. She shared some dried meat with Tomas, broke the ice on the stream so the animals could get at water without too much difficulty, and left Tomas guarding the horse. He whined a protest; she repeated her order and limped briskly away.

Initially, she had intended to hike the last ten miles to the village, wary of the fox-faced Syl's reconnaissance skills. Now, however, she'd be lucky to manage five miles without having her leg seize up on her. She had brought snowshoes but only needed them from time to time when the drifts grew deep. Finally, at three in the afternoon, she caught her first whiff of wood fires, and she stopped to rest, eating handfuls of dried fruit and venison, drinking still-warm tea from the vacuum flask, and rubbing at the burning muscles in her thigh. The minute she stopped moving, the nerviness was back in force, urging her to hurry up, not to bother with doing this from hiding—what did it matter? Just walk up and say hello, let me see your secrets....

But if she was going to do this, she should do it right, raw nerves or no. So she sat and twitched, every sense quivering, until dusk came and she could approach the town without being seen.

Movement was a relief, the distractions of purpose allowing her to push the feelings to one side, where they remained but did not get in the way. She could concentrate on her more immediate senses and finally peel the cover from whatever it was that Miriam and Isaac and the others had not told her.

The first thing she saw was an adolescent boy chopping wood. That would have been troubling enough by itself—Dian winced every time the heavy double-bitted ax flew down toward his fragile boot—but then a woman came out of the nearby house and, instead of taking the dangerous object away from him, she merely gathered up the split logs and went back inside.

Five minutes later, a heavily dressed person carrying a rifle came down the lane toward the wood-chopper. Dian's first reaction was of relief, that one of the village guards would now intervene with a scolding, but the guard merely greeted the boy, exchanged a few words, and went on.

Worse yet, the guard's voice had been far too low to belong to a woman.

And it went downhill from there.

When she'd first laid eyes on these people back in August, Dian's immediate reaction had been how eerily like one of Kirsten's tales they were, riding blithely through the hazards of the countryside with a couple of menfolk. That night in their village, watching and listening, her underlying reaction was precisely the same: who did these people think they were, residents of that safe haven Before, the twentieth century? Sure, boys wanted to flail away at frozen wood with razor-sharp axes and men wanted to be in the front lines with the guns, but how could that be permitted? Axes slipped, enemies shot back. Even small cuts turned septic, and the world Dian knew could not afford to lose even one man through carelessness, not when males died as fast as they did through the myriad diseases of infancy.

Yet here were men, carrying guns and acting as if

the past fifty years had never happened. They even moved differently.

A scant half hour of this, and Dian had to retreat. Taking care to move only where others had trod the snow, she walked out of the village until she came across a rough shed filled with firewood. She was not hungry, but she made herself eat and drink, and when she had put together her thoughts, she returned for a more methodical survey of the village.

It was the dinner hour, and most of the houses were bright, warm beacons in the darkness. Most of them had men in residence, and a high number appeared to have only one wife. Miriam's claim of nearly a third male population was not too much of an exaggeration.

As with the Valley, houses staggered their dinner hours to accommodate the shifts for the night watch. Around seven o'clock, three heavily bundled figures carrying guns came down the road Dian had retreated up. One of them walked up to a house whose family had just finished their meal, knocked and entered, and came out two minutes later without the gun. On the guard's heels came a similarly bundled woman, calling good-byes into the house. She slung the rifle over her bulky shoulder and pulled on a pair of gloves. The day guard continued down the row of houses until she came to one where the windows showed a neatly set table and last-minute preparations in the kitchen.

A few minutes later, the solitary guard was joined by two others, and they went back the way the first three had come. Dian stayed where she was, among the branches of a yew tree, and sure enough, half an hour later the same ritual was repeated with the guards from the other side.

She could not be sure, but of the six guards, three had seemed to be men.

As she prepared to move her position, the door of the house opposite came slowly open, and out stepped a toddler: a boy child. He was lightly dressed and wore only soft leather slippers on his feet, but he clearly had a purpose, for he sat down to negotiate the three steps from the porch and set off down the muddy road.

A girl toddler would have been bad enough, but watching idly as a boy was swallowed by the dark was agony. It was all Dian could do not to go after him, but she really did not want to immerse herself in the lengthy process of making her presence known, especially with the sensations of impending disaster plucking at her skin. She watched the child closely, knowing someone would notice the open door in a moment, knowing the child was not about to wander off into the woods, but scarcely able to breathe while he was out there.

No one came. The open door continued to pour light and warmth into the night, the toddler stumped away down the deserted road, and Dian began to moan with tension. All right, she finally decided; give the kid until the last house before the road bends, and if they haven't spotted him, go after him.

The tiny figure closed in on the bend in the road; the bright happy houses on either side continued their nightly revelries; the house opposite poured its life out unknowing; and at last, one split second before Dian stepped out from the thick branches, she heard an exclamation from the hallway. A girl of about fifteen pulled the door fully open, revealing an entrance hallway with a braided rug and mirror. She peered out, then stepped back in and shouted over her shoulder. Turmoil erupted: women and men spilled into the hallway and out onto the porch, lights shifted through the dark rooms of the house, searching the upstairs rooms. The child was still there, squatting in the road, but in a minute he would not be.

Finally, the adults came out, three of them, pulling on coats and boots, holding lamps and lights, conferring and peering until Dian felt like shouting at them, "He's down there!"

And then a small sound came through the frigid air, and all three whirled in the child's direction. Two of them set off at a run, and Dian dropped her head into her hands, light-headed with relief. She barely heard them return, the child crying now at his cold feet, the adults torn between sympathy and recrimination.

How could they live like that?

And more immediate, how could the Valley risk the consequences of allowing that casual attitude so near? It was hard enough to soothe and distract the Valley's menfolk into safer paths; with this degree of freedom on their very doorstep, how long would it be before young Salvador pressed to join the guards, or twelve-year-old Harry ran away to the woods for a hunting trip? Before Peter refused to go to the caves in an emergency?

No wonder Miriam hadn't told them everything.

And Isaac... That little deception about archery skills was the least of it.

She'd seen enough to know what the problems were. Now she had to decide: were they dangerous enough to require an immediate ban? Or did fairness, and a recognition of the benefits these people would bring, require that she give them an ultimatum?

If she did that, if she stood up now and found Miriam and told her, "We'll let you come to us if you can find a way to keep our menfolk safe from your irresponsible attitudes," what would these people do? Was it even possible to reshape the ingrained habits and attitudes of an entire village?

She didn't think so.

Everyone assumed that someday the viruses would lose their potency and men would slowly return to their previous numbers. Alongside this came the acceptance that menfolk would then take back some of their traditional authority; indeed, nearly every woman Dian knew secretly longed to see an adolescent boy freely testing his limits and wished to live among men who didn't have to watch their every step for the benefit of their community.

Which might explain why this village was a throwback in its social structure: its freakish numbers had not required them to accept the immense changes the rest of the world had been forced to make.

However, Dian did not think that the rest of the world was about to catch up to these numbers anytime soon. And inviting the attitudes of freedom could prove a contagion with disastrous results.

She stood among the dark branches, the cold eating into her bones as she tried to decide what to do: show herself and deny these people the Valley, or consult with Judith first and, if Judith agreed the risk was too great, then get a message to them some way—sending Sonja home would do it nicely.

She might have had an easier time deciding if she hadn't been so preoccupied with the ever-mounting prickly feeling running up and down her spine. It was hard to think rationally. But really, did she absolutely have to do this now? Could she think about it and come back? Talk about it with Robin, maybe?

The more she considered this scenario, the better she liked it. Robin was a man who cut wood and carried a gun, and although she was not entirely comfortable with either of those things and did not completely understand why he needed to be alone, she did trust him enough to be willing to talk this over with him.

As if to force her hand, two women came out of a house, attracted by the commotion of the rescued toddler; one of them was Miriam. The adults called back and forth, the child began to cry in earnest, and they all retreated into their houses. The doors closed, leaving the street deserted and Dian still silently in her place of hiding.

Yes, she seemed to have decided to think about this for a while.

One thing she would do before she left. She took from her pocket an object she had prepared back at Robin's, a carefully split walnut with a note inside, sealed shut and coated with wax, then bound all over with a length of thin wire coated in red plastic, salvage from an old telephone line. She chose a snowdrift she thought likely to last until spring, against one side of a picket fence, and dug down to bind the bright wire to the slat. It would be noticed the instant the snow receded. The note read simply: *Dian was here.*

She dusted the snow back into place and stood back to admire her work. The revelation that the fox-faced Syl had spied on the Valley right under her nose had rankled for weeks. This should pay her back, if Dian decided not to return. And as she turned to pick her way back into the woods behind the houses, she suddenly realized where the tiny woman had picked up her competence in the woods. Syl was "the girl" who had blackmailed Robin into teaching her tracking skills. She smiled, imagining the woman's face when the brightly wired walnut message appeared in the spring.

Once away from fear of detection, however, her boots crunching softly through unbroken snow, Dian's smile faded. The incipient panic played at the ends of her nerves, building and flooding in tenfold; by the time she found Tomas and Simon in their makeshift shelter, she was near to running through the night forest. She also knew that the nameless threat concerned either Robin or Isaac. If Isaac, there was not a thing she could do, but Robin... Without pausing for food or sleep, she stripped off Simon's blanket and threw the saddle over his back, relying on moonlight, memory, and Tomas's senses to keep to the path.

It had taken her two and a half days to reach the village. On the return trip she was forced to lay over when the moon went in, when she realized she was getting lost, but in the gray predawn she was on the path again, unmindful of the threat of other travelers, pushing herself and her animals. They slid over the top of the last ridge just a bit after noon on the second day; Dian smelled it before she could see it.

Smoke lay heavy in the air. Tomas's hackles went up and she had to call him back to her side, where he paced, stiff-legged, a growl rumbling in his chest. She dismounted well back from the clearing, but she need not have worried; the intruders were long gone.

The barn had collapsed, the cabin was a crackling black skeleton; Robin's unburned possessions lay scattered across an expanse of slowly refreezing mud that four days before had been clean snow. Glass shards sparkled in the sunlight; half the greenhouse panes had melted, sagging and dripping back from the great heat of the burning cabin. Broken dishes lay in heaps, a pan lid had lodged in the branches of a huckleberry bush, the beautiful woolen blanket from Robin's bed lay torn and trampled at the base of a tree. And brooding over it all, the blackened stones of the chimney and a few stinking beams that clung precariously together.

She walked forward slowly, but there was no body among the ashes, no smell of burnt flesh to give the remains an even more nauseating undertone. Near the barn she found a manure shovel with a smear of blood on one end and picked it up, sharply gratified to see strange hairs, bright blond in color: Robin had not gone without a fight.

But if they'd surprised him in the barn, why hadn't he had his handgun with him?

Because he'd gotten out of the habit of wearing the thing, her mind answered, *with you here to back him up.* She dropped the shovel as if it had bitten her.

She went over to the giant slab of granite that had been Robin's porch step and found it still warm from the fire. She found something else as well: after she'd been sitting there for a while, she became aware of faint movement and looked down to see Cat, her odd gray-brown fur filthy and scorched in places but relatively uninjured. Dian pulled off her glove and held out her hand, and a minute later the fur brushed against it. Cat crawled into her lap, head buried in Dian's coat, purring desperately. She even stayed there when Tomas came over and nudged her with his nose.

At Dian's feet lay one of Robin's delicate herb baskets, undamaged although its contents had spilled out onto the ground. Turning it over in her hands, she looked up and, halfway between the house and the barn, saw something that made her heart stop in her chest. She put the cat down and walked numbly around the rough circle of exposed earth to stand staring blankly at the charred remains of Robin's books. The murdered authors of a world gone past lay cremated, deliberately piled up and set aflame. She knew the intruders for what they were, and she felt the rage begin. It grew like the growl in Tomas's chest, this revulsion and fury at life's Destroyers. These were not human beings who had been here, though they walked on two feet. These beings were a throwback, the spawn of the creatures who had brought on the

Bad Times, who had killed Kirsten's father and thousands more in their riots, who had poisoned water supplies and burned libraries and set bombs and murdered anyone tainted by a connection with technology and education. Great as her rage was over Robin, her revulsion at the way he had been taken was even greater. She dropped the small basket and sprinted for her horse, consumed by the need for venting her fury.

When her hand was on the pommel, however, she did not mount. A small cold voice spoke through the heat and asked her what she would do if they did not have Robin when she caught up with them. Would she be able to meet them on their own level and exterminate them regardless? Or would she be forced to back off and return here to a very cold trail? Should she even go after him at all? She stood for several minutes leaning against the saddle, willing the voice of reason away, wanting to be gone. In the end, though, cursing herself under her breath, she removed the bridle so Simon could scrape in the snow for grass and went to find a hefty branch to sort through the smoldering remains.

Ninety minutes, a sliced finger, and numerous painful little burns later, Dian was satisfied that Robin's body was indeed not here. With a degree of grim humor she gathered together some of the larger scraps of unburned wood and lit them a second time, setting Robin's largest pan, dented but whole and filled with ash-flecked snow, onto the resulting fire. While the water heated, she scrubbed her face and blackened hands with snow and set off in a wide circle, scouring the hillside for any trace of Robin, any hint that he might have gotten away. There were none. The pan sent a geyser of steam into the air, and Dian poured the boiling water into the thermal jug, threw in a few tea leaves, screwed in Isaac's wooden stopper with care, and stood up. Her eyes went to

Tomas, lying on the warm granite-slab step, Cat tucked fastidiously against his flank. The dog's head was between his paws, and he was watching her intently.

First, Cat. Dian spent a few minutes further collapsing the inner wall of the greenhouse, dragging some branches over to shut it off. It would be cold, but protected. She went back to the slab and stroked the frazzled fur. "Sorry, lady, but you're going to have to fend for yourself. You can get in out of the cold in the greenhouse, and there'll still be plenty of mice near the barn." Dian gathered up what few edible bits of scorched food she could find, then retrieved the sad heap of Robin's blanket and dropped it in front of the dog.

"Tomas, find Robin. Go to Robin."

Dian was surprised at the speed of his response—he seemed almost to have been waiting for just that command. Certainly he did not bother to sniff at the blanket but rose and trotted off in the direction of the footprints, and her heart lifted a bit at this appearance of Culum's lightning intelligence and wisdom in his son. She picked up the blanket, shook it out carefully, and folded it away into her saddlebag. On another whim she included the small basket of herbs. Sentimentality, perhaps, but it was a light enough thing to carry; the blanket, anyway, might come in useful. She bridled the horse, mounted, and followed Tomas down the hill.

Dian had not even stopped to consider the potential consequences of going after Robin. She owed him a life, and to do otherwise was unthinkable. Nor did she reconsider her actions now, merely putting out of her mind—or, at any rate, putting in the back of her mind—the niggling voice that asked, *But you're pregnant now, and walking into danger: do you owe him two lives?* She rode along immersed in what her eyes were seeing, all her attention on the path of trampled snow that stretched before her. There were eleven horses, she decided, five of them being led. Two would be those that belonged to the woman who had killed, and been killed by, Culum; two would probably be the gang's own packhorses. She would assume that the fifth horse they led bore Robin, captive but alive and no doubt as well as they could keep him: Destroyers might burn books, but a healthy man would be a commodity too valuable to risk. That meant six strangers, which matched the footprints at the cabin. They were apparently unconcerned with anyone wanting to follow them, for they were making no attempt to conceal their tracks. Good. Even better was the news that the lead rider left occasional spots of blood in the snow.

Not so good was their goal. Assuming they had taken Robin in order to sell him—and it was unlikely that a roving band of half a dozen women would wish to be burdened with such a valuable and vulnerable, to say nothing of potentially dangerous, individual for very long—the most obvious choices were either Redburg, nearly a week to the south in this weather, or Ashtown, five, maybe six days' reasonable ride from Robin's cabin. Ashtown, whose walls had held Isaac in as a child. Ashtown, the thought of which had caused a seasoned Traveler in Jamilla's cozy parlor to shiver and a Meijing guard to go grim. Ashtown, which lay straight in the direction of the line of hoofprints she was following. Five days away, and by the signs, Robin a day and a half ahead of her. The weather would hold, her skin told her that, and she could ride by moonlight. Her thigh ached already from the demands of the last few days; it would just have to ache.

And if, as her rational mind told her was all too possible, she failed to catch up with them in time?

Two choices then, discounting the third possibility of
simply turning her back on the whole problem and
abandoning him: she could retreat all the way back to
Meijing, borrow enough money to buy him out, and
ride back with that perilous amount of silver calling
out to three hundred miles of countryside, to the clear
possibility of finding him long since suicided and
buried; or she could go in after him. Enter Ashtown,
with its fearsome reputation, and steal him back from
that walled and guarded city.

Neither choice bore thinking about. She would just
have to overtake them, she told herself, and put her
heels mercilessly into Simon's sides. She stopped at
full dark, cleaned the two hares she had encouraged
Tomas to take during the afternoon, and risked a
small fire to cook them. She dozed, wrapped in
Robin's filthy, smoke-thick blanket, then mounted
up again with moonrise. At the dark before dawn she
stopped again, slept for an hour, and dragged herself
from her sleeping bag. After sharing the last of the
cooked meat with Tomas and giving Simon a large
double handful of the spilled grain she had scraped
from Robin's wrecked barn, she pressed on. At midday Simon threw a shoe, and she began to walk occasionally to spell him. The endless day passed, a never
ending, never changing cycle of dark tree and white
ground, skirted rocks and crossed streams, and always
the trail, the mashed-up stretch of hoofprints in the
snow, wider now across a meadow, single file in the
woods, never seeming any fresher, always mocking,
drawing her hypnotically on.

The day trudged toward darkness in increasing
pain and exhaustion, relieved only when she found a
wooden button, half-buried in the snow, that had
been torn from Robin's coat and tossed—deliberately?
by Robin?—to one side. Later, by moonlight, she
found where the party had spent its third night, and

the trail leaped half a day nearer. Both discoveries refreshed her more than the snatched two hours of sleep between impassible dark and moon's light, and she drove on, all three of them limping now, Dian walking as much as she rode.

The following dawn it took her ten minutes to creep from her sleeping bag and knead the worst of the fire from her cramping thigh. Three hours later they passed the fourth campsite, where Tomas caught a raccoon attracted by the scraps. It was old and tough, but it was food, so she stopped briefly to clean it, giving most of the innards to Tomas and stuffing the rest in her pack to eat raw. The snow was deeper now, but the trail was broken already, so tantalizingly fresh she could almost smell her quarry. She would have to kill five armed, well-fed, rested women, but she would do it, and Robin would not be taken in by Ashtown.

At dusk, Simon went lame. She turned him loose in a meadow over which a Remnant house brooded. She hoisted her possessions into a tree and stumbled off, carrying only her rifle, binoculars, food, and sleeping bag. The trail was fresh now. She would make it. She would.

When it was too dark to see the trail, she fell into her sleeping bag next to Tomas, woke reluctantly three hours later, shared out the rest of the cold, raw raccoon, and dropped her trousers to urinate. When she glanced down at the moon-bright snow, her ears suddenly filled with a rushing noise and dizziness threatened to knock her over. She had to strike a light to be certain.

She was bleeding. Not a lot, not yet, but shockingly red and alarmingly steady. She let the handful of dry needles burn out, and after a while her eyes readjusted to the low light.

Bleeding. If she went on, she might well lose this baby.

If she stopped here, she would almost certainly lose Robin.

Dian leaned against the trunk of the tree, staring unseeing at the path of churned snow winding away before her. In the shifting moonlight she could all but see Robin, straight-spined with despair, riding away from her. Eventually, with the movement of an old woman, she reached down for her rifle, and took one step, then another. The being lodged within her was little more than an ounce of organized tissue, whereas Robin...

Robin was real. Robin was family. He had taken her in despite the threat to his life and his freedom; he had saved her life and given Culum burial; he needed her now, not seven months from now. The hypnotic trail pulled her along and she pushed forward, Tomas close by her side as he led her, stumbling and falling, in Robin's wake.

She could smell them. At dawn, she thought she saw them through the trees on the very brow of the opposite hilltop. An hour later, she came upon their final campfire, not yet cold; twenty minutes after that she saw clear signs of where Robin had thrown himself from his horse and tumbled down a steep hill, which cost his captors at least half an hour and cost him, going by the dots on the snow, a bloody nose in retribution. The blood was still red, the horse droppings barely cool, and Dian pushed herself into a shambling run.

She could smell them, see them, could almost hear them across the crisp air. She could do everything, except catch them.

From her vantage point up a tree two miles away, Dian's old binoculars showed her the party approach-

ing the city, eleven horses with seven riders merging
into the market crowd outside the gates. She lost
sight of the bright blond head on the black horse at
their lead, then saw her reappear from behind a pavilion. Dian watched until Robin had disappeared
through the Ashtown gates, swallowed by the city. It
looked very final.

She sat back against the tree, eyes closed, for a long
time, until a faint whine from Tomas below roused
her to descend reluctantly from her perch. Utterly,
bone-achingly weary, she dropped with a jar from the
tree, pulled some fir branches into a rough shelter,
and with Tomas beside her, she slept.

When she woke, as tired as if she had never closed
her eyes, she turned her back on Robin and walked
through the beginnings of a dull snow, curiously
thick flakes that fell against her cheeks like cold spiders, making her way back to the meadow where she
had left Simon, the meadow overlooked by the Remnant of some rich person's vacation house. One side
of the building lay smashed beneath a fallen tree, and
the oak floor of the remainder was buckled into
waves where the rain had entered, but the other wing
seemed secure enough and would at least keep her
dry.

She let Simon into an entrance vestibule with an
ornate fitted stone floor, shut him into these impromptu stables by dragging the remains of a dining
table across the hallway, then took a brief walk
through the rest of the house, watching for signs of
bear or cougar. She found none, only abandonment
and decay. A small closet off one of the musty bedrooms held a store of sheets and mouse-chewed blankets, and she scooped up an armload of the stained
and frayed fabric to soften the warped floor. The
whole time, from when she jumped down from her
vantage tree until she pulled the patched sleeping bag

around her head, she continued to feel the slow,
sticky ooze of blood from her womb.

She lay like a dead thing for fourteen hours, Tomas
at her back for warmth. When she woke, she let him
out into the snow to hunt, took the rabbit he brought
to her into the house's once-grand living room. The
scenic wall of glass, mostly broken now, made it into
a drafty shell with owls and bats in the high roof
beams, but the broad stone fireplace was still functional, and there were plenty of dining room chairs to
cook over. She ate, then slept again. The bleeding
slowed, turned to spotting, and on the third day
stopped entirely. She still had the baby; only time
would tell about Robin.

Tomas continued to act as provider, and one day
she shot a deer that ventured too close to the front
drive. Simon's poor grazing was supplemented by the
sealed jars of oats and wheat that she found in a
pantry off the ornate and useless electric kitchen.
And at night she lay with a small kerosene lamp that
was more decorative than illuminating and read from
the books she found in one of the bedrooms, children's stories for the most part, familiar and comforting. The days passed, fifteen of them, each one
returning to her a degree of strength, if not enthusiasm. And each day saw the same cycle of inner dia-
logue.

I have to do this.

No, you don't. You're pregnant, that changes everything.

I owe him my life. And Culum's burial.

You don't owe him your child's life. Isaac's child's life.

Robin will die, in Ashtown.

Robin's a survivor.

Not of this.

That's his choice, then. You didn't put him in this

position, and just shut up about his not wearing the handgun, that's not your fault.

I can't leave him.

He wouldn't want you to come after him. You know he wouldn't.

I owe him.

If you go, it's because, deep down, you don't want this child. Don't want what it'll do to you, tie you down, change you.

Shut up.

It's true, you know it.

It's for Isa—I mean, for Robin.

Yes, what about Isaac—whatever happened to telling Miriam her people would not be welcome in the Valley? If you go after Robin, who'll be there to warn Judith?

Plenty of time for that. Plenty of time.

What if there isn't?

If there isn't, then Judith will deal with it. But there is time enough.

You don't have to do this. Turn around now, Robin will be fine.

I do. I do have to do this.

The argument went around and around in her head, as maddening as it was unproductive. One night Dian had a nightmare about a maggot-infested otter rising sleekly from its grave and attacking the child she held in her arms, but even that did not turn her completely from Ashtown.

In the end, the decision made itself, just as Dian's initial impulse to follow Robin's abductors had made itself: her feet simply could not imagine moving south, to safety.

She waited two weeks, both for the sake of her body and in order to avoid any possible link between her arrival and the party that had preceded her. For fourteen days she lived among the ghosts in the wing of the lodge, and on the morning of the fifteenth day, a gray dawn that declared its intention of snow by nightfall, she saddled Simon and turned his head in the direction of Ashtown.

CALIFÍA, QUEEN OF CALIFORNIA, [RODE] TOWARD
THEM EQUIPPED FOR BATTLE.

TWENTY-TWO

DIAN RODE SOUTHEAST, OR AS CLOSE TO THAT DIRECtion as the terrain would allow, doubling back in order to join with the main north–south road and appear to be just another Traveler from the south. Once on the road, she was fortunate, for the signs showed a band of half a dozen horses an hour or so ahead, and she was followed by a slow-moving group of wagons, three miles behind at mid-morning, considerably further back when she stopped to rest the animals and take a cold meal at noon.

At three-thirty Ashtown appeared in the distance, and Dian was shocked at the icy stomach and loose bowels that seized her at the sight of its wall and roofs. Simon startled, lost his footing briefly, and distracted her into self-control. She reined in and sat looking at it for some minutes. When she nudged the horse back into motion with her knees, her face was grim.

Five miles from the city she caught up with straggling riders from the party in front, two women on a single horse and leading a gelding gone lame. Dian's first impulse was to drop back, but after watching them undetected for a while she decided that they did not feel dangerous and that the advantages in appearing at the gates as part of a group might justify the small risk that these two represented. She rode on, into a bad moment when the woman riding pillion spotted her and reached for her rifle, but the woman left it half-drawn at Dian's raised and open hands and slid it back into place when it became apparent Dian was alone. Their trust did not extend to wanting a stranger at their backs, however, and they sat and waited for her to come up to them. She stopped twenty feet away and pushed her hat back on her head. The woman on the horse's rump took this as a conversational opening and nodded her head.

"Afternoon."

Dian agreed.

"You, eh, you alone?"

Dian turned and glanced behind her at the stretch of trampled snow and mud that curved off into the trees.

"Looks like it," she answered. There was a pause.

"Going to Ashtown?" the woman asked.

"Thought I might." Another pause stretched out, not tense, but in need of filling.

"You part of the bunch up there?" asked Dian, raising her chin at the road ahead. A flake of snow drifted down, and another.

"Yeah. There's a baby; they went ahead to get out of the cold."

Dian nodded, and as at a signal both she and the rider in charge of the horse pressed their heels in, so the horses moved northward again.

"You, eh, you don't live in Ashtown, do you?"

"Not yet," Dian answered. "Heard it might be a good place."

"Oh, it is, it really is," the woman enthused. "There's a lot happening there, some good schools—I don't know whether you have kids or not—and it's safe, not like down south—"

"Jesus, Mares, you sound like a chamber of commerce or something." The other woman spoke for the first time, growling but not unfriendly. She tipped her head to look at Dian. "Name's Dee," she offered. "She's Maryanne."

"Dian."

"And what's that?" grunted Dee. "Baby moose?" She was looking down at Tomas, who walked between his mistress and the strangers, watchful but not overly concerned.

"That's Tomas. He comes from nowhere, he is bound for salvation, for he moves on a holy quest." Dee and Maryanne looked startled, as well they might.

"What seeks he?" Maryanne finally ventured.

"He seeks the genetic improvement of his race throughout the north. He seeks the creation of a race of superior dogs, great in body and spirit, and has humbly dedicated his life to the cause."

Dee and Maryanne stared at each other over Dee's shoulder, looked at Tomas and carefully at Dian, and finally decided it was a joke. They burst into laughter, Dee's giggles strangely girlish for such a large woman. Tomas cocked his eyebrows quizzically and wagged his tail, which set the two off again. Maryanne finally rearranged her face.

"It is a just cause, Tomas. May the Heavens bless your—your work," she spluttered.

"Thank you," Dian answered seriously for him.

"He is a fine dog," Maryanne said. "A good head. I'd like a pup, if you know of anyone whose bitch is, eh, participating in Tomas's holy quest." The two women again collapsed in giggles, somewhat excessively for such a mild jest, Dian thought. Maryanne finally wiped her nose on the end of a scarf, and then tipped her head to Dian in a conspiratorial aside.

"You'll have to watch that kind of joke in Ash-town, though, Dian. They're a little, um, straitlaced there. Not too much of a sense of humor, some-times."

"But then, what can you expect," muttered Dee, "in a city full of guardian angels?" Maryanne gaped at the back of her partner's head, glanced uneasily at Dian, and to Dian's amazement clapped a gloved hand over her mouth and began to snigger. The tips of Dee's ears had gone bright red; the two women looked for all the world like a pair of kids making dirty jokes about the head of the family.

"Shit's sake, Dee," Maryanne sputtered, "talk about watching your jokes," and she took her hand from her mouth to jab the other woman hard in the ribs. Dee shrugged, but it was an uncomfortable, tight motion, and she did not look at Dian for some time.

So, mused Dian, it would appear that a person did not jest about certain things in Ashtown, a town where streets were safe, the children were schooled, and jokes that linked sex and religion were considered daring—even these two had been shocked, though they regarded themselves as too sophisticated to show it. Interesting. And what the hell had Dee meant by "guardian angels"? Dian had four miles, maybe an hour, to pump these two and discover where the ice was apt to be thin beneath her feet in Ashtown.

Dee and Maryanne were part of a large family of trader–farmers, twenty-four women, seven men (which numbers indicated that they were a successful family of traders), and a variable number of children. The six now on the road had been part of a group trad-ing in Meijing and south into the Valley when, in Au-gust, Dee's cousin had been knocked under a wagon and broken her leg, very badly. They had intended to ride for home in September, but the leg was not expected to heal until October at the earliest. Normally they would have left her, to make her own way home or to be picked up the following summer, but—she was pregnant. It was all extremely inconvenient, and Dee personally thought the woman had known her condition before they left Ashtown in June, but in any case by October she would be six months along, and the healers and midwives all agreed that in view of the accident, she'd be a damned fool to travel. So half the group, five of them, had stayed behind. The baby, a girl, was born six weeks early, in the beginning of December, but was healthy, only slightly small, and ate heartily. As soon as the mother's bleeding stopped they had bought heavy fur parkas and left for Ashtown. They were looking forward to getting home (which at this time of year was a house, or several connected houses, within the city walls) and to seeing the children, one of whom was Maryanne's.

Dian admired the frayed sepia photograph of a gap-toothed, pigtailed child in a summer dress and returned it to the proud mother, commented untruthfully on the resemblance, and asked what the family did in Ashtown during the winter months.

From Maryanne's description and Dee's grunts, Dian pieced together a picture of the town as a bee-hive of activity under its blanket of snow. Politics—three of the family were on various governing bodies, municipal and school boards, and Dee's mother was a past Mayor. Culture—the city possessed two movie theaters and four live stages; Maryanne's sister played in the city orchestra; nearly everybody was involved in some sort of dramatic society, even if she only painted sets or sold tickets. Education—school for the children was mostly in fall and winter, and public lectures abounded. And for plain entertainment, there were a number of nightclubs and dance halls. Yes, Maryanne loved her city, and even the more phlegmatic Dee seemed in agreement.

"It seems like I chose the right time of year to come," said Dian. "What about your army?"

The ice went abruptly paper-thin, and Dian could hear the cracks spreading out as Dee looked back over her shoulder at Maryanne and then away.

"What about it?" asked Dee.

"A lot of towns use the winter to practice drills, teach the kids to shoot, that kind of thing," said Dian smoothly.

The two women looked at each other again and relaxed slightly.

"No," said Maryanne, "we don't have an army."

"No army? How do you protect yourselves?"

"We—the city—have an agreement with Queen Bess. She has an outpost only fifty miles from here."

"Ah. Taxation?"

"Some. Not much, considering the security."

"I suppose not. And inside the city? Do her troops police the streets?"

"No," said Maryanne, sounding offended. "We have the—we have our own police force. They're very...efficient." The force's efficiency was obviously regarded as a mixed blessing, and Dian thought she could put a name to the local militia: these would be the city's guardian angels.

"I see," she said, and did, a great deal: external tribute and an internal police force so effective that it inspired fear even in such prosperous, law-abiding citizens as Maryanne and Dee, coupled with the privilege and corruption that Isaac had fled.... "I see. Tell me about the schools. What grade is your daughter in?"

Relief washed over the woman's broad features as she realized that Dian was only asking reasonable questions after all, the sort of questions to be expected from a stranger shopping around for a safe haven for her family. She told Dian about the skills her child was learning, and Dian made interested noises and thought furiously.

Half a mile from the gate, with the snow falling on the roofs and tents that had begun to appear along the road beside them, Maryanne stopped in the middle of a sentence and turned to Dian with the air of a remiss hostess.

"But you, Dian, do you have a place to stay? Friends?"

"Not yet. I'll find work."

"What do you do? I've been chattering on so . . ."

They waited for her to answer. She could feel their eyes on her and knew what she had to do. She took the role open to her and stepped into it. She would not need to appear as a member of a group after all—indeed, it would be better if she did not. She turned to them with a small, tight smile on her cold lips.

"Truth to tell," she told them, "I'm a guard." They reacted exactly as she had expected. Dee's hands jerked on the reins and her stolid face went pale. Maryanne actually swallowed.

"Mercenary?" Dee asked carefully.

Dian neither confirmed nor denied it.

"I got tired of the South," she said, and chose not to notice that they were not beside her as she lifted her face to the city and rode forward.

Under ordinary circumstances, the discomfiture inflicted on the two harmless women might have troubled Dian, but circumstances would not be ordinary for a long, long time, and her mind was very much occupied with other things. She could think only of what she would have to do in the next minutes, while Isaac's past and Robin's present bore down on her and the nervy feeling of impending evil built into the intensity of a toothache.

Ashtown's walls had been modeled on those encircling Meijing, though with considerably less in resources and imagination and no concern whatsoever for aesthetics. Much of it incorporated the backs of buildings, their windows bricked up and the gaps between them filled with a mixture of bound rubble, sheets of rusting metal, and rough logs. It should have looked slapdash and homey, but it did not. It looked brutal, solid, and effective. Although, Dian tried to reassure herself, from the inside the walls would surely not be difficult to scale. Twelve-year-old Isaac had gone over them; so could she.

Holding that cold comfort to her, Dian approached the left of the two entrance portals, the one that declared itself to be for *Strangers*. The guard cubicle was empty, as opposed to *Residents* on the right with its line of tired travelers being harassed by an equally tired-looking woman in a dark blue uniform studded with shiny buttons and draped with scarlet braid. She was arguing with a short, blocky figure in a coat of ratty wolf skin, both of them waving papers. Between them and the gate stood two big women in black, a dull, unrelieved black that seemed to suck the color from anything nearby. The women were standing in front of a smoking brazier, warming themselves and looking bored. Two old but well-cared-for shotguns leaned against the wall, ten feet away. Each of the guards had an odd black tubular object strapped to the outside of her forearm, some nine inches long and slightly thicker than a thumb. Some sort of Artifact, from its appearance, vaguely similar to objects she'd seen on the Meijing guards along the Road—communications device, or weapon?

The *Strangers* door was tightly shut, with neither uniformed official nor black guard in sight. The two

women in black smirked at Dian's indecision and ignored her. With that smirk Dian's path was set. She
dismounted slowly, feeling their watching eyes. She
eased her back and squatted down to dig the ice
from Simon's hooves, then did the same for Tomas's
paws before rising to rummage through the saddlebags for a couple of half-frozen rabbit legs that she had
roasted over the lodge's fireplace the night before. She
stripped one bare, giving the meat to Tomas and sticking the bones back into the saddlebag; then, carrying
the other leg and leaving Tomas to stand watch over
the horse, Dian walked across to the ornately uniformed bureaucrat. The two big guards by the brazier
watched her approach. One of them turned her back
and made a remark to the other, who laughed through
yellow teeth. Dian ignored them both, instead walking straight up to insinuate herself between the paper-
waving duo, where she stood, stripping and chewing
the meat while she looked from one to the other with
undisguised interest. The woman in the wolf skin
looked irritated, and the uniformed official stopped
what she was saying.

"Lady, you'll have to get in line," she told Dian
rudely.

"I am in line," said Dian. She gestured with the
gnawed rabbit leg past the woman's nose at Simon
and Tomas, chewed, swallowed, and smiled. "Do I
just go in?"

"Of course not. You'll have to wait until the atten-
dant returns." She moved to look around Dian at the
woman in wolf skin. "Now, your pass says you'd be
back by—"

Her voice ended in a squeak of pain and astonishment as Dian's greasy fingers shot out to dig into her
jaw, forcing her head around. Dian continued to smile
into the woman's frightened eyes.

"And how long will that be, please?"

"I—I don't know. Twenty minutes?"

"Good." She let go of the woman's face and patted her cheek affectionately. "Twenty minutes. If they're not here by then I'll come back and join your line. Right?" The bureaucrat swallowed and swiveled to look for her two black-clad guards. One of them had her gun, the other was still fumbling. Dian faced them: dead silence, two guns aimed at her, the surreptitious noises of people behind her moving briskly away. She held out both hands, empty but for the half-stripped leg, and shrugged at the two guards. "Just asking a question," she said mildly. She raised the meat to her teeth again, sucked off the last shreds, chewed, swallowed, and gave the guards a wide smile.

Then she tossed the bone over her shoulder and walked off, unarmed and covered in freezing sweat, walking up the row of stalls as if to investigate their few offerings, leaving horse, rifle, and possessions under Tomas's watchful eye.

A Meijing copper bought a cup of hot broth, and a small silver gained her two meat pies. She strolled back at a leisurely pace that belied the pounding in her veins, ignoring the eyes on her and the ice in her guts. She gave one of the pies to Tomas, nodded politely at the black guards and their ready weapons, nodded again and smiled to the suddenly nervous bureaucrat, and settled her back into a comfortable squat against the logs of the wall to eat her own pie.

She nearly laughed at the absurdity of it, the ease with which one person can terrify another merely by ignoring her sacred symbols of power. She ate the last of the pie, pleased that she could swallow around the dryness in her throat, washed it down with the dregs of the broth, stood up (seemingly oblivious of the jittery reaction her movements set off on the other side of the entrance), and walked back down to return the cup to the vendor. All the way down she felt the eyes

of the crowd on her; on the way back she felt like a
wolf strolling past a flock of penned sheep. Dee and
Maryanne, standing at the rear of the *Residents* line,
would not meet her eyes, but she nodded at them anyway, and smiled, and smiled.

She stopped halfway between the portals, pulled up
her sleeve and peered elaborately at her bare wrist,
and, grinning merrily, looked over at the uniformed
official, who dropped her papers on the muddy stones.
Dian walked over and squatted to help the woman
gather them up.

"How stupid of me," said Dian, and held out a
sheaf of papers. "I don't have a watch. Has it been
twenty minutes?" The woman gulped, reached for
the papers, and backed away from Dian, who followed
her with a look of polite expectation arranged on her
face. The woman stopped and cast an appeal at the
guards.

"I suppose, uh, that is, she doesn't seem to be there
yet...."

"No, she doesn't, does she?" agreed Dian. "Ah,
well, that's all right. I'll just come through your side."

"But I don't have the forms," the woman squeaked,
"the authority—"

With that, the blunt barrel of a shotgun came up to
rest on Dian's chest.

Dark, dead eyes, rotten teeth, an ill-healed knife
scar on her face, an inch taller than Dian and thirty
pounds heavier. Dian looked over to where Tomas
crouched, quivering, and pointed a commanding forefinger at him until he subsided. She glanced over at
the other guard, down at the gun barrel, into the eyes,
and smiled.

"It's just that I had some business inside, and I'd
rather not wait out here all night. I need to see somebody, and there's obviously no one of any importance
out here. But if you insist that I should wait..." She

took a step back and caught the look the second guard
threw up at the overhanging wall, a look of triumph
consulting authority. The moment's lapse, the gloating relaxation of the closer guard, and the knowledge
that the person she needed to see was watching from
above coalesced into movement. Dian's arm came up
under the gun, which boomed past her ear and sent
the remaining onlookers diving for cover while her
forearm continued up to slam the heavy double barrel
upward and hard into the woman's face. Before the
woman had staggered back, Dian's legs were already
launching her at the other guard, whose gun was coming up but not fast enough. Dian tackled the guard at
knee level and her gun, too, fired, a window high
above them tinkling into fragments. They rolled, and
Dian drove the base of her hand up into the woman's
chin. The guard's eyes fluttered.

Dian reached up through the tangle of woman lying on top of her, found a wrist, and struggled to her
feet with the woman's arm pushed high behind the
dark back. Out of the corner of her eye she was aware
of women diving behind walls, horses rearing and
slipping, but she was only concerned with Tomas,
standing teeth bared over the guard with the bloody
face.

"Tomas, enough. Fetch the gun," she ordered quietly. Reluctantly, one hundred fifty pounds of dog
wrapped its lips back over its teeth and went, stiff-
legged and huge of ruff, to bring his mistress the
heavy metal stick with the foul smell. She took it
from him, broke it to knock out the remaining shell,
and tossed it next to the other one.

"Guard the guns, Tomas." He stalked over to the
weapons and placed himself over them.

The forecourt was now so silent, even above the
ringing in her ear Dian could hear the wet snuffling
and outraged curses of the guard with the crushed

nose, the raised shouts down the road, the nervous jangle and snort of the horses, and—and a voice from within the walls. She searched for its source, found the narrow slit fifteen feet up the wall, saw someone behind it, and forced her mouth into what felt like a rictus of death but she hoped looked like an insouciant smile.

Show no fear, not any, she thought incoherently: *only confidence—spark curiosity—put on a mask.* But what if I'm wrong, what if there is no authority behind the wall—or if there is, what if it's just as brutal as these two, no brains, the fear that unseen figure inspires nothing more subtle than the fear of a mad giant with a stick, what if I'm wrong, she'll cut me down and I've failed them all, Robin and Judith and Isaac and Culum and—

Stop. No fear. The guard she was using to block her body from a potential shot out of the window had recovered from the stunning blow to her chin and was tense under Dian's hands, spoiling for a fight but not willing to sacrifice her arm for the pleasure. The other guard was getting to her feet, and Dian knew that in seconds she would no longer control the courtyard. Unless . . . She let go of the guard's wrist and held out her hands.

The guard stumbled away, leaving Dian completely exposed, unarmed, her hands spread open away from her sides. She was gambling all on the ability of an unseen presence to control her troops; she did not hear the low command from above, she simply stood, for an endless string of seconds, twisting her palms up now in a gesture of waiting, ever smiling at the hole in the wall, eyebrows lifted in a secret amusement, smiling. The bullets did not come. Ten, eleven, twenty seconds, and she started to lower her hands when it came, a crack that hit the stones ten feet behind her, and even as her body was trying to react, her mind was furiously countermanding the movement, so that she twitched violently but did not actually move from her place.

"Leave it, Bernie," said the voice from above, and a moment later snarled, "I said leave it!" Dian turned her head slightly to look at Bernie with the broken nose, the red blood covering the lower half of her face to glisten against the flat black of her garment. There was rage in her eyes and in her stance, and the black forearm tube was now in her hand, held in precisely the same stance Dian had last seen during the fight on Harvest Day between Laine and Sonja. A weapon, then, but not a gun.

With great deliberation Dian turned away from her, wiped her palms off on her coat, and walked over to her frightened horse. She wanted nothing but to sit down and shake for a while, or to sprint for the hills, but forced herself to gather up Simon's reins, talk soothing nonsense to him, and stroke his flaring nose.

The *Strangers* door opened and out came two more black-clad women, these with rifles over their shoulders. They marched past her without so much as a glance, over to where the two failed guards sat, both of them cursing and packing the one woman's broken nose with snow. The *Residents* line formed up again hesitantly, its first member a good fifty feet away and ready to leap for cover.

These new guards did not look the type to leave their weapons out of reach, Dian thought. Bernie and her friend apparently knew they were outclassed, or outranked, because they followed the newcomers' curt orders to leave without much argument. Dian watched in amusement as the two tried to decide what to do about their shotguns, still straddled by Tomas's legs, then tensed as one of them took a step forward with the black weapon tube in her hand— whatever those things were, Tomas would not know how to deal with them. However, the older of the new guards shouted at them to leave the guns and, cursing with great violence and little eloquence, they both spat imprecations in Dian's direction and went through *Strangers*. She smiled, and the door shut behind them.

The guards got the line moving again, and the uniformed woman began briskly to funnel her charges through their gate. Dian leaned against Simon's reassuring flank, and picked her teeth, and wondered what the hell to do now. It was cold, it was getting dark, it was beginning to snow in earnest, and her leg ached from knee to waist. In ten minutes the last of the travelers had gone through and the first of the stall-holders was being passed, and although the two guards were including Dian in their watch, nothing else happened.

Had it not been so damnably cold, with so much at stake, it would have been funny. Dian felt a sudden confirmation of respect for her opponent in the room above, but it had to end, one way or another. She pushed away from Simon's shoulder, pulled off her hat and slapped it against the saddle to free both of snow, put it back on, went around to put her foot in the stirrup, and mounted. She circled Simon around until she was facing the upper window, and though it was too dark to see inside, she knew the woman who commanded the guards was there, watching her. Dian could feel her. She raised her voice to carry through the ramshackle wall.

"I thought you might have need of someone with a bit of talent." She showed her teeth in a grin, as if it mattered not at all. "Guess I was wrong. Tomas, heel," she called and, pressing her boots into the horse's ribs, turned confidently out into the snow.

If the woman called, it would be within twenty yards, before Dian reached the stalls. The call did not come. Ten more seconds went by, seconds filled with the beginnings of bitter self-recrimination and her mind's angry demand for an alternative plan, when the voice followed her down the road. A single word: "Stop." It was spoken in a low voice but a carrying one, and Dian did not think it a good risk to pretend she had not heard it. The owner of that voice would not repeat herself. She reined Simon in and circled him around to wait. In less than a minute, the *Strangers* door opened wide, and a woman stood within, darkly indistinct but surprisingly small in the gloom.

Dian took a final look up at the looming, ugly walls and wondered if she would be able to maintain the matching facade of cold brutality that the next weeks were going to require of her. Then she thought of Robin somewhere in there behind those walls and decided the attitude on her part would not be entirely a facade. She urged Simon forward, back to the city, to enter the city's gates.

...SHE DESIRED TO RULE OVER ALL MEN, NOT

BY MEANS OF SHARPNESS OF MIND,

BUT RATHER BY FORCE OF ARMS.

TWENTY-THREE

IT WAS A SMALL WOMAN WHO WAITED, A FULL HAND shorter than the smallest of the four guards Dian had yet seen, but her body was hard under her closely fitted black clothes. She was a white woman in her late thirties with cropped brown hair and a look of patience on her face, and other than her odd amber eyes, at first glance she appeared nondescript. The tube on her forearm was silver, and she wore an automatic handgun at her hip. Dian swung off Simon, downed Tomas, and approached her. With every step, Dian's sense of the woman's power grew, and as she stood looking down into the older woman's face, she could feel the sweat trickling into her hair: nondescript was the last thing this woman was.

"Why did you damage my women?" the shorter woman asked after a minute. There was no threat in the low voice, but it was far from reassuring. Dian felt, rather, that behind the cool words lay a menace more terrible than any posturing or snarl. This woman had no need to assert herself to anyone.

It took a considerable effort to keep her own response equally calm, but a matter-of-fact answer was her only hope. "I only damaged the one," she answered.

"It seemed a better way of getting your attention than filling out forms."

The amber eyes studied her, then went to Simon, and rested a long minute on Tomas before coming back to Dian. She tipped her head to speak to someone over her shoulder.

"Take her to Center. Give her a bath. Food if she wants it. Bring her to me in an hour." She paused, and her eyes shifted. "She's not to be damaged."

"Yes, Captain."

The eyes came back to Dian. "My women will care for your horse. They will return your possessions after they've been through them, if it is decided that you still need them. And the dog is to stay behind when you're brought to me."

"Very well."

The Captain turned on her heel and swept away, two black figures at her back, and the bare inner courtyard suddenly gained ten degrees and a supply of oxygen. Dian drew a deep and shaky breath, surreptitiously wiped the sweat from her brow, and followed the guard into the city, through narrow passages and oddly vacant streets to a door in a solid, unmarked, unwindowed building, one in a solid block of similar buildings. Her two guards, one in front and one behind, silently marched her up a flight of stairs and down a passage that was much too long for one building, a passage that could only have been made by joining up all the buildings in the block. Up another stairway a door was opened, and Dian was escorted into a bleak, bare room lit by a dim electrical ceiling light covered by a wire cage, showing a rough mattress on the floorboards, no window, and two more doorways. The leading guard walked over to the left-hand door, a closet, and pulled out a stained, once-white robe, which she dropped on top of the mattress's two folded blankets as she passed to the other doorway. She went through it; Dian heard the screech of a tap turning, followed by the splash of water. The woman came back and looked at her partner, who had not moved out of the doorway.

"Strip," ordered the woman at Dian's back.

Without hesitation Dian began to drop fur hat, fur parka, belt, knife, boots, sweaters, shirts, trousers, socks into a heap on the floor. The cold of the room bit at her flesh. The guard reached up to run her fingers carefully through Dian's hair, then stood back.

"Squat," came another brusque command.

"No, I don't think so," said Dian easily. "I don't think that's part of your orders, and I don't want your hands poking me. Nothing personal, you understand, but you'll not do it short of, er, 'damaging' me. Sorry." She hid her apprehension behind a taut smile, extended her hand out flat to keep Tomas in his place, and waited.

"We'll see what the Captain says," the guard said finally, and the other began awkwardly to gather up Dian's shed clothing. They left, and a pair of bolts slid to on the other side of the heavy door.

Dian picked up the robe and went into the bathroom, where she found the lack of anything that could be fashioned into a weapon carried to an extreme. No mirror, a small wooden brush with soft bristles, but no comb, one small flat control knob and a faucet that would have required a crow bar to pry from the wall, and a toilet with neither seat, lid, nor tank, flushed by a knob in the floor.

"Nor iron bars a cage," she commented aloud to Tomas and anyone else who might be listening, although as she climbed into the barely tepid bath she doubted that her mind was innocent or quiet enough to regard this place as a hermitage. As she sank gratefully into the water, she found herself wondering just when her mother had implanted that little snippet of poetry into her mind, and then wondered further what Mother would say at her daughter's current circumstances. There was no doubt about it, though: even a tepid bath was heaven after two weeks of scrubbing with melted snow. She soaped all over with a rough yellow bar that smelled of dead sheep, drained the gray water, then filled the tub again, lying back to study the ceiling. It was clean. Everything was clean, if minimal, and how the hell was she going to get out of this alive, and with Robin? Tomas came in after a while to drink from the water lapping around his mistress's knees. Dian held her fist in the water and squirted him playfully; he bit twice at the jets, then turned around and around next to the tub and flopped down on the tiles with a sigh.

The water became cold, and no more warmth could be coaxed from the tap. Dian left the wooden plug in the hole, in case Tomas wanted another drink, and dried herself with the towel that was threadbare but clean. The short bristles of the brush made no headway into her wiry hair, so long now that it brushed her shoulders, so she ran her fingers through it a few times, then dropped the sacklike robe over her head and went to sit in the cold room, legs crossed, on top of the blankets that she was no doubt meant to huddle under.

They came for her before the hour was up, the same two as before. She stood up smoothly, told Tomas to stay, and went with them. They bolted the door on Tomas and took her away without a word.

Down several different corridors and stairways they walked, passing numerous women, all dressed in dull black. Dian revised drastically upward her estimate of how many women it would take to guard Ashtown from itself. Two hundred? More elite guards here than there were adults in her Valley, apparently. Her escort stopped in front of one of a series of undistinguished doors, knocked once, pushed it open, and stood back. Dian entered, and the woman shut the door and turned the lock from the outside.

Another windowless room, larger but no more luxurious than the one she had come from. It was nearly as cold as the cell, and although there was more furniture, the four wooden chairs looked less comfortable than the mattress had been. There was a table, and an electrical lamp to supplement the two ceiling bulbs, but other than those it was bare of bookshelves, cushions, rugs, or pictures on the wall. Dian chose a chair, tucked her bare feet underneath her, and resigned herself to a wait.

It was forty minutes before the inner door opened unceremoniously and the small Captain came in. She closed the door and walked across the boards to sit in the chair across from Dian. Dian dropped her feet to the floor, and as she waited for the woman to speak she knew she'd been right not to fuss about the rooms, not to break down doors to prove she could, but merely to wait by sitting, rocklike and patient. This woman might employ blusterers and bullies, but she led by the absolute rule of being the most dangerous animal in the jungle.

"Your name?"

"Dian."

"Where are you from?"

"South."

"Where?"

"South."

"Do you have a reason you don't want me to know?"

"Not particularly."

"Why did you come here?"

"I told you. I was looking for work."

"Why here?"

"It's cold out there."

"It's warmer in the South."

"Too warm."

The woman thought about this for a moment. "Why should I let you in? You're not here half an hour and I've got blood on the ground and lose two of my Guard. You're trouble."

"I'm good."

"I've got good people."

"And I won't make trouble with them. Those two you put out in the snow, they were temporary gun-toters, taken on because they're tall and mean. Put their guns halfway across the yard and go stand near the fire—that's the work of rank amateurs. Real guards I can work with."

"And if I put you to work with 'gun-toters'?"

"Do you have many like that?"

"Answer the question."

Dian shrugged. "If you told me to, I'd try."

"Why are you here?"

"It's cold, and I heard of Ashtown."

"Where?"

"Meijing."

"Is that where you're from?"

"Most recently."

"Doing what?"

"I was with their road guards, for a while."

"The Meijing guards? You're not Chinese."

"Wall guards are Chinese, the rest can be anything," she said truthfully.

"Why are you here?"

"I got bored, for Christ sakes."

"You're bored, you're probably in trouble in Meijing, and I should let you join up? You'd piss off as soon as I put some pressure on you."

A fractional drop in the Captain's eyelids told Dian that they had suddenly reached the crux. There was more here than she could immediately identify, but she did not hesitate.

"Pressure I can take."

"And . . . discipline?" There was a caress in the word, affection and anticipation that caused warning bells to start jangling in Dian's head, but the only indication of it was the brief twitch she felt along her jawline. She hoped the Captain had not noticed.

"I told you," she answered, "I'd get along with the others."

"That's not discipline, and you know it. Discipline here is putting up with anything—*anything*—that I say you put up with. I say you crawl, your chin is on the ground. I say you submit to a strip search, you spread 'em before I finish the sentence. That's what discipline means in my guard, and frankly, I don't think you can cut it."

"I thought those two were just throwing their weight around. If I'd realized the search was your order—" She made to stand up.

"Sit." The captain leaned back and studied Dian. "So you can take discipline?"

"I understand discipline," Dian replied evenly, but by God the room was cold, cold.

"Do you, now?" the woman drawled. After a minute she rose and went to open the door she had come through. Two large and eager women came in, all but rubbing their gloved hands together at the sight of Dian in the chair. They were followed by another, who bore a more than passing resemblance to Dian's interrogator, although her eyes were darker. This woman pulled a chair up next to the one the orange-eyed woman had occupied. The Captain came back and stood looking down at Dian while she addressed the two big, gloved women behind her.

"You know the rules. Blood I don't care about, but nothing more permanent than a week, and any bones broken, I break the same on you, and maybe another for good measure. You," she addressed Dian. "Two of my guards are dead because of you."

"*Dead?* But I didn't—"

The Captain's small, iron-hard palm shot out and cracked Dian's head around.

"You will not interrupt me," she said mildly. "Two of my guards are dead, and that is not permitted. You will sit in that chair and you will make no move to protect yourself. If you do, or if you get up from the chair, you will be taken to the city gates and you will leave immediately and you will not come back, ever, on pain of death. Do you agree?"

"I told you," Dian croaked, "I understand discipline."

"Right," she said, and turned to her chair.

"You . . . they called you the Captain?"

"They call me Captain, yes."

"What is your name?"

"If you ever have reason to speak to me after this evening, you will be told my name. Now, are you finished delaying? Good. You may begin," she told the two, and sat down in her chair to watch.

Her mind gibbering at the impossibility of sitting still while appalling things were being done to her body, Dian felt her arms gathered high behind her, and the shorter of the two women, the one with the much-broken nose and many scars, came to stand in front of her. She tugged at her sleek black gloves, studying Dian like a butcher about to fell a steer, and it was intolerable.

"*No!*" Dian heard the sharp edge of terror in her own voice, and she modified the protest into a hoarse whisper. "No. You can't do that."

Something in her attitude caused the gloved woman to hesitate and look to her frowning Captain for instruction.

"You want to leave?" the Captain asked. Dian jerked her head in a negative. "Then what is it?"

"I . . . you mustn't. Not there. I—" She gritted her teeth and pushed it out. "I'm pregnant."

"Ah. That does change things a little. First time?" Dian nodded. "And you're what, twenty-eight, nine? Bit of a surprise, then?"

"God, yes," she blurted, and then clamped down her jaws, hard. No weakness, none; never.

"That's the real reason you wanted to come in from the cold, isn't it? First time preggers and nervous with it. Yes?"

She took Dian's silence for a humiliated admission of weakness, which was not far from the truth. Dian wondered in despair what punishment the woman would devise as an alternative, and closed her eyes briefly and missed the Captain's nod.

Dian's leg exploded with agony and she screamed with the suddenness of it as the chair flew out from underneath her. She caught her breath on the floor, looked up at the two waiting, happy women and then at the two in the chairs, the orange eyes speculative, the dark eyes even darker and in a face that had taken on a faint flush. One of the women by her side reached down, set the chair upright, patted the seat; the other grinned through gaps in her teeth; but the decision had been made, and Dian would not unmake it now.

She did not scream again, made no noises other than the choking sounds of expelled breaths. Her silence may have accounted for the misjudged blow that finally rendered her unable to crawl back up to the chair, as an increasingly irritated guard, tired of being limited to her victim's extremities and growing annoyed at Dian's lack of response and dogged return to the seat of torture, slapped once too hard. After Dian hit the floor that time, she did not get up again.

"HOW CAN MY ARRIVAL HAVE FAVORED MY
ENEMIES AS WELL AS MY FRIENDS?"

TWENTY-FOUR

DIAN WOKE SLOWLY. AWARENESS BEGAN TO UNFOLD IN tendrils, one by one, delicate tendrils requiring careful consideration. Breathe. In. Out. The air tasted warm: inside air. And the light: gray under the slits of her eyelids. Dull, distant sunlight, not electricity, or oil, or candles. Which meant there was a window nearby, although why this should be of interest did not occur to her. Next, some minutes later, emerged a sense of smell, bringing the evocative odor of freshly ironed linen. Home. Cleanliness. Mother. Then the harsh tang of something medicinal, farther off but pervasive. Two senses, smell and light, linked her to the world, and after a while a third. Hearing brought the muffled sounds (*blankets*, she thought, *pulled high—I am lying in bed*) of people, of distant conversation, and of feet moving in a large building. Everything muffled, feeling slightly drunk, feeling— no, oh, no, mustn't feel, don't want to feel, don't move, breathing is enough. Breath by shallow breath she grew more awake and knew that she was about to open a door and walk into a black room in which a cougar crouched, waiting for her to walk in, to wake up.

And then, sudden as that cougar's pounce, a nearby door slammed and, with the involuntary wince of reaction, every abused muscle in her body seized up tight. Instantly she was lying on a bed of fire, knives were sliding into her arms, her thighs, stabbing over and over, and even though it was essential, so utterly vital *(why?)* that she not scream, she could not help the short chuffs of breath that leaked from her closed throat, short, breathy near-moans. She was only dimly aware of feet and a voice, the blankets being pulled back, and a sharp prick on an otherwise pain-free hip, then the blankets being draped carefully across her taut and quivering body.

"Try to let the muscles relax," said a voice in her ear. "The shot will help, but let them go soft. Concentrate on your breathing. If you go limp, you won't hurt as much. Relax." The voice continued in this vein for several minutes, counteracting the tense *huh, huh* of her breathing, and finally, just as she was becoming dreadfully certain that she was going to have to shriek to rid herself of this awful tightness and agony, the spasm let her go, as suddenly as it had taken her, and she lay limp and trembling and drenched with sweat.

"Good. Now, don't move for a little while." There was a rustle and the scrape of a chair on floorboards, and a shape moved into her vision. A dark, round face looked at her with something of the detachment of a doctor, tempered with a healer's empathy. "Good morning. Though I don't doubt you've had better ones. My name is Margaret. Your baby's still in place, and by tomorrow you'll just be in pain. Nothing broken but blood vessels and skin. Today we'll drug you a bit to take the edge off and let you sleep. In a few minutes I'll get a couple of people to help me shift your position so you don't lock into a statue. By tonight you might be able to move a little on your own without going into spasms."

Whatever had been in the needle, it was fast working its way through Dian's mangled nerve endings, dulling them and leaving her to float, a torso without extremities. She made an effort with her mouth, which was a peculiarly unwieldy shape, and got out a sound which was meant to be "Tomas" but only puzzled Margaret. Her jaws ached, her cheeks and lips were swollen, her tongue felt as if she had bitten it, and a tooth was loose, but she finally pushed out an intelligible syllable.

"Dog."

"The dog? He's certainly healthy, though I don't know if the door will stand if you're still in bed tomorrow. We gave him some food, but he hasn't eaten it yet."

No, thought Dian muzzily, he won't take food from a mistrusted stranger, but he has a whole tub full of water; he'll do. God, I'm tired, and with that she fell asleep.

The light was of a different quality when Dian woke again, a late-afternoon light that came through the curtains, illuminating Margaret and the book she was reading. This time it was a true awakening, not slow unrelated tendrils, and she took great care not to move. After a minute Margaret looked up, somehow determined that the slits of Dian's eyes were focusing on her, and rose from her chair.

"Welcome back. Let me get you another shot and then we can move you around a little."

"No." It came out without the consonant, but the intent was clear.

"You'll have to move, you'll stiffen like wash on a line in January if you don't."

"No shot." Shoh.

"You don't want a shot?"

"Huh."

"Oh, don't be stupid, girl. Or did you enjoy that spasm this morning?"

"No shot."

"Okay, you try it if you like. But if you start seizing up again, I'll inject you whether you want it or not. I have to answer to the Captain for your health."

"Where?"

"Where? Where is the Captain, you mean?"

"No."

"Where are you? This is your room, child, one of them. Or didn't you know? You passed your initiation. You're an Angel now, honey. You're one of us." Dian squinted to see the woman's face more clearly, wondering if she'd heard a thin edge of bitterness to the words, but the room was too dim, her eyes too swollen to focus. Margaret changed the subject. "Do you think you could swallow something? You haven't eaten anything in nearly twenty-four hours, and if it goes much longer I'll want to put a drip in your arm."

"Yes." Yesh.

"You want to try now?"

"Yes."

The next couple of hours were a period of infinitely slow movements and intense concentration, using her mind's self-control to keep her body from feeding back into its own pain. The closest she came to losing it was when two black-clad guards—Angels—came in her door looking eager, but they radiated only a habitual and general menace, and none toward her specifically. Instead, they gently lifted her up and carried her off to a room down the hall and, under Margaret's watchful eye and snapping tongue, let her down into a long wooden tub filled with a warm, slightly pink, gelatinous substance. Margaret positioned Dian's head on a cushioned rest, turned down the lights, and left her.

The slimy gel was both unpleasant and comforting. It was eerily alive, seeming to echo her pulse as its buoyancy wrapped and massaged her injured flesh and drew out the pain and the heaviness. It was also remarkably conducive to the beginnings of rational thought: about Angels and Captains who sat watching in cool speculation to judge how a woman took to being beaten bloody; about the experience the Angels had in inflicting pain without permanent damage, and the care they took in healing the pain afterward. And about the initiation process itself, which she intuitively knew was not completely finished with her.

In half an hour Margaret returned to stand at the foot of the tub with her hands on her hips. Now that the swelling around her eyes had begun to go down, Dian could see the woman more clearly. She was dressed in the same flat black as the other Angels, but she was an entirely different physical type, smaller than the Captain or any of the other Angels Dian had seen, but more than the height difference, she struck one as being delicate and round. The only hardness in her was in her mouth and the merely muscular strength in her hands and arms.

"Better, isn't it?" she asked Dian.

"Much." Her lips could even form a resemblance of the *M*. "What is this?"

"You've never been in a restoration bath before? Surely they must have them in Meijing."

"I 'as never hurt in Meijing."

"Meijing was after you got those scars on your chest, then. That explains why they healed so badly. What was it?"

"I 'as a kid. A game called Stakes and Ladders. Someone pushed me off a ladder, and there was a stake underneath."

"I've heard of that game," said Margaret slowly.

So had Dian. The areas where it was played, far to

the south of the Valley, tended to have disastrously high rates of birth defects; the lethal game was one way of ensuring that the slower children never made it to breeding age. Coming from the sort of area where children played Stakes and Ladders would explain much about the person Dian was trying to be while in Ashtown.

"This stuff feels alive," she commented. Her words were slurred, but Margaret either had a good ear or was accustomed to deciphering speech from swollen mouths, for she understood immediately.

"It is, more or less. It's a culture, like yogurt or something, but I don't really know if it's the organism or the heat and texture or the electrical current that does the job. All of them, I guess. We turned down the heat and the power for you, because of the baby. You can have another half an hour, and another hour in the morning."

"Have to see Tomas. My dog."

"Tomorrow. Captain's orders. He's fine, we threw the clothes you were wearing into the room, and he's scratched them into a pile and is lying on them. He still isn't eating, though."

"He won't, not 'less I give it to him." This would probably not be true forever, considering Tomas's age, although Culum might well have starved rather than take food from an untrusted hand. Still, it was better to give the impression that she was irreplaceable, for now.

"Well, he won't starve before tomorrow, and he's drinking from the bath. Half an hour," she reminded Dian, and left her.

At the end of it Dian could stand unaided under the hot shower, but her bad leg crumpled and she would have fallen had not her Angels caught her, gently, under her arms. Back in her rooms she ate a bowl of eggy custard, which Margaret fed her since her fingers could not close on a spoon, and drank a cup of hot, thick soup that was laced with something, for her sleep was unnaturally deep and lasted until dawn.

Breakfast, too, consisted of milk and eggs, and she commented on the fact to Margaret.

"Do you have hens that lay through the winter here, or do you reserve eggs for people with sore teeth?" The words were only slightly slurred this morning, she was pleased to hear.

"Angels always have eggs," Margaret answered ambiguously. "More?"

"Thanks."

A different pair of Angels appeared to carry her to the gelatin bath, stiffened as she was by a night's immobility, but afterward she walked back, limping heavily and leaning on Margaret's shoulder but nonetheless under her own power. At her door she noticed a small metal plaque screwed to the wall next to the doorknob, saying:

DIAN
C

Margaret opened the door for her, and although she felt like going to bed she steered an uncertain path over to the sofa instead and eased her body cautiously onto the edge, leaning back. Margaret followed her in, closing the door behind her.

"If you sit like that you'll find your arms ache. Rest them on a pillow. You should also keep your legs up as much as you can, they'll heal faster."

"What's the *C* mean?"

"C? Oh, on your nameplate. That's your rank."

"Is that the lowest?"

"Not quite. Ds clean the toilets and haul off the dead bodies from the practice rooms." Dian thought she might be joking, but it was hard to tell.

"How do you raise your status? What letter are you? If that's not prying."

"I'm a B1, one step short of A4, and you raise your rank by making the Captain happy."

"Somehow I thought that might be the case. Now, about Tomas."

"First food, then you have some business to attend to, then the dog. You are hungry?"

"I am hungry."

"Some crumbly bacon?" Margaret grinned wickedly, and she was instantly transformed into a gamine in unlikely clothing, impossible not to respond to. "Nice crunchy buttered toast with raspberry jam? A small steak?"

"Jesus and Mary," Dian groaned, "you are an evil woman. There's nothing wrong with my taste buds—you have bacon?"

"Of course, and it's goood, all salty and crisp and chewy, to sink your teeth into."

"Egg custard. And in a week's time I'll tie you down and stuff some down your throat."

Margaret bounced out the door and leaned back in.

"Sausages," she crooned. "A juicy apple. Crisp hash-brown potatoes." The door closed, and most of the room's energy left with her.

Dian gave herself two minutes and then forced her unwilling body to stand upright. These were her rooms; she would see them under her own power. This was the living room, with sofa, two soft chairs, and footstool upholstered in an inoffensive if uninspired rough brown cloth, low table in front of a fireplace that was laid but not lit, and a desk and chair next to a window. She hobbled over and pushed the drapes aside with the back of her hand, to look out onto—a surprise. It was a large garden—a small park, actually, a totally enclosed rectangle comprising a couple of acres of snow-covered grass, an assortment of bare trees and half a dozen evergreens, mounds of sculptured shrubs, a little pond, frozen over at the moment, with a scattering of benches. It appeared to be the inside of a city block, which had been gutted and turned into a private space for the Angels to sit in the sun and smell the flowers, away from the public eye. Assuming Angels smelled flowers.

She let the drapes fall shut and went to the internal door, through which she had been carried but not yet walked. To the right, toward the inside of the building, was a small bathroom, with toilet, basin, bath and shower, all shiny enamel, bright paint, and thick towels. To the left, with its own narrow window overlooking the park, was a small kitchen—a table and two chairs below the window, metal sink, small wooden preparation area with three drawers below, black stove with three flat grids of concentric rings that she took to be electric heating units, an actual, humming refrigerator only slightly smaller than Ling's tucked under the tiled surface next to the stove, and overhead cabinets. And I am only a C, one step above the lowest of the Angels, thought Dian, looking at a row of brightly glazed mugs hanging on hooks under the cabinets. Angels always have eggs. Angels also have electricity, and warmth, and a higher degree of technology than she'd seen coming through the city. And if Angel technology includes planes and artillery, she thought, then God help Meijing—God help us all. She glared at the humming refrigerator as if its bland front concealed a launch button and continued to the fourth door, the bedroom. Her bedroom.

The bed had been neatly made. (By one of the lowly Ds, she wondered?) There was a chest of drawers, whose handles looked beyond her abilities at the moment, but a closet door piqued her interest. She got her hand around the knob, but tightening the fingers sent shooting pains up into her shoulders and across her back and made her break out in sweat. She gritted her teeth—figuratively if not literally—shifted the position of her palm, and by moving her entire body finally succeeded in rotating the knob the necessary distance to free the latch. The door opened, she loosed her hand and leaned against the wall to catch her breath.

"Minor victories," mocked Margaret's voice behind her. "Hardly worth the effort, considering what's in there."

Dian pushed the door open with a hand inserted in the opening, found a light switch, and surveyed her new, hard-won possessions. One black robe such as the one she was wearing, one black allover jumpsuit, one black shirt, one pair of black trousers, one black padded jacket. And one stunning, brilliant blue jumpsuit of heavy silk that practically leapt out of the shadowy space at her.

"They should all be close to a fit. Their previous owner is about twenty pounds heavier than you but about the same height. She was happy enough to trade toward some new things, so you'd have something without having to wait."

"I'm surprised at the blue."

"Wear what you like in your rooms, honey. Anything or nothing, just so you put on your blacks when you go out. Breakfast?"

Dian followed Margaret into the kitchen and lowered herself onto one of the chairs. On the tray in front of her lay two bowls and a mug, all ceramic and all lidded, and to the side a curious object, a twist of what looked like aluminum, incorporating a kind of cuff from which came a wide strip with a convex curve, which in turn ended in a truncated spoon.

"That's an elaborate contraption," she commented. It also looked well used.

"You've never seen one before?"

"No, but I can guess." Margaret watched while Dian threaded her hand into the object. The bowl of the spoon was cupped in the palm, and the whole was very light and quite secure. Margaret lifted off the lids for her, and she dipped the spoon carefully into the bowl that was steaming, a puree of cooked apples and some grain. The motion put strain on her tender muscles from elbow to shoulder blade, but freedom was not a thing to be spurned, and she managed eight spoonfuls before the tremors became uncontrollable. Margaret fed her the rest of the puree and the egg custard and helped her cup the mug in her bandaged hands, then took the tray away. The self-feeder she left on the table, and Dian studied it with distaste. How many damaged hands would it take before such an instrument became a necessary part of the Center's equipment? It did not look terribly old; it was certainly not an Artifact. Nonetheless, it was scratched and bent, reshaped and mended twice.

Margaret had not said when she was coming back, though Dian remembered that there was "business," then Tomas. Thinking about it, Dian decided that she could as easily await whatever the business was reclining on the sofa as sitting here, with considerably more dignity and comfort than if she had to pick herself from the floor, which is where she'd end up if she remained on the kitchen chair much longer. By more or less lying across the table, she eased herself upright and scuffled into the living room, cursing the stiffness that came back whenever she remained still, collected some pillows and dropped two, and edged her way onto the long, wide sofa with great relief. She couldn't get her right foot up onto the cushions, but half was better than nothing. Slowly and deliberately she relaxed all her muscles, one at a time, and gradually she

dozed, and ached, and tried to visualize a process of
rapid healing, with no particular success.

It was the first time outside the pink bath she'd
been able to relax and let her mind go free and, free of
all the other pulls, it riveted, straight as a needle snapping to magnetic north, to the thought that had lain
beneath everything else the last two days, to Robin.
How to get him out of here? And, perhaps even more
urgent, how to let him know she was here, for if he
knew of her presence, at least he would be reassured
and be less inclined to slit his wrists—assuming he
hadn't already. The sooner she was active (Heal,
legs!), the better would be her chances of finding the
men's quarters, and its weaknesses. Would a closely
confined and tightly suppressed community of males
be more or less likely to help one individual? Certainly they would if it meant an improvement in the
status of them all, but a single man, when it involved
an escape for which they might be punished (Were
men beaten here? Or was a more sophisticated punishment reserved for them?), and a newcomer at
that . . . She had to know more about them before she
could decide, which would mean at least one visit to
the men's quarters, and that, she was certain, depended on her active assumption of duty. Eggs and
milk might come free, but she rather doubted that access to men was on the same scale.

This circular and unfruitful logic was interrupted
by the door being flung open (did no one knock in this
place?). Margaret stepped in, but Dian's greeting was
cut off when the woman stood back stiffly and faced
the doorway in an attitude of attention. Dian struggled painfully to rise and had accomplished—with
great internal cursing and greater trepidation—both
feet on the floor and an upright back against the soft
cushions when the Captain entered, followed by a
middle-age Angel carrying a leather bag similar to the

one Ling used for her medical kit. The Captain's eyes swept over the room and the very furnishings snapped to attention, but she waved a commanding hand at Dian.

"Sit."

She continued across to the window, this taut, muscular woman a head shorter than Dian who wore her simple black uniform as if it were armor, who moved with the arrogance of command and the constant readiness to fend off attack, who looked out of the curtains with an air of automatic but preoccupied reconnaissance while behind her Margaret closed the door and the strange Angel took up a position in front of it. Dian was distracted from the Captain by the vibrations of apprehension, of fear, coming from Margaret, but the woman would not meet her eyes, and Dian looked back at the Captain, who had let the curtains fall closed and was circling the room. She ended up in front of Dian, practically on Dian's toes, and when she sat on the edge of the low table before the sofa, their knees almost touched.

The Captain's face was, as Dian had thought in the *Strangers* entranceway, undistinguished—oval face, hair so short as to lack texture, ears flat. A slight gap between her two front teeth lent her an incongruous air of congeniality, rather like the woolly face of a lamb concealing a wolf's fangs, for no one who saw this woman's eyes could ever think her simple and congenial. Set beneath nicely arched brows and between full lashes, her irises were a peculiar light orange-brown darkening to black-brown at the edges. They drew a person. They invited confidences. They were the eyes of a fanatic, of a mesmerist, of a woman to love and to hate and to kill and to die for, and for several long seconds Dian forgot the grinding aches in her limbs and head, and saw only the Captain's eyes.

The amber gaze blinked, finally, slowly, like a reptile,

and the Captain tipped her head slightly toward the closed curtains.

"Eyes hurt?"

"Head," Dian admitted.

"I told Margaret to give you painkillers."

"She did. I stopped it. I don't like what they do to my brain."

"The hell with what you don't like, I want you next week."

For a startled instant Dian heard the words as a lover's assignation, but on the heels of this came the awareness of the Captain's flat disinterest—this was only a command to report for duty.

"You can have me today, what there is of me."

A very slight sharpening of the orange gaze was the only outward sign that she had heard the words, but Dian was in no doubt that she was pleased. The feelings this woman gave off, even in Dian's present low state of sensitivity, were unmistakable, great waves, powerful and primitive that shifted now to a humorous approval that made her paradoxically even more dangerous.

"That's true" was all she said, and broke her gaze to nod at the women near the door. The strange Angel brought the medical bag and put it on the table, then knelt on the floor, opened its mouth, and reached inside with the attitude of a person putting her hand into a nest of snakes. However, she merely drew out a piece of paper and a stained and battered metal ink pad, laying both on the table next to the bag. She took a pen from an invisible pocket inside the neck of her shirt, uncapped it, and looked up.

"Name?" the Captain asked Dian.

"Dian."

"Family name."

"MacCauley." Rarely used, nonetheless it had belonged to Judith's mother, so it was Dian's.

"Birth name."

"Why?" Dian started to ask, but before the syllable was even out of her mouth the Captain's hand flashed out, unbelievably fast and with absolutely no warning. Dian grunted involuntarily at the pain that reverberated up and down her extremities until her fingernails ached; after a long minute she eased herself back upright. The face in front of her was neither less nor more friendly than before.

"Birth name," the Captain repeated.

"Elizabeth. My birth name was Elizabeth MacCauley. Middle name Escobar."

The kneeling Angel wrote the names on the paper and placed it in the Captain's hands. She in turn held it out to Dian and waited until Dian's recalcitrant fingers had closed against it before she let it go.

"Read the words." Some vague shift in her voice lent the brief command weight, as if she were edging into liturgy. Dian looked at her sharply, then at Margaret, but received no clue. She ran her eyes down the page:

> I, Dian Elizabeth Escobar MacCauley, do swear, by the strength in my hands and the blood in my veins, that I shall serve my Captain and my fellow members of the Ashtown Guard, that I shall obey her commands and dedicate myself to her happiness, and declare that from henceforth all the days of my life, if it be her pleasure, I shall lay me down and die for her.

Dian read it again, deciding against a mild jest based on the lack of strength in her hands, and commented lightly on the implications of a latter phrase. "Sounds pretty final." She was unprepared for the response of her audience. The Captain sat up sharply, the guard

twitched, Margaret almost cringed against the door
when the yellow and brown eyes sought her out.

"You did not tell her?" the Captain began, her
voice silky. "You did not prepare this woman for her
vows? You were told—"

"Yes," Dian interrupted rapidly. "I'm sorry, but,
yes, she did tell me. I forgot." The fanatic's eyes
loosed Margaret and came back to stab at Dian.

"You would protect her?" she asked Dian.

"Only against unfair accusations," Dian replied
evenly, and added in a flat voice, "I am not in the
habit of giving charity."

She endured the Captain's hard scrutiny without
giving way to the urge to squirm, until the Captain
looked away at Margaret and then at the guard.

"The Hand," she ordered. The guard opened the
bag wide and gingerly drew out a heavy glove made of
metal cloth, large of finger and thick across the palm,
with a plate of metal embedded there. It was evil,
Dian's mind whispered to her, it was death, and the
Captain took it with a casual familiarity and began to
draw it over her right hand.

"Speak the words," she intoned. "Speak the words,
that you may be bound by them." Dian tore her eyes
from the living machine into which the Captain's
hand had been transformed, and looked at the words
on the paper, and knew that she had no choice. She
cleared her throat, suddenly tight and very dry.

"I, Dian Elizabeth Escobar MacCauley," she began
to read, and although she had no intention of keeping
this promise extracted under duress, she could not
keep herself from wondering, superstitiously, if she
would ever see Judith again, ". . . and die for her."

The assistant Angel flipped open the ink pad, took
Dian's right thumb and wet it against the frayed surface, then positioned the thumb over the paper and
pushed down, rocking it slightly. Then she held out

the pen, saying, "Sign your name or a mark on the line." Dian managed an *X* on the line beside her black thumbprint. Her hand was shaking badly, not only from the injuries already inflicted on it, but from the danger warnings that were pouring into her, from all three women and from the silver glove, and from the sure knowledge that there was not a thing she could do to protect herself from whatever was coming.

The Captain took the pen, signed on the line below Dian's mark, folded the paper, and dropped it into the bag. She flexed her hand lovingly inside the glove.

"Prepare her."

The Angel and Margaret came around the back of the couch. Margaret undid the loop fasteners at the top of the robe Dian wore and opened it to expose Dian's upper torso, oddly pale and free from bruising below her breasts. The women each took one of her arms, firmly but not without gentleness, and stretched them out across the back of the sofa. The Captain shifted forward to wrap her knees around Dian's legs, hooking her feet under Dian's ankles. With her victim now completely immobilized in this intimate embrace, the Captain leaned forward to look into Dian's face. Dark, orange, gloating eyes, glowing with passion and terrible joy, met tight blue ones fighting fear, and losing. The Captain laid her gloved hand, cold and soft and alive, across the top of Dian's left breast, nestled its flexible mechanical weight into the burgeoning softness of early pregnancy.

"You are mine, Dian MacCauley. From this day forward you belong to the Captain of the Ashtown Guard, to have and to hold. When I and my successors say 'breathe,' you will draw air into your lungs. When we say 'die,' you will cease to live. You will honor and protect me, and in my turn I will give you all. From this day forward, Dian, I claim you as mine."

Then came the pain, first a sharp, wounding jab

deep into the breast, and then the fire, the glove growing hot and then hotter, burning itself into her flesh,
building into something beyond fire, into acid that
seared and bubbled its way deep into her, and there
could be no fighting the body's response to it, no self-
respect or control, no dignity, nothing but the pain.
Dian arched back against the glove and a scream
came from deep in her throat, a full, deep shriek of
outraged agony. After long seconds something inside
the orange eyes was satisfied, and the glove was withdrawn.

The imprisoning arms instantly let her slump into
the soft cushions. The Captain sat back, untwined
her knees from Dian's legs, removed the glove and
tossed it casually into the open mouth of the bag, and
sat studying Dian. Under her gaze Dian fought for
control, forced down the whimpers spilling from her
throat, tried to make her lungs breathe normally instead of grabbing great gulps of air, concentrated on
relaxing the bruised muscles of her yammering arms
and legs and head, fought more than anything to keep
from her face any sign of the hatred she felt for this
woman, sitting patiently between Dian's trembling
knees, watching her calmly, oblivious of the sickly
stench of burning flesh that filled the room.

I will kill this woman, Dian swore to herself, kill
her and bring the place down around her ears. In response, the Captain's jaws clamped down as if she
was biting through something, and she leaned forward again and slid one hand around the nape of
Dian's neck, pulling her forward until her mouth was
on Dian's, forcing Dian's lips apart with her slick,
cool tongue. Before Dian's abused limbs could react,
the wicked, hot taste of blood washed into her mouth,
and then the Captain sat back, pulling a clean square
of white linen from a pocket, deliberately wiping the
smear of blood from her lips while before her Dian

gagged and spat and dragged her sleeve painfully across her mouth in a desperate urge to be rid of this woman's lifeblood. The Captain paid her no heed but folded her handkerchief, stood up, and looked down at Dian's face, filled with loathing and mortal fear. She smiled gently.

"You are mine," she said conversationally, "and my name is Breaker."

...THE QUEEN WAS A DOUBLE PRISONER OF
BOTH HER BODY AND HER HEART.

TWENTY-FIVE

WHEN MARGARET CAME BACK IN SHE FOUND DIAN
naked in the bathroom, water running in the basin
and the sour smell of vomit strong in the air. There
were droplets of blood sprayed across the basin, the
floor, the mug, and the toilet, most of it from a new
gash in Dian's hand where she had hammered at the
tap in a fury of frustration. Margaret soundlessly
wrapped the ice she carried into a wet cloth, replaced
the cloth Dian was holding to her breast, and went ef-
ficiently about the business of cleaning and bandag-
ing the new cut.

"Fuck," croaked Dian after a few minutes, "what
was in that glove? I can't get it to stop burning."

"You won't. It fades with time, but it never goes
away. Some kind of acid. It irritates the nerve endings
but doesn't quite kill them. You do get used to it," she
added, and under her breath, "sort of."

With exquisite care Dian peeled the cloth from the
angry flesh and saw, for the first time, the emerging
brand that she would live with until the day of her
death: a stylized figure an inch and a half tall, two
sweeping lines forming a rough triangle surmounted
by a pair of wings. An angel.

"But why? It's—diabolical!"

"Oh, yes. It's a very effective reminder of who we are. You know what they call us?"

Us, thought Dian. *Us.* "Angels?"

"That's nothing, even we call ourselves that. The civilians call us Vampires, when they think we can't hear. It's not allowed, of course, but they whisper it among themselves, write it on walls sometimes. Can I get you something to drink, other than the water?"

"Something hot and sweet. And can you help me up first, I can't—"

Margaret put an arm around Dian and pulled her up onto the toilet seat, rubbed her hand in simple affection between Dian's bony shoulder blades, and went out. Dian heard the sound of water running into the kettle, and as if in sympathy her gorge rose, vomiting the water she'd drunk back into the basin. In a minute, Margaret returned to bathe Dian's face with a wet towel. Dian rested her bruised cheek against the porcelain and closed her eyes. It's over, she told herself. She'd wanted in, and she was in, and that she had paid a price did not change that. In a few minutes she vomited a final time and allowed Margaret to clothe her in the other black robe from the closet. She sat on the toilet and tried to gather the shattered pieces of herself together. In a few minutes Margaret brought her an infusion of hot mint and honey, brushing casually against the door in passing so that it swung nearly shut. The Angel held the cup to Dian's lips and helped her to drink. The process was painful, but the tea warmed her and cleansed her mouth of the raw taste of bile and the lingering impression of another's blood.

"The bathrooms aren't usually monitored," Margaret said in a low voice.

"What?"

"The other rooms in our apartments occasionally

have listening devices and viewholes, but we're allowed the privacy of our bathrooms, so long as we don't seem to be ducking in too often."

"I see. Thank you for the warning."

"You didn't give me to her today."

"No. Why didn't you tell me? I thought she was going to rip your head off when she saw I didn't know what was going on."

"I don't know why I didn't. No, really, I don't. Stupid, my God, but the idea of preparing you—I started to, any number of times, but I just couldn't face it. It wouldn't have made any real difference to you, though, even if I had," she added.

"I see," Dian said again, and she did, if dimly. "But look, next time you get the urge to commit suicide, give me a chance to get clear first, okay?"

"I know. It was a hell of a thing to do. Temporary insanity," she said, and smiled, not very successfully. Dian smiled back, with her eyes if not her swollen lips.

"Help me to bed," Dian asked, and once there she touched Margaret's hand and said, "I'll have one of your painkillers, I think. A mild one." Margaret went away and came back with a needle, and Dian slept until the afternoon.

A knocking woke her, followed by the deep burn of her breast and then the tedious shooting aches and pains in the rest of her. The knock came again a minute later, and she realized it was at her door.

"Come in," she called, and heard the sound of someone opening the door in the next room, depositing a rattling tray in the kitchen, and Margaret was at the bedroom door.

"You knocked," Dian commented. "I didn't think anyone here bothered."

"Not for a C, no, but as of noon you're a B4. You got status now, lady. Can you get up?"

"I think so. Open the curtains a little, would you?"

"Glad your headache's going. Can't say the same for the women who have to work down near where your dog is kept. He's howling now—at least, they assume it's him and not a banshee or a generator about to blow up."

"That's Tomas. Can I get him now? Thanks." This last was for Margaret's help with an errant and ridiculous fuzzy slipper that had appeared at the side of the bed while Dian slept.

"Eat first."

"I'd rather get Tomas first," she protested, although the smells that awaited her at the door to the kitchen sent sudden spurts of saliva into her mouth.

"Orders," Margaret said succinctly, and handed Dian the wrist-spoon. She managed most of her lunch before the muscular shakes set in, despite the morning's treatment, and told Margaret she thought her teeth could manage something firmer that evening. She half-expected a joke about bacon or steak, but Margaret only nodded, deposited the bowls in the sink, and disappeared into the bedroom. She came back with the black jumpsuit over one arm.

"Think you can get this on without help? It has a zipper," which put it into a realm of luxury goods beyond anything Dian had ever owned before, including the Meijing silk blouse—God only knew where it was. "Can you handle the zip?" she asked a few minutes later. "I tied a loop through it."

Dian did manage it, by hooking the thumb of her left hand through the loop, though she needed help getting the soft cloth shoes—black—onto her feet. She followed Margaret out, and as they turned left into the maze she glanced at the plaque next to her door. It did indeed say *Dian—B4*. Thoughtfully, she followed Margaret through the hallways filled with Angels. Before long she could hear Tomas, whose full-chested, eerie hound howl made even Dian's hair stand on end and set her teeth on edge, two changes of level, a ninety-degree turn, and a hundred yards of corridor before reaching the room where he was being kept. She stood outside the remembered door, and the next time he paused to draw breath she addressed the wood with one sharp word.

"Tomas."

The silence was deafening. Two half-shouted conversations down the hallway cut off abruptly, and half a dozen Angels looked out from various doorways at Dian, relief dawning on their faces. She nodded at them and turned back to the door.

"Tomas, down on the bed," she ordered, and heard an instantaneous scrabble and thump from within. She looked at Margaret.

"He's going to need to run it off. Is there someplace I can let him out? He'll hurt himself in the hallway."

"There's an entrance to the garden straight below. Will he be dangerous when you let him out of there?"

"Oh, no, just fast."

"I'll have someone spread the word downstairs, then. How long?"

"Ready when you are."

"Three or four minutes ought to do it. Hold on a second." She went to consult with one of the onlookers, who made rapidly for a door and disappeared. Dian waited for Margaret to come back and work the bolts, and she went in.

Tomas lay on what was left of the mattress, onto which he had pulled what had once been Dian's clothes. He was barely down, lying up on his haunches, quivering all over like a huge furry pressure cooker about to explode. She did not look directly at him, lest she set him off, but limped across to the bathroom door, saw that he had been drinking, stepped around several putrefying hunks of meat and his chosen toilet corner (what room lay beneath this? Dian wondered, secretly amused), and went out the door.

"Heel, Tomas," she said. One huge bound brought him halfway out into the hallway, another one and he was rigidly attached, six inches from her left leg, his nose seeking her hand. She allowed him to have it, to snuffle her palm and lick her, even let him nibble at her fingers, the pleasure of the contact overcoming the sharp twinges of pain that shot up to her shoulder. He stayed at her side, holding perfect obedience down the awkward stairway, out the door, adjusting his eagerness to her slow gait with tight jerks, down three stone steps that were wet with half-melted snow, on which her leg failed and she would have collapsed but for Margaret's arm, out into the mushy parkland grass of the hidden garden. Finally she stood still and looked down at him, at his bristly face and open mouth, eagerly pricked ears, the blatant joy of the dog at his heart's return. She grinned back at him through a tight throat, stepped back, and swept her arm out in a broad, all-encompassing wave that freed his bonds.

The dog shot out across the stunted, half-frozen winter grass and a hundred yards away dove into a stand of rhododendrons, which heaved violently and spewed hunks of sodden snow in all directions to record his passage. At their end he erupted out again into a mad racing turn, skidded and recovered and turned to cover the ground between himself and Dian in two score of ground-hugging, overlapping, spine-flexing bounds. Twelve feet from her he launched himself into the air. As Margaret exclaimed and reached out belatedly for Dian's right shoulder, he soared at chest level an inch from her left one, landed in a huge spray of gravel behind her, and raced past

them to circle around the rhododendrons and do it all
over again. Half a dozen times he raced and circled
and flew, but on the seventh time, instead of pelting
up to them and launching himself, he slowed to a trot
and came to stand in front of his beloved mistress,
heaving and blowing clouds of steam and looking up
at her through bushy eyebrows with eyes that held no
reproach, no question, only love and joy at her return.
Her heart went out to him then, in a way it had not
in the Valley or on the road, in a way she had never
given of herself to anyone but Culum. She dropped
painfully to her knees, hardly noticing Margaret's
hand on her elbow, and when he came forward to butt
his head against her chest, she draped her arms
around him, sinking her face into the thick, foul-
smelling hair over his shoulders. His solid presence
and utter faithfulness were infinitely comforting, and
despite the pain in her knees and breast and the cold
and the wet that was seeping into the legs of her
trousers, she remained bent over him for a full
minute before she put up her arm for Margaret to help
her rise. In her affection for this woman who had
risked befriending her, she took Margaret's hand,
wrapped it gently as far as it would go around the
dog's heavy muzzle, and nodded his head with it.

"Friend, Tomas," she told him. "This is a friend.
Margaret. Margaret, meet Tomas." She turned to look
into Margaret's eyes and abruptly realized that she had
made a bad mistake. Revealing her vulnerable spot,
her love for this dog, to Margaret might not be a problem—somehow she knew that Margaret was to be
trusted that far—but the windows that opened onto
the garden . . . Nothing to be done now—and the worst
thing that she could do would be to ignore or try to
hide this, her one weakness. She tried for a smile.

"You're safe around him now. He would probably

even take something to eat from you. He'll regard you as a friend."

"I'm very glad he's not an enemy," said Margaret, eyeing the animal whose shoulders came to her hip, who outweighed her by a good thirty pounds. "I thought he was going to knock you into the next building. Can we go inside now? I'm not dressed for this, and you're turning blue."

Dian deferred to Tomas. "Are you finished, Tomas? Yes, I think he's finished for the moment. Would you like some food, Tomas? Food? I'd say he was distinctly interested, wouldn't you? Yes, let's go in. On you go, Tomas," and he leapt gaily up the steps, tail high and flailing furiously, waiting as his new Friend helped his Dian up the stairs. His mistress was back in her heaven; all was right with the world.

Dian was granted thirty-six hours of peace. She ate, began cautiously to chew, took three more pink-gel baths, had a haircut, and slept twelve hours at a stretch. Tomas ate, was bathed, combed, and exercised by the increasingly infatuated Margaret, and slept in profound satisfaction on the floor beside Dian's bed. Dian's headache faded, her ears stopped ringing, the bruised flesh turned yellow and her eyes returned to normal, bandages and one set of stitches were removed, her fingers regained their skill and a portion of their strength, she met two of her neighbors and the D who cleaned and brought her supplies, she was measured for clothing, and on the morning of the fifth day, four and a half days after she had first entered Ashtown's gates, the midwife came and Dian heard for the first time the amplified heart sounds of the being that lay in her womb, a breathless bird-beat that shook her more profoundly than anything that had happened since Robin's abduction.

The midwife had no sooner left than another knock came at the door and Dian, thinking it was Margaret, called out her permission to enter. It was not Margaret, but another Angel, whose face was familiar but whose name Dian did not know. She wore a handgun at her hip and spoke with a military formality that did not mask her underlying scorn.

"The Captain will see you now," she said. "You are to bring the dog."

Dian did not say anything but went for her cloth shoes—a pair of boots had arrived, but their laces were difficult unaided and they pinched her still-swollen feet. She sat on the bed and pulled them on, slowly, of necessity as well as to gather her thoughts, which had scattered unreasonably at the sound of the rapid *thuppa thuppa* given out by the midwife's Artifact machine pressed to her belly. There was no more time for disability or woolly-headedness, no time at all for weakness. She was, for better or for worse (*in sickness and in health*, her mind threw in, *all the days of my life*) an Angel, and her Captain was summoning her. An Angel among Angels, as brutal as was required to do the job. She would find Robin, and she would get them both out, but in the meantime she was her Captain's Angel. She had a hard moment with her jacket, half on and her arm awkwardly stuck, but she forced it up at the price of awakening her shoulder, took a deep breath, and went out to join the guard.

"Tomas, heel," she said as she passed through the room and walked briskly away in what she hoped was the direction of the Captain's rooms, so that the other Angel was forced first to close the door and then to scurry in order to shoulder Dian aside and take over the place in front.

"Your name?" Dian asked the back, but the woman walked directly on. Dian followed but deliberately slowed, exaggerating her limp and smiling now, and the woman would have lost her had she not waited at the next corner. Dian sauntered along with a hand resting on Tomas's back, and spoke to him in a casual but carrying voice.

"You know, Tomas, one of the difficulties of coming into a system like this is, you don't have any way of learning the ins and outs of how things work unless someone tells you or you see it in action. Take official duty, for example," she went on, and grinned wickedly at a startled D pushing a cart of cleaning supplies. "Some places, guards on duty aren't allowed to talk outside of transmitting orders. That's fine. That's how it works. Other places, now, guards running orders from higher up start to feeling that the orders are theirs, that they're every bit as big as those who actually gave the orders." Dian was strolling now, baring her teeth in mock cheer at any passing Angel, even at her guide, whose back was becoming increasingly rigid. "Now, that's just plain foolish, wouldn't you say, Tomas? Yes, I thought you'd agree. You're very sensible, 'cause you know, once that happens, once a guard starts imagining rules that aren't there and other people find out about her attitude, well, now, it's not too long before someone comes down on that guard like a ton of bricks. Sometimes it's someone from above, sometimes from her own level; either way, that guard is pretty flat. All because of making up some rule that isn't there, in order to feel important. 'Course, if it is a rule, nobody's offended. But if it's not, and people find out it's not, well—"

"Delia," the guard hissed at Dian over her shoulder. "The name is Delia. Now, would you get moving?" Dian agreeably sped up her stride to a fast crawl, smiled widely, and shut up. It was good to know that word of her actions outside the gate had spread and survived the night's beating. Perhaps, come to think of it, even been fed by it—certainly this guard seemed hesitant to cross Dian openly. However, she might be a lowly messenger. Have to find out Delia's rank, thought Dian, and then they stopped in front of a door. The Angel knocked twice, and at a brief mutter from within she opened the door, then shut it after Dian and Tomas.

The Captain sat in a soft chair with her feet stretched out to a wood fire. Next to her sat the woman whom Dian had seen the night of the beating, who resembled the Captain although her eyes were closer to brown—sisters according to Margaret, or by blood, maybe cousins. Between them rested an ornately carved low table with a silver tray and coffee service, two translucent cups and saucers, and a plate of small cakes. The two women studied Dian with their similar eyes, those of the strange woman analytical rather than compelling, and cold where the Captain's hinted of passion. Dian held her hand out, the fingers gesturing down, and Tomas sat. The gazes of both women went to him.

"He's very obedient," the other woman commented at last. Her voice was slightly nasal, as if the resonators had been blocked or crushed, and the effect was slightly creepy. It was not a voice to obey, but definitely one to avoid crossing.

"He's young, but he's intelligent and wants to please," Dian agreed, and waited for further sign of what was demanded of her. Finally, the strange woman turned back to the Captain and leaned forward with her hands on the arms of the chair.

"Must go. I'll let you know what they decide, shall I?" Something about the thought seemed to cause her secret amusement, as if the offer were a joke shared by two adults over the actions of infants. The Captain seemed to agree with the attitude, if not the humor.

THEN SHE TOOK UP HER SWORD WITH BOTH HANDS

AND WENT TO ATTACK HIM FULL OF RAGE.

TWENTY-SIX

SPRING CAME, EVEN TO ASHTOWN. TO DIAN, THOUGH, the fragrant sweet-pea blossoms that splashed up the walls and tumbled from window boxes, the birdsong and the kites in the clear blue sky, the rich smell of new-mown grass and freshly turned earth and the voices of children playing out of doors all had an air of unreality, of stage dressing—like, she thought in one of her blacker moments, some diseased whore in skillfully youthful makeup.

Her mood that gentle late-March morning was black indeed, and she stalked the streets, savage and short-tempered and every bit as dangerous as the person she had, for two and a half endless months, been pretending to be.

There were a number of reasons for her blind and savage march through Ashtown's gleaming roads. For one thing, she'd been inside this putrid, cheerful little town for nine godforsaken weeks and two days, while the time left to inform the Valley of what was on its way built, crested, and passed: Miriam's people would be packed and on the road south, with nothing but the briefest of greetings from Dian to give them pause. She had not confronted them that snowy evening, she had not returned from Robin's cabin; she had failed, and Judith would pay the consequences.

It might not have been so unbearable if she had been able to relax occasionally, but for every hour of every one of her sixty-five days here, she'd had to be on her guard against softness, friendship, self-revelation. Every person she encountered hated and feared her for what her uniform meant. The only exceptions were themselves clothed in black: Angels inside the Center, where the camaraderie of soldiers provided a veneer of friendship; Margaret, who remained an enigma despite daily familiarity and physical intimacy; and Captain Breaker, whose emotions, often unfathomable to Dian, most emphatically did not include fear—or even, Dian suspected, its corollary, hate. In all that time she had not seen Robin once; she was no closer to seeing him than the day she'd arrived. Nor had she seen a trader with bright blond hair, although she hadn't expected to: anyone who would Destroy books would scorn to live in a city that cherished its amenities as Ashtown did.

Added to those frustrations was this pregnancy, nearly two thirds of the way through now, which meant she had to piss every ten minutes, couldn't eat anything interesting without suffering the most ungodly heartburn, had to see the midwife every two weeks (and was finding it increasingly difficult not to murder that good woman, to wrap her own stethoscope around her neck until she gagged on her platitudes about proper diet and positive attitude and exercise and breathing and goddamned nipple preparation, for shit's sake), and was nudging toward the time when she would be forced into maternity leave, lest her soft outline make an Angel an object of amusement in the streets.

But the final straw, the panic that pressed in on her

and was about to drive her off the edge into desperation, was the sure knowledge that she was losing Tomas.

Breaker was clever, Dian gave her that, as clever with dogs as she was with people. Four weeks of seeing Dian regularly, always with Tomas present, developing a simple friendship with the big, unsuspecting animal. Then a month of gradually increasing independence with him, of reason and absolute authority saying, "He has to learn to obey me, Dian," and "It's not a good precedent, Dian, for an Angel to have a weapon her Captain can't handle," working up to "He handles better when you're not looking over his shoulder, Dian, why don't you leave us alone for an hour?" Then last week the arrival of a very large but exceedingly stupid smooth-haired bitch, some kind of Great Dane mix brought south through Portland from Idaho, all this culminating in that morning's command—not request, command—that in six weeks Tomas would accompany Breaker on her four-day trip north to meet and escort Queen Bess to Ashtown for her annual visit. Without Dian.

Savage and ugly as an ink smear across a watercolor of spring, she prowled the tidy streets and alleys of her self-imposed prison; poor Tomas, pacing beside her with her fingers brushing his shoulders, had no idea what had put his mistress into this foul mood. She barely noticed the alacrity with which the road in front of her opened up, or the way children were snatched from her path, or the sudden gulping silence that eddied through the streets as the citizens became aware of this black Angel bearing down on them. Dian: the embodiment of uncontrollable fury and irrational death that they put up with, and turned very blind eyes to, as the price one had to pay for security; one of the Vampires *(whisper it!)* who occasionally snatched up a citizen *(but surely only those who deserved it, and not one of mine, not my family, not today).*

Dian took no notice of the averted eyes, tight lips, and rigid shoulders. She was entirely taken up with her own impotent rage, with fury at the delay and at the visibly rounding belly pushing out the front of her black tunic under the jacket, with the maddening, never-ending burn in her left breast, like some small, sharp-toothed animal that always gnawed harder on bad days, and the throb in her apparently healed leg that on cold days and depressing ones demanded that she consciously suppress a limp. She ached with the frustration of suppressed violence, she longed to let go and do something truly vicious, to anyone, but she held herself in, feeling herself a maniac under tight but marginal control, and continued her patrol.

Halfway through the morning, she dropped by the Angel station located next to the smaller of the town's two movie theaters, quiet still. She lodged a report and used the station toilet, then came out and turned down the street to the stall that sold cups of thick, sweet coffee, the kind the midwife forbade her. She took the cup, put her coin down, and walked away, so the woman could take the money without trepidation. Most of the Angels just took—and often considerably more than cups of coffee—but from her first patrol Dian had made it clear that she accepted no gifts. Word had spread fast, and by the end of the day the shopkeepers were all aware that the new Angel with the dog paid her way, that she was polite, but that when she put on that smile, you'd better back off, fast.

The morning was uneventful, perhaps because her mood preceded her in the street and instantly doused any potential hot spots. The closest she came to action was when she approached a pair of furious merchants, so deeply immersed in their argument they did not notice the nervous silence that fell over their neighbors. She had tapped them each once on the shoulder with her unpowered wand; two red and irritable faces turned in her direction, then went abruptly pale, and the two frightened women faded away with identical sick smiles, in opposite directions. Dian slid the wand back into its clasp on her arm, and went on, even more infuriated now at this reminder of the daily intimidation she practiced, and at the spineless acceptance of her black-clad presence by the people of Ashtown.

There was no violence all that morning, not even any graffiti. No one came to her for help, but then that was hardly out of the ordinary. Angels were not there for helping, except under the very direst of straits; as for settling disagreements, one might as well submit to the judgment of a venomous snake. Angels were for repression, pure and simple, to carve away troublemakers with swift efficiency and thereby smooth the lives of decent, law-abiding citizens. At any rate, so the law-abiding citizens reassured themselves, and the town lawmakers always voted for the continuance of the Ashtown Guard, for their salaries and equipment and steady increase in numbers. Some of the more sensitive might have difficulties sleeping occasionally, as they recalled the smirk on the face of Captain Breaker's sister during the discussions on these matters, and in the still, dark hours they might wonder if the town Council controlled the Guard, or the Guard controlled the town. Come morning, however, their worries seemed silly. Hard times called for hard measures, and the Angels were an important tool for the preservation of order. A sharp tool, granted, and one with no apparent safe handle, a tool that could slice the unwary. Best to avoid Angels, at all times. But they were only a tool.

And I, thought Dian, *I am an Angel. That smirk is*

on my face too, because I can see who controls this town. We do. I do. It was a thought as sour as her stomach, and it wormed its way into her more deeply with every snatched-up child and averted pair of eyes.

The woman with the mule did not see Dian until it was too late. Dian came around a corner from a shadowed alleyway into the afternoon sun and was greeted by the sound of thick blows on flesh and one voice raised over a confusion of others. Above the crowd of perhaps two dozen heads an arm emerged, grasping the light end of a heavy-handled crop. The stubby butt end flew through its arc and disappeared, landing on some unseen but solid body at about shoulder level. A burst of voices, most raised in protest but a few in encouragement, nearly covered the bray of the victim, and Dian did not wait for more. With Tomas at her knee, she snapped the wand down into her hand, thumbed it to a mild charge, and slapped it indiscriminately against anything in her way. With a series of singing cracks followed instantly by stifled curses and outraged gasps, her path cleared miraculously, to open on a tableau consisting of: a mule with blood running down its unkempt neck, ears back and four feet planted in an implacable refusal to carry a load larger than it was; the broad back of its infuriated owner, flaying those ears with slurred but blistering imprecations and the upraised crop; and the half-circle of onlookers, backing away rapidly at the unheralded but not unexpected irruption of this dark harbinger of violence. Dian ignored them and reached forward to lay the heavy hand of authority on the sweaty, muscular shoulder in front of her.

Perhaps what followed was Dian's fault. Her failure to take normal precautions, or even to duck more quickly, may have arisen from her secret hunger for something, anything, to happen. Perhaps it was only an awful mistake on the part of this trader, a relative stranger to Ashtown who had not been here often enough to develop the automatic caution of the native, a Traveler whose small voices of warning were swept away by her drink-fueled fury at being crossed by the stubborn animal, by the power of bending the dumb beast to her will, and by the glory she felt at the scene she was creating among these rustic Ashtowners. She, too, was someone who liked a good fight, and she felt the hand on her shoulder as the opportunity to indulge in something more exciting than beating a mule (which she'd have to stop doing in a minute anyway before she killed it and had to carry the load herself). In either case, the result was the same: the woman's instinctive response to the interfering hand was a sharp backward jerk of her upcoming elbow. It connected, hard, with Dian's mouth.

The woman turned with the crop raised, filled with the anticipation of a spot of dirty fighting, and then she froze in horror at the sight before her: a tall Angel in black, blood on her teeth, wand at the ready, murder in her icy blue eyes. The woman barely noticed the huge and angry dog at the Angel's knee, crouched quivering beneath the restraint of his mistress's outstretched fingers, the circle of rustics held rigid as if by the same gesture, their apprehension giving way now to open fear. The onlookers' collective gasp that had accompanied the impact of elbow and mouth had cut off into silence, instantaneous and absolute. A leaf could have been heard dropping to the street, had it dared move. Certainly the only sound was the slobbering breath of the injured pack mule and the macabre strains of an accordion from the next street over. Dian began slowly to smile, and the trader's befuddled brain finally recognized what she was facing. The bloodied crop fell to the ground, and she would have moaned had her throat been capable of it.

Without taking her eyes from the woman's, Dian deliberately rotated her head, spat a gob of blood into the street, licked her split lip with a contemplative tongue, and allowed the grin to come back onto her mouth. She reinforced her command to Tomas with a tiny push of her hand toward the paving stones, then reached over with her free hand to click the wand back into place on her forearm. Thus unarmed, she crouched slightly, her hands at waist level; the fingertips of both hands twitched inward, inviting the stranger to come at her. To the onlookers she looked like a cat with a mouse. Or, with the blood trickling from her lips, like a Vampire at midnight.

The artificial stone-cold sobriety that results when alcohol is converted by terror had hold of the trader now and, knowing she was a dead thing, she answered the invitation in the only way possible. There was a knife in her hand moving toward Dian's belly, and the blade might easily have gutted the pregnant Angel had its wielder been more sober and less afraid. Dian turned it easily on the guard built into her left sleeve and stepped forward so that her rigid right hand could deliver a straight-fingered thrust directly into the woman's stomach. The fight was over before it began. With the trader retching at her feet, Dian turned her back and picked up the woman's two weapons. The crop she tucked under her arm. The knife she used to slice through the pack's belly bands, then she drove it deep into the load and tugged. The animal skittered away from the sliding packs, stepping on its owner's hand and kicking her leg before it came near enough to the onlookers for a woman to reach out reflexively and grab its halter. The trader had regained her breath and squealed at these additional blows. She snatched her trampled hand to her chest and sat hunched up, cradling the cracked bones and squinting up at her attacker. Dian contemplated the knife, testing her thumb against the wicked point; she stood over the woman for a long moment, then flipped the knife over in her palm and threw it hard and deep into the woman's packs.

A brief wince at the damage being done to her property gave way to disbelief and the faint beginnings of hope as the woman realized that she was not about to have her own knife turned on her. She began uncertainly to answer Dian's unfailing smile with one of her own.

"Get up," Dian invited her. The woman climbed up from the street and swayed, confused but willing to be wrong about the murderous tendencies of Angels. The Ashtown onlookers had their doubts.

"I'm sorry about the—" the trader began, and with that the cutting end of her own crop hit her full on the face and knocked her stunned to the street. Dian, jiggling the crop in her hand and waiting for the woman to push herself up from the street, felt more alive than she had in months, filled with an exultation that soared and swooped with her, restoring to life the parts she had thought were dead and gone, carrying with it a surge of strength and joy and power, feelings that were right and good and as heady as strong drink, more satisfying than sex. Angelic rapture held her, the ecstasy of action after close confinement, of clear purpose after the indecisive days and months, the joy and craving for blood and the surge of hatred given a rightful target. She loved this ugly, drunken woman, loved what she, Dian, was about to do to her. The woman staggered to her feet.

"We don't like it when strangers beat their animals in our city," Dian told her politely. "It disturbs the children and leaves a mess on the streets." Then she belted her again. This time the woman decided that anything beyond the sitting position was a dangerous occupation. Dian, however, was not finished, was, in fact, only beginning to give herself over to this mad, glorious, and instantly addictive sensation of being the wielder of complete and uncurbed power.

"We also do not consider it polite to sit in the presence of a guard unless invited. On your feet." The woman peered through her good eye at the crop, and at Dian, and staggered despairingly to her feet.

"Now you may sit," said Dian, and hit her. The woman put her arm up against the blow, and for some obscure reason this weak attempt at self-preservation—tardy, ineffectual, and not even from one of Ashtown's own—was the straw that nudged Dian over the edge into madness, and she hit the woman again where she lay, and then again, and again, and yet again. At first her small grunts of effort were lost in the trader's noises, but in a short time the woman fell silent, and Dian's rage fell on this inanimate lump at her feet.

She almost killed her. She would have killed her, would have flailed away until something vital was broken, had it not been for the gentle interruption of a man's husky and sardonic voice from the crowd of unwilling witnesses.

"Mother of God," said the voice, "imagine having an Angel for a mother."

Ice and fire tingled down Dian's veins and froze her where she stood, right arm raised. A collective sound came from the people around her, equal parts strangled gasp and moan—if they had been frightened into immobility before, when Dian had an object for her Angelic wrath, they were now in the grip of sheer terror, for God only knew what she might do at this. A pinless grenade dropping into a locked room was no more sure to cause destruction than an Angel crossed, and by a male, who could not (could he?) be harmed, even (surely!) by an Angel. Paralyzed by horror and an unspeakable anticipation, the crowd cringed, and waited.

Dian's face must have held all the shock she was feeling, although none of the women could have guessed the true cause. She straightened. Her arm went down, and she slowly pivoted. Two very unhappy private guards edged reluctantly aside from their charge—this was one thing they could not protect him from, and both of the women knew that they would be lucky to keep their heads, much less their jobs, for their failure to protect him from his own insanity. They each took one step away, and there he stood, chin raised, face calm, brown of skin and eyes, perfumed and pampered and effete of dress, wearing an almost parental expression of withering disapproval: censuring, disappointed, devastating.

Robin.

SHE WAS SHOCKED TO SEE HOW HANDSOME HE WAS.

Twenty-seven

Dian turned away from that expression, back to the bloody, welted, half-naked trader. She let the gory crop fall to the ground and deliberately pulled a clean handkerchief from her pocket, wiping her face and hands with it, then discarding it onto the woman's body. She looked around and chose with her eyes two women who had made encouraging noises while the mule was receiving its beating.

"You, and you. Clean this mess off the street. Get a stretcher if you want, take it to a clinic if you like, just have it out of here in ten minutes."

They left at a near run. Dian surveyed the other faces, and as an Angel was satisfied with their state.

"The rest of you, clear out. You," she said to the woman still holding the mule. "The mule is yours. Sell what's in the pack, everything but the rifle, the food, and one change of clothes. Pay whatever bills that creature adds up in the clinic," she pointed her chin at the unconscious trader, "and if it survives give it the gun and clothes. The rest is yours." She turned her back on the woman's stunned thanks to make sure Tomas would stay put. He had spotted Robin, and it would be disastrous if he were to greet his lost friend as enthusiastically as he so obviously wished to.

"Tomas, stay. You can't have him," she said for the sake of the retreating ears. "He's mine," and she bared her teeth evilly as she stalked up to Robin.

"Go," she dismissed the two guards. One of them opened her mouth, snapped it shut at Dian's glance, and backed away several steps before turning to walk down the street. The two women stopped uncertainly at the next corner, and Dian allowed them to stay there, within sight but not earshot. The two stretcher bearers returned, spilled the body onto the stretcher, and hesitated.

"Pardon me, ma'am, do you want us to ...?" She waved her hand at the stains on the cobblestones.

"No, the street cleaners will get it later. Take the crop and the rubbish." They gathered up the soggy bits with profound distaste, piled them onto the stretcher next to the trader, and scuttled away with their burden.

Dian stood for a long moment looking at the stains on the street, still wet and bright in the center, browning rapidly at the edges, and was visited by the same sick sobriety that had hit the trader a short time before. Mother of God, she thought, what have I become? She felt a trembling start deep inside her, and the desire to vomit, and with a great wrench pulled herself up into the top of her mind, checked on Tomas, and turned at last to Robin.

"I'm sorry," she started to say, but he cut her off with a flash of his eyes.

"You must not look like you're apologizing. Forget it."

"Yes. You're right. Oh, Robin, my God. I thought I'd never find you."

"You thought I would slit my throat before you found me," he corrected her.

"I—well, yes. I've been here nearly three months."

"A bit less than that, isn't it?"

"You knew I was here! But how—"

"The Men's Quarter knows all the gossip. Some of it does get a bit distorted, I admit. The first rumors had you killing three Angels, wounding the Captain, and entering the city with either a mountain lion or a timber wolf at your side. Don't laugh, they're watching. I am very glad you already had Tomas down. I've taken to wearing perfume, but I don't know if that would put him off."

She showed him her teeth, for the benefit of other eyes.

"Probably not. Oh, God, it's good to see you, Robin. I was going crazy." She stopped, and said in a different voice, "I really was going crazy, wasn't I? Christ, another month and I'd have turned into an Angel for true. I feel like hugging you and dancing through the streets."

"Not a good idea."

"Oh, hell, nobody expects rational behavior from an Angel."

"Except another Angel."

"Do you see one?" She tensed, but did not turn her head.

"No, not yet. You do not look well, my friend." He searched her eyes, and her own gaze slid to the side.

"It has been a long three months," she told him. "I feel considerably better now. Robin, we must meet."

"We've met."

"I mean to talk. We have to get out of here, there isn't much time left."

"Isn't it better to wait until the child is born?"

"I will not have my child born in this place." She spoke with the flat intensity born of desperation, and after a moment he nodded, and asked an odd question.

"Have you been initiated?"

"What, as an Angel? Of course. Why?"

"Later. Just don't make your Captain angry."

"I try not to. Have you met her?"

"I have met her," he said, and there were unpleasant connotations lurking behind his even words. "Dian, I mean it. Neither of us will leave this place if you make that woman angry."

"Right. Okay, I won't, but we must talk. How can I get to you?"

"As I said, we've met. Now you can ask for me next time you come to the Men's House. I'm on duty all next week." His voice was light but sharpened abruptly at Dian's reaction. "Don't touch me, and for God's sake don't look like that. That's better. Ask for me; they call me Robby."

"Robin, if I ask for you, after what happened today, they'll expect me to take you to pieces."

"Not necessarily. 'Nobody expects rational behavior from an Angel.'"

She began to laugh, saw Tomas ooze forward another half-foot, and ordered him back.

"Angels coming," Robin murmured. "Two of them."

She looked into his sweet, wise, weary face.

"Be strong, Robin. I'll get you out of here. See you Monday evening." She put up her hand to pat his cheek, then with the footsteps behind her she slid her hand caressingly down and dug her thumb and fingers into the pressure points of his neck. Before his hands could pry her fingers away, before the surprise on his face could change to alarm, he was unconscious. She winced inwardly at the thud he made hitting the ground, but outwardly she smiled down at him as her two colleagues came up to her.

"Looks like I got me a new playmate," she told them happily, whistled Tomas to her side, nodded her permission to the two private guards to approach what their appalled expressions said they thought would be a dead male, and continued her patrol through the warm spring afternoon, humming under her breath. Perhaps Ashtown was not so very hideous, after all. If one could leave.

In the bewitching hours, long after midnight, Dian came awake in her room, knowing something was wrong, not sure what it was. Margaret slept quietly beside her. Tomas snored in his place on the floor; there was no intruder. Her ears held no echo of a noise, from inside or out. She could smell nothing out of the ordinary. An overactive imagination, she told herself, go back to sleep.

The tadpole-baby stirred within her body, a weak surge but already stronger than the feather-tickle of a month ago. In the darkness she allowed herself to explore the unfamiliar shape of her belly, to lay both hands on the mound and feel the motions of the person she and Isaac had created in their pleasure, almost half a year ago. It stirred again. A small knob (a foot?) pressed against the palm of her right hand, and she smiled a private smile and felt the sting of tears in her eyes, tears of great tenderness and ferocity and sadness. She had meant what she said to Robin, although she had not voiced it to herself before: she would not have a baby born into Ashtown, not this baby, not to survive. Even a girl she would rather kill with her own hands than have it, a child of Isaac's, trapped here. Yet if she left, the hard journey south would very probably be the death of the child. This was not one of her "feelings"—those had faded into vague uneasinesses, a process that made her feel like a victim of cataracts, going slowly blind. It was merely a feeling, and an observation.

And now she knew what was wrong this night,

because she had felt it three times before. Both times since she came to Ashtown she had managed to keep it from the midwife, but this time—she had an appointment with the woman tomorrow, and even that stupid individual could hardly miss the symptoms. Dian lay in the night and ground her teeth in silent rage at her body's betrayal, but there was no way around it—she well knew how the Guard worked, and had no doubt that suspicions would be raised if she tried to avoid the midwife. She would eventually be found out, and the fact that she had tried to hide the problem would make life very difficult for her, would certainly lose her the freedoms she had so laboriously gained, the freedom of movement she must have in order to get Robin and herself out. After a while Dian reached over and switched on the electric light, and as Margaret roused in sleepy confusion Dian pushed the sheets aside and looked down at the brilliant red blood splashed across the white cotton. It wasn't that much—considerably less than what had spilled from the trader (Dian's little grunts of effort)— but it was too much to hide. Margaret came awake, and saw, and with exclamations of distress went to summon help while Dian lay back on the pillows and put her arm across her eyes.

Dian was confined to bed for four days, after which she was granted four days of limited mobility, to be sent back to bed on the second of those when the spotting started up again. She lay fuming beneath the medications for days, then sat and stared out the windows for the better part of a week. When the bleeding was thoroughly stopped, Dian alternated between pacing the halls and sitting like an invalid in the sun, throwing a ball for Tomas and agonizing over Robin. Finally, after twenty days of sick leave, Dian blew up at the midwife and threatened to break all her fingers, whistled Tomas to her side, and stormed off past a protesting Margaret to the duty officer to insist that she be placed back on the patrol roster.

Margaret stood at her shoulder and shouted furiously at the officer in charge, until finally Dian heaved her bodily out the door and locked it. She went and sat across the desk from the bemused Angel, and grinned crookedly.

"She's so damned protective, you'd swear it was her baby. I was stupid, you probably heard about it; I beat up some idiot Trader instead of using my wand and I started to spot, but that was three weeks ago. I'm going off my rocker—next thing you know Margaret'll have me knitting goddamned booties. Put me back on duty, even if it's half-days; I promise I'll take it easy and use the tickler instead of my fists."

"What does the midwife say?"

"Oh, you know her. She makes Margaret look irresponsible."

The Angel laughed. "I shouldn't have anything to do with it, but with this visit from Queen Bess coming up, we're too tight for words. There's been more graffiti than we can keep ahead of, even had some rock-throwing day before yesterday—you can imagine how the Captain loved that. If I could put you someplace visible but safe, even for half-days, it would free up someone else for the tougher stuff."

"That'll do, just to get me out of this place before I start drooling. Thanks, Donna."

"Anytime, glad to put people to work. I'll have to clear it with the Captain, of course, but there shouldn't be any problem."

There wasn't. Dian was back on the streets the next day, with dire warnings from midwife and healer ringing in her ears and the knowledge that Margaret was moving her stuff out of Dian's rooms in protest,

THEY SAT ON THEIR ROYAL CHAIRS THAT WERE FINELY

DECORATED WITH PRECIOUS STONES...

TWENTY-EIGHT

MORE THAN A HOUSE, LESS THAN A CITY, THE MEN'S Quarter of Ashtown was a world unto itself, obedient along certain lines but with a distinct air of aloofness, of uncertainty, as if a woman could not fully depend on not being laughed at behind her back while walking its corridors. Or even—and this was the spice of it—count on not being physically attacked. Not that violence occurred here, or if it did, it was rare, and then usually between men. Or, even more commonly, one man against himself. It was difficult to say exactly where this air of threat came from, for it was by no means overt, merely an awareness of the potential for teasing cruelty such as that possessed by a cat, a desire to pounce and tear that the animal's owner had no control over.

The eeriness of the place was underscored by the women who worked there, all of whom would have been exposed at a crossroads by less-civilized peoples. Each had been touched somehow, physically or mentally twisted and deformed. Dian assumed that they had been chosen for the work in order that the men might not be tempted by their servants, but she was not certain. She had no idea who did the choosing here, or their motivations.

The Men's Quarter was part harem, part boarding-house, all stronghold. Under the pretext of keeping the valuables in a safe place, Ashtown's menfolk were concentrated here, under lock and key and behind high walls. Some of them were members of a family and actually spent most of their time in their own private home with their wives, although theoretically even they lived here. Others were clearly courtesans, owned only each night by the highest bidder. Most were somewhere in between, independent but with certain duties to the city. Newcomers without money, such as Robin, were indentured slaves; it could take a long time for a man to work off his purchase price. Dian had no idea what the blond woman had received for him, but the price was sure to have been high, and unless he caught the eye of some wealthy family, his indenture would be long. The knowledge of the burden each carried did not help the morale of the men, and she had heard that a few years ago, when repression was particularly strong under Breaker's predecessor, there was an uprising one night that saw six Angels and nineteen men killed. Since then a state of cautious truce had prevailed, and women walked softly inside the walls of the Quarter.

Dian presented her identity badge at the desk and gave her knife to the woman there—her wand she was allowed to keep, both as her unremovable badge of authority and because everyone knew that a wand was useless to anyone but its coded owner anyway, and no man could manipulate it as a weapon against himself or others. It seemed that she had a lot of credits; what was her preference?

"I have an appointment with a gentleman by the name of Robby."

"An appointment?" said the woman. She pulled open a book and ran the tip of her finger down the columns with the distrust of a near illiterate, her eyes

narrowed and her mouth laboriously forming each
name. She had a severe facial defect, a twist across her
mouth that joined her upper lip with her nostrils and
made her speech almost impossible to understand.
"Didn't think Robby was on tonight," she finally
muttered. "No, I'm right. He's not due to be available
until Wednesday." She was clearly delighted at being
able to thwart an Angel, although she was careful not
to show it too openly.

"Tell him I'm here. I think he'll agree to see me."

"Not until Wednesday. Only three days. Or could I
call someone else? If you like the quiet ones, there's
Jacky. Or we have a new one, who'd cost you a lot of
credits but—"

"Robby," said Dian very quietly. "Now. Please."
She shifted her arm so that the wand rapped once
against the wood of the desk, then moved her hand
away from a small glint of silver on the counter; it instantly vanished. Bribery was not encouraged, especially by Angels, but this particular woman was well
known for her talent at slowing and obstructing the
process with small irritations, which slid away on
the grease of a silver coin. Dian had heard her called
the Ferryman.

The woman made a show of looking up Robin's
room location, sent a message off by a runner, a child
of fourteen with an artificial leg (Was every woman
here given the job for which she was least suited,
wondered Dian?), and allowed Dian a chair in the
next room among the other clients.

One by one names were called and women went
through the ornate gilded doors at the far end of the
room. No men appeared. Dian sat in the ornate and
diabolically uncomfortable chair with her legs
stretched out before her, a dark island avoided by the
stout and pompous merchants and the less prosperous, nervous middle-class types alike. After a while

another Angel came in, gave Dian a nod, and sat down across the room to set up an island of her own.

Dian had just concluded that a) the men themselves had designed this system to keep the women of Ashtown in their places, and b) the Ferryman's fee must have risen, when her number was called—outside the Center, Angels did not have names. She ignored the inaudible ripple of relief that went through her neighbors as she rose and followed the summoning crone through the encrusted doors. The woman, a twist of bone who barely reached Dian's chest, hobbled ahead of her to the registration desk. The woman there was nearly normal in outline but afflicted with some skin disorder that had left her with blotches of color ranging from Jamilla-black to Willa-white. The piebald effect was startling but not entirely unattractive. Apparently the woman herself thought so as well, for her dress was so scanty as to leave little to the imagination. She held out a pen between black thumb and pink forefinger and waited for Dian to sign for the authorization to transfer credits. Dian looked at the paper, then looked more closely with her eyebrows raised.

"This is a mistake," she said. "I only want the one man for half the night, not six men until noon."

"No mistake, ma'am," the woman said in a throaty voice that intimated she would happily perform other functions than that of accountant. "Robby's new, quite vigorous, and most creative in his services. I think you'll be pleased with him. In addition, there is a surcharge for his being off duty and the additional medications it will necessitate."

Dian took the pen and smiled thinly, tempted to drive it through the hand that lay on the desk.

"You misunderstand. No medications are required. The services I require will not prove...taxing on his strength." She crossed out the total and wrote in a figure one quarter the original, signed it, and handed it back to the piebald woman. And bared her teeth. The woman's superior facade cracked slightly, and she held the paper as if Dian had smeared it with something foul.

"One moment, please," she said, and ducked through a door. Dian leaned against the counter, studied a bad painting of a nude male on the wall, and cleaned her fingernails. After a considerable time the woman reappeared and put the paper in front of Dian, then put another beside it, and took a small step back. The figure had been changed again, twice Dian's offer and half the original, and initialed. Not, thought Dian, by this woman herself. The other paper was a short typed statement to the effect that she, City Guard 820, agreed that if she were to cause injury or damage to Robby VanDerHue (was that really Robin's last name, she wondered?) she would agree to pay an additional sum, which would bring the total up to the first figure that had appeared on the paper. Ah, she thought, amused: word of her encounter with Robin had reached the Quarter, and they were afraid she might be here for purposes of revenge. Stupid, really, to think that they could control the actions of an Angel.

Dian took up the pen again, signed the statement with a flourish, drew a line through the new figure on the other page and wrote one that was halfway between their second offer and hers, and initialed it herself with *D* and her number. The woman bit her lip and could not keep from glancing briefly at the sleek black wand strapped to Dian's bare arm. She was gone for a shorter time, then returned without the papers, looking relieved. Wordlessly, she took a key from a large rack and handed it to the child who rose from a seat at the end of the counter. As wordlessly, Dian took the key from the child's hand, reached across the counter to put it back on its hook, and chose three others at random. She handed them to the child, who seemed too stupid to be either frightened or confused but who moved placidly away with the top key held in front of her nose. Tonight Dian would choose her own room. The price extracted, over twice the normal, would pay for all but the most luxurious suites.

The three rooms she looked at were almost indistinguishable, each being impersonally furnished, tidy, but with the mustiness of ingrained grime and stale passion. She took the second one, slightly larger and not quite so tawdry in its decorations, and prowled around nervously while Robin—Robby—was brought. The curtains felt greasy and the window looked onto the back of another building, gray wood on top of two stories of brick, all in the shadow of the taller building Dian was in. The window across from her held three anemic potted plants, their leaves pressed up to the glass like the fingers of wistful children. Dian made a short sound of irritation and let the curtains fall shut, then went to sit on the room's single chair.

Robin knocked before entering, and Dian had to stifle the urge to leap up and fling herself on him. It was as well she satisfied herself with a laconic "Enter," because he was not alone. The placid child who had brought her here followed him into the room, each of them carrying a heavy wooden box. The child put hers down on a table and left. Robin put his down beside hers and straightened his back.

"What is—" she started to say, but he was already talking.

"I brought the music you told me you wanted. I wasn't sure you were still interested, after all this time, but it's here if you want it." His eyes were full of warning, and she answered carefully.

"Yes, you were right. Is any of it good?"

"Some of the records are badly scratched, but, here, I'll set it up and you can choose one." He was already pulling from one of the boxes a venerable black and silver record player and its attached speakers. He set them up on the table, rummaged in the box and came up with an extension cord that was more mend than original wire, and crawled under the bed to plug it in. He went to the other box, took off the lid, and slipped out half a dozen black discs separated by sheets of soft paper.

"What do you fancy, slow or fast?" he asked, giving a nod on the first option.

"Slow, I think, at least to start with," Dian answered obediently, with only the vaguest idea of what was happening. He selected a record, laid it on the turntable, and in a few seconds a hiss and the regular thump of a scratch filled the room, and then a rich syrup of music arose, and Robin moved forward with his arms slightly raised. It appeared that they were going to dance.

It took Dian a while to remember where her hands went and how to be led rather than lead, but after she'd stumbled twice and nearly sent Robin sprawling, they both shortened their steps and it worked fairly well. He was, to her surprise, a good dancer. She put her face awkwardly alongside his.

"Either you've gone completely crackers," she whispered into his ear, "or you think there are listeners."

"Can't be sure which microphones are working and which aren't, but it's best to be careful."

"No watchers?"

"I don't think in here, but again, if you assume there's an eye at the keyhole, you won't step wrong." He winced. "Speaking of which, could you take off your shoes?"

She unlaced her tall black boots and they met again

in the middle of the floor, some male voice crooning about the impossibility of leaving his love. Dian draped herself across Robin and spoke urgently while keeping her face without emotion.

"I'm sorry, Robin, I started bleeding before I could get here last month; they wouldn't let me out. I couldn't think of any way to get a message to you."

"I'm glad you didn't try," he murmured. "I heard you were sick, glad you're better. Is the baby all right?"

"What? Oh, yes, fine. Look, Robin, we have only three weeks. Queen Bess will be here after that, and with her and her garrison camped here, it'll be impossible until early July." Too late—but he knew that. She described briefly the preparations, how Breaker would leave the city, taking nearly a quarter of the Angels with her, for a period of five or six days.

"It's got to be then, Robin. Before that the clampdown will be hard, getting the people well-behaved. Without Breaker here, we'd have a chance. There are two problems. First, we'll have to have some help from inside the Men's Quarter. You'll have to find someone willing to risk a bribe to get you to me. Once out I can get you over the wall. The second involves Tomas. I may have to leave him behind." She explained about the Captain's plan to take Tomas as part of the escort. "There are choices. I could injure Tomas slightly so she couldn't take him, but it'd have to look worse than it was or he'd slow us down. Or, if you could suggest something to make him sick but that he'd recover from in a day or two, I could use that. I don't know, though, Robin. I can't afford to make her suspicious. I love Tomas, almost as much as I loved Culum, but if it's a question of staying here or losing him, there's no choice. If having Tomas with her makes the Captain feel that I'm safely pinned down, so be it."

Robin said nothing, but his body and hands were gentle, comforting. Not in the least erotic. They danced for a while without speaking, and when his voice came in her ear it was in the tones of a man who had something very definite to say.

"We'll try. About the other. There is...unrest in the city."

"You know about it?"

"I told you, the Quarter knows everything, if a person can sort sense from nonsense. I hear everything. In fact, I'm known as something of an old gossip."

"You?" The very idea was absurd.

"Indeed. Most of the tales in circulation have passed through old Robby. They change a bit sometimes, coming out. The number of injured men grows a bit, the weakness of the Angels gets exaggerated. Some tales even get started here. The one about Breaker's sister. Heard it?"

"About her being a—about her odd taste in food? I found some graffiti about it the other day. God, I hope you're careful, Robin."

"Oh, I'm subtle with it," he said, not really answering her question. "If I can't be free, I might as well indulge my unexpected taste for anarchy. Which brings me to the point. There are twelve good men and true, ready to lead a bid for freedom. Half a hundred more who would be gathered in if the wind were strong enough. Dozens willing to be blind. Three weeks is short to bring it to a head, but I can try."

"Robin, what on earth are you talking about? All we need is someone to let you out and a minor distraction on the other side of the Quarter, not a riot."

"Revolution is more what we had in mind."

"'We?'" Dian stopped dead; he got her moving again. "My God, Robin, what have you been doing here? What kind of ideas have you been putting into their heads?"

"The ideas were there. Surely you've heard what happened five years ago? Twenty-two Angels dead, half again as many men?"

"No, no, it was six and nineteen."

"I've seen the records, Dian. Twenty-two and thirty-seven known dead, with five more missing in the fire. The men nearly had the city then, or enough to bargain with, but they hadn't the weapons, and when the Angels took back the Quarter and went on a rampage, they sealed their fate. Before that night it might have been different—negotiation, relaxing the restrictions, small breaks in the walls. Not now. Nobody's forgotten a thing. Listening to the stories, you'd swear you could smell smoke and see blood seeping down the stairs. It's gone underground, but it's very much alive. There's not a man in here, even those who were children then or have come since, who doesn't believe with all his soul that sooner or later he'll walk out of the Quarter a free man, and most of them know in their hearts that it'll be over the bodies of Angels. The Angels know it too. You never see one in here unarmed, they never eat or drink in here, very rarely stay the night. No, I haven't contributed any ideas that weren't here already. Helped give it some focus, started it coming together perhaps. But the process itself is inevitable."

Robin continued to steer Dian's unresponsive body around the floor until the record came to an end, and went to turn it over. He came back and took up her arms again.

"There'll be another slaughter," he continued. "One that'll make the last one look like a cart accident. Unless cooler heads retain control over the Angels, in which case it'll be just our ringleaders castrated and hanged and the rest of the Quarter sold and traded to the four winds or kept sedated for the rest of their days."

"Robin," she said finally, "this isn't your business."

"It is," he hissed, and the venom in his voice was a revelation. "By God it is. I didn't ask to be brought here. Not a man here deserves to be sold and caged like an animal. This city has to be taught that no human being has the right to do that to another."

"Revenge."

"Righteousness. Justice, if you prefer. It'll happen, Dian. And there'll be a bloodbath on both sides. Unless you help."

"Robin, for God's sake, I can't smuggle guns into the Men's Quarter," she said flatly.

"Oh, no, my dear, nothing so complicated. All I need from you is information. For one thing, does Breaker have large-scale weapons?"

"What, like artillery? I'm sure she has some portable things, grenade-launchers and the like, half a dozen machine guns, two armored cars, and a store of fuel to run them with. But I've never seen or heard of anything bigger. I think someone told me that there had been a half-repaired airplane once, but Bess took it. She's the one with the weapons. Breaker has mostly riot gear."

"She also has a certain device, and we absolutely have to know where it's located. It's bound to be somewhere Breaker can get at quickly, a small room near her quarters, even a closet. Don't worry about how to use it, we can figure that out. We just need to be able to find it without wasting our time searching." And he told her then what the device was, and with considerable satisfaction told her how it would be used, and it was as well that no one was watching them because very soon Dian gave up all pretense of dancing and reared back her head to stare at him, openmouthed.

"*All* the Angels?" she whispered, aghast.

"Not you, of course, I'll take care of you," he began, and then he realized that what he saw on her face
was not just surprise but horror. Revulsion. He let her
go and took a step away from her, and with that small
movement the stubborn faith that had brought her after him, that had bound them together and given
them both purpose through all the dark nights, quiv-
ered like a spider's gossamer in a strong wind, and a
great hungry chasm yawned up at their feet. In ten
seconds Dian watched him age a decade, and his eyes
sagged and looked at her with fear.

"Oh, God," he said. "What have I done? At least
promise me you won't report us. You owe me that,
Dian. Please."

Robin begging was more than Dian could bear. She
grabbed his hand as if to keep him from falling into
the rift between them, or perhaps to keep herself from
falling, and she wrapped it between both of hers, holding it against her chest.

"Robin, please, don't look like that. Of course
you're safe with me. It's just—you're talking about
mur—about killing more than two hundred people, in
cold blood. And not all of them deserve to die, really
they don't, Robin. There's a lot...Some of the Angels..." She took a deep breath and started again.
"Look, let me think about it, see if I can come up with
something else not quite so...drastic." Barbaric. Terrifying. Their hands lay just above the rise of her
belly, and she held them there until she saw most of
his fear subside. Nonetheless, the memory of it stood
between them, and changed everything. She moved to
lessen the damage.

"I mean it, Robin. I will think about it, I promise
you. But honestly, I think it would be a great mistake
to wipe out all the Angels. For one thing, it probably
wouldn't take out the top echelon, certainly not
Breaker or her sister. For another, I swear to you that

there are some Angels who would make valuable allies and friends, and you—the men—would be fools to cut yourselves off from them. Surely you can figure out how to make this...device...selective?" She was now the one to plead, and Robin saw what this meant before she did: she was more than halfway committed to this act, because it was he who asked it of her. She was an Angel, yes, with power of life and death over him, but she was Dian, and she would hold to her faith, if it cost her more than her life.

In the end they agreed to meet in two days. Robin would talk with the men. Dian would find the room. She left, not looking at him, her hands cold but her black uniform clammy with chill sweat. She felt as though her forehead were branded: *Escapee. Mass Murderer.* And worst of all: *Traitor.*

That night Dian could not eat dinner, could not sit still, lay awake restless until Margaret (who had never actually moved out despite her threat) finally asked her what was the matter. Dian snarled at her and got up, went to the kitchen and made herself a cup of hot whiskey-tea, and took it to drink in the dark living room.

Thoughts flew about her head, as uncontrollable as if she were already drunk. God, what had he gotten them into, stupid goddamned male ruled by his balls, I thought Robin had more sense. Some distraction that would make: the Quarter rising, men spilling out in all directions and setting the whole stinking city on fire, Angels dropping like flies, nobody'd take much notice of two horses making their way off. Tomas—no, can't think of Tomas, too excruciating, think of Tadpole inside, no longer a tadpole, kicking out as the whiskey hit it, punching too, on the other side, bossy damned kid, Don't drink, Mama. Oh, God, Robin, what have you done to me? If I stop you,

you're dead, and half the Men's Quarter with you, but if I go along I put the necks of every single one of these women I've lived with, fought beside, slept next to, under a guillotine blade controlled by a lot of power-drunk adolescents with testosterone in their brains. And Breaker won't even be here, damn your eyes. If Breaker were here, if I could be sure your rioting menfolk would get their greedy hands on her, God, I don't think I'd hesitate, not even for Margaret, but the witch will be out of reach, safe with Queen Bess—until she comes back to crush you all. Wait until she's home? And with Bess inside the city walls too, take out the both of them at once—but no, not possible, there'll be too many guns without Angel implants waiting to cut down untrained rioters, male or no. Jesus and Mary, I need another drink, go to sleep, Tadpole, Mama's gonna get smashed.

But the alcohol did not remove the thoughts flying about in her head, only slowed them, simplified them, made them all the more stark and terrible.

Could they—could she—trust the men? That was the question gnawing at her mind like a living thing. Given the tool for murder, would the men use it well, use it to carve for themselves some freedom of movement, or would the revolt be only a carnage of blood-thirsty revenge, like the story Kirsten had told once about what happened Before when groups of well-meaning animal lovers loosed the wild tigers and lions from their cages? What had started as a personal and private bid for freedom had exploded into . . . this, and too many lives were at stake. Too many women. Too many—ah, yes, that was the point, wasn't it? Too many friends.

Thirteen weeks was too long to remain aloof. The Ashtown Guard was no longer an anonymous mass of black-garbed monsters. On the day she had finally met Robin, she had told herself that everyone hated and feared her, but it had not been true; even then she had known it was not. Yes, some of the Angels were sadistic horrors, but she had found those to be surprisingly few, had discovered the disquieting fact that most of the Angels, behind the closed doors of the Center, revealed themselves to be strong, capable women, not unfriendly, not without humor, with an above-average complement of intelligence and a powerful sense of loyalty.

She liked them. To her amazement, considerable consternation, and occasional self-loathing, yes: there were some she would count, were she honest with herself, as friends.

And Margaret. What of Margaret? They had become lovers a little more than a month after Dian's arrival, for a complexity of reasons Dian still had not sorted out. Loneliness was part of it, odd in itself for a woman who by her nature preferred solitude. Simple animal affection entered into it, a response to the one hand held out to her on her arrival, and wanting to give something in return. The surface reasons—that it made her stand out less among the other Angels, that it fit the role expected of her—she no longer even considered, because whatever it was that existed between Margaret and herself, it was not surface.

The edifice she and Margaret were creating had lies and deceptions for its foundation, but the building itself was an honest one. Moreover, as the superstructure took on more weight and substance, it was settling down and compressing its false base into a real one. Somewhere she still knew herself to be Culum's Dian, Judith and Kirsten and Isaac's Dian, but that woman of the South was fading, turning into an insubstantial ghost at the shoulder of the Angel Dian, that Vampire among a community of creatures bound by the taste of a Captain's blood. Dian had proven her worth: a dependable guard, formidable despite her current condition, silent and steady and working her way rapidly up toward A status, her Captain's fair-haired girl.

Sometimes at night she would get out of bed and stand in front of the bathroom mirror, naked but for the identity tags on the thong around her neck, trying to discern what those around her were seeing, what the Captain, Margaret, the Angels thought was there. She herself saw nothing, only an ever more blatant and bitterly ironic contrast between her swelling belly and breasts and the increasing angularity of her face, bordering on gauntness and dented with the beginnings of what in a few years would look like the lines carved by chronic pain. Her face looked older than Judith's, her breasts full and nubile, her belly ageless. She would look again at the lines beside her mouth that had not been there in August, flush the toilet, and return to bed. On the nights Margaret was there, they would make the awkward and ultimately unsatisfying love Margaret seemed to want, and lie back to back in the night, pretending to sleep, obscurely comforted.

She took her drink into the bathroom, closing the door and turning on the light. Tonight when she dropped her robe in front of the mirror, her skin was flushed with the alcohol, and the scar of the Angel on her left breast looked almost like fresh blood. It had begun to pull as the tissue beneath it expanded, a minor discomfort, little more than an itch on top of the deep and perpetual burn. She touched it faintly with the fingertips of her right hand, traced the familiar shape of it, and thought with a remarkable lack of fear about what Robin had told her, the truth of what lay beneath the scar, the truth that explained how the two guards whom she had bested on the snow-covered forecourt back in January had come to drop down dead before the day was out, how Angels who

displeased their Captain tended to have heart attacks
out of the blue. Beneath this brand in her flesh lay the
ultimate power of Ashtown's Captain, the key to her
authority, the secret weapon that Robin proposed to
hand over to the men, Robin's own gentle, cold-
blooded, and utterly ruthless means of striking back
at this nest of snakes that had drawn him in.

 If she gave him what he asked for, paid what
seemed to be the Quarter's price for Robin's and her
freedom, if she led them to the small room with the
transmitter device, who, then, would die? Number
489, perhaps, Alicia of the beautiful hands and the
delicate watercolors and the earthy jokes? Or 314,
middle-age Johanna, who cried whenever she thought
of the granddaughter who refused to see her? Or 824,
gorgeous lithe black Dinah, just joined at age seven-
teen and gently troubled by the morality of her
choice? Or Suellen, the D who cleaned Dian's rooms,
placid and big of heart? Or Lani, the oldest Angel in
the Center, white-haired and straight-backed and
lightning with the wand and generous of her time to
teach the newcomers? And what of Laura, she of the
wide mouth and dark moods, who had once when in
her cups admitted to the embarrassment of having
two escapees in her family, a pair of cousins named
Miriam and Isaac? Would all those numbers, walking
their patrols, running perhaps through the halls of the
Center to the alarm bells, stop in their tracks with a
faint look of surprise and then collapse as the cap-
sules beneath the Angel brand—those tiny receiver,
trigger, and poison devices implanted by Breaker's diabolical metal-cloth hand—burst open to release their
silent death?

 Not the Captain, oh, no. She would have no capsule burning her breast.

 And not 820; Robin would cut Dian's from her in
time.

But number 749? She of the firm and gentle hands and the profound sense of the ridiculous and the deep doubts about the rightness of what she was doing: what of Margaret?

Dian traced the upswept wings gently, then suddenly scrubbed the heel of her palm hard across the mark two, three times, with no result but a momentary sharp pang where there was normally an ache.

Dian supposed she loved Margaret. It was a form of love, anyway, this coming together of two mismatched souls. However, if truth is in wine, then strong spirit holds the stronger truth, and in her near-empty cup Dian could only see that Margaret was not to be trusted. From the very first, she had seen the Angel healer's flirtation with death and disaster, and the whiskey told her that Margaret, given the tools, would not be able to resist pulling it all down on their heads. Unwillingly, unconsciously even, but she could simply not be trusted with a secret. Short of kidnapping her, or knocking her out and cutting the capsule out of her, there was no way of saving Margaret other than putting her life in the hands of the men.

She raised the bitter cup to her mouth and drained it, then reached down for her robe, flushed the toilet, and went back to her bed.

"DO YOU ESTEEM MY STRENGTH SO LITTLE THAT
YOU PLAN TO DEFEAT ME WITH STICKS?"

TWENTY-NINE

THREE WEEKS.

Twenty days, twenty elongated, slowed-down, stretched-out days, every tick of the clock spanning a slow breath and each evening an eternity from its morning, and yet, as with any event of massive import, the hours seemed incongruously to tumble one upon another in uncontrollable panic as the end loomed inescapably closer and closer. The days gathered tension to themselves as an avalanche gathers pieces of hillside, and the nights—the nights were sheer hell.

No one must know. Margaret must not guess. Breaker must catch no faint whiff of suspicion or she would be on it in a flash, and all would be lost. Utter and absolute normality, the mask she had held up in front of her since the day back in January when she had ridden up to Ashtown's snow-covered forecourt, must be maintained. Nothing of the massive land-slide of tension thundering through her could be permitted to show. The appearance of normality was urgently, hugely important.

It was also quite impossible.

She maintained the facade for a day, two days,

three, with nothing more than an odd glance from Margaret and an offhand joke from one of the other Angels to rake her raw nerves.

And then on the fourth day she knocked the midwife unconscious.

From the first visit the woman had made Dian's hackles rise, for no discernible reason other than her perpetual cheeriness and jocular nagging. This time she was jovially displeased about Dian's blood pressure and launched off on a lecture concerning Dian's activities, scolding her about her visits to the Quarter and threatening her with bed rest. It was this last that caused Dian to lose control—only briefly, just one fist, but the midwife was not really an Angel and was unprepared. Instruments scattered and a chair was flattened in the impact, and Dian stormed out past the woman's assistant, knowing that disaster had just struck.

Two hours later she was summoned to the chief healer's offices near the infirmary. She had seen Margaret's superior only two or three times, and on each occasion she had been struck by the woman's quiet calm and her sense of burdens borne. She reminded Dian of a sad Ling. This time was no exception. The healer took Dian into her office, sat for several minutes with her fingertips on the pulse in Dian's wrist, then moved her chair around to face her patient.

"You find Charlotte difficult?" were her first words.

"I'm sorry, I do. But hitting her was unforgivable."

The healer smiled gently. "You didn't hurt her, and you may have taught her a valuable lesson. I assure you, you're not the first to find Charlotte's style of midwifery oppressive. Personally, if I were to find myself under her care, I'd probably strangle her. You will come to see me for the remainder of your pregnancy. No, don't worry, I enjoy birthing—it's a pleasant change from broken bones and concussions. I always look forward to Charlotte's 'rejects'—they're generally more interesting than her star pupils." She laughed, a cough of humor. "But I'm afraid she is right: you are doing too much for your health and the health of your child. You're also worrying, and you're not sleeping well. You're an Angel, but even Angels have to recognize that they are primarily women. I know it's difficult. It's not easy to think that you're heading into a period of relative helplessness. The stress," she added, "being on *relative*. Your training, your very personality go against accepting a degree of dependence. However, you must learn to accept it, and relax, or you're going to be ill. Now, how do we do this? Do I take you off the street?"

"No! I mean, please, I really would crack up if you locked me away. That's why I hit her—the thought of bed rest . . ."

"I see. Nonetheless, you must cut back. I will allow you to maintain a quarter-time schedule, three half-days a week, for the next month. After that you will simply have to find other outlets. And speaking of which, your visits to the Quarter. You told Charlotte that you do nothing more physical there than dancing. Is that so?"

"Yes."

"Make sure it stays that way. Also, I want you to promise that you will lie down for one hour every afternoon."

Dian was glad she was sitting; she went lightheaded with relief. "All right," she managed to say. "Thank you."

It was as simple as that. Word spread, as always in the Center; the other Angels made their subtle and accustomed adjustments to this latest manifestation of the mild craziness of all Angels, and made no further reference to Dian's pregnancy, not to her face.

Dian knew there were numerous remarks and humorous glances when her back was turned, but she gritted her teeth and encouraged the attitude. It gave her fellows a focus well away from the true source of her worries.

Fifteen days left to the rising. A new series of graffiti appeared overnight, an odd pointy squiggle of bilious green paint, like an upside-down mountain range, soon interpreted as two long fangs on either side of a row of pointed teeth: Vampire teeth. The Ds were busy all day painting the marks over; the next morning they were back again. Rocks flew out of nowhere at Angel heads, a pair of teenagers was found painting a fence with a vaguely similar green color, and the arrest edged into a near-riot before an alibi was provided. Sharpened stakes fell out of doorways, trip wires in alleyways sent bucketloads of filth onto Angel heads, and a pail of green paint fell from a roof, spattering the double patrol with indelible, pus-colored smears.

Inside the Center, tempers flared. The Captain raged, Ds and newcomers collapsed in tears, quarrels escalated into drawn weapons. A minor disagreement with Margaret blossomed into a crisis, ending late at night with a hysterical and very drunk Margaret slamming out Dian's door. Dian gave her half an hour to calm down and then followed her to her rooms and spent the next three hours comforting her, listening to her weepy plaints and apologies, and feeling gray exhaustion creeping up. The next day, for the first time ever, Dian canceled a patrol and stayed in bed, knowing that the authorities would have heard of her night and been displeased if she had pushed herself onto the streets.

Fourteen days; thirteen. A messenger Angel at her door: her presence was required by the Captain. Dian's heart beat heavily in her chest and a hissing built in her ears, but although she felt giddy and shut the door with a degree more abruptness than was good manners, she did not faint. She changed into her newest and most voluminous tunic and, Tomas as always touching her left fingers, walked with the messenger to their Captain's door. The other Angel raised a hand to knock, but Dian forestalled her with a question.

"Say, Violet, you've done some work on security, haven't you?"

"Some, yes."

"Well, I was talking to Lieutenant Carmela last week." This was the woman in charge of the Center's internal security. "Something she said made me think about this wing, and I've been wondering if there's any way we might improve it. I know the Center's tight, but if—God forbid—some crazy got inside, she'd be sure to aim for the Captain. What I was thinking was, is there someplace—even a small room—that's fairly secure already and would only need to be strengthened?" Violet's eyes flickered to one side, and without following her gaze Dian went on. "Just a space for the Captain to be absolutely safe until we could get her out. It's not urgent, I suppose, certainly not worth bothering the Captain over until after the Queen is gone, but think about it, huh?"

The Angel nodded and turned back to the door, and Dian with her, but afterward, coming out of Breaker's rooms furious and humiliated and relieved and desolate, her eyes went to the spot that had drawn Violet's eyes. It was an awkward corner, created when two neighboring buildings had been joined, but the paneling was broken in a door-sized rectangle, and a small plate of polished black glass, nearly hidden behind an ill-lit statue of a nude male, covered the number-pad release for a high-security door. Dian noted its position mechanically and walked away.

She walked alone.

The pain of Breaker's order, the emptiness at her side, made further explanations about her state of nerves unnecessary. It also submerged the anxiety almost completely. Several times over the next days she forgot entirely, found herself thinking, *When Breaker comes back and I have Tomas again*—only to remember that, no, she would not see him again, ever. Unless she failed.

Margaret came in that evening to find Dian sitting in a cold, dark room, staring unseeing at the ashes in the fireplace, a half-empty bottle of Ashtown rotgut on the table before her. Dian did not look up at the movement of the door, seemed not to notice the sudden illumination of the room, and Margaret, after studying her for a long moment, shrugged out of her jacket and took it to the closet, went into the kitchen and put the chicken she'd stewed earlier back into the oven to heat, rubbed out the note she'd written on the message slate asking Dian to put the dish in, made two cups of strong tea, and carried them out into the living room. Dian had not moved. Margaret put the mug down in front of her, laid and lit a fire, closed the curtains, and took the bottle out into the kitchen. She came back to sit near Dian, tucked her feet under her in the chair, and blew at her cup.

"What happened?" she asked quietly.

For half a minute more Dian sat unheeding, and then blinked and looked at the fire, then at Margaret.

"Tomas. She took Tomas."

"The Captain?" Margaret was surprised, not at the idea but at Dian's reaction. Breaker often kept the dog with her for hours, half a day at a time.

"Bitch," Dian spat out. "Worse than a bitch in heat. Shameless." Margaret could hear the slur of Dian's voice now and knew that she was indeed profoundly drunk. She had never seen it before and was alarmed at the thought of listeners, but there was no stopping Dian. "Been after him for months. Stupid fucking dog, can't see into her. He's not mine anymore. Wouldn't go for her if I ordered him to, not now. Not mine. Never again. Gone. He's gone. Stupid damned male, thinks with his—" She stopped dead, slapped her hand over her mouth, and turned so pale that Margaret hurriedly put down her cup and scrambled to her feet, looking desperately for something Dian could vomit into.

Dian dropped the cup she was holding, fumbled to retrieve it, then abandoned the effort and struggled, heavy now and awkward, to her feet. She turned her back on Margaret and walked with swaying dignity out of the room, but she did not pause in either bathroom or kitchen. Instead, Margaret heard the bedroom door close softly, and the creak of the bedsprings, then silence.

She sat down on the sofa in Dian's place, filled with bewilderment and uneasiness. Surely Breaker would return Tomas after Bess's visit. He was much too valuable to sell or give away, and what on earth could she do with him in the Center if not return him to Dian? She couldn't possibly spend the time on him that Dian did, nor was she a stupid woman, willing to cripple one of her Angels just to demonstrate her power. But Dian had sounded so final. And the hand over the mouth—that had not been the stomach's rebellion, but almost a parody of shut-my-mouth, especially accompanied as it had been by a strange expression of—what? Drunken slyness? A shaft of sober fear? Alarm, certainly. Because the thought of listeners had suddenly broken through to her? Somehow Margaret thought not. And the uncertainty made her unhappy.

It had to be connected to the guilt that Dian had been demonstrating in recent days; of that Margaret was certain. Her sudden interest in the Men's Quarter, her jumpiness and absentmindedness, and tonight's abrupt self-interruption while referring to male intractability—yes, no doubt about it: there was a man in it somewhere.

In the dark bedroom Dian lay staring up at the ceiling, nowhere near as drunk as Margaret thought, but far more so than she should have allowed herself to be. She lay staring at the ceiling, imagining ways to kill her Captain, the woman who had stolen her dog's loyalty, who had toyed and teased Dian with Tomas's obedience, taken such languid pleasure in demonstrating her power over the dog, reveling in Dian's helpless rage, and finally been both amused and aroused by Dian's hatred of her. She had kissed the nape of Dian's neck in mocking affection, and laughed aloud in sheer happiness when Dian came within a breath of attacking her.

God, she hated Breaker, loathed her, wanted nothing more in life but the pleasure of killing her. Almost nothing, she corrected herself. First she would thwart Breaker and her city, walk away from its prison bars and loose the menfolk on it: freedom, whatever the cost. She would give Robin that, and (she was becoming more sober, depressingly so) she would carry out her responsibilities to the child in her womb, Isaac's child.

Someday, though, she would return. Someday.

Twelve days. Dian woke to find herself alone and bereft, but safe: the Center thought she was going nuts with her pregnancy, the Captain saw her being pushed off center by the loss of Tomas, and Margaret read her anger as guilt; all were, in part, correct. As long as Dian refrained from disillusioning any of them, she and the men were safe.

Eleven, ten, nine days. The Angels cracked down

hard, drew the curfew back an hour, punished anyone found with paintbrush or rock in hand. It appeared to be working; things calmed down, the Vampire graffiti failed to appear one morning, the turmoil within the Center calmed somewhat. Breaker walked with a swing in her stride, believing her hard hand had done the trick. Dian knew the truth: the men didn't want to risk her canceling the trip north.

One week before Breaker was due to leave for the rendezvous with Queen Bess, Dian went to the Angel in charge of the duty roster and told her she wanted to start her maternity leave.

"About time, I'd say. Effective today?"

"If it's convenient."

"Sure. Things have been quiet lately. You'd never've thought so a couple of weeks ago, but the problems just faded away. Bit of graffiti last night, but we haven't had anyone throwing rocks in days. Must've been a phase of the moon or something."

"Funny."

"Yeah, it is. Anyway, sure, this is a fine time to get you off the streets. We may need to call on you once the Queen arrives, but there's nothing urgent until then. You want a job in the meantime, or some time off? You have the credits."

"You know me, I've got to have something to do. A desk job, or teaching?" she suggested, knowing she'd never finish any class she started.

"Can I put you down for tutoring duty? Nothing too physical, maybe wand and guns?"

"Sure. Archery if you want it," Dian offered. "Or staff, if I wear a padded vest."

"I don't know about the staff, but we were just saying the other day that we should do a refresher in archery. I'll see if I can put together a class. You get more credits for a group," she added, and made a note in her ledger. "Might even join myself—I did a bit as a kid, but it would be fun to pick it up again."

"Fun, yes, well. Schedule it whenever you like, two or three days a week. See you," she said, reflecting that she probably would not, ever again.

"Sure. Say, where's the dog?" the Angel asked innocently. Dian paused, her hand on the door frame, searching the woman's face for mischief and not seeing it. She was that rare creature, an Angel who missed out on the gossip.

"With Breaker," Dian said finally.

"With—oh, yeah, come to think of it I did hear something. You know, I don't think I've ever seen you without him. Must feel funny."

"It feels like I've had an arm amputated," she said flatly, and went out the door.

It was the truth. She felt the loss of Tomas even more acutely than she had Culum. Then she had the distraction of fever, and the death had been noble and clean; this, however, was neither. It was betrayal, it was selling the dog into slavery, and the thought of Tomas working with Breaker was almost as repugnant as the idea of giving birth to a citizen of Ashtown. That Tomas was young enough to recover from her absence, that he would be pampered and valued the rest of his life, almost made it worse. Death in battle would have suited him better.

She was also quite simply not herself without Tomas. Since she had taken her first steps, Dian had never been away from her dogs for more than an hour or two at a time. The dangling fingers of her left hand were continually startled at encountering nothing but air. She kept thinking she was hearing things, only to realize it was an absence, not a presence, of the click of canine nails on pavement. The nights rang with emptiness, and she often jerked awake in alarm at the lack of grunts and snores from the floor beside the bed, imagining the silence to mean Tomas sitting up, pricking his ears at an intruder. Every time her hand went out in a command as automatic as breathing, she was brought up hard by the realization that the human partner at her side was not about to respond. Her reaction time was shot to hell; she really had no business patrolling the streets.

It was true that she was not needed, that the turmoil which had been building throughout the spring had abruptly tapered off. Breaker would leave with a confident mind, and Dian, too, was reassured, though for markedly different reasons: the quiet streets demonstrated more than Robin's words that the Men's Quarter had a greater degree of control, over events and over itself, than she had feared. Perhaps utter disaster was not to be the inevitable outcome of this.

Eight, seven. Dian went to the Quarter that afternoon while Margaret was on duty in the infirmary, spent two hours with the syrupy music blaring, and when she left, the route to the small locked room was in Robin's head. She did not know how the menfolk would get in, either to the Center or the room, but she assumed that there must be some way to overcome the numbered code behind the black glass plate— after all, what if Breaker died without telling anyone the code? Actually, she did not much care; if the men couldn't figure it out, that was their problem. She and Robin would be gone.

Six days, five. Four. Less than forty-eight hours before Breaker left, and coming up from the bowels of the Center where she'd been coaching the new Angels in the use of the bow and arrow, Dian turned a corner and there was Breaker with Tomas at her knee. Both Dian and her dog reacted instantaneously, he leaping at her like a puppy and biting affectionately and stropping his hundred fifty pounds of enthusiastic muscle against her legs and flailing his tail around so hard that the next day she had bruises along her shins, and she thumping him and tugging his ruff and slapping at his grinning mouth and shaking his lower jaw with her hand and feeling his tongue slobber and work against her palm and his teeth chew gently. It was perhaps thirty seconds before Dian remembered.

She looked up slowly into a pair of yellow eyes utterly devoid of any human expression, and a cold shiver of fear rose through her. Not for herself, but for Tomas. She extracted her hand and stood away from him.

"Tomas, heel," said Breaker in a gentle voice that held a razor's edge, but Tomas was having none of it and would not be stood away from. He ignored Breaker completely.

"Tomas!" she said again, and this time his ear twitched, but he did not budge. Dian reached down with both hands and seized the fur along his jaws, and bent her forehead down to touch his, holding it there for a moment. When she stepped away this time, it was final.

"Tomas, go," she said firmly, and without looking at Breaker she began to move away. He made to follow her, and she brought out the voice saved for the direst of sins, the voice that combined shock and disappointment and hurt and a hint of anger, the voice of a condemning god. "Tomas! Bad dog. Go."

He froze, and she turned and stumbled off.

Dian was not a weeping woman, but when she had reached the refuge of her rooms she gave herself over to it, and allowed Margaret to hold her and comfort her, and wept for that too.

The Men's Quarter was slightly more than a sixth of the city in acreage, slightly less than a sixth in population. It was in the northeast quadrant of the roughly heptagonal city, a rounded-off triangle surrounded by three wide, flat boulevards that were lit harshly at night, with access to the Quarter only through barbed wire and broken glass and alarms. The closest the Quarter came to Ashtown's perimeter walls was a fourth of a mile from its northernmost point. The southeastern tip of the triangle was half a mile from the wall, and the western tip was buried in the city, a few hundred yards from the Center. The men would make their break halfway along the Quarter's southern wall. They would head west to the Center; she and Robin would make due east for the outside wall.

Breaker left at night lest the populace take her departure as an invitation to mischief. Dian did not see them off. She was in the shooting range buried far beneath the Center, plugging copious quantities of bullets into paper figures that looked like Breaker.

One more day and its night, and then another day, the last day, never again to see a dawn in Ashtown. The thought was powerful, life-giving, and she kissed Margaret with more affection than she'd demonstrated in some time. She felt—dear God, she was happy, for the first time in forever. When had she last felt like this? Childhood? Then she remembered: the intoxicating hours of freedom after leaving the Valley the previous October, before finding Willa. The exhilaration of action, movement, anything to stir the stagnation that had tugged at her, clung to her, turned her into a fat old pregnant woman. God—the first few nights I'm probably going to bitch at how hard the ground is, she thought, and grinned to herself.

"You're in a cheerful mood this morning," said Margaret from behind her, sounding mildly suspicious. Dian finished pulling her tunic over her head and reached for her brush, and then turned and directed her grin at Margaret.

"I know. It's crazy, but I just decided, what the hell.

I *do* want this baby. And I'm *not* going to allow the Captain to screw me into a corner. Let's do something tonight. What time are you off?"

"Early shift, I'll be home by four."

"Great. Let's get out of the Center. Dinner somewhere where they won't act like we've got the plague. And there might be a decent movie playing. Yes?"

"You are in a funny mood," Margaret insisted, but now a smile of her own was tugging at the corner of her mouth.

"C'mon. What I really want to do is stuff myself silly and dance until dawn, but I can't do either right now, so we'll have to practice decorum and be in bed at ten o'clock like the old folks. You game?"

"I'd love to, Dian."

Somehow Dian got through the day. Somehow she kept enough of her mind on the movie to know when to laugh. Later she managed to eat the food that cost her as much as a night in the Quarter would have, aware of Margaret oohing and ahing over the delectable dishes and the glamour of the restaurant, though Dian could only grimly think that it was as well to tuck away as much as her crowded stomach could bear, because it might be some time before she had another hot meal. It could have been stewed wood chips, for all she tasted it. She gave Margaret champagne, and wine, and brandy, and scandalized eyes were averted from the sight of two Angels in their black uniforms, one markedly pregnant and the other decidedly drunk, helping each other out the door.

Margaret sang rude songs and giggled in the open horse-cab, and once home fell headlong into Dian's bed and lay senseless, snorting occasionally. Dian removed Margaret's boots and tucked the blankets over her, and then, before turning off the lights, she eased back the heavy hair that tangled onto Margaret's face and placed her lips lightly on the skin behind Margaret's right ear. Margaret grunted and muttered. Dian smiled, sadly, and closed the door quietly, and went to make herself some coffee. She sat with the lights out and the curtains open, looking down at the Angels' private inner garden, its blossoming trees ghostly in the dim light of lamp and half-moon. She sat, and breathed, and felt the beating of her heart, and waited, and when at twenty-three minutes after midnight the first sirens sounded, she relaxed.

The waiting was over.

She picked up her cup and carried it to the kitchen, washed it, dried it, hung it on its hook over the sink. When the alarm bells began to clamor in the hallway, she went in to Margaret, shook her shoulder gently.

"Margaret, there's some kind of problem. I'm going to see if I'm needed. Don't bother getting up, they'll send for you if they need you; I just wanted to tell you where I was going. And to say thank you."

Margaret backhanded the hair from her eyes and squinted groggily up at Dian.

"F' what?"

"For tonight, of course. And for everything since January, I suppose. Go back to sleep now, sweet girl. I'll see you later."

"Be careful."

"I will."

She leaned down and kissed the woman lightly, drew the quilt up over her shoulders, and left her. With any luck, Margaret would never know for certain. Bones would no doubt be unearthed in the cooled debris, and what was to say that some of them were not those of one pregnant Angel?

Dian took her wand from its recharging unit beside the door, strapped it on, reached into the closet for her thick, short-sleeved flak jacket, tight across the belly now but with inner pockets that would not show the items she had secreted there earlier—extra socks, a flint and matches, a few fruit-and-nut bars, a twist o. plastic film holding a few tablets, mostly antibiotics in case she and Robin did not come through un scathed. And a long, thin, strong rope. She did up the jacket's buttons and reached into the closet for the rest of her riot gear, issued to every Angel but worr only in the rare event that the Angelic mystique of in vulnerability was actively, massively challenged. The rifle, her personal choice over the more commonly used shotgun, she slung onto her back; the belt, bris tling with ammunition and gas grenades, wen around her hips; the claustrophobic helmet she tucked under her arm, and let herself out into the cor ridors.

Downstairs it was incredibly noisy, but no chaotic: give Breaker her due, she may be an absolute tyrant, but her women were trained to function with out her. There were three people at the communica tions desk instead of the usual one, all speakin; stridently into radio telephones with hands flattene over their free ears. Dian gave her number to the Lieu tenant in charge and was told to get to the northern end of the Men's Quarter, where there was apparently a mass breakout attempt, reports of twenty, forty mei already over the wall. Dian obediently left the Quar ter, stopped outside to buckle on her helmet and un sling her rifle, and then took off—east, not north North was the decoy.

In five minutes she trotted up to one of the mino entrances of the Quarter. The single guard ther greeted her with furious questions.

"Fucking hell!" she exploded. "What's going on? can't get anyone to stop and tell me."

"Don't you have a radio?" Dian asked her.

"They said to shut up and get off the air."

"They probably won't have told you, then. You're wanted in the north end. I'm your relief."

"What is it?"

"Breakout attempt and, from the look of it, fires. Better hurry up if you want to get in on the fun."

"I should go back for my gear."

"The Lieut said no, just get your ass up there. Oh, and you're to go around the east end, round up any stray Angels you see, and send them up too."

The woman hesitated no longer, but grabbed her equipment and set off at a run down the lit boulevard. Dian let out a sigh of relief. She'd been prepared to wand the woman, or shoot her, but deceit was far better. She tapped twice on the thick wooden door. She felt eyes on her but nothing happened, and then she remembered that she was completely anonymous, and hastened to raise the obscuring faceplate on the helmet. The door opened instantly, and she slid inside.

"You'll have to put someone on the door," she started to say, but a black-clad almost-woman was already pushing past her to the guardhouse. She nodded and turned back to the dark passageway, which her senses told her was full of people. The door behind her shut, the lights went back on, and, prepared though she was, she took an involuntary step back at what confronted her.

The room was filled with men, moreover, a group of men surrounded by the clear, taut aura of violence. It was a scene few women living could have witnessed: a small male army, armed to the teeth, knives and clips of ammunition strung around their bodies. It was a scene straight out of Before, when men were the warriors, something out of a storybook or the grainy, flickering movies Margaret liked, although Dian had always found the idea of a male army so unlikely as to be amusing, and slightly embarrassing. It did not strike her that way now. She found these men noble, determined, and very impressive; they smelled of power and death.

The impression lasted only a moment, until she blinked and saw before her twenty-seven edgy, self-conscious, out-of-shape, overarmed men, but the vision stayed with her and erased the last traces of her doubt and condescension. These were hardly prime male specimens. A few of them had muscles, but several were distinctly pudgy, and all of them were typical overfed and underworked pampered city-dwellers. However, she would now trust them to know roughly what needed doing.

She straightened, realized that she was gripping her half-raised gun with unnecessary fervor and let it droop, and scanned the faces for Robin. She missed him at first, started to open her mouth with an angry protest, and then her eyes snapped back to a familiar woman: Robin, in a padded vest as of old, dressed as an Angel. All the men wore black, some more successful imitations of the Angel uniforms than others. Two of them held helmets, all had false wands—reasonable facsimiles—and the variety of guns was sufficiently Angelic to pass. However:

"Couldn't you find black boots?" she asked. Some of them looked taken aback, and she had to admit it was an odd note on which to begin a heroic evening.

"Oh, my dears," a voice drawled from the back. "If only I'd known the proper fashion for a revolution. This is just too humiliating."

Laughter woke the little passageway, nervous, basso, and relieved, but Dian did not join it.

"The brown ones will pass in the dark," she persisted, "but you'll have to do something about the lighter ones. You'll be spotted from a mile off. At least rub some lampblack into them, anything." A pot of some black greasepaint was produced and depleted, and at last Dian was satisfied.

"Robin, the supplies?" She handed him the Angel knapsack she'd secreted away. "Put whatever you have in here with some grenades on top in case it's checked. Now, who's heading this?" Glances gave her the answer, an unassuming middle-age bookish sort with implacable eyes behind wire spectacles. She held out a scrap of paper that held a few lines of names and numbers. "I've given you everything you asked for," she told him. "In another ten minutes the Center will be virtually empty, and the route Robin gave you is the safest and most direct. I can't do anything about the door lock, but you knew that, and I assume you have something in mind. I've done my part," she stressed. "What I want in return is these twelve lives spared. These women do not deserve death, and if you deal with them honestly, they could be of great value to you. Also, I suggest that you consider sparing anyone whose number is higher than eight hundred. Anyone over that has only been here for a year or so, and a lot of them are new recruits under sixteen. Children. And all the numbers above one thousand are servants, whose only sins were to cook and do Angel laundry. If you refuse to save these women and girls, there is nothing I can do. But I ask it of your honor to try."

The man studied her eyes and then took the paper from her hand, looked at it, and buttoned it into a pocket. He nodded once, and she told him, "I probably don't need to mention that, if you are captured, that piece of paper would be the end of those twelve."

"No," he said, and again she was, irrationally, reassured. She held out her hand to him, and he took it.

"Good luck," she said. She slung her rifle again across her back and moved to the door, then stopped. "Two more things. One, none of you saw me tonight.

I am missing, dead, but you never heard of me. Second, I suppose it doesn't much matter what you think of me, but I'd like you to know that I'm not a traitor. I came to Ashtown to get Robin out, and that's what I'm doing. I've never been an Angel in anything other than appearances. I tell you this so you know that the information you have and the names on that list are clean; they come from someone whose word is solid."

The man smiled then, just a little with his eyes, and he was no longer unassuming.

"Good luck to you too, Dian," he said, and laid his hand in a brief blessing on Robin's shoulder. "Goodbye, Robby. We'll name a street after you," and he pushed them out the door. The false Angel put his head through the archway.

"Anything?" she asked him.

"Half a dozen Vam—Angels running by a minute ago, nothing since."

"Good." She pulled off her helmet and gave it to Robin, shook her head again at his shoes, and showed him how to drop the visor. "I don't suppose that jacket is armored," she asked.

"No, just warm."

"Well, stand behind me if bullets start flying. And if anyone comes up to us, do something to keep them from looking at your feet. Ready?"

"As I'll ever be."

"Are you scared?"

"Be a fool not to be."

She laughed happily and slapped him on the shoulder. Call her a fool, then, but she felt like she was crawling out of the grave, more alive every minute.

"Come on, then," she said, and strode off big-bellied down the middle of the deserted boulevard with Robin at her heels.

In January she had reassured herself with the warm thought that escape from within the walls would be an easy thing, and to her surprise it proved to be true, particularly for an Angel of the streets who had spent hundreds of hours patrolling every twist, turn, niche, and pile of builder's rubbish with precisely that goal in mind. Dressed as they were, no citizen questioned them, though many an eye peered out of curtains at them; the few Angels they passed made only the most cursory and preoccupied of greetings. She came to a point where the wall formed an angle and pushed Robin into a doorway that she knew to be boarded up from within. She looked at her watch.

"We made good time," she whispered. "Now, if your engineering wizard knows his stuff, the lights will go off in five minutes. If not, we get to climb over the wall in full light. Can't risk shooting them out." Guns had been heard from the north for the last few minutes, single shots, a few automatic bursts, and two explosions of grenades, but there had been nothing closer yet.

"You have a rope?' asked Robin.

"A gorgeous one, cost me two weeks' pay. I'll go up and tie it to that standard there, you see?"

"Oh, for heaven's sake, Dian. I know I'm just a man and no Angel, but I can climb and I'm not seven months pregnant. I'll go up, drop the rope down for the pack and then you."

"Well, all right," she said reluctantly, "but I want you to wear this jacket as well as the helmet."

"Agreed. But you take it back on the other side." They made the exchange and then settled to wait in silence. After a while the wind shifted, and it smelled of smoke and something more pungent: tear gas.

"How long do you think they'll hold out, in the north?" she asked.

"Hours. They're well entrenched and supplied. Been collecting stuff for this move for years, ever since Howard saw the failure of the last one." Howard was the man with the wire glasses. "He's an unlikely-looking revolutionary, but the perfect combination of chess player and assassin. The other day—"

The lights went out. Dian never did find out what had happened the other day, because Robin was already edging out of the doorway, blind but with the terrain firmly planted in his woodsman's eye. Dian followed his progress with her ears: up a drainpipe, along the top of a bay window, onto the roof, over to the next roof, and finally a scramble onto the building whose end formed part of the perimeter wall. There were voices coming from the upper floor of the middle building, and candles were lit there and in the ground floor of the end one, but in the darkened street she and Robin were invisible.

She heard a faint slithering noise and the nylon rope was there. The pack went up with only two thumps; the rope returned. She tested it, found it secure, and pulled her way up it, slowly but silent. Once on the top they reversed the process, and Robin ended by climbing down the doubled rope (which Dian had bought long for just that reason, in order to reach twice the height of the wall) and pulled it down after him.

They were out. They were free. Now there was only the getting away.

Dian led him along the wall, skirting shacks and dwellings, freezing at dogs and voices that were beginning to be raised as the disturbance inside the wall built. Finally they were at one of the Angels' three stables. The guard there was awake, until Dian strode up to the woman in full riot gear while Robin came up from behind and cracked her on the head. They left her tied, drove off all the horses but two, and stole every bit of gear they could manage, chucking most of it into a ditch outside the town.

They stopped only once, while Robin took out the

alcohol, needles, and the scalpel he'd somehow got his hands on and subjected Dian to a quick, messy, and unanesthetized surgery on her upper breast. It hurt like hell, but at the end of it, she was no longer an Angel.

[CALIFÍA] HAD MORE BOLD ENERGY AND

MORE FIRE IN HER BRAVE HEART

THAN ANY OF THE OTHERS.

THIRTY

THE SUN SHONE; THE RAIN REFUSED TO FALL; THEIR tracks lay open on the soil for all to see.

Late on the third morning the maps failed them. Where there should have been the gentle slope of a creek bed and the Remnants of a narrow roadway, there was only an apparently endless expanse of boulders and scree that stretched around the corner half a mile away, debris that once had been part of the overhanging hill. Bomb, earthquake, or natural landfall, it hardly mattered, for the way was impassable. They filled their bottles from the trickle's pools and turned back to follow the ridge.

An hour later they were leading their horses along the shaky, sparsely treed ridge when some vaguely remembered urge caused Dian to look over her shoulder. At that distance she might have dismissed the figures as a herd of elk fleeing wolves, or a group of wild horses, but they were not.

"Robin," she said. Startled, he slipped and nearly lost his footing, recovered, and looked at her. She tipped her head at their pursuers, and saw the bones of his face emerge, taut in fear. She looked away.

"Shit," he said. "So soon. I thought we'd throw

them with that business at the creek and the rocks. All that delay for nothing. They must've picked up one of Queen Bess's trackers; I don't think there's anybody that good in Ashtown."

"No, it's not one of Bess's," she said, her voice quiet and even and filled with rage and despair. "It's the Captain herself. She's using Tomas."

"No," he exclaimed. "It can't be, she'd never come herself, not with the city burning."

"No? What can she do about the city but put it under siege and wait for reinforcements from Portland? She might as well come after us. Pride, you know. And I imagine the touch of using Tomas to track me down proved irresistible."

Wordlessly, Robin took the binoculars from his saddle and focused on the specks ten miles away, but Dian did not need glass lenses to see her dog. He was there, on a long lead, no doubt, fastened to the wrist of Captain Breaker. She turned back to the ridge, and after a few minutes Robin followed.

They made it past the slide, and once they had regained firm hillside Robin called a halt and made her eat some bread and dried fruit. It tasted like sand, but she obediently chewed and swallowed while she sat with her eyes studying the opposite hilltop. Robin ate silently and put the food in the bag when they had finished, then came to stand beside her.

"So," he said. "You know the dog better than I do. How do we shake him? Short of flying?"

"We don't. I take up a position on that hill with the gun. You go on ahead."

"No."

"Oh, Robin, please. No heroics. There's only the one rifle. I'm a better shot than you. I can pick off...I can kill Tomas and the Captain when they come up to the base of the slide, and probably three or four others, depending on how they're arranged. Chances are better than even that without her they'll turn back home. Even if they don't, they're still three hours behind us. I'll catch up with you and we can set up a second ambush. Guerrilla warfare."

"No."

"Robin, damn it—"

"I have the right to choose, Dian," he said evenly, and she could not insist, could not help seeing that were she to force him, it would be as if he had not left Ashtown, and she—she would be stamped irrevocably as an Angel. She squinted at the opposite ridge for a moment, and then held out her arm.

"This wand," she told him. "Its charge stays full for over a week. Everyone believes that a wand only works for its owner, but actually all it needs is for her thumb to be on the indentation—see here? This is the power adjustment; top is full power. At that setting it kills, fast. They say there's no pain. Surer than a rifle bullet. You just have to be sure my thumb is on the dent. Doesn't matter if I'm alive or not. It should have two minutes of full power. One second kills." She snapped the wand back into place, and looked up at him to see if he had understood. He had. Neither of them would return to Ashtown. Not alive.

Forty minutes later they were on the opposite knoll. Robin led the horses down the hill away from the creek to tether them while Dian trimmed the brush to make an overhanging shelter. She lay down at full length under them, grunted at the pain in her breast, and set about creating a bowl for the globe of her stomach in the hard ground. She had to settle for a doughnut of branches, and then when that threw off her position at the rifle, she devised more rocks and branches to hold her elbows up at the proper level. Robin returned with a pair of blankets, which helped, and shoved in beside her under the scrub. He set out their bottles and a leather bag of food, took up the binoculars and lay quietly next to her, looking down-stream while she fiddled with the telescopic sight and the props. She felt as if she were lying on a basketball and her breast burned like the living hell, but it was the best she could do. She brushed the hair back from her forehead and took a long pull from her water bottle, then she too lay quietly. The air was hot and still, and after the months of breathing concrete and tar-mac, the odors were sweet and subtle.

"You know," she mused after a while, "I was lying under a bush with a pair of binoculars when this whole thing started."

"This is not the end," said Robin, without taking his eyes from the binoculars.

"You don't think so?" she said softly, and for the seventh time reached out to rearrange her meager supply of long bullets. He did not answer, and they lay, silent and invisible companions, and waited for the end to begin.

It did not seem long, although it was nearly an hour, before Robin stirred.

"Something startled a jay."

Dian wiggled her fingers rapidly to limber them up and bent to her gun. One minute stretched out, two, infinitely slow now, and when large and abrupt fig-ures loomed into her scope it was a shock, as if the al-ready familiar arrangement of boulder, brush, and tree had suddenly given birth to a dragon. She shook her head free of all thoughts, and put her finger on the trigger.

Tomas. Tomas first, a stout lead connecting her to—damnation, not the Captain! An Angel, but not Breaker. Donna, usually in charge of the duty roster? What the hell was she doing out here, a city girl? Dian ran the scope across the growing crowd of Angels and strangers milling about excited on their horses, ges-turing and miming their exclamations at the land-slide, until suddenly a ripple spread through them like a boulder dropped into a pond and Captain Breaker was there. The Captain, looking—sweet Mother of God, look at her face. Rage, controlled but visible, the lust for murder mixed with pleasure and anticipation. And complete confidence. Dian shivered at the thought of what those hands would do to her, and to Robin, and waited for an opening.

None came. The women moved up the hillside, Tomas disappeared and reemerged, never near the Captain, never both of them clear, and it had to be both. Agony, frustration, near premature tightening of her forefinger before Robin spoke.

"They'll have to follow our way up the ridge, and they'll be strung out then. It's further away, though. Will that make a difference?"

Dian released a breath, let go of the gun, eased her rigid neck.

"No problem," she said. "No problem."

She squirmed backward out of the bushes, got to her feet, went off to urinate in the brush, drank some water, thought of nothing at all. After fifteen minutes she went back to her hiding place, rested the smooth gun comfortably into her shoulder and her cheek, and began the last wait. Her mind remained mercifully blank, with no past, no future, only necessity and the open hillside across from her, and the gnats whining in her ears.

Forty-five minutes after leaving the slide, the pursuers appeared on the hillside. Tomas was surging up the hill in the lead, bounding eagerly at the freshness of Dian's scent, his muscles yanking at the arm and shoulder of the human he was yoked to as she stumbled up the rough slope trying to keep up with him. A few riders were still on their horses, most were on foot. No sign yet of the Captain. Tomas was halfway up the open patch of hillside, eighteen or twenty women straggling behind him. Dian and Robin both lay taut, waiting for Breaker to appear. Tomas was twenty yards from the first trees now. No Captain. Fifteen yards. A drop of perspiration ran down Dian's face, and she dropped her head to her sleeve to clear her eyes. Robin stiffened and Dian snapped back up to see her Captain's unmistakable gray stallion with a pair of legs behind his belly. Too canny, the Captain. It would have to be Tomas first, then, and hope for the best. No thinking now, and Dian shifted to the dog, her dog, the dog she had bred and helped to whelp, the dog she had held from the hour of his birth, who had taken his first meat from her hand and received her training and become her partner, who had saved her life more than once, who loved her so much he would betray her and the man she was responsible for, the dog who was eight yards from safety and straining happily against the leash, smelling her nearness, and she centered his chest in her crosshairs, gently squeezing the ridge under her finger, aiming at where the fullness of his chest would be in the instant it took the bullet to travel the distance, and the trigger went back, back, and the gun jolted against her shoulder.

Dian slammed another round into the chamber, but Tomas was down and tumbling, thrown aside by the force of the impact, brought up short by the taut lead attached to the wrist of the Angel, a woman with much faster reactions than Dian would have credited her with because she followed his pull by throwing herself to the ground and lying still, but there was no time for her now, not with the Captain loose, and the scope's vision stuttered across the confusing litter of moving people until it found the gray horse, half-rearing and being pulled down from the off side, the woman's legs mingling with the horse's. Right, then, have to take the horse out first, and when he had

come full around to face downhill, she put two rapid
bullets into his chest and neck and he collapsed, kicking, but the Captain was still not exposed, she went
with him, huddled behind him and invisible but for a
hand here and a glimpse of hair there. The hillside
had erupted into movement, women diving for cover
and hauling their horses up and down the hill, a
scurry of body parts in the powerful scope. Dian
aimed at any woman who came near enough to the
Captain to be of any help, so it was not until Robin
made a noise that she realized that something other
than her rifle bullets was happening below. She had
hit three women, but there were at least six absolutely still bodies, including Donna where she lay
with her arm outstretched toward the body of Tomas.
Dian lifted her eye from the limited field through the
scope and saw a guard on a horse tumble limply to the
rocks, another one stand up from behind a boulder,
put a hand to her chest or throat, and collapse as if
poleaxed. All Angels, she could see, none of the
Queen's guards. The men of Ashtown still held the
city and had finally managed to boost the transmitter's signal enough to reach here. Too late to save
Tomas. Too late.

Within two minutes, silence had descended opposite, the silence of dead Angels and bewildered Queen's
guards clutching the reins of their mounts among the
trees as if the horses could save them from this terrifying plague. Another minute, and a voice through the
utter, shocked silence, the words unintelligible but the
personality and intent unmistakable: the Captain,
mustering the remnant of her troops. Figures began to
assemble along the top of the hill, then at a signal they
all moved down at once, horses protecting bent-over
women, moving in front of and around the gray stallion's body. Dian kept her sights on the Captain, although short of slaughtering every horse on the hill,

which she did not have the ammunition to do, she could not prevent Breaker from gaining the protection of the trees. However, just before she disappeared into them, the hated face peered incautiously over the withers of her four-legged barricade and seemed to look straight into Dian's eyes. There was madness there, and wild laughter and rage, and Dian had the pleasure of seeing her duck at the last shot.

The battle was over. Looking a last time at the tawny figure among the black-clad ones, Dian could not say it was won.

The dust settled. Crows began to call. Within a very few minutes the first vulture had begun to circle overhead. Robin finally put down his binoculars, dropped his head onto his arms, and took a shaky breath.

"Will she come after us?" he asked finally.

"No. She'll be halfway to Ashtown by now, to see what she can save. She's crazy, but she's not stupid. We're safe."

"I'll go down there after dark to get Tomas's body."

"No. We leave now. There will be one of the Queen's guards sitting very still and waiting for us to come down, and probably two working their way in this direction."

"How do you know?"

"It's what I would do. No, we're safe from Breaker now, unless she finds Ashtown totally lost to her and Bess unwilling to support her. Then she'd come after us, but not before. Let's go."

"Dian, I am so utterly sorry."

"Shut up, Robin. Just shut up. Bring the water, and let's get out of here."

...WE DECLINE TO SAY MORE OF WHAT BECAME OF

THEM, BECAUSE, IF WE WISHED TO DO SO,

IT WOULD BE A NEVER-ENDING STORY.

THIRTY-ONE

AUGUST, AGAIN. HEAT LAY ON THE VALLEY, CHILDREN shouted and shrieked from the millpond. In the fields, the orchards, the barns, women and men labored. The harvest was under way, and although it was not a bounty such as last year's, it would be adequate, with care, to hold them through the winter. God was good.

Judith was working her way down the row of bush beans with her hoe. In a few minutes she would be at the fence and could start up the next row, and so it had gone all morning. She liked hard physical labor. The mind had no place in it, just grit and stamina, very satisfying and incongruously restful.

She reached the end, walked over to the shade under the young mulberry tree where she'd left her water bottle, drank, walked back, and began the next row. She and Isaac had chosen to do the entire field themselves, although he was up at the house at the moment. They often worked together, pulled into each other by the vacuum of Dian's absence. He was a good partner. He didn't insist on making conversation. That was restful too. Back up the row, the uneven rhythm of chop, scuffle, pull, chop, pull, scuffle, chop, leaving drifts of wilting weeds in her wake where she had freed the beans of their competition, mindless and necessary work.

What would Dian have thought, told of her sister's uncharacteristic affection for brute labor? She wondered, as never a day passed without wondering, if she would ever know what had happened to her sister. She'd left a note in the snow for Miriam to find, a maddening little note saying only, *Dian was here,* and then nothing. The world was just too big, and the expansion of this Valley into the land beyond the waterfall was only another symptom of its uncontrollability.

She increased her pace and was soon soaked in sweat. Her mind's jabber retreated.

Up the row, turn the corner, back down to the fence, stop to swallow some lukewarm water, up the next row, turn the corner, back down. Soon it would be time for lunch, her breasts told her, though she would like to keep on with this until darkness came and she could fall exhausted into bed, or until the earth came up around her legs and swallowed her up. Chop, scuffle, chop, pull, scuffle.

What?

It took her a moment to realize that Isaac was shouting at her. She straightened her back painfully, and then the bell's clamor rang out and she looked, startled, up the hill and saw women running toward the houses, and beyond them men—David and Salvador, Peter with Jon on his hip—sprinting up for the high meadow with a woman behind—Consuela?— urging them on. Hanna went pounding by up the road with two dripping children in her arms and three more at her heels, shouting unintelligible words while Carmen bellowed for *Laine!*—who would be sleeping after her night watch, Judith thought, but not Sonja because she'd gone out with a scavenging group—but Laine had heard the bell and burst out of her house at the run, half-dressed and a rifle in one hand as she pelted barefoot down the dusty road toward the bridge—all this in an instant, and Judith let the hoe drop and was moving fast in the direction of the mulberry before her head had finished turning to see what was coming at them. As Judith scrambled over the fence without seeing it, Laine passed her, shoving her shirttails one-handed into her waistband, shouting an order to Judith to get to the caves, accelerating into the turn of the road with her rifle at the ready. Then between one step and the next, all urgency left her, as her shoulders came up and she decelerated to a flat-footed halt in the space of five strides. Judith glanced toward the tree and trotted into the center of the road to see what Laine was looking at, with her rifle barrel pointing so casually off to the side. The road's bend and the height of the corn kept Judith from seeing, but she could hear hooves, a lot of them, crossing the mill bridge, hoofbeats her mind insisted were coming at an easy, nonthreatening walk. Judith came up beside the armed woman standing openly in the middle of the road, watching the approach of:

Jeri, grinning fit to split her face, escorting what looked at first glance like:

A hundred ebony-haired, green-uniformed, armed and mounted Meijing guards, at whose head was:

A tall Chinese woman balancing an absurdly pale white-blond toddler on her left thigh with great aplomb, and riding beside her:

A man, stocky and dark-skinned, a tiny infant tucked to his chest, and gamboling amid his horse's hooves:

Two ungainly, huge-footed, long-tailed puppies, one brindled, the other jet black. Beside them, on the outside where she had just come into view—or where Judith's eyes had finally acknowledged her:

Dian. No Culum, no Tomas, but with another tiny baby strapped to her chest.

The leading Meijing soldier put her right hand into the air and the entire black-haired cavalcade drifted to a stop, except for Dian, who rode forward, dismounted, and walked the remaining distance until she stood in front of her sister.

"Hello, Jude."

"My God," Judith finally forced out of her throat. "My God, we thought you were dead."

"I know. I couldn't get a message to you until five weeks ago, and then nobody would bring it here because of the hill tribes, and that's why half of these technicians are here, to set up a communications system—oh, sweet Jesus, Jude, I never thought I'd get home again," and then the sisters were in each other's arms, crying and laughing and hugging until the mite on Dian's chest bleated in protest, and Judith stood away with a question in her eyes. Dian edged the sling away from the flat face, revealing a shock of thick black hair on the small head.

"Your nephew, Jude. My son." She half turned and held out her hand to the man, who dismounted and walked up to them. "My sister, Judith," she said to him. "Jude, this is my friend Robin. And the one he's carrying is your niece. My daughter."

"What? Dian, what is this?" Judith was torn between laughter and disbelief as she touched first one black head, then the other.

"Twins. I never believed in doing things halfway. Oh, and that's Willa, on Mai's lap." She pointed at the pale toddler. "She's mine too, in a roundabout sort of way. She was named for Will. Jude, I'm sorry." She reached out to touch her sister's arm, but her motion was arrested by the sight of a very dirty naked little boy baby who was trying to crawl onto the road from the shade of the mulberry tree, to be thwarted by the lowest rail of the fence. Realizing his failure, he pulled himself upright and bellowed. Judith shook her head, went over to retrieve the child and his shed diaper, and brought him back on her hip.

"Will," she said, "this is your aunt Dian. What's wrong?" she asked, seeing her sister's face change.

"I thought . . . I dreamed." She stopped, and her eyes rose involuntarily to the empty attic window in the big house. "Kirsten."

"Dian, I'm sorry. She died, just before Christmas. In her sleep one night. She told me she'd had a dream about you, a couple of weeks before. She would have been so happy to see you."

Death came when I grew old enough to understand what it took to make a life. . . .

"Yes. Yes, I dreamed about her too." She turned her back sharply on the house, thus missing the figure who stepped off the veranda, slowly, as if unsure of his vision. "Judith, this is Mai; she came as a friend, and as an official Meijing representative. Do you think we can find them something to drink? We won't have to house them, they'll bivouac down by the bridge, but a stab at hospitality would be a good start. I thought I'd ask Ling to put Robin up for a few days, until he decides where to go."

Judith cast an eye on the invaders, who actually numbered fewer than thirty, and began to call out to the others, asking Lenore to organize beer and lemonade and maybe some ice, sending one of the girls to retrieve those who had sprinted for the caves at the sound of the bell, catching Susanna's eye and sending her off to summon up quantities of food from across the Valley. She looked back and found Dian watching her, eyes sparkling. She grinned in return.

"What are their names?" she asked.

"I didn't name them yet. I thought, since Isaac missed everything else, the least I could do was to let him—" Her eyes went past Judith up the road, to the burly, bearded figure slowly approaching. When Judith turned back, she saw all the emotions flood into her sister's face, the yearning and the joy and the hope and the fear that he, that they...Dian hesitated, and Judith gave her the answer.

"God, he's missed you, Dian."

Wordlessly, Robin handed Dian her daughter, and watched as the two figures met on the road, the man's hand trembling as it touched her face, his tears visible from here. Yes, Robin thought, this man is worthy of her.

Judith led her unexpected guests up the hill to her home, and when Laine turned to follow the last jingling, polished horse and its rider, Dian and Isaac were still bent over, huddled together, blind and deaf to anything outside of themselves, and their children.

EPILOGUE

From a distance, there was nothing on the hillside, nothing but the dry grasses of late summer and the encroaching scrub trees of the Northern California forest.

The turkey vulture had spotted him some time ago and begun to glide in lowering arcs. She remembered this place, if birds can be said to have a memory, where one bright, hot morning earlier in the season she had circled down over a positive mountain of food, only to have two parts of it stir, rise to their feet, and walk away. One of them had moved slowly and the other with the awkward gait of an animal about to give birth, but despite these hopeful signs they did not seem in any immediate hurry to provide her importunate fledglings with breakfast. The horse they left behind, however, was more than adequate.

Now there was another meal waiting at precisely the same spot, stretched out among the long-cleaned bones and the scattering of cloth and metal objects that the two figures had abandoned and the grass had not yet covered. It was certainly skinnier than the horse had been; still, even the bony ones had their tasty bits. She dropped down lower yet, eyeing the figure cautiously. Doesn't do to hurry, not with these kind that had teeth and a temper: she had a scar on her left wing to remind her of that.

By the time she decided that the corpse was going nowhere, she had half a dozen companions. Ever philosophical, the vulture knew that the object below would feed them all, but she was becoming impatient and dropped down to land, first in the snag of a dead tree, then on a tall Remnant of a chimney, and finally to bounce along the ground toward this tawny, bony, toothy lump of meat. She paused, spread her wings slightly, and hopped up onto the log beside the dry bones—and then she was flapping frantically for height when the tawny corpse came back to life and snapped at her. She retreated with dignity to her perch in the dead apple tree and, folding her wings, settled herself with the others to wait. From the looks of it, it would not be long.

The day wore on, the shadows shortened and then grew long again, and still the animal snarled and snapped whenever one of them approached, once coming away with a mouthful of feathers. There were now eleven patient vultures in the tree, murmuring encouragements to one another and outwaiting the dog.

Finally, when the shadows of the hill had begun to swallow up the objects below, their potential breakfast struggled to its feet—stiffly, with only three of his paws touching the ground, but nonetheless standing. The front of his chest was a mess of scabs and scars where the infection from the bullet was still fading, his left ear dangled and oozed from a fight with a coyote two days before, and the bones of his noble spine and hips poked up into the matted, brittle drape of his fur, but he was on his feet, limping slowly away to the south. Inside his chest the great heart beat on, unflagging, as Tomas followed the long-ago footsteps and faded scent of his own, his beloved. His Dian.

ABOUT THE AUTHOR

LEIGH RICHARDS is a third-generation native of California, born, raised, and now living in the same area that *Califia's Daughters* is set. She is better known as *New York Times* bestselling mystery writer Laurie R. King. Her most recent acclaimed mystery novel is *The Game*.